Seeking Justice

by
W. Ward Neuman

ISBN: 978-0-557-73933-2

This book is dedicated to...

my family. No one could ask for a more loving, understanding, patient, forgiving, and supportive clan.

Acknowledgments

I appreciate the efforts and encouragement of the many individuals who contributed in so many ways to my first attempt at fiction. Special thanks to my favorite daughter, Nicole, for her excellent editing help. My other two favorite daughters, Nadine and Naomi were also very supportive.

Prologue

Continental Airlines flight 2360 was landing in Guatemala City. Most of the passengers were traveling for the usual reasons: business, vacation, or family. But that was not the case with four men from Chicago. They were on a most unlikely mission, and it was possible, perhaps even likely, that not all would be returning.

Wade Courtland was the de facto leader of the group, and he could not help but wonder what he, two other retired multimillionaires, and a veteran police detective were thinking when they decided to undertake this dangerous project. They had spent the last few months successfully completing several less challenging missions, which would, hopefully, serve as preparation for what they were about to undertake.

They call themselves The Payback Team.

Having been successful in their careers, they decided to use their energy, determination, and drive to the benefit of those who lack the ability to achieve justice on their own. Most of them had already suffered physical injuries, some had spent time behind bars, and one had experienced a blow like none he could have possibly imagined.

Seeking justice comes at a price.

Wade looked at Tommy Martin and Michael MacMillan, his friends since seventh grade, and remembered how the three of them had dispatched Luis Medrano, a guy who beat the wrap for raping and murdering a young girl, due to evidence that was gathered illegally. The system had failed, but a failed system was not about to keep them from seeking justice for the girl's family.

He remembered how they had handled the situation with Dr. Edmond Crowley, educator, respected pillar of the community, family man. At least, that was how all but a few saw him. Unfortunately, his wife knew the other face of Dr. Crowley: the drunken, wife-beating one.

When he glanced at Sean Callahan, a recently retired cop, and the newest member of the team, he recalled their first meeting. Neither much liked the other. Wade was in the hospital, recovering from a gunshot wound that nearly finished him, and the detective wanted to get information that would help him with the case, but Wade dummied up. Callahan knew that he was planning to seek "vigilante justice," and that was the reason he wasn't cooperating.

Things took an ironic turn when the trio helped the detective with a case that involved the kidnapping and death of a young boy. "The system" was not about to resolve the issue, and Callahan knew it. To paraphrase Harry Truman, sometimes "the system isn't worth a bucket of warm spit."

As he reviewed these and several other events, Wade couldn't help but wonder if all of the experiences they had gained from their previous ventures would enable them to achieve their objective in Guatemala.

Finally, just as the plane's wheels made contact with the runway, his mind drifted back to the morning, several months earlier, when his short-lived retirement took an unexpected, irreversible detour.

Chapter One

Surviving the First Day

At 8:00 on a beautiful spring morning, Wade Courtland mumbled two words after swallowing his first sip of coffee. "I'm bored."

Paula, the love of his life for more than twenty-five years, glared at him for a few seconds, shook her head, and announced, "I knew you wouldn't make it past breakfast."

"What are you talking about?"

"I've been telling you for the past year that you need to find something to do after the sale of the company is complete. Yesterday was your last day, and already you're complaining. We both know you need something to keep you busy just about every waking minute, or you go completely wacko. You have just about as bad a case of attention deficit disorder as anyone could possibly imagine. I don't know if you even remember me discussing this with you."

"Okay, I get the point. But you know how it's been. Getting this company sold was almost harder than what it took to start it and run it over the past twenty years. Lawyers, accountants, not to mention all the government agencies and red tape; we had to satisfy the FTC, the IRS, EEOC, OCHA, and the FEPC. I'm surprised the ASPCA didn't jump in and try to kill the deal as well. And to top it off, I was never completely determined to sell in the first place. It's just that the price was right, and I didn't think another opportunity like the offer they made would come along again for who knows how long.

"But the reason I hadn't thought about what to do after the sale is that I was supposed to stay on as a paid consultant for two years. I had planned to be working just as hard, making sure that all of the new people kept the momentum going, so that I could realize the full payout. Then, at almost the very last minute, it was decided that I should leave, and they in turn would waive the delay in my receiving the full amount of the buyout. So I got a sixty-million-dollar paycheck and a pink slip all in the same day. I guess somebody decided that I could get in the way of some of the plans they had for the company if I stayed."

"Honey, it's not like I haven't heard all this before. But why don't we try to focus on a solution. You know, it's really a pretty nice problem to have, more money than we could ever spend, and plenty of time to think about how to spend it!"

"Okay, good. Let's focus."

After about two minutes, Wade stood up and started pacing. "Okay, I focused. But I didn't come up with anything. Got any ideas?"

"Well, I have had an idea for quite a while now, but I've been afraid to bring it up for two reasons. For one, I knew you would not have been able to concentrate on anything I could have said that didn't concern the sale. I know that you have really been under tremendous pressure trying to run the company and work on the details of getting it sold, all at the same time."

"You're probably right. But you said there were two reasons?"

"Well, the other one is that, I was afraid you weren't going to like the idea."

"That's ridiculous. You had an idea, but you didn't want to tell me because you thought I might not like it? Is this a women-are-from-Venus-and-men-are-from-Mars thing? Stop worrying about what I might think and just tell me. How else are you going to know if I like it?"

"Okay, but I'm going to stand over here by the door in case I have to make a quick exit. Here goes. Remember when you said that if you hadn't started the company, you might have liked going into law? You always felt that the little guy often gets screwed and you just hate it when there is no effective system in place to help some of those who need it the most. I can quote you word for word: 'I would spend twenty percent of my time doing pro bono work, because so many people who need legal help can't afford it.' You also said that a lot of people who need help don't know how to go about finding it, and that you would go after some difficult cases even without being asked. I loved it when you used to talk like that. Deep down, I know what's in your heart: you can't stand it when you see injustice going unpunished.

"But, Babe, I realize that you haven't really let these feelings surface for awhile because of your focus on business. But maybe now it's time to look into how you can help the little guy...those who really need it."

"If you think I'm going to spend the next three years in law school just so I can—"

"Wade! You aren't seeing the big picture. You don't have to be a lawyer. In fact, we both know that using the law to resolve injustice is usually way too time consuming, as well as horribly expensive. Calm down and concentrate for a minute on what I'm saying. Of all the ways you could use your time and *our* money to help others, this may be the best, where you personally make it happen. If you donate to a charity, they will obviously use the money in ways of their own choosing, and they typically don't need any of your time. But if you pick the cause, take over and get personally involved, and use your time and our money to settle an injustice done to others, you are finally doing something that will keep you from telling me you're bored. You and I know we've been very fortunate, and that now it's time to give something back. There, now I've said it all, and I've got my hand on the door, in case I need to make a run for it!"

What followed was a long silence. Paula could see the look of intensity on the face of her soul mate, a look she had seen countless times before. It always amazed her that while Wade was a textbook example of attention deficit disorder, he could focus like a laser beam to a distant target when it suited him. She knew that it was this strange mix of qualities that had enabled Wade to start a company from nothing and turn it into a sixty-million-dollar payday.

Finally, Wade broke his concentration. "Okay, fine. Give me an example."

"It's right here in the paper, three inches from your elbow. Look on page three. You'll see an article about a tourist bus hijacking in Guatemala. The banditos took everyone's money and jewelry at gunpoint. The article says that the government isn't doing anything about it either, even though two of the passengers who didn't cooperate were shot and killed. It's supposed to be a very corrupt country; no doubt payoffs are involved. I noticed the article because this is exactly what happened to your aunt two years ago. And she said that they took two young girls with them and that they were never seen again.

"Do you remember what you said when you heard that some of the passengers are being kidnapped? You said you would like to go down there yourself and put these guys out of business."

Wade did not respond as she thought he would. He said, "You better put your hand back on that door handle. If you think I'm going to go to Guatemala in order to—"

"Okay, fine. I know this is not something that you should try to fix on day one, but it's something you could work up to. The funny thing is that I know you could do it. You could get your buddies, Rocky and Cheech to help, and—"

"It's *Chico*, Rocky and Chico; you never get that right," corrected Wade.

"Whatever. Have you forgotten that they talked about teaming up with you on a project or two when you get your company sold? Since Rocky sold the last of his pawnshops last year, and Cheech, I mean Chico, retired from actively running his management consulting firm, they must also have a lot of time to spare. And I know that money is not a problem for them, either. Now that I think of it, how come they each moved into beautiful homes and we still have the same house we bought before you started the company, when it was all we could afford? And don't give me this story about how Warren Buffett has lived in the same home for over thirty years."

"Paula, Paula, please. Don't change the subject. One thing at a time. I was starting to like the idea until you threw that Guatemala thing at me. Tone it down a notch and come up with something a little closer to reality. And by the way, thanks for thinking I could pull off something like that. I know that your confidence in me has had a lot to do with the success of our company. See, I said it that time, *our* company."

"Okay, you want to start at the bottom? How about this for starters? Your nephew, Ralphie."

"What about him?"

"Go collect some of the debts he was crying about last month," answered Paula.

"Oh, yeah, I remember that," Wade said. "He was really pissing and moaning there for awhile. I know I thought it was a pretty shitty deal, and I told him if I had time, I would help him do something about it."

"You never told me any of the details," replied Paula. "What happened?"

"Well, as you know, he was running a Monday night poker game for a couple of years. I went there two or three times when he begged me because he was short a couple of players. I even got Rocky to go with me once. The kid ran a nice game. The food was good, plenty of whatever anyone wanted to drink, and everything was pretty much straight up. He treated it like a part-time job and worked hard to make sure he was taking good care of the players. He told me that after expenses, he made three or four hundred a week. The players paid a 'rake,' meaning three or four dollars came out of each pot to compensate him for having the game, food, drinks, etc. He told me that it was a lot more work than anyone realized—shopping, setting everything up, getting the seats filled, cleaning up, and a lot more.

"Then everything fell apart at the end. Three or four players were 'on the books,' meaning that he had loaned them money to play in the game in order to fill the seats, and two players outright stiffed him. It turned into a classic cash-flow problem, just like we had in our business a couple of times back in the early days. Only thing is, Ralphie didn't survive and had to shut down the game. He told me that most of the ones who were on the books are paying him back a little each month, and one or two of the others are 'tap city,' so he will probably not collect anything from them. But what really got to him was the two guys who just plain stiffed him," said Wade.

"How? Explain."

"One guy wrote him a check for five hundred dollars and then closed the account the next day," explained Wade. "When the check came back to Ralphie, he called him and the guy gave him some bullshit and made some promises, and then stopped returning calls. Then Ralphie sued him, and got a default judgment because the guy didn't show up in court. But when he tried to collect on the judgment, the guy couldn't be found. He's a bartender, and he often jumps from one job to another, and moves from apartment to apartment. He had to hire a skip tracer to locate him. That's a guy who supposedly can find anyone. So with all of his court costs and two hundred bucks for the skip tracer, he was starting to wish he had just dropped it because right after he was located, he moved again. Finally, Ralphie gave up. If it was me, I would have gotten the money on principal, especially when Ralphie told me that he had found out that the guy had borrowed money from several other people and stiffed them also. Ralphie told me that this guy was going to get what was coming to him someday, but I remember thinking that it would be nice if that day would come like real soon, instead of down the road a few years."

"What about the other guy?" asked Paula.

"Another screw job. Hard to say which story pissed me off the most. The other guy lost over 1,500 dollars in one night and told Ralphie he had to go out to his car to get his checkbook, and never came back. I know, you're thinking 'why didn't Ralphie get cash each time he sold someone chips, like in a casino?' Yeah, that would be ideal, but after a while, he felt like he could trust these guys. Now he knows that was a mistake. Anyway, Ralphie was never able to speak to him again. He wouldn't answer his cell phone, and Ralphie had lost the guy's business card. The guy owned a used car lot, but Ralphie didn't know where and wasn't even sure of his last name. I know it doesn't sound very businesslike, but after the guy came to the game five or six times, I guess he started to get comfortable with him. The final straw was when someone who Ralphie knows saw him at a local casino, and the guy said that the reason he wasn't going to pay Ralphie was that he was cheated. Paula, I've been to that game, and I know Ralphie. That's bullshit, and I know it really hurt him. I'm getting angry all over again just thinking about it. Someone should have fixed those guys clocks and gotten the money."

"Wade, *h-e-l-l-o-o-o*. Do you see what's happening here? You've just proven my point. You've got that fire inside of you that says 'this shouldn't happen—it's not right'. Now, today, you've got the time, the money, the desire, and the ability to make it right. So, now, are you ready to stop being bored?"

Chapter Two

Chico and Rocky

Wade, Chico, and Rocky met in seventh grade on the north side of Chicago. A lasting friendship began almost from the start, and had recently passed the forty-year mark.

They grew up in a tough neighborhood, about two steps from the bottom of the socioeconomic ladder. It didn't matter much to them, however, and they didn't even know that their families were considered part of the working class poor, until they entered the local junior college and met a few kids from the other side of the tracks. The environment they grew up in taught them the kind of street smarts that would come in handy in the future, but about their second year at the community college, they realized that if they wanted to get to the other side of the tracks, a sound education would be a necessity.

And without a doubt, they planned to make it big. Nobody ever figured out what the psychological ingredients were, which drove them to seek success and to achieve wealth, but no one doubted that they were going places. They never told anyone, but the day after they received their associate's degrees, they took a blood oath that they would become millionaires by age forty. They argued for years about who came up with the idea, but most likely they each contributed a part of it. They even remembered arguing about where to make the incision with Wade's knife and finally thought that their index fingers would work best.

This ceremony would have sounded idiotic to almost anyone they might have told about it, but there was no doubt that some compelling power developed as a result of it. Certainly none of them wanted to fail the others in their unusual quest, so the result was probably inevitable. They all made it.

Everyone called Michael MacMillan "Rocky" because they thought he looked like Rocky Balboa. At six feet four inches and close to two hundred and forty pounds, it would take a suicidal maniac to want to challenge him to anything other than a spirited game of checkers. Even after he told people his last name, many still thought he was Italian, just like the Rocky in the movies.

Chico was born Thomas Martin, and nearly everyone called him Tommy. In fact, the only people who referred to him as Chico were Wade and Rocky. The three of them were the only people on the planet who knew how the "Chico" thing came about. In their early twenties, they were out clubbing one night, and when they left the last place, some drunken moron followed them out and went up to Tommy and started hassling him. In those days, Tommy had what he called his "Frito bandito mustache." And on this particular night, some far from sober young woman in the club put a sombrero on his head, and he was still wearing it when the drunk approached him. With spit coming out of his mouth with every word, he shouted at Tommy, "Hey, Chico, how come you messin' with my woman?"

It wasn't until this moment that Rocky and Wade realized that Tommy could be mistaken for someone from south of the border, especially in the evening light and by someone who was only semi-coherent.

"Hey, man, I don't even know which one is your lady, so just forget it. Let it go, okay?" answered Tommy. But that wasn't good enough for the drunk.

"You're goin' down, Chico." Two punches missed their mark, and signaled Tommy that this incident was just getting started and wouldn't end until someone was looking up from the sidewalk. The next punch was more like a roundhouse swing and caught Tommy on the left side of his head, nearly knocking him down.

Until the punches started flying, he had hoped that this could be ended peacefully, but the punch that landed both hurt and angered him. Using a technique he had learned in one of his martial arts classes, he folded the fingers of his left hand and pressed his thumb against his index finger. His arm shot out so fast that there was no time for the drunk to react. Tommy's knuckles found their way straight to his opponent's throat, and it was clear to everyone that this fight was over. The drunk fell to his knees, clutching his neck. Tommy put his foot on the guy's chest and gave a hard push, knocking him flat on the concrete. As the drunk fell, Tommy said, "*Gringo estupido. Adios, cabron.*" That's Spanish for 'fuck you, asshole'." He was trying to mimic the accent of a Hispanic kid from his neighborhood, and to everyone present, it sounded like he had just crossed the Rio Grande. Tommy was about to deliver a well-placed kick to the man's gut, but Wade and Rocky thought that leaving was probably a better idea, so they pulled him away.

From then on, to Wade and Rocky, he was "Chico." Tommy didn't like it at first, but after a while, it served as a reminder of how he had put the guy in his place, and "Chico" was just fine with him.

A couple of months after their blood oath, they split up for the better part of two years as each of them went off to different state universities. Although their grades qualified them for entrance to almost any private university, their finances did not. This didn't bother them at all, as their goal of getting a college education was the main thing, and the specific name of the institution was unimportant from their point of view.

After graduating, they each did what was expected of them and got a job. Wade went to work managing a fitness center. Chico's degree was in business, so he accepted an offer from a management consulting firm. Rocky was having difficulty deciding which of several offers he should take when fate took over. His uncle owned a successful pawnshop, but it started a downward spiral after he suffered the first of three heart attacks. He insisted he could stay in control and turn it around, but the family knew it was only a matter of a year or so before the "GOING OUT OF BUSINESS" sign would have to be posted. Rocky was pressured into helping his uncle run the shop, but it was agreed that it would be just until his uncle's health improved.

During these early years after college, they met often and discussed their progress toward their "blood oath goal." It wasn't long before they all realized that "working for the man" was not the way to go about it. They couldn't name one person who had achieved success, at least by their definition of success, who was working for someone else. Conclusion: they needed to be out on their own. But how?

In Rocky's case, the answer came unexpectedly. His uncle had his fourth and final heart attack, and at the wake, his aunt asked Rocky to take over. They could work out the details of the transfer of ownership, price, and terms later, but she assured him that it wouldn't be something he couldn't handle. The funny thing was that Rocky had come to love the pawnshop business and had done a pretty good job of not just holding things together, but actually helping to turn them around.

It wasn't long before an opportunity to buy a distressed pawnshop a couple of miles away came up. At first he thought that the idea of trying to run two shops when he had only been at it for less than three years was a little more than he wanted to take on. But the price, next to nothing, was just too good to pass up. He could sell the entire unclaimed inventory, close the shop, and make about four times what he was paying for it, so it was a slam dunk. Within six months he had started showing a profit, and it kept growing every month. Now he knew he was going to be the first of the trio to reach the "blood oath goal," and he knew he would make it well within the time frame. He figured he would achieve millionaire status within ten years, well before the age-forty deadline. All he had to do was buy a couple of more shops and everything would fall into place.

And that's exactly what he did. He not only reached the goal well before the deadline, but by the time he turned forty, he was already thinking about what to do when he retired. Ten years later, after considerably more profitable growth, he decided that he would turn things over to his trusted second in command, a guy who had worked for him almost from the beginning. Rocky felt that he would rather receive a large, really large, salary as the semi-retired owner than to sell out completely, which would result in some rather unpleasant tax consequences. He could watch things from the sidelines, step in if any problems came up that were too much for the general manager, and spend the rest of his time doing whatever appealed to him.

Things were going in the right direction for Wade also. He was starting to be looked on as the "boy wonder" at the health club. His interest in fitness was being aggressively applied in his work, and everyone seemed to notice, especially his clients. Wade had been able to position himself as a personal trainer at the club for a few of the more committed members, and when he wasn't handling his management duties, he was able to work with them one on one for an hour at a time, ten or twelve times each week. This involved a lot of unpaid overtime because his paycheck as manager of the facility wasn't meant to compensate him for anything over and above his job description. But that was just fine with him. The way he figured it, the club was paying him to get the experience he would need some day to run his own show. And it looked like that day was soon to arrive.

Wade had developed an amazing ability to find exactly the "training threshold point" for each of his clients. That's the term he invented, and he kept the details of the process to himself. It involved determining the exact maximum training intensity for each client, bringing them to this point in their workouts, but making certain that they did not surpass the threshold. That way, they would receive the maximum benefit, but without sustaining an injury. Nearly all of his clients were starting to demand more hours of Wade's time every week because they could see and feel the results.

But Wade knew that leaving a steady paycheck and starting his own facility was way out of his reach financially. Rent, equipment, insurance, and salaries all added up to a fortune, and that's before the first paying member walked in the front door. But then the unexpected happened. One of his clients was the vice president of a venture capital firm and spelled out what looked like a very profitable opportunity for Wade. His company would put up the front money, and Wade would be in business. This arrangement is what got him on the path to eventually realize his "blood oath goal." The client was kind enough to put a provision in the contract to enable Wade to buy out the venture capitol firm after certain conditions were met. These conditions were difficult, but they provided even greater motivation for Wade to make a success of the business, because he didn't want anyone owning a piece of it other than himself.

Growth, profit, and success followed fairly quickly. It became obvious that he was soon going to outgrow his existing facility, but he realized that expansion and further growth would only add to the seventy hours he was typically putting in each week. His client, the venture capitalist, mentioned the concept of franchising his systems and techniques for running a fitness business. Wade had heard the word "franchise" before, but didn't have a clear understanding of how it worked. Then the client mentioned the example of how McDonald's had achieved phenomenal success through franchising, and it wasn't long before Wade could see the light. Within twenty years, Wade's fitness business had grown to over 400 locations in the United States. Wade was worth a fortune. The next step was to spread out internationally, but Wade felt that taking this step would again bring him back to seventy-hour work weeks, so he started thinking about selling the company and moving on. When an offer came in sooner than expected, he decided to pursue it, and after working out all of the complicated details, he wished the new owners the best and walked away.

Things did not go quite as well for Chico. He did make the deadline of age forty, but only by a few months. He struggled with a serious age problem with the management consulting firm he started out working for. The problem was that he was twenty three, but looked to be even younger. What fifty-year-old businessman was going to pay any attention to what a twenty something kid had to say? The firm thought they had the solution: send him to the companies that were new in business and run by young entrepreneurs. There were plenty of young tech savvy geniuses who had great ideas, but next to no clue about how to run a business. The concept worked fairly well on paper, but in reality, not many of these guys could afford their consulting services. It was a classic catch twenty-two; those who needed help the most could afford it the least.

So, Chico struggled on for a few years without any significant increase in salary. Fortunately, he didn't have a wife or family or mortgage, so he was able to get by. But somewhere along the way, he became an expert at seeing how certain long-range planning strategies could guide and direct companies that had any kind of promise of making it. He could analyze where a company was at a given point in time and help them develop an effective five-year plan. More importantly, he could guide them on a month-by-month basis on how to revise this plan when necessary. It was as if he could see around every corner and adjust course to avoid obstacles that the owners of the companies he was advising had no way of seeing on their own. Several times, when a plan he had come up with started to fall apart, even when things became screwed up beyond all recognition, he was able to calmly scramble his way into a solution that would get the company back on track.

Then he used his planning skills to come up with a five-year plan for himself. He had signed an employment contract with his firm that forbade him from doing any consulting work for any existing clients after he left the firm. He knew from past experience that the company would take aggressive legal action against any former employee who tried to violate the contract. So, it looked like leaving and starting with nothing would be his only choice, but this would very likely result in several years of near-starvation existence. Fortunately, the contract said nothing about doing private consulting work on the side during the time of his employment; he just had to make sure any new client he chose was not associated in any way with his firm.

He had extremely good instincts about which of the company's potential new clients were destined to make it and which would wind up spinning their wheels for a few years before failing. Naturally, a lot of these companies decided that they could not afford his firm's services after the initial presentations were made, so Chico started approaching some of the more promising of these firms and offered his part-time consulting services for free. He explained that by the word "free," he meant that they would pay him nothing, but they would work out a long-term stock option plan, and if the client achieved certain objectives over time, he would be able to convert these options into an equity position in the company.

He chose his new clients carefully and was able to sign up several over the course of the next three years. The plan could backfire if the firms he was advising didn't make it, but he knew he had chosen wisely. The plan could also go up in smoke if he didn't have the ability to sustain a very heavy work schedule, putting in an effective forty hours with his employer and another thirty hours with his new clients each week. But he knew he could do it because he was motivated to succeed, and he was deeply committed to his plan. It also helped that he loved the type of work he had chosen for his career.

It took several years before he saw the results that he knew would inevitably come. In his early thirties, he borrowed against part of the equity he had acquired in some of these companies; he was able to give suitable notice to his firm and, finally, get out on his own. Because he had been highly regarded by his employer, the company made a point of referring businesses to him that they had decided to reject as potential clients for one reason or another.

His new company grew slowly in terms of the number of clients, and Tommy never had more than ten employees. So in one way of looking at it, he was running a relatively small business, but the value of the stock he owned in his clients' companies was well into the millions by the time his fiftieth birthday arrived. After so many years of long, challenging work weeks, he decided it was time to pack it in. He sold his firm to three of his junior partners, cashed in about five million in stock in his clients' companies, went to his farewell party, and never looked back.

Chapter Three

Taking the First Big Step

Paula knew that the best way to get Wade to go along with any of her suggestions was to put it on the table and then walk away from it for a day or two. She knew that he wouldn't be able to get it out of his mind without giving it some serious consideration, even if he said nothing about it for several days, which was usually the case.

And if she brought it up again too soon, it would only serve to irritate him, and he would likely stop thinking about the idea from that point on. Paula knew that the best way to have any degree of control at all over her man was to take the opposite approach: act like she didn't care at all one way or the other, and then wait for him to reach the right conclusion: *her* conclusion.

So on the morning after she had laid out her plan of how he could fill his suddenly open schedule, she sat quietly at the breakfast table, waiting for the inevitable.

"You know, I've been thinking about our discussion yesterday," said Wade. "I think it's a good idea. I could do it, and I know I could really get into it, once I get going. And I think that getting Rocky and Chico involved would result in a kind of synergy that would be unbeatable. You were right, by the way; they've been looking for something a little more constructive to do with their free time. I think they would probably like this whole concept of trying to settle the score for people who don't have the resources to do it on their own.

"But listen, this thing down in Guatemala, I'd really like to do it, and I think we could figure out how to pull it off, but I'm not ready to take on something like that for openers; maybe after we get rolling. And it could be something we could put in the back of our minds, work on it every now and then, until we know we're ready. Not sure how long it would take before we'd be ready; depends on how much experience we would gain working on a few less complex projects."

Not only had Wade come around to Paula's way of thinking, but just like she figured, he was starting to act like he had come up with the idea on his own. And as she saw it, that was probably for the best. That way, she knew he would put everything he had into the project, just like he had done to build the business.

"Do you think you are ready to call Tommy and Michael, or do you need to work out more of the details first?" she asked.

"We're meeting for lunch today. I can't wait to see their reaction when I lay it all out for them." replied Wade.

"Sounds good. By the way, did you notice that I have stopped trying to refer to them by those silly nicknames you have for each other? Seems like I always get it wrong. And you know, you promised you were going to tell me how they came up with that stupid name they have for you: 'Spike'."

"It takes too much time to go into right now. I've got a few things to take care of before I leave for our meeting, and I want to get outside for a run before I leave."

"Okay, I won't forget. And maybe we can also talk about getting us a house that's a little more suitable for us, one where I could keep a horse. I've been away from riding like, forever. After all, both Tommy and Michael bought beautiful homes for their wives long before—"

Wade cut her off. "Okay, fine, but I've got a lot on my mind right now. Maybe later, I promise." She lost track of how many times she had heard that line, but this was not the time to make a federal case out of it. So she just smiled and watched as he got up and left the table, content that she had gotten most of what she had wanted out of the conversation. She knew that their lives were about to head off in an entirely new direction, one that would include excitement, adventure, danger, and probably a whole lot more.

Chapter Four

Road Rage, Extreme Road Rage

With so many questions and concerns swirling around in his head, like the numbered balls in a lottery machine, Wade decided to go on an extra long morning run. This daily ritual was usually where he did his best thinking and problem solving. No telephone interruptions, no "urgent" e-mails to respond to, and no one telling him that they needed "just a minute of his time." It was just him, alone in the great outdoors, with almost no distractions. He didn't even mind those days when the weather was less than ideal; he simply had to choose the right combination of what to wear, and then he could conquer anything that Mother Nature threw at him. And on those rare days when ice covered the pavement, he would resort to the treadmill, but fortunately, this particular day was just about perfect.

Whenever possible, he preferred to run on country roads—less traffic, relaxing scenery, and much more peace and quiet, but this was not one of those days. He knew that in addition to focusing on the new challenge that he had decided to take on, he had to remain aware of potential traffic hazards. He was no match for a vehicle doing the unexpected. He remembered the day, six or seven months ago, when he visited one of his running friends, Hank, in the hospital. Hank was a victim of something totally unnecessary and utterly vicious. A car full of drunken teenagers lobbed an empty beer bottle at him, fracturing his skull. No doubt it hadn't occurred to them that since the car they were riding in was going in excess of fifty miles per hour, the beer bottle was also traveling at that speed.

After about thirty minutes into his run, Wade came to a four-way stop and was proceeding across the intersection between the two white lines provided specifically for pedestrians. He got to the middle of the intersection and was about to cross the remaining two lanes when he saw the Corvette approaching from his right. The Vette had rolled through the stop sign, and it was clear that the driver had no intention of waiting while some "asshole jogger" crossed in front of him, even though the Vette did not have the right of way. This certainly was no time for Wade to get into a battle of wills when he had no chance of winning. He was forced to stop in order to avoid becoming a statistic. As the Vette passed through the space that would otherwise have been occupied by Wade, the "asshole jogger" got a good look at the driver and noticed the look of smug satisfaction, as if he had just won a clever victory.

Knowing that there was not much he could do about the situation, Wade simply put his hands on his hips and glared at the rapidly vanishing vehicle. The driver saw this in his rear view mirror and chose to take it as a sign of defiance and disrespect. His look of "smug satisfaction" instantly turned to anger, and he decided that there was no reason why he should put up with the likes of some wise guy pulling a number like this on him.

Wade then saw that the incident was far from over as the Vette made an illegal U turn and promptly burned rubber when the driver floored it and headed straight back to the intersection, which Wade had just finished crossing. The smart thing would have been to keep on running, preferably to some area accessible only to a pedestrian, like the city park just a couple of hundred feet away, less than a thirty-second run, even at half speed. But curiosity took over. What exactly was the driver going to say or do when he got within shouting distance? Why would someone almost run him down and then come back for a further encounter?

The driver pulled up close to Wade and then passed him and cut in front of him and hit the brakes, so that Wade had only two choices: reverse direction or wait for whatever the driver had in mind. He decided to stop and wait it out, realizing that it would not be a good idea to do anything to allow the situation to get any more out of hand than it already had.

"Got a problem, pal?" Wade was looking into the face of a very hostile "Type A Personality," with an obvious look of road rage for added emphasis.

"No problem, really," replied Wade, "except that I had the right of way, and if I hadn't been paying attention, you would be facing a charge of vehicular homicide, and I'd be on my way to the morgue."

Well, so much for trying to keep things under control. Wade said what he was thinking, but he quickly realized that he should have avoided this clash of egos. Nothing good could come of it. One of the little self-improvement issues he had been working on was not to let outrageous individuals get to him, but this occurred to him just a second too late.

As he got out of the Vette, the driver ramped it up another notch by shouting, "You're really a smart ass motherfucker, aren't you?"

Although he felt himself starting to get angry, Wade decided to let his intellect overrule his emotions and walk away before someone got hurt. Actually, the odds were pretty good that the one doing the hurting would be Wade, even though the driver had a solid forty pounds on him and a couple of inches in height. This would be a great time to use some of the martial arts skills that he had worked on for years, but standing over a crumpled, battered piece of shit that really deserved it would not be worth it in the long run. How was he going to prove who was at fault? The "authorities" often look at the guy who got the shit kicked out of him as the "victim," and thus, by conclusion, the other guy is the "perp." This would likely turn out to be the classic no-win situation.

So Wade decided to pack it in and bail. Walking around the back of the car, he figured it would be a good idea to head for the park, but not before deciding to get in the last word. He gave the trunk door a slap of his hand as if to say, "This is what I think of you and your Corvette that almost ran me over." As soon as his hand hit the car, he knew he had acted out of anger and that the Vette owner was probably going to retaliate in some way, so his instincts told him to take note of the license plate for possible future reference. It read FAST 1. It really fitted the guy's nature.

But, of course, it was far from over. The driver reached into the glove compartment and grabbed something and started after Wade. Clearly, he wasn't about to suffer any further disrespect by letting the asshole jogger rudely walk away before he finished telling him off. Wade couldn't make out what the driver was shouting, and he wasn't sure what he had grabbed from the car, but he knew it was time to put it in passing gear.

Seeing Wade sprinting away from him was more than he could take. Not only was he an asshole jogger and a smart ass motherfucker, but he was rapidly putting himself out of reach of suffering anymore of the driver's rage.

Wade heard what sounded like two firecrackers, but he didn't have to think too hard to figure out what it really was. He continued his sprint, but as he got to the entrance of the park, he felt himself slowing down. He wasn't sure why he was nearly out of energy, as the speed and distance were well within his capability.

Then he felt it. Like ten hornets stinging him in the same spot on his upper left arm. He grabbed at his arm and felt something warm and wet. He was now about fifty feet inside the park and unable to run any further. As he fell to the ground, he looked back at the Vette. The man who had shot him smiled at his accomplishment, then got into his car and slowly drove away.

Chapter Five

The Payback Team Gets Started

It didn't take long for Chico and Rocky to figure out that there was a problem. When Wade didn't show up at the restaurant exactly at noon, they knew something was wrong. Wade was never late. Never. Not for a business meeting, not for a get-together with his two lifelong friends, not for anything. One of his favorite sayings was a quote from one of his heroes, Vince Lombardi: "People who aren't on time aren't committed."

A phone call to Paula only proved that their concerns were well-founded; he never returned from his mid-morning run. The three of them spent the next two hours in a state of panic. The last phone call got the results that they had feared: he was in the hospital. To add to their unrest, the hospital refused to give any details other than the fact that he was in surgery.

Nobody tried to count the traffic laws that were broken in the next few minutes, but somehow they were able to get to the hospital in record time, only to be told that Wade was in recovery. But recovery from *what*? Heart attack? Unlikely. He was in great physical shape. Car accident? Impossible, both cars were still in the garage. Then what had happened? Just when the speculation was getting totally out of hand, they were told that Wade had been assigned to a room, and it was okay to see him.

They were greatly relieved to see Wade sitting up in a chair, laughing and joking with a doctor and two nurses. Normally, Wade would have taken advantage of their concern and would have concocted some really wild story, just to pull their chain a little. It was sometimes his nature to use his offbeat sense of humor to make light of a serious situation. But he decided that this was not the right time, since he could tell that Paula had been crying, and he had never seen Chico or Rocky quite so distressed about anything. Plus, it would be hard to come up with a story stranger than the real one. So he told it straight, just like it happened.

All of them were greatly relieved that this was not a life threatening issue, and it helped to see Wade in a pretty good mood. They didn't like hearing that he would have to endure several therapy sessions, but the doctor assured everyone that he would be back to one hundred percent before long.

Wade wanted to conduct the business that he had planned to cover at their aborted lunch meeting, but he was quickly overruled by everyone—the doctor, Paula, Rocky, and Chico. Anything other than "Goodbye, see you tomorrow" would have to wait. When he was informed that the bullet had severed an artery and he had lost about four pints of blood, he finally figured out that they were probably right.

He was told he would be in the hospital for a few days, and since he would have nothing else to do other than lie around and regain his strength, there would be plenty of time to discuss the new plan and start developing a strategy for carrying it out. Wade didn't want to interrupt his growing obsession with his new mission, but he knew that he also needed to begin his rest and recovery period.

During the next few days, a series of discussions took place in Wade's hospital room. Sometimes Paula was present, but usually, it was just the three old friends. Wade's son and daughter were away at college, and although they insisted on coming home to see their dad, Wade was able to persuade them that he was fine and that they needed to focus on their studies.

Chico and Rocky were completely sold on the concept of using their time and resources to seek justice for others. Their enthusiasm was increasing every day, and soon they realized that there was no turning back. The idea of taking another blood oath was brought up, but Chico pointed out that Wade had recently lost a good portion of his blood supply, and that he probably couldn't afford to part with any more, so they just laughed and forgot about it. They realized that they were sufficiently committed without having to repeat their previous ritual.

Wade was shocked that Rocky wanted to start right in by going down to Guatemala to gather more facts, in order to start working on a strategy for shutting down the bad guys. It took a lot of persuading, but he finally backed off and agreed that they should work on a few less dangerous challenges initially. Wade and Chico both felt that Rocky tended to be the most impulsive of the three, and they also knew that they would have to keep an eye on him so that this trait didn't get out of hand. But they wanted to go about it in the most effective way because they needed everyone to maintain a high level of commitment and enthusiasm.

Then the term "vigilante justice" was brought up, and as hard as they tried, they couldn't keep these two words from popping up. Finally, they decided to face reality: what they were contemplating was, in fact, just that, vigilante justice. There was no getting around it. Taking the law into one's own hands to right a wrong is illegal, plain and simple. So now what? What would happen if they got caught trying to solve someone's problem that the law couldn't, or wouldn't, address? Was it enough to explain that they meant well? They knew the answer, and it wasn't one that they liked.

They realized that they were facing a paradox: how could they help others without hurting themselves? Then two decisions were reached that got them a little closer to coping with the dilemma. The first was deciding that they would call themselves "The Payback Team." And the second was that they were going to work on finding a way to minimize their chances of being detected.

Chapter Six

The Road Rage Incident—Payback Time

Finally, Wade reached the point where he had just about made a full recovery. He had actually enjoyed his three days of rest in the hospital, and he felt that the time he was able to spend talking with his two friends about plans for The Payback Team was worthwhile. He was also pleased with the progress he had made in his therapy sessions. Initially he had doubts, but after he got started, he quickly discovered that the method of therapy that was prescribed was going to be effective.

For the most part, his concentration during this time had been focused on recovery and working on plans for The Payback Team. But he certainly hadn't forgotten about the guy with the FAST 1 plates; after all, the incident nearly caused him to bleed to death. It was only a matter of luck that a medical student was sitting on a park bench nearby and knew exactly how and where to apply pressure after Wade had passed out.

But it was also the med student's lucky day. A great number of doctors start out owing a fortune in tuition bills before they earn their first dollar. This one didn't realize it yet, but her slate will be wiped clean the day she earns her medical license. Maybe she will put two and two together, but she'll never be able to learn the identity of her benefactor for certain.

Wade decided it was time to enjoy a run in the country, and while about in the third mile, his thoughts became focused on what to do about FAST 1. This piece of shit needed to be slowed down a few notches, but how to go about it? He had a couple of good ideas, but he planned to run them by Chico and Rocky to get their added input.

He realized that they had been right; this would make an ideal inaugural project for the new Payback Team. Wade couldn't help thinking how ironic it was that he was going to be the first person for whom the team was going to seek justice.

Wade was certain that Chico was going to prove invaluable at fine-tuning some of his ideas into a workable scenario. And as for Rocky, well, Wade felt that Rocky would no doubt become quite capable of turning a plan into action and then getting the desired results. They would definitely become indispensable in their new roles as members of The Payback Team.

When he was in the hospital, he had tried a couple of times to come up with a game plan regarding FAST 1. But it seemed like nearly every time he started to focus, a detective named Sergeant Callahan would show up and try to get to the bottom of what happened. It was clear he had been shot, but Wade insisted it must have been a random shooting. No one in the park had seen the Corvette, but several strollers had heard the two shots. The cop knew that Wade was full of shit, so there was nothing he could do except walk away. Wade pissed him off big time when he asked him if he didn't have something more important to do, so the cop decided to let him know he didn't like being jacked around.

"Listen, Courtland, I know what you're thinking. You're going to try to settle this on your own. Fine. But if you do try to settle it on your own, you'll be in just as much trouble, maybe more, than the perp. Then we'll see who has 'something more important to do'. Thanks for nothing, asshole." Then, as he walked out of Wade's room for the last time, Wade could hear him muttering "Jesus Christ, why do some assholes have to be so goddamned uncooper..."

But Wade was certain he had made the right decision. There was no way to match the bullet with the gun because there was no bullet. There was no way to place the perp at the intersection because there were no witnesses. This was the classic your-word-against-mine scenario.

And in addition, there was the possibility of a serious downside to cooperating with the police. If Wade blew the whistle on FAST 1, the perp would then have access to Wade's identity, and if he knew a couple of git-'er-done dudes like Chico and Rocky, finding out his address wouldn't be much of a challenge. And after that, Wade would have to watch his back, and it could very well become a case of who gets whacked first.

Wade didn't like the expression "vigilante justice", but he had to admit that it pretty well described the new role he had chosen. So, now, the question became: how to even the score without setting off a flair that would lead Callahan to his doorstep? He decided that the Vette was the key he had been looking for. What Corvette owner doesn't love his beautiful, powerful toy? This one was new, without a scratch or ding anywhere, and perfectly clean. Psychologists say that, in some cases, a car is an extension of a guy's persona, but Wade didn't really care about all of that. What he was sure of was that if you take away a child's toy, he's going to be pretty upset.

So now, he had the start of a plan. He was ready to approach Chico and Rocky and ask them how they could improve on the plan and what would be the best way to pull it off. This had turned out to be a very productive run that was going to result in payback time for a guy who really deserved it.

When he laid out the basic plan to his associates—steal the Vette—they laughed for a full minute. Then they looked at each other and laughed again until they had to wipe the tears away. Then, when Wade asked why they were laughing, they laughed some more.

"Alright, I get the point," said Wade, "you guys find something funny about my plan. So how about cluing me in?"

Rocky was the first to respond. "The point is some lunatic shoots you for no good reason, you almost died, spent three days in the hospital, had to undergo a few weeks of painful therapy, and you want to get even by stealing his fucking car? Are you fucking serious? We figured you were going to ask us how to make this asshole disappear."

Then it was Chico's turn. "Unreal. You must have totally lost it this time. Why don't we just wave our finger in his face and tell him not to do it again or we're going to get really mad. That ought to put the fear of God in him."

Wade gave them both a long, disgusted stare before speaking. "Okay, fine, so you don't like the plan. So let's work on it. But no one's going to cancel this guy's ticket, at least not this time."

Chico thought about it during the silence that followed. Then he said, "Wait a minute. You're right, let's work on it. What if we steel all of his Vettes? It'll drive him completely crazy."

"Now you've lost me," Wade said. "Far as I know, the guys got one Corvette. You know something I don't?"

"You know, it amazes me that you built a company worth tens of millions, and yet, sometimes it seems like you are one sneaker short of a pair. Why don't you just think about this for a minute? What's a guy who owns a Vette going to do when someone steals his ride?" replied Chico.

"Buy another one?"

"Bingo, dipshit. Of course, he will. And when we heist that one, he'll buy another one. And after his insurance company starts raising his rates, and at some point cutting him off, he'll have to dig into his own pocket to finance his Vette fetish. And the final blow will be when he has to step down a notch or two to buy a used Vette, and then who knows what after that? All I know is that it's going to cause him a whole lot more pain than if *he* got shot in the arm."

"Chico, you're a genius!" Wade exclaimed. "I knew you'd come up with a winner. But how do we steel his Vette, okay, his Vettes, and what do we do with 'em when we get 'em?"

It was time for Rocky to climb on board. "Hello, did you guys forget about me? That's where I come in. Don't worry about it. I know this one guy who can steel any set of wheels, anytime, anywhere. And I know this one guy who can come up with a fake title, and another guy who can get the ride down to Tijuana where we can get fifty cents on the dollar. Piece of cake."

"Beautiful. I knew if I could get you clowns to stop laughing, you'd come up with something workable. But why don't we just give the Vette away, or junk it. We don't need 'fifty cents on the dollar," Wade said.

Things got quiet for several minutes as both Wade and Rocky stared at Chico. They knew it was only a matter of waiting patiently until Chico came up with the solution.

"I've got it!" stated Chico.

"We knew you would."

"Let's give the money to charity—in his name," added Chico.

Wade didn't get it and asked, "What's that going to accomplish?"

"Think about if for a minute. What would happen if you sent a nice check to a charity of your choice, with a letter saying that you were so moved by their cause that you sold your beloved Corvette in order to help with their needs?" asked Chico.

"Well, I suppose they would send a receipt so I could deduct it from my taxes, and probably a thank you letter telling me how generous I was to sell my Corvette," answered Wade.

"Right," continued Chico. "And how do you think Mr. FAST 1 will feel when he finds out that his cars are selling for half what they're worth? In fact, now that I think about it, who cares? The point is when he gets a car stolen two days after he buys it, and ten days later a letter thanking him for his kindness—and this happens over and over—how long will it be before he completely loses it? This is so much better than whacking him."

Wade was starting to catch on, but he still didn't get the big picture. "Okay, I like it, but how do we get him to send the letters to the charities?"

Chico rolled his eyes and let out a sigh of disgust. "Spike, you are s-o-o-o s-l-o-o-o-w. He doesn't send the letters, we do. We send a cashier's check with his name on it, a letter with his signature at the bottom, and an envelope with his return address. Everything traces back to him. Now do you get it?"

Wade was about to express his approval when Rocky cut him off. "This is a work of art. Let's do it! Can we start tomorrow? I can call my—"

"When we come to the end," Wade interrupted, "meaning when he is out of insurance, out of money, and out of his mind, let's make sure that we arrange a confrontation where we sit him down and set him straight, let him know why we busted his balls, and inform him that it's not nice to shoot people, that sometimes the other guy shoots back."

Chapter Seven

Getting Ready to Launch

"I know this one guy—" Rocky started out, but was unable to finish.

"Rocky, it seems that half your sentences begin with 'I know this one guy,'" Wade cut him off. "The only thing more monotonous than that is when you tell, or I should say retell, your story about the time a guy came into one of your shops and tried to pawn ten live hand grenades."

They had gotten together not long after their last meeting to go over some of the details of how The Payback Team was going to officially get started.

"Okay, fine, whatever," replied Rocky. "But I do know a guy who can help us with one of our major problems. Remember when we debated the fact that we are out of business, not to mention completely fucked, if we get busted? And unless we come up with something to greatly minimize this possibility, we should probably just think about trying to work on our golf handicaps, especially you, Chico. I remember the last time we played eighteen holes. You really—" He didn't get to finish.

"Would you mind sticking to the subject?" interrupted Wade. "Go back to the part about 'I know this guy.' It looked like you were about to say something important for a change."

"Asshole," muttered Rocky. "All right, the guy I know can help us in a big way. With his expertise, we will have a greater chance of keeping under the radar. I'm all for seeking justice for those who can't do it on their own, but if we get caught, our operation not only is permanently shut down, but our reputations will be worth less than yesterday's newspaper. I don't want to try explaining to my kids through two inches of Plexiglas on visitor's day that Daddy meant well."

Wade jumped in again. "Okay, so who is this guy, and why do we need him?"

"I'm getting there," Rocky replied. "Just put a lid on the interruptions, okay? This guy can help us with the identity issue. By that I mean that he can get us legitimate identification documents so that, if we are ever caught and locked up, they will never be able to track us after we make bail."

Chico was intrigued. "Who is this guy, and how does he do it?"

"He is right below the HMFIC of the witness protection program. He has owed me a huge favor for—"

Wade was confused and interrupted Rocky again, asking, "What's HMFIC?"

"So much for not interrupting," grumbled Rocky. "Spike, you used to be just about the sharpest knife in the drawer, but now I wonder if maybe your parents were first cousins. HMFIC means 'head motherfucker in charge.' I thought everyone knew that.

"Anyway, several years ago, his kid was locked up on an attempted murder charge. I put up a hundred grand on a million-dollar bond because daddy didn't have a dime to his name. So this kid gets out of the can, but now he needs a mouthpiece. So I spring for another fifty large, and when it's all over, the kid gets off—happy ending. I got paid back a long time ago, but every time I see him, he tells me that he is in a position to do something for me in return, if I ever need it.

"Until now, I had no intention of collecting my marker on this one, but now I'm going to take him up on it."

Chico had a question. "Why did you say legitimate identification documents instead of phony IDs?"

"That's because he is going to fix us up with identification papers of real people," Rocky answered. "We will assume the identification of someone else. We are each going to get a wallet with all of the types of things we have in our own wallets: pictures, business cards, credit cards, licenses—the whole enchilada. Our social security numbers will match up, he's covered everything."

Wade was not convinced. "I see a flaw here. What's to stop the person whose identity we are assuming from blowing the whistle if he gets wind of this in some way? I think if I found out that someone else was going around trying to be me, I'd get a little pissed."

"That's because the real person we are talking about is no longer with us," explained Rocky. "Meaning he's dead. That's the beauty of it; he's not around to complain. See, here's how it works. There are a couple of cops who work the part of town that most people try to avoid, the place where alkies go to take their last step to oblivion; skid row is what we used to call it. So, sometimes, they find one of these guys frozen in an alley before it's reported. Then instead of following procedure and calling for the paddy wagon to take him to the morgue, he just disappears, and no one knows about it. Except that the two cops are a couple of grand richer, and now there's a real identity for someone else, namely, us, with the help of my friend, to takeover."

Wade and Chico were almost convinced, but, as usual, Wade wanted to be certain. "Is this foolproof? Is there really no way that this thing can get tripped up?"

"I wish I could say yes, but nothing's 100 percent," Rocky responded. "It's just an attempt to tilt the odds in our favor. The likely scenario, if we get caught, is that we are taken into police custody, then we prove who we are, then we bond out, then we eighty-six the wallets, and then there's no way to trace us because they will be looking for someone else. If they really want to do some serious checking at the police station before we're released, we may have a problem, but that's not likely since everything looks like we are who we say we are."

Chico was pretty much satisfied and asked Rocky, "I like it. What do you need from us to get started?"

"Just your driver's license number. That way, he can check with one of his contacts at the secretary of state's office and make sure that your picture gets on the new license. You don't have to do anything else except wait about a week, and then I'll hand you your new wallets. Hope you guys like the pictures of your new wives and kids."

Wade put another problem on the table. "What do we do about our vehicle? How do we get around someone recognizing our ride, or worse yet, taking down the license number?"

"I know this one guy who juggles license plates pretty well," said Rocky. "What I mean is that he goes to the long-term parking lot at the airport and takes the plates off two vehicles, one of which looks just like our vehicle, and that set goes on our ride. So when someone reports our plate number for whatever reason, the law checks it out and traces it back to the owner of the vehicle that matches ours. That way, if a cop runs a random check, he sees that it belongs to a vehicle that matches the description of ours.

"And this guy is pretty thorough. For example, he runs the plates before we ever see them. Imagine if Murphy's Law kicked in and he swiped plates off a stolen vehicle, or if the owner had a couple of warrants out on him. Wouldn't that be a ball buster?"

Chico had a concern. "But the guy who is missing the plates would have reported them stolen."

"Remember: I said he jacks two sets of plates," Rocky reminded him. "The other set goes on the car that looks like ours. Now the guy who owns this vehicle doesn't report his plates stolen because he still has plates on his car. It just takes him awhile to notice that they are the wrong plates. And I know this one guy who will let me know when the plates are finally reported stolen, and then, because we are nice guys at heart, we mail the plates back to the owner with a nice note thanking him for lending them to us. Then the process starts all over again."

Chico couldn't help but wonder about the inconvenience that The Payback Team's tactics would occasionally cause other individuals. "I can't help but feel sorry for some of the innocent bystanders who are going to be unwillingly involved. What about these poor guys who are going to get jacked around with their missing plates?"

Wade was the first to respond. "Yeah, I've given that a lot of thought. We've got to carefully assess each situation to see if any possible problems we may cause are worth it in relation to the end result of settling a score that needs settling. Sometimes, we'll just have to decide to back off."

Then Rocky added a few words. "Now, I can see a little more clearly why the law doesn't want John Q. Citizen trying to take over their job. Problem is, they don't always do their job, and I guess that's pretty much why guys like us come up with the idea of The Payback Team."

Chico had one more important point to cover. "Let's get back to our list of concerns because I have one more thing to bring up. What about someone recognizing us? For the most part, we have all kept pretty low profiles, at least considering our status in the business community. We're not like Donald Trump, where we go out of our way to get on the front page, but we do know a lot of people."

Rocky answered, "Good question, and I have two responses. First, I know this one guy who can help us with disguises. I don't mean anything elaborate, but he can alter our appearances with wigs, tinted contact lenses, facial scars, beards, etc. He's even got these plugs we can stuff inside our cheeks to alter the shape of our faces. You want to look bald? He can take care of that in less than a minute. You know, this will really be an important issue once we get going because, as we all know, these days, there are cameras all over the place."

Wade sounded his approval. "Good thing for us you know so many guys. But you said that there were two answers to Chico's concern."

"Right," said Rocky. "The best way to keep from being recognized is through subcontracting."

Wade didn't get it. "Okay, now you've lost me. Explain."

"By subcontracting, I mean to hire out a lot of what needs to be done. I know this one guy who can take care of anything for the right price. You want somebody found? He'll find 'em. You want somebody tailed? He'll stick to 'em like he was their shadow. You want somebody tied up in a pretty pink ribbon and delivered to your doorstep? No problem."

Chico had to know. "Holy shit! Where do you find all of these guys?"

"You'd be surprised," replied Rocky, "about the guys who have walked into my pawnshops. I remember, one time, this guy came in trying to pawn ten live hand—"

"Stop already," Wade cut him off. "We've heard that one too many times to count."

"Okay, fine, some other time. But I think it's probably time for us to invite him to one of our meetings. I know you're thinking he must be about one step away from being a hit man for the mob, but the fact is, he's a pretty solid citizen. Major Robins. Twenty years in the marines, then ten years as a covert operative for who knows what; perhaps the CIA. For the last five years, he's been one of the most

35

successful bounty hunter's around. We can get a lot done through him, stuff that stops with him and can't be traced back to us. But he ain't cheap. Spike, he'll put a nice dent into that sixty million of yours before long, depending on how much we want to use him," explained Rocky.

Wade was ready to wrap it up. The meeting had lasted a good part of the morning, and the coffee had long since gone cold. Also, he was aching to get out for a run. "I can see where we could put him to good use. Okay, then, next meeting it is."

Rocky wasn't quite ready to end the meeting. "So when do we get to hear more details about the Guatemala gang, and when can we get started on accumulating a few Corvettes?"

"Bring it up at the next meeting. I promise we'll talk about it."

Chapter Eight

The Payback Team Meets Their First Subcontractor

"Guys, meet Major Laurel Robins," said Rocky. "Major, meet Tommy Martin and Spike—I mean Wade Courtland. I forgot he doesn't like to be called Spike."

Major Robins was just over six feet and about two hundred pounds. He wore a sleeveless camouflage vest, making it easy to notice the *semper fi* tattoo on his right forearm. With his marine haircut, chiseled, muscular features, perfectly flat midsection, narrow waist, and disproportionately large upper torso, he could almost have been mistaken for the guy on the marine recruiting poster. The only factor that didn't fit was his age, which Chico and Wade figured was somewhere around the early fifties. He could also be likened to an older version of one of those ultimate fighters seen on cable TV. Any mugger who chose this guy as a victim would quickly find out that he had chosen the wrong profession.

After the handshakes were completed, Wade asked, "So, do we call you, Major? Laurel? What's your preference?"

"Only person calls me Laurel is my mother, so I guess Major will be just fine," replied Robins. "But here's the thing, 'Major' was just a nickname I picked up in boot camp, and it kind of stuck. I actually never got above the rank of lieutenant."

By the looks on everyone's faces, it was clear that he would need to explain further.

"Well, this is what happened. The finest marine I ever met was our drill instructor in basic training. He motivated me more than I could ever have imagined was possible. I went out of my way to be the perfect marine, and he noticed. I had the shiniest shoes, the best pressed uniform, and the snappiest salute of anyone in our squad. He was constantly using me as an example. He must have said it fifty times: 'Why can't you guys be more like Private Robins.' Just about when they were sick of hearing it, we had bed inspection, and I was the only one who passed. So he lined us up, stood us at attention, and started his lecture. He said, 'You guys are a sorry bunch of losers. Why can't you be more like Private Robins? He is a major asset to this squad, but no one appreciates it.'

" 'More like a major asshole,' someone said in a loud whisper. When the sergeant tried to find out who said it, everyone dummied up. 'All right, fine,' said the sergeant and ordered everyone to drop and give him fifty. Worse yet, he said he had to get to a meeting, and he said, 'I'm putting Private Robins in charge of seeing that everyone completes their pushups.'

"Now, here's an example of why I loved this guy. He took me outside and said he realized he had made a big mistake. He had been building me up to be the squad leader because he thought I had leadership potential, but now he knew he had pretty much blown it. So he told me to leave them alone for a few minutes, go over to his office and bring back two cases of beer. So when I got back with the beer in about five minutes, I asked if everyone had completed the punishment. Naturally, they all said yes, and naturally, I said, 'Good. Now, since I am in charge, I say we all should have a couple of beers and take the rest of the afternoon off.' That really saved my ass from being the outsider from then on, but naturally, the name 'Major' stuck. So that's my story. Now, what about the 'Spike' thing?"

Wade shot a look of disgust at Rocky and said, "I'll get to that later, but first let's get down to why we're here. Did Rocky fill you in on why we contacted you?"

"Yes, but it doesn't make any sense," replied Robins. "You guys want me to help you with a couple of assholes who owe your nephew a few hundred dollars? By the time you collect from them, you may very likely have spent way more than they owe. Isn't that a little like taking a cannon on a squirrel hunt? Why not just give him the money and forget about it?"

Wade gave Rocky another angry look. "Apparently, Rocky forgot to mention that these are just kind of warm-up exercises and that we intend to branch out into other, more complicated and serious ventures — the kinds of situation where someone has been wronged big time but doesn't have the resources to do anything about it. I'll give you an example in a minute, but let me try to put this in a little more perspective by asking you a question. What would you do if someone ran up to you, grabbed cash out of your pocket and took off? And let's say that you chased the guy and got the license number of someone who was waiting for him around the corner. Keep in mind, of course, that going to the police will probably just be a waste of time because he will have fifteen relatives who will all swear that he was with them at the time of the robbery. So it's your word against his, and you're gonna lose."

Major Robbins took the bait. "Let's put it this way: by the time I got through with him, he would have wished he had been caught, convicted, and gang raped while serving time in prison."

Wade was pleased with the answer. "I guess you get the point. It's the same thing; in both cases, you were robbed, plain and simple. So there's a lot more to it than the money. He should pay for the crime. It becomes personal, and someone has to seek justice. It would be great if we could count on our legal system to always come through and handle it for us, but we all know that this is often not the way it turns out."

"Okay, I'm starting to like it. Got any examples of where else you're going with this?" asked Major Robins. When Wade explained the Guatemala situation, Major Robins thought for a moment before replying. "If you guys want to try something like that, I'd say you've got a whole lot of 'warming up' to do, as you put it a minute ago."

Chico jumped in before Wade could bring up the example of FAST 1, saying, "I haven't said anything about this until now, but I've got a situation to bring up that would fit in as a great warm-up exercise. My wife has a friend in her bridge group who is a victim of wife battering. This lady has most everyone convinced that she bruises easily and was taking some self-defense courses that got pretty physical at times. But Christine began asking questions about the class, and it became obvious that she was just blowing smoke. So she took her out for coffee and pried it out of her. Her husband is one of those Jekyll-and-Hyde cases: upstanding citizen as far as the community is concerned, but a real monster when he's had a few too many or if he's had a bad day at work or if the Cubs lose or whatever. You know the type. This guy needs a lesson, big time."

Rocky chimed in. "I can top that one. It was in the paper the other day, really sad. My wife was crying about it, and I have to admit, I felt like crying, too. It's that case about the guy who raped and murdered a fourteen-year-old girl, but he got off when it came out that the police had violated his rights when they illegally gathered evidence. Well, the news story was about the girl's mother. She had a stroke a couple of days after the case was dismissed, and now she is in a coma and not expected to recover. And she has two younger kids at home. Now, I could really get my teeth into that one."

The major had heard enough. He said, "I can help. I can definitely help. In fact, I like what you are doing. I'd like to say 'put me on the team and I'll work for free,' but I can't. I have my own team, my staff, and they are going to have to get paid. It'll take more than just me to handle most of what you guys want me to accomplish. The good news is that I won't charge you for my time, plus, the guys I will be using will be far removed from you, with almost no chance of anything coming back to bite you in the ass."

Chico asked, "Can you give us some idea of how you will charge us for your work?"

"It's not really possible to predict in advance, but I'm sure you wouldn't want to get a big surprise each time you get a bill, so let's leave it at this. I'll send you a bill, itemizing each detail of our work, and if you don't like it, don't pay it. Then I'll walk away, and we're done. That way, the pressure is on me to make sure that I am more than fair, and it will ensure our chances for a long-term relationship. How does that sound?" asked the major.

No one answered directly, but by the nods and looks on all three faces, it was clear that this arrangement would be more than satisfactory.

Wade had heard enough and said, "Well, then, let's get started. What do you need from us?"

"Give me any details you have about the two guys who stiffed your nephew."

"Well, Ralphie used to have the business card of the guy who accused him of cheating. His name is John, and his last name starts with V," replied Wade.

The major got up and started to walk toward the door while saying, "Okay, that's enough for me. I'll be back by noon tomorrow with his full name, date of birth, social security number, address, and phone number."

All three caught Wade's look of bewilderment and laughed for a full minute. But Wade didn't get the joke.

Chico was the first to catch his breath and said, "Spike, it's amazing how, on the one hand, you are a really intelligent guy, but on the other hand, sometimes you are so clueless. Maybe someday they will have 'dumb Wade jokes' instead of dumb blond jokes. Don't you get it? The major is fucking with you. The fact that your nephew used to have a business card is of no relevance. It's just not enough to go on. You need to come up with a lot more than this."

Rocky and Chico both looked at Major Robins, shook their heads, and gave a smirk that implied that their friend was beyond help.

"Okay, fine. Maybe I'm just a little too focused on getting started to remember what complete assholes you guys can be at times, like just about always," said Wade. "Here's what I know: he owns a used car lot in the Gary/Hammond area, lives in Hanover Park, and I heard he occasionally plays no limit hold 'em at one of the Indiana casinos. And the other guy's name is Stuart Stedman. He's a bartender, and he used to live in Franklin Park. His father has the same name and also lives in Franklin Park. Ralphie had the father's address at one time, but he shouldn't be hard to locate because Ralphie said he's in the phone book. So just as soon as you can get back to us with enough information, I think we are ready to take the next step and contact these guys. We'll need to decide what we're going to do when they refuse to pay up, and that's going to be when the fun comes in. And as far as FAST 1 is concerned, Rocky, I think you should have your guy run the plate, get us a name and address, and then tell your other contacts to start hijacking some Corvettes and start shipping them off to Guadalajara, or wherever the hell they're going."

Rocky concluded the meeting with one word, "Finally."

41

Chapter Nine

Making Progress

Things were starting to come together. In the week between meetings, a lot had happened. The three old friends were so full of enthusiasm that each tried to outshout the others in order to be the first one to be heard. Wade finally raised his hands in a "whoa/stop" motion and told Chico to settle down and let Rocky go first.

Rocky blurted everything out in one long sentence. "I've got your wallets with your new identities, I've got some good news from Major Robbins, I know where the asshole who shot you lives, we have now stolen our first Corvette, it's on it's way to Tijuana, I've got some information on the guy who gave Ralphie the bad check, and we are close to finding out about the other guy who said Ralphie had cheated him."

Chico was waiting for the slightest break in Rocky's speech and wasted no time in jumping in. "And I've come up with some plans about what we should do with Ralphie's two friends, assuming we still want to try to pressure them to settle up."

Wade liked the first part of what Chico had just said, but was surprised and curious about the second part. "What are you talking about? Why are you questioning the issue of going after them?"

"Well, I was running my ideas past Christine, and she wondered why we would want to mess around with a couple of little weasels like these guys. She reminded me about her friend who is a punching bag for her psycho husband, and wants to know why we don't focus our energy on something more important."

Wade hesitated for a minute and then responded. "I've thought about this a lot. In one regard, you're right. Why should three millionaires in their fifties screw around with a couple of lowlifes like these two jerkoffs? And I keep coming up with the same answer: before we move on to more worthwhile challenges, we need to fine-tune our act. Frankly, if we can't pull this off successfully, The Payback Team should probably consider dropping any plans of staying in business. Also, I keep putting myself in Ralphie's shoes and I know how I'd feel if the same thing happened to me at his age. Remember what the major said? If it happened to him, the guy would prefer jail time to the consequences he would dish out."

Chico responded, "That's pretty much what I told her, but I just wanted to make sure that everyone felt the same. So, do you want to hear my plans for these guys?"

Rocky was the first to comment. "Of course, we do, but if you'll back up a couple of steps, you might remember that Wade gave me the floor first, and you pretty much interrupted." Chico mumbled something that sounded like "fucking asshole", but neither of the other two heard it clearly, and neither one cared. Rocky continued. "Our Corvette friend's name is Everett Flanagan, and he's a stock trader. Very rich. Lives in a gated estate up in Barrington Hills. So we need to try a slightly different tactic because this guy can afford to buy a new Vette every week for the rest of his existence. I still think copping his rides is a good idea, but it's just not going to hurt as much as we had expected—more of an inconvenience than anything else.

"And with regard to Stuart Stedman, the major located him. We now have his address, and he even found out where Stedman works; he's a bartender in DeKalb. The major got all this information by scamming the guy's old man. Told him he went to high school with his son and he was trying to get ahold of him regarding a class reunion. So now we're ready to proceed on this one.

"As far as the other guy, John V., is concerned, Major Robins has one of his guys asking around in the casinos down in Indiana, and it looks like he plays in the poker room at Harrah's Horseshoe Casino in Hammond just about every Friday afternoon. So we're close on this one also.

"So now, Chico, pal, it's your turn. I can tell you're having trouble waiting for me to finish, but at least you didn't interrupt this time."

Chico looked like he was about to mumble something else about his opinion of Rocky, but decided he had more important things to cover. Instead, he said, "Thank you for finally finishing. Now, here's what I think we should do. First off, we need a work vehicle. I suggest we get a work van, the kind that has no side windows. The windows in the rear doors should be heavily tinted. That way, all three of us can sit in the back, along with whichever asshole we want to take a ride with us while we discuss business, and no one can see what's going on inside. Typically, it won't be practical to try to meet with these guys in their homes or offices, except under unusual circumstances, because then they would have the home court advantage, not to mention access to their weapon of choice.

"We can use two of those 'three across seats' that detach from an SUV, one on each side of the open space in the rear of the van, facing each other. And I suggest we use one of the major's staff as our driver. Maybe Rocky can go out and pick up a nondescript van, registering it to his new identity, and then get one of his contacts to furnish us with plates. And I think we should get a series of magnetic signs to stick on the sides and on the back. Like 'Johnson's Meat Market' or 'Henry's Mobile Repairs,' complete with a company logo and phone number, so it looks innocent and legit. And we should change to a new sign each time we use the van."

Chico could see that his ideas were being well received, maybe even better than he had hoped for, so he decided to continue. But before he got the next word out, Wade cut him off, saying, "Why do we have to change the signs every time?"

Chico looked annoyed when he said, "Spike, I was betting that you would ask that question. Rocky, do you want to explain it to him?"

"Yeah, sure, I knew he wouldn't get it," replied Rocky. "You see, we want to attract as little attention as possible. If the sign changes all the time, no one's going to see a pattern or remember anything about us. Do you think Stedman is just going to stand there and wait for us to grab him every time he sees a van that says 'Wolf's Heating and Air Conditioning'? Do you want to be the one to chase after him when he takes off like the Road Runner on steroids? Different signs put the element of surprise on our side. Now do you get it?"

Wade didn't try to hide his irritation. "Why do you guys have to be such smart asses? Can't you just—?"

Chico decided that what he had to say was more important than listening to Wade, so he cut him off. "I think we're ready to go and have a little chat with Mr. Stedman. Let's wait outside the bar he works at, and then have him join us for a little ride. We'll explain that a friend has asked us to collect the money he owes, and we'll be careful not to let him know that it's Ralphie. Remember that he knows where Ralphie lives, and if he makes the connection, it could spell trouble for Ralphie. Since this guy apparently owes plenty of people, he shouldn't be able to make the link. And we are going to collect more than what he owes Ralphie because we're going to explain that there are interest and late fees involved. This accomplishes three things: one, in terms of payback and justice, there should be a penalty; two, he won't be able to link the figure we come up with to the amount of money he owes Ralphie; and three, we can use a little extra to compensate us for the expense of hiring the driver. Anything left over goes to charity. I'm sure we are not interested in personally profiting from any of our little projects. I'm guessing that with court costs, the cost of serving the summons, and the cost of the skip tracer, your nephew is out about nine hundred bucks. So I think two grand should just about cover it."

Wade was looking a little uncomfortable. "What makes you think he's just going to hop in our van, and why would you think he would have two grand on him to hand over to us?"

Chico was ready with an answer. "Take a look at our friend Rocky over there. Don't you think he's capable of 'persuading' just about anyone to get in the van? And yes, of course, he's not going to have that much cash on him. It's our job to explain to him in terms that will make him realize that not paying carries much more consequences than forking it over when he does get the cash. We'll give him plenty of time, let's say a whole week to get it and we'll tell him to have it on him because we'll be meeting him again to conclude our little chat. But we'll pick him up somewhere else, like when he gets home, or when he leaves for work since who knows what he might have waiting for us in the parking lot outside the bar?"

Now, it was Rocky's turn to express a concern. "Okay, getting him in the van is a slam dunk, but what if he doesn't have the cash after a week?"

"That may happen," replied Chico, "but it's unlikely, once we explain the consequences of not paying. And I'm not talking about violence, at least not with this guy; we'll save that for someone who really deserves it, like the wife beater, or the guy who raped and killed the teenage girl. We'll ask him how he feels about having his wheels 'repossessed' or how he would like to come home and find everything he owns sitting in a busted up pile on the front lawn of his apartment building. There's lots of ways of getting him to cooperate, we just gotta be a little creative with our 'motivational techniques'."

Both Wade and Rocky looked like they were satisfied with the plan, but Rocky was the first to speak. "You said you have plans for both of Ralphie's deadbeats. What about John V.?"

Chico responded, "Hey, it's been a long day, and besides, I'm dying to see what's in my new wallet. For now, why don't you work on getting the van and the plates, and when that's done—and you get a driver lined up—we'll head over to the bar, and on the way we'll go over what to do about John V. And, by the way, I was listening when you mentioned the part about FAST 1 being loaded, and that does present a new twist to our payback plan for him, but I think I can come up with a solution. We'll talk about that next time also. It's four o'clock, so we still have time to grab a couple of cold ones and get home in time for dinner. Meeting adjourned."

Rocky and Chico got up to leave, but Wade wanted to get in the last word. "Just one more thing, don't mention anything to Paula about FAST 1's gated estate. That's exactly what she wants us to look into. But there's nothing wrong with our house. It's where our kids grew up and—"

There was no way he was going to finish the sentence. Rocky and Chico both interrupted, but Rocky was the loudest, who said, "Spike, you cheap bastard, give the woman what she wants. You've got just about the best wife in the world; she'd have to be to up with an asshole like you, and you've lived in that house forever. Thanks for bringing this up. I'm gonna make a point to take a video of the estate, and guess who's gonna be the first one to see it? And you know what else? The place he lives in is like horse country. There are horses all over the place. That'll remind her that she wants you to get her a horse. It's about time, don't you think? *Now*, the meeting's adjourned."

Wade stood up in disgust and headed toward the door. He was mumbling to himself, but the others had no trouble understanding the words that came out of his mouth. "Beautiful. Fucking beautiful."

Chapter Ten

The Big Day Arrives—Almost

Wade was reaching for the phone just as it rang. It was Chico. "Hey, I was just going to call you. What's up?"

Chico had a slightly depressed tone in his voice. "You know, I'm really not comfortable with this Stedman thing. I know we're supposed to leave in a few hours to go and have a little chat with him, but I just don't see the point in trying to collect two grand from some stupid shmuck who cheated your nephew. And what if we ultimately have to use force or mess him up in some other way? Is that right? Is it worth it? Why don't you and Rocky handle this one? I know we're supposed to be a team, but I'm just not—"

"Okay, fine," Wade interrupted; he didn't need to hear anymore. "Maybe if I tell you why I was trying to call you, you might see it differently. There's been kind of a new development. I've already called Rocky and asked him if he can reschedule the driver and put this off until tomorrow. We need to get together to go over a couple of things. Rocky will be here in thirty minutes, and I was about to call you to tell you also. Get here as soon as you can. It's important."

Paula was nice enough to make everyone sandwiches on short notice, even though she had better things on her agenda. After everyone sat down, Wade explained that he had called his nephew the previous evening to let him know that he was going to be meeting with Stedman. Wade wanted to know any additional details that might be helpful in their attempt to accomplish their mission.

Wade spent the next ten minutes talking without interruption. He explained that this guy, Stuart Stedman, was actually a likeable, friendly guy. He had borrowed from a lot of people and stiffed just about all of them. But it was not because he was a thief by nature, but because he was an addicted gambler—big time. He was twenty-four years old, had lost his wife and the custody of his two kids, had a car repossessed, had been thrown out of a couple of apartments, and hadn't been making alimony payments, all because of gambling.

49

Whenever he ran out of cash, which was often, he got hold of money any way he could, usually by borrowing, and then it was only a matter of time before it was gone again.

"I've had a complete paradigm shift about this guy," said Wade. "In fact, I now see our whole mission a lot differently as a result of that conversation with Ralphie." Wade caught Rocky's look and knew he had better explain what he was talking about. "A paradigm shift occurs when something causes you to change your point of view. I remember I once heard a story in a psychology class that illustrates this. A father got on a commuter train with his two young boys. In no time, they were out of control, terrorizing the car, running, jumping, yelling, annoying everyone, and the father seemed completely oblivious and lost in his own world. An irate passenger walked up to the father and asked him why he didn't take control. The father looked up with tears in his eyes and said, 'I don't know what to do. We've just come from the hospital. My wife has gone to be with the Lord. I don't know how to tell them. I don't know, I just don't know.' He then buried his face in his hands and began sobbing. Now, it was different, the paradigm shift having occurred. Instead of anger, the passengers were showing compassion. Several were trying to entertain the boys, and two elderly ladies were trying to comfort the father."

Now that Wade was satisfied that Rocky was back on track, he continued where he had left off. "I think we've been too focused on punishment and retribution. We've thrown around words like 'justice' and 'payback.' Is that how we want to see ourselves? As avengers? Sure, sometimes we will have no choice, like the guy who raped and murdered the young girl. I think about that every day, and I can't wait for Chico to come up with a plan for how to take care of that sick psycho. But what about Stedman? Should he be punished or helped? Or maybe both? And what about the wife beater? I'll bet if you look into it, you'd find that one of the reasons she doesn't leave him is because she loves him, and most of the time, they have a good marriage. Same question: should he be punished, helped, or both?"

Wade paused for a moment and noticed that his words were having a positive impact on Chico, and Chico also noticed that Wade hadn't taken a bite out of his sandwich, while Chico and Rocky had already finished theirs. Rocky was the first to break the silence. "I pretty much agree with you, but what about someone like FAST 1? How do you 'help' a guy like that? Isn't punishment the only answer? He didn't shoot me, but damn it, I felt just as mad about it as if he had."

Wade had an answer. "Thank you for saying that, I appreciate it. I don't really know if he can be helped, but I'm just saying that we shouldn't only be about punishment and justice. Maybe, sometimes, the best thing we can do is to turn someone in the right direction. What if we could get Ralphie's money back and get Stedman into Gamblers Anonymous?"

Rocky blurted it out first. "How the hell are you going to do that? And what about John V.? The major's guy caught up with him, and I've got the complete rundown on him. His name is John Vargas, and—"

"Let's not get off course here," Chico cut him off. "Spike, I like where you're going with this. One of the reasons I was starting to get a little uncomfortable with our mission is that it was a departure from where we were in our business careers. How many times over the years did we meet and discuss business? And we always came up with the same conclusion: first, do right by others, and then, hopefully, they will do right by us. We applied this principle to our customers, our employees, and our suppliers, and it paid off. Spike, I kept the sign you gave me. Remember? It hung on the wall behind my desk at work, and now it's in my study at home. At the top of the sign it says, 'Rules for Treating Customers.' Below that it reads, 'Rule Number 1, The Customer is Always Right' and below that 'Rule Number 2, If You Think the Customer is Wrong, Refer to Rule Number 1.' The point is, it's a little one sided for us to just punish the perpetrator and make it right for the victim. Why not look at the perpetrator as someone who needs help also?

"And I'm back on track with Stedman. And I think I know how we can accomplish both, getting the money and getting him into GA. We do it through the old man. There are at least a couple of clues that they are close. Notice how he tried to be helpful when the major was pumping him for information about how to get in contact with his son? And, Spike, didn't you tell us that he lived in the same town as the old man for awhile, Franklin Park? Guys who don't get along with their parents don't usually want to stay close by. I'd make a large wager that the old man knows nothing about his kid's addiction and would be quick to take action if we inform him. Plus, I'm not above recommending some intimidation tactics if that doesn't work."

He could tell that his ideas were being well received, so Chico decided to continue. "I've even got an idea about how to deal with FAST 1. Stealing his Vettes is still a good idea, but it's not going to have as much effect as we originally thought. The annoyance factor will be effective, but not the economic factor. So when we have the sit-down with him that Spike proposed, let's get him to discuss the shooting, and let's get it on tape. Then we will tell him that he needs to do two things in order for the harassment to stop. One, turn himself in or we will, and two, complete an anger management class. That may not help, but at least there's a chance. You can let him know that if he does what we ask, you will go to court and recommend leniency, thanking him for being a good citizen and turning himself in, etc."

Wade wasn't satisfied. "Wait a minute. What makes you think he's going to give us a confession? I don't think there's a chance in hell that—"

Chico couldn't wait to blurt it out. "Spike, have I got a surprise for you. I was setting you up for this one, and you took the bait. Predictable as usual. Now, here's the thing: I told Rocky to have the guy who heisted the Vette to get FAST 1's piece out of the glove compartment. It's a Smith and Wesson snub nose .38 caliber, and we've got it. So let's put it in a plastic bag and show it to him. And we tell him that his prints are all over it and that when ballistics matches the slug pulled out of your arm, there's no way that he's—"

Wade didn't let him finish. "But there was no slug in my arm. The bullet went completely through and..." Wade stopped in mid-sentence when he saw that both Chico and Rocky were shaking their heads and rolling their eyes in disgust. Then he paused for a few seconds while he figured it out. "So you're saying that we let him think that the police have the slug because there's no reason for him to believe otherwise. I get it. That's beautiful. Nice going. I'm even going to overlook the fact that you can both be such complete assholes most of the time."

"Well, I'm glad you like the plan and that you were able to figure it out on your own without our having to spell it out for you, as usual. Now, Rocky, what were you saying about John V.?"

"He's a complete sleazeball, and I'd love to see how you're going to transform this guy," said Rocky. "He runs a used car lot in Gary, Indiana, and it's at least his third one. He'd open them up and then had to shut them down a couple of times, the major had found out. He specializes in the cars that nobody else wants, makes enough cosmetic improvements to make them look saleable, hides the mechanical flaws, and then sells them to people who can't afford to buy a set of wheels in the conventional way; charges them a small down payment and a huge amount of juice. The state's attorney's fraud division has closed him down more than once, but then he opens up in another location, changes the name, and fixes it so his name doesn't show up on any of the business application paperwork. And get this: he's served time for fraud, embezzlement, passing phony checks, and is now on probation for possession of stolen securities. Your nephew picked a real winner."

Wade responded, "I'm not surprised. Sounds like your classic sociopath. And before you both think I've gone totally soft, let me tell you without a doubt that there are some hardcore cases that only deserve punishment, or at least the threat of punishment. Did you know that the most unfortunate characteristic of a sociopath is that he doesn't have a conscience? Isn't that amazing? No conscience. In general, about four percent of the population is comprised of sociopaths; that's one in twenty-five. But in prison, it's several times as high. Easy to see why. When we're dealing with someone like this, there's no hope, and we would only waste our time trying to change his behavior. In some countries, once they have determined that a criminal is sociopathic, they don't even try to rehabilitate him. They just put him away for as long as possible and keep him out of society."

Rocky was fascinated. "Really, a person without a conscience? How can you tell? Are they born that way? How do they get that way?"

"No, we're not gonna be able to tell for sure," replied Wade. "The shrinks know how to figure this out, but there are some traits that offer clues. Usually, they are very narcissistic, often have trophy wives because this makes them look good, and they thrive on being envied and recognized. They are often charming, but if you look carefully, you will see that it is a phony kind of charm. And very importantly, they are incapable of loving others. It may seem like they love their spouse, but typically, it's just for show because they want to be well thought of. They are often addicts—whether drugs, alcohol, or gambling—because without true love to fill their lives, they are easily bored and seek thrills and excitement in abnormal ways. This is also the kind of person who is most apt to beat his wife and cheat on her as well. As far as nature or nurture, no one is sure, but most psychiatrists give the edge to nature, meaning that they are hardwired from birth. Sad, but probably true."

Wade paused while he finally finished his sandwich. "Fortunately, not all sociopaths are dangerous or criminal because they are typically intelligent enough to realize that the laws of society are going to apply to them as well as those of us who do have a conscience. It's just that the rest of us try to obey the laws of society because we know it's the right thing to do and because we care for others and their rights."

It was time to end a very productive session. Wade could tell that all present felt that things were on the right track and that they were now more excited than before about proceeding with their mission. "Okay, looks like we're in sync. Rocky, have the driver pick us up at the same time tomorrow, and Chico, see what you need to do to revise the plans you were going to cover with us. Remember, we were going to discuss this on our way to Stedman's bartending job."

Chapter Eleven

The Payback Team's First Encounter

Wade was just returning from his morning run when he saw a van pull up in front of his house. The sign on the side of the van read BENSON'S BAKERY, so naturally he had no idea why the van was stopping at his house. He knew it couldn't be Rocky and Chico because they weren't due for over an hour.

As he started to walk in the front door, Rocky jumped out of the van and hollered at Wade that he needed to hurry and get ready to go. He explained that he had tried to call him and had left a voice mail, but since Wade had been out on his run, he wasn't aware of any change in plans.

"What's the rush?" asked Wade. "You guys aren't due here for at least an hour."

Rocky told him to hurry and get ready, and they would discuss the details in the van. He also reminded him to be sure to bring his new wallet.

Instead of the usual half hour it would have taken him to shower and change, Wade was ready in about fifteen minutes, but that wasn't good enough for Rocky. "What took you so long? My wife can get ready for a formal dinner party faster than—"

Wade cut him off. "Never mind about your wife. Get to the point about what's going on."

It turned out that they wouldn't be heading to the bar after all. Major Robins had called Rocky early that morning with some new information. It seemed he had done a lot more than he was asked to do. One of the major's staff had checked with the bar and gotten Stedman's work schedule and found out that he was not scheduled to work until the weekend. The guy had also taken the time to go to Stedman's apartment complex, locate his pickup truck, and attach a tracking device. Then the major called about an hour later to say that Stedman was at Hollywood Casino, in Aurora. Rocky explained that they needed to leave ASAP before Stedman busted out of the poker game or blackjack or craps or whatever method of going broke he had chosen. Wade asked if maybe Robins had assumed a little too much responsibility, including racking up a fair amount of expense, but Rocky pointed out that their time was of more value than any of the other considerations. Did they feel like wasting a two-hour round trip out to the bar in DeKalb? The answer was obvious. In fact, they all decided that Robins was showing the kind of initiative that was needed. Chico made reference to Robin's story when they first met him about how he was a "major asset" to his squad in basic training, and pointed out that he was also becoming a major asset to The Payback Team. It was only a half-hour drive to Hollywood Casino, just enough time to go over how they were going to handle the meeting with Stedman. Chico had wanted to go over his plans for John V., but that would have to wait for the ride home.

As soon as they located Stedman's pickup truck, Wade started to complain about how long they might have to wait for him to leave the casino. Chico mumbled something about Wade being the most impatient person he had ever met, and then bet him a hundred dollars that he would have Stedman approaching his truck within ten minutes. He then picked up his cell phone and called the casino. When the operator answered, he said, "Hi, I'm looking at a blue Dodge pickup truck, Illinois license number B 24 331 with the lights on. Someone's going to have a dead battery before long. Hope you have a way of notifying the owner." The operator must have thanked him because he ended the conversation by saying, "No problem. Bye." Eight minutes later, Stedman showed up. Wade was shocked, but handed Chico the hundred dollars.

Stedman was a pleasant-looking guy and appeared much younger than the twenty-four years that Ralphie had mentioned. No doubt this guy would be carded until he was at least thirty. When comparing notes as they saw him walking toward the truck, it turned out that each of them had the same initial feeling about Stedman: he sure didn't look like a deadbeat or a sick gambler or a divorced father of two who was behind on alimony. One of them even commented that he looked like the kind of guy he wouldn't mind having for a son-in-law. Finally, they all shared the opinion that this was someone who they wanted to help, and that this was quite a departure from their original goal.

Stedman was of average height and weight, so getting him in the van was not going to be a problem. The van was parked about fifty feet from the truck, and the driver did exactly as he had been instructed. The van drove slowly toward the truck, timing the speed so that it would arrive at the truck at the exact same time as Stedman, but from the opposite direction. Chico was in the front passenger seat and rolled down the window, smiled at Stedman and asked if his name was Stu. The second he heard the word "yes," Wade slid open the side door, Rocky jumped out, picked up Stedman, and put him in the van. Immediately, Wade closed the door and the van drove off. Elapsed time: six seconds.

After driving about three blocks, the van pulled into a nearly empty parking lot and parked behind a large trailer. There was just enough room between the trailer and the brick wall of an apartment building for the van to fit, briefly hiding it from view. Art, the driver, had been carefully scanning the approach to the casino parking lot to try to find the best location for what came next.

Chico got out and removed the magnetic signs, in case anyone saw Stedman being hustled into the van and reported it. The most distinctive thing they would have remembered would have been the sign. But now, that was no longer an issue. It was just another ordinary vehicle. He also changed the plates. Rocky had a friend who owned an auto dealership and just happened to owe him a favor. So Rocky became the custodian of a set of dealer plates. When he noticed that these plates came with two long, narrow magnets attached to the back side, he decided that all of The Payback Team's plates should be set up the same way. So Chico was able to get out the front door of the van, remove the three signs, change the two license plates and get back in the side door in about thirty seconds.

When Chico got back in the van, he noticed that Stedman was trying to say something, but he couldn't get it out. Not only did he have the classic deer-caught-in-the-headlights look, but it looked like the "deer" was going to pee in his pants. If they had expected resistance, they were very mistaken. Rocky had been ready with duct tape, in case there was going to be a lot of screaming, but that never happened. This was not turning out at all like they had expected.

Wade decided he would have to revise his opening remarks a little and focus on calming him down before anything was going to sink in. "We're not going to hurt you, at least not today. We're just here to explain a few things in order to make life a little easier for you. If you listen carefully, you will leave here no worse than when you got in the van, and if you listen real carefully, your future will be even brighter than before you met us. Does that sound fair?"

Stedman realized that it would be a good idea to agree, so, still unable to speak, he nodded his head.

Wade continued. "You're in a lot more trouble than you could ever possibly imagine; that's the bad news. But the good news is that we have a solution that is going to make everything right, and you'll never be in this situation again. Do you understand what I'm talking about?"

Finally, it looked like Stedman was starting to relax, if only slightly. Relaxed enough, at least, that they thought he was listening to what Wade was saying. But just as they expected, his look showed that he had no idea what Wade was talking about. Chico had gotten in back, and he and Wade were facing him, with Rocky on his right. Trying to get out of the van would have been nearly impossible, with Rocky between him and the back door and the other two on the other seat across from him.

Wade decided it would be a good idea to slow things down a little. Stedman was clearly overwhelmed at the sudden detour his day had taken, and Wade knew that his fear was interfering with his ability to fully comprehend a lot of what Wade was saying. So Wade paused for a few seconds, smiled, and said, "Tell you what. How about something to drink? Art, our driver, was nice enough to bring a cooler. Want a can of pop or water, or how about some juice? Maybe that will take the edge off things a little. What do you say?" Without waiting for an answer, Wade slid open the divider that separated the front and rear of the van, reached up front and brought back the cooler and opened it. With the front of the van partitioned off, it was impossible for anyone to see what was going on in the rear of the van. "What would you like?"

Stedman was still taking the silent approach, but he did point to a can of diet Coke and seemed to relax a little more when Wade handed it to him.

Everyone else grabbed a can, and after a minute or two, Wade began again. "Okay, let me spell it out for you. It must have occurred to you that the day would come when one of the people you stiffed would want to call in their marker. If you borrow money from enough people without paying them back, sooner or later someone is going to cause you to regret it. You're a gambler, so you know about odds and probabilities."

It was clear to everyone that Stedman was finally processing what he was hearing, and it almost looked like he was about to get in a word or two of his own. Wade continued. "Well, a very good friend of ours has asked us to collect what you owe him. You might not even remember who it is because it's been a while, but it doesn't matter. When you add interest, plus some reasonable collection fees, it comes to about two grand, and he wants it within a week. But here's the funny thing. He said he thinks that, basically, you're an all right guy, and he doesn't want to see you getting into a situation like this again. He said he knows you've screwed a lot of people, and that unless you stop now, someone, someday, is gonna fix it so you'll never be able to do it again, if you know what I mean. But don't worry. That's not why we're here. He wants us to tell you three things, and if you take his advice, you're gonna be real grateful that we showed up today."

Wade purposely stopped talking and was determined to wait it out until Stedman asked the obvious question. For a couple of minutes, the only sound was the van's engine, as it cruised on city streets within three or four miles of the casino. Finally, Stedman was able to get a few words out. "What three things?"

It had been decided that Chico would take over at this point. He said, "One, we're gonna call you at the bar in seven days, and you're gonna tell us that you've got the cash; we're gonna tell you how to get it to us. Two, borrow the money from your father because our friend knows you're gonna pay him back. It wouldn't be right for some other sucker to get stiffed just so you can pay off our friend. And three, get into Gamblers Anonymous. He says you gotta quit gambling; that it's the only way for you to have any kind of future."

No one spoke for nearly a minute. Art had been listening to the conversation that came over the speaker connected to the front and rear of the van. He was now headed back to the casino, as he could tell that they were nearly finished. It looked like they would be within a mile or two when the conversation was finished. Wade noticed this and decided that he would compliment Major Robins for selecting Art to be their driver. Truly a professional.

Now it was Rocky's turn to chime in. "One last thing. Our friend wanted you to know that there will be consequences if you decide to ignore any of what you were told." At this point, it was clear that Stedman was concerned about what he had just heard, and Rocky knew he had to address this concern. "I can tell by the look on your face that you would like us to elaborate, and that bothers me. Why would you care about the consequences, unless you don't intend to follow these three simple things? Look, I'm starting to get really irritated. Do you think that the four of us felt like wasting half a fucking day on a slimy little weasel like you? We're in the 'collection' business, pure and simple. Last time someone fucked with us, we took him for a one-way ride in a chopper out to the middle of Lake Michigan."

Earlier, on the way to the casino, it was decided that they would play "good cop, bad cop" if the opportunity came up, and Rocky seemed to be the natural one to get to be the bad cop. And it looked like he was really getting into the role. Chico and Wade knew that Rocky would be bragging about his performance for at least a week, but they had to admit, it was having the desired effect.

Good cop Wade jumped in with just the right timing. "All right, all right, that's enough. Forget about what he just said, that was a special circumstance. You know, we're not used to this. Usually, we just collect, that's what we do. But our friend had these extra requests, so we gotta make sure that you get the cash and do what he asked. All you have to do is follow these three things and you won't see us any more. But you know what? The more I think about it, he's doing you a big favor. I think you will live a much longer, happier life if you do what he says. In fact, I know you will. You seem like a nice, reasonable guy, so I'm gonna leave you with some free advice. If you get yourself straightened out with this GA thing, you're never gonna have to deal with guys like us again. No one's gonna come around some day and make life difficult for you. But that's where you're headed, believe me. I've seen it plenty of times. Now, we're just a couple of blocks from the casino. We're gonna drop you off here, and maybe you can think about making the right choice while you walk back to your truck."

The Payback Team had discussed what to do when the conversation was over, and they decided that they would not return to the pickup point, just in case someone had seen Stedman being unwillingly put in the van. So Stedman was let out of the van and sent on his way. And a couple of blocks later, the driver pulled over to another spot that he had located during the time they were cruising with him. Chico got out of the van and installed new magnetic signs and license plates, letting John Q. Citizen know that this truck belonged to the Majestic Concrete Corp. If Stedman tried to memorize the plates when he walked away from the van, the information was useless.

"Wasn't that convincing?" were the first words out of Rocky's mouth. "I thought I really—"

Wade cut him off. "Save it for later. We need to sit down and analyze what just went down, and discuss how to improve on it for next time. I thought it went pretty good, but I know we're all a little keyed up right now. I think we should all go and grab a cold one. Art, do you want to join us, or do you have to report back to the major? And by the way, you did a great job. We really appreciate it."

Art had other things on his agenda, so he drove to the spot where he had met Chico and Rocky. Then The Payback Team, and their unrecognizable van, headed straight to a local sports bar.

Chapter Twelve

Taking Time to Plan and Reflect

The waitress brought three pint glasses of Guinness draft, with just the right amount of foam on top. One sip told them that this place knew how to serve Guinness—just the right temperature, and the glasses were the perfect shape. And it was obvious that the bartender knew the right way to fill the glass: start on a forty-five degree angle, pause just below the top of the glass, turn the glass straight up and then fill to the top. To a serious beer lover, this made all the difference.

Rocky decided he wasn't finished congratulating himself. "It's like I practiced this routine for a month. I was really convincing. In fact, I even—"

Chico looked like he was about to throw up. "Hey, I've got an idea. How about you putting a lid on it so we can get down to business here?"

Then Wade added, "Hey, I've got a better idea. How about we giving him exactly one minute to unload, and then we never hear about it again for the rest of our lives?"

Now, it was Rocky's turn. "Hey, I've got the best idea. How about you guys both pound brass tacks up your ass?"

Chico decided it was time to get serious. "You know, one thing I liked was the grab. Now, that really went well. I don't think he knew what hit him until he was in the van. He didn't have time to think or react. We've got to try to make it work like that every time." Rocky was shocked to hear what actually sounded like a compliment. He was about to expand on what a good job he had done, but Chico was quick to cut him off. "And there's something Rocky said that got me thinking. It was that thing about the chopper. I've thought of a few ways we can use a helicopter to our advantage on some of our future projects. Rocky, do you know if Major Robins has access to one?"

"I don't know about the major, but I know this one guy who runs a flight training school up in Milwaukee, and he owns at least two of them, plus a couple of single engine planes. He owes me a favor, so getting him to help us shouldn't be a problem. Plus, I guarantee he'd do just about anything we want, for the right price, no questions asked."

Chico was not about to let on that he was pleased with Rocky's answer. Instead, he decided it was time for another put down. "Do you know any guys who don't owe you a favor?"

Wade felt it was time to get down to business. "Look, we're here to discuss what happened today, and what we're gonna do to complete this project. For my money, it went much better than I thought it would. It looks to me like he's gonna come up with the two grand, and I actually think he's done gambling. So we really helped two people today, Ralphie and Stedman, just like we planned."

Shaking his head in disbelief, Chico gave his opinion. "Spike, you're so naive. Do you really think it's that simple to get someone to quit a gambling addiction? Yes, I think he's going to come up with the two grand, which is the first of the list of three requirements we spelled out to him. Spike, think carefully about this before you answer: where do you think he is right at this minute?"

After thirty seconds, Wade made his guess. "I'd say he's in his truck either heading back to his apartment or over to his father's place to explain what happened."

This conversation was going in the exact direction that Chico was steering it. "Okay, you gave your opinion. Now here's mine: I know exactly where is, and I'll bet a grand to your C-note that he's right where he was this morning, at the casino."

Wade turned this over in his mind for a few seconds, long enough to decide that the odds were too good to pass up, so he accepted the wager. "Okay, you're on, but there's really no way to prove it. Even if we call him and ask him, we can't be totally sure he'll give a straight answer."

Before Wade finished talking, Rocky had pulled out his cell phone. He pressed a couple of keys, and then looked over at Chico. Both he and Chico shook their heads and rolled their eyes. "Yo, Major, this is Rocky. Give a quick look and let me know where Stedman's truck is right now." He paused a few seconds, then thanked him and hung up. He looked at Wade and said just two words, "Pay up."

Wade gave a look that showed he was disappointed, both because he was out another hundred dollars, and because he had forgotten about the tracking device. "Okay, fine, you got me. Here's your damn money. But how could you possibly have known where he—"

As he neatly folded up five twenty-dollar bills, Chico responded, "Well, unfortunately, I've had some firsthand experience with gambling addiction. You see, I—"

Wade interrupted. "Oh, jeez, Chico, all these years I've known you, and I never knew you had a—"

Chico quickly cut him off. "No, no, no, shit-for-brains, not me. It's Christine's brother-in-law. Until we got him into Gamblers Anonymous, he was a real fucked up mess. If I hadn't jumped in, he would have lost his house and his family. It got to the point that some of the kind of guys like we are pretending to be with Stedman were about to make him sorry he ever saw a deck of cards or a pair of dice. This all happened about fifteen years ago, and it had been going on for a few years before anyone knew about it. Sick gamblers develop ways of hiding everything, their losses and their whereabouts while they are out gambling, the people they associate with, and the ones they owe money to. They don't want their loved ones to know because, for one thing, they would not approve, and also, they don't want anything to stop them from going out to try to win back the money they've lost. Plus, they really crave the adrenalin rush they get from gambling.

"It's really strange how Christine's sister found out about it. She was at the hairdresser's, and the lady next to her said that the newspaper must have made a mistake because they had her house listed in the public notice section as one that was going to be sold at the sheriff's auction. So she checked it out, and it was true. They were about to lose their house, and she had no clue. Amazing. So she comes to me like I'm supposed to be responsible for getting them out of the mess Chuck got them in. You know, in one way, I wanted to let him lose the house to teach him a lesson, but then why should his family have to suffer? I actually liked him, he was an all right guy, and I was just as surprised as anyone that someone as straight as he appeared to be could wind up like this. I guess some people just shouldn't drink, and some people just shouldn't gamble.

"Anyway, I bought the house at the sheriff's sale, on the condition that he would get into GA. You know, the surprising thing is that he didn't want to do it at first. Can you believe he didn't think he had a gambling problem? At least, he thought it was something he could control. Now that's just wild, but that's how they think. You know what they say, 'you have to realize you've hit bottom before you're willing to get help'. So what we did was this: we had a 'family intervention.' Christine and I, her sister, and Chuck's parents all sat him down, and every one of us told him we were going to walk away from him if he didn't get into GA. It wasn't really true. I mean, I don't think his parents were going to disown him, for God's sake, but he didn't know that at the time.

"He had to be dragged to his first couple of meetings, but after a while, he was able to see that he had a problem. I'm not saying he got straightened out right away because there were a couple of relapses. And this was not a surprise because they told us that a lot of people relapse at least once or twice during recovery.

"Well, the good news is that he kept up with the meetings, went into the twelve-step program, and he's now a recovered gambling addict. And that's not all. A couple of years ago, he became a sponsor. That means that he's reached the point where he is assigned to be kind of a 'big brother' to other GA members who are trying to get straightened out.

"So that's how I know about sick gamblers. Now, Spike, you want a chance to get your money back? Remember the three conditions we gave Stedman? I've already proved it's unlikely he's anywhere close to quitting gambling, and I've agreed that we'll probably see the two grand, but how about the third stipulation, borrowing the dough from his old man? I'm gonna offer the same odds on this wager, that he doesn't tell his father about this because that would mean coming out that he has a gambling problem. He's just not ready, and no way is he gonna walk into a GA meeting. So do you want a shot at getting even, or are you starting to catch on?"

Wade saw the light. "Okay, so it looks like we're gonna score on only one of the three conditions. But it's a start. Knowing you, the great planner, or I should say *schemer*, you've already thought about this. Wanna clue us in?"

Chico looked down at his empty glass. "Yeah, sure. But it's time for another round, and before I get into that, I want to talk about John V. That should really be the next order of business because I'm really anxious for us to pay him a visit. I'd like to get down to Indiana first part of next week. That okay with you?"

Chapter Thirteen

Preparing for the Trip to Indiana

Although The Payback Team was starting to unwind, they nevertheless kept their focus on business. They had agreed to pay a visit to John V.'s used car lot, so they needed to discuss Chico's ideas about how to handle the situation. And they also needed to decide what the next step would be with Stedman. There was the matter of how to go about picking up the money. They realized that what they had done that day involved, as a minimum, unlawful detainment and, possibly, kidnapping. Would Stedman have a surprise waiting for them if they decided to approach him directly? They felt that this was very unlikely, but they decided not to take any chances. Besides, they needed to find an effective way of going about this now, because there were bound to be similar circumstances in the future with individuals who would be a whole lot more capable of turning the tables on them.

It was Rocky who came up with an idea that they liked. He told them, "I know this one guy who was supposed to go in the witness protection program, but instead he decided to leave the country and try to survive on his own. He's over near London, and he's got one of those mail drops. You know, it's got a street address, with a suite number, but the suite number is really just a mailbox that he rents. He pays someone to go and pick up his mail once a week; he doesn't even go there himself. He checks to make sure the guy isn't being followed before he meets him and gets his mail. So why don't we have Stedman send two thousand dollars in US postal money orders to that address? My guy will let us know when it arrives, and he will wire us the money. After a couple of weeks, if we haven't heard from him, we'll know Stedman stiffed us, and then Chico can figure out what to do next. How does that sound?"

Wade nodded and told Rocky to get back to him with the address. He would make a point to call Stedman later that day and give him the instructions, making a mental note to tell him to check at the post office to make sure he attached the correct postage. He also decided he would remind him that there would be consequences if *all* of the three requirements were not followed. Finally, he picked up his cell phone and double checked to see that he had remembered to block his caller ID.

Next, Rocky gave a report on the latest development regarding FAST 1. One of Major Robins's staff had let Rocky know that FAST 1 wouldn't necessarily be rushing out to buy another Corvette because he owned other vehicles that he could use until he got around to replacing the Vette. Currently, he was driving a one-year-old Lexus, and he also had a vintage Mercedes Roadster, which rarely left his five-car garage. His wife drove an Escalade, but Rocky recommended leaving her out of the picture, at least for now. The major's associate reported that FAST 1 drove the Lexus to the train station parking lot every weekday, so Rocky explained that he had told Major Robins that the Lexus should be picked up from the parking lot and shipped down to Mexico.

Much to Rocky's surprise, Chico asked him if he could call the major right away and stop him from heisting the Lexus. "Listen, Rocky, I've been thinking about what you said about the chopper. Remember your guy up in Milwaukee? Could he rig up something so that he could pick up the Lexus with his chopper? Can you find out if he has one with enough power? What I'm thinking is that we dump the Lexus in his pool. With the way you described his estate, I'm sure he has one. Think about it: his Lexus is ruined, plus, how is he going to get it out of the pool? This is gonna be a real cluster fuck for him—his worst nightmare. Remember, we said we can't hurt him as bad as we want from the economic side; we have to find some other way to mess with him." From their looks of approval, Chico knew he had scored again. Rocky promised to make some calls and set it up.

Then a final thought occurred to Chico. "Oh, and one more thing. Tell your friend to get a picture of the Lexus from his chopper after it goes into the pool. We can send it in to the newspapers; that oughta fix his clock. And you know what I just thought? Paula would love to get a good look at the estate from the air. It sounds exactly like the kind of place she'd like Spike to buy for her. And if we're really lucky, there might even be a horse or two in the picture. That's what friends are for, right?"

If Chico and Rocky hadn't been so busy laughing and doing a high five, they would have heard Wade's response: "Couple of complete jerkoffs."

Rocky brought up one last piece of business. "I know if I bring up the subject of the Guatemala project, you guys are gonna say that it's premature to be talking about it now, and I agree. But let's not get so wrapped up in what we're working on right now that we forget that we really have bigger things in mind down the road. If all we're gonna do is hassle guys like John V. and Stedman, then it's gonna get old real fast. And what about the wife beater and the rapist, you know, the motherfucker who killed the—"

Wade interrupted. "Calm down, Rocky. You know we all agree on this. You don't have to remind us. Yes, these things are very much on my mind, and I'm guessing that Chico has given some thought about what we can do with these two assholes. Chico, how about bringing us up to date on your ideas for these guys on our way down to Indiana?"

Chapter Fourteen

Heading Down to Indiana

The Payback Team enjoyed a beautiful late-spring weekend. A round of eighteen holes on both Saturday and Sunday, followed by a barbecue at Wade's house on Sunday evening, left them relaxed and ready for Monday's business. They had discussed some of the details and progress with their growing list of challenges during their golf games, but there was still a lot to cover during the ride down to John V.'s car lot.

This time there was no need to rush. Major Robins' people had found out that John V. worked the lot alone from 10:00 A.M. to 6:00 P.M., Monday through Thursday, and he had a partner who was there on Friday and Saturday. The major had supplied them with a picture of John V., taken in the poker room at Harrah's Casino, so they would have no problem making sure that they were dealing with the right guy when they arrived at the car lot. Just to make sure, Wade had shown the picture to his nephew who confirmed that it was John V.

Wade was waiting in front of his house when the van from "MidTown Flower Shop" pulled up. He introduced himself to the driver, whose name was Blake. It was pretty easy to determine that his name was Blake because he was wearing a blue work shirt with his name on it. The driver was not at all what Wade had expected. He was used to the clean-cut, marine look, but this guy was bald, had a scruffy red beard, and a port wine birthmark covering most of his right cheek. Wade did his best not to stare, but it didn't seem to matter to Blake, as his appearance was clearly not important to him. When Wade got in the back, Rocky started to ask him if he had remembered his new wallet, but Wade waved him off with a gesture that said, "You worry too much."

After Rocky passed the picture around, they spent a few minutes discussing their impressions. Rocky and Chico felt that he definitely had the look of a used car salesman, and they also had no doubt that he had spent time in prison. He had dark wavy hair, a couple of teeth that didn't seem to line up with the others and a complexion that indicated he had gone through his teen years with severe acne. Wade commented that it's really impossible to draw conclusions just by looking at a picture, but he did agreed that it didn't look like John V. was going to be the cooperative type.

Chico had decided that they would take the friendly, direct approach when they got to his car lot. They would ask to go inside so they could sit down and explain that a friend had had some business dealing with him and was out roughly three grand, including a reasonable amount of interest that had accumulated. They all agreed that there was little chance of them leaving with the cash, but it would at least be a starting point. Chico would then be able to decide what to do after getting his reaction. After everyone was comfortable with who was going to say what, including Rocky getting to play "bad cop" again at the right time, they spent the rest of the ninety-minute ride discussing other business.

Wade reported that he had spoken with Stedman and explained that it sounded like he was going to send the money orders to England. He mentioned that Stedman sounded relieved to find out that paying the money did not involve getting picked up and thrown in the back of a van again.

Next, Rocky explained that he also had followed through with his phone calls. It turned out that his guy in Milwaukee did have a helicopter capable of picking up the Lexus, but he explained that he would need to get it done as quickly as possible, due to the air control restrictions within a thirty-mile radius of O'Hare airport.

Then Rocky called the major and went over the details of how one of his staff should connect a harness to the Lexus just a couple of minutes before the chopper arrived. They needed to coordinate every step of the plan in advance—the exact location of the parking lot, the directions to FAST 1's estate, and how the harness was to be attached to the fifty-foot line hanging from the chopper. By now, they realized that nothing was too complex or challenging for the major and his staff to handle. They couldn't wait to see the picture of the Lexus at the bottom of FAST 1's pool.

Finally, just a few minutes before arriving at John V.'s, Chico gave his update. He explained that he had tried to work on a plan for dealing with the wife beater, but that he was going to need a lot more information before he could proceed. "Rocky, can you talk to Major Robins and see if he can find out a few things for us? Is there any record of her calling 911 about her husband? Are there any police reports? Did she ever go to an emergency room for treatment? Has she ever been to one of those battered women's shelters? I need to know as much detail as possible. For one thing, we need to pin down that she really is a victim. I know there are instances of a woman bringing down the hammer on her old man because she wants to pay him back for cheating on her, or maybe even for a reason that only exists in her twisted mind. I'm sure it's legit in this case, but we have to make sure. None of us wants to bust the wrong guy's balls.

"And as for the other guy, you know, the rapist that got off on a technicality? I want to make sure we do the right thing by him. I figure we need to find a way to put him where he belongs, which is in prison. I thought about putting his lights out permanently, but I don't think any of us is ready for something like that. I'm not saying I couldn't do it; in fact, it will become necessary if we take on a project I am thinking about after we complete the thing down in Guatemala."

Wade raised his hand and said, "Whoa, you're going a little too fast. One thing at a time. How in the hell are you going to put this guy in prison? The prosecuting attorney and the judge couldn't do it, so how do you think we—"

Chico cut him off. "I know, I know. Remember, I said 'we need to find a way.' I didn't say 'I know the way.' I don't have the answer yet, but I'm working on it."

Rocky was about to ask about the new project Chico had referred to, but Blake's voice came over the speaker. "We're two blocks from the place." They had decided to get out a short distance from the car lot so that John V. would not be able to see the van. As soon as they got out, they realized that their new surroundings pretty much fit the impression that they so far had formed about John V. It was about as low as you could get, a good example of complete urban decay. Broken windows, trash everywhere, a couple of abandoned vehicles, one burned-out apartment building and one boarded-up house. A couple of gangbangers, with their baseball caps on sideways and their baggy pants almost falling off their hips completed the picture.

When they spotted the car lot, it became clear that John V. was in the vulture business. He picked over the remains of those who had nowhere else to turn. The cars were cleaned up junks that no one but the most needy would even look at. What they had been told by the major was now completely verified. But, sadly, this was not a circumstance that they would be able to rectify. Putting John V. out of business would be a small improvement to the neighborhood, but this lowlife and his business were symptomatic of a much, much larger societal problem, one that they were not qualified to solve. Before approaching the lot, Rocky spoke to the driver and pointed out the exact spot where he wanted him to wait until their business was concluded. They needed him to be close by in the event that they needed to be picked up in a hurry. Rocky had also picked out a spot a couple of blocks away where it would be safe to change the plates and signs after their business was done. He was trying to plan ahead in case John V. ran out of his office after them and made note of the license and signs.

John V. was outside, walking around, and as far as they could tell, he was counting hubcaps. There were about twenty cars on the lot, and a quick glance showed that one or two were missing a hubcap. Their best guess was that the most valuable cars were worth about two to three thousand dollars, assuming that there were no major engine or transmission problems, but that assumption was probably unwarranted in more than a few cases.

As soon as he saw them, John V. put on a phony smile, something that was no doubt second nature to him, and started to reach out his hand to give Wade his most sincere used car salesman's handshake, when it dawned on him that these three didn't fit in. The smile vanished and the hand pulled back. "Whadda ya want?" was the not so friendly reception that greeted The Payback Team. When they compared notes later, all agreed that it was clear at this point that this was not going to be a slam dunk.

Wade tried to maintain a calm, pleasant tone, even though he had just come across possibly the most obnoxious person he had ever met. "Well, we have some business to discuss. Could we go inside and sit down for a few minutes while we explain?"

Without saying a word, John V. went inside. They followed him in, even though they were not specifically invited. John V. walked behind a beat-up wooden desk and sat down. He crossed his arms over his chest and leaned back in a gesture that said, "You're in my domain now. I'm in control."

Knowing it would be a waste of energy, but nevertheless attempting to appear friendly and nonthreatening, Wade put out his hand and said, "My name is Allen Harris, and this is—"

Ignoring Wade's outstretched hand, John V. said, "I don't give a flying fuck who you are. You're obviously not the heat, or I would have seen a badge by now. So get to the point and then get out."

Wade sat down on one of the two chairs in front of the desk, and Chico sat down next to him. Rocky stood off to the side of the desk. John V. gave a brief look that said, "Who invited you to sit down?" And then Rocky noticed that John V.'s eyes shifted over to the top left desk drawer, which was partially open, but not quite enough to see what was inside. From that moment on, Rocky kept his gaze focused on two things: the drawer and John V.'s eyes.

Trying to make his voice sound as pleasant as possible, Wade answered, "Well, our friend, Harry, was involved in a business transaction with you. And his position is that he was not treated fairly. He is out three thousand dollars, and he asked us to relate this to you and to ask you to do the right thing and settle up. So we came here to—"

John V. was now laughing so hard that it was pointless to continue. Then he stopped abruptly, curled his lips in a threatening manner, and shouted, "Some asshole tells you to come over here and fuck me out of three grand? Get the fuck out of here, now!" Then he did exactly what Rocky expected him to do. He looked over at the drawer. When his eyes looked back over at Wade, his left hand slowly opened the drawer. He assumed that his uninvited guests were more intent on his shouting and would not notice the drawer, and in the case of Wade and

Chico, this was, in fact, true. "You don't leave now, there's gonna be big trouble. No one comes in here and tries to rob me. You're trespassing. I can make you real sorry real fast that you ever walked in that door."

Rocky had waited until he was sure that John V.'s attention was focused on hollering at Wade and adjusted his position just enough to look inside the drawer. After a quick glance, he was no longer curious about the contents. He knew that John V. would have to stand up, due to the position of his chair, in order to reach into the drawer, and he was waiting intently for any motion that indicated that he was about to get out of his chair.

Chico had been holding his cell phone in his left hand, out of John V.'s site, and now that he sensed they were nearing the end of their little chat, he quietly opened it and punched a couple of numbers without looking at the phone. He waited a few seconds, and then closed it. It would now be a matter of less than ninety seconds before the van arrived at the pickup point.

Wade, knowing that they were getting nowhere, and that there was a good chance that violence was about to erupt, nevertheless wanted to make his point clear. "Listen, if you don't do what we're asking, there's definitely going to be big trouble, as you put it. But it won't be like you think. Our friend is very persistent, and he expects us to—"

John V. had heard enough. "Okay, fine, now you're threatening me. Here comes trouble, motherfucker."

Rocky saw the movement the split second it happened. He had moved one step closer to the desk so that he would be in the exact position he needed to be at just the right time. As John V. stood up and reached his hand into the drawer, Rocky's timing was precise. With his right hand, he slammed the drawer shut as hard as he could, catching John V.'s hand just below the knuckles. Chico and Wade could hear the simultaneous sound of the drawer closing and bones cracking. But Rocky wasn't finished. In the same instant that he removed his hand from the drawer, he pressed his left knee against it, pinning John V.'s hand half in and half out of the drawer. With both arms free, he wrapped one around John V.'s neck and began to squeeze tightly. At the same time he reached around his head with his other arm, accomplishing two purposes: John V. was unable to make any audible sound, and Rocky was in a position to snap his neck like a pretzel stick.

With an equal mixture of extreme pain and fear for his life, John V. made the first intelligent decision since he met up with the trio: be quiet, listen, and don't struggle.

Rocky was ready for another academy award performance. "You try to pull a gun on me, you motherfucker? You try to pull a gun on me? Last time some son of a bitch did that, I put all six pieces of him in the ground, four feet under somebody's grandma's casket. Now when her loved ones go to the cemetery, they're also paying their respects to some lowlife pissant like you. Get ready to die, motherfu—"

Right on cue, Chico interrupted. "Stan, no! He's not worth it. That's not why we came here. Harry just wants his money. Mister Vargas, you've made a big mistake. Unfortunately, you didn't give us a chance to tell you exactly who you're fucking with. But that's okay, you'll see us again. Remember when Allen used the word 'persistent'? Well, you're gonna find out about persistence—that's a promise. Stan, let him go. It's time to leave. I don't feel welcome here anymore."

Rocky moved his knee and took a .357 magnum from the drawer; not the best weapon for the occasion, but it definitely would have gotten the job done. Then he decided to take one more crack at the Oscar. "Listen, asshole, do you think I enjoy fucking up jerkoffs like you? Well, okay, actually I do, but that's not the point. The point is that it didn't have to happen like this. All you had to do was behave. And as for your little toy, we're gonna take it with us. You shouldn't be playing with guns anyway, because you could get hurt. Now listen, this is important. Next time we see you, and it's gonna be soon, have five large in your pocket. That's the only way you're gonna end this nightmare."

John V., now grateful that he wasn't going to be sliced into six pieces, and temporarily forgetting about the pain, looked like he had a question. But Wade saved him the trouble of asking. "Yeah, we did say three grand, but that's before the nice warm reception you gave us. Now, like Stan said, the figure is five. Don't forget, and don't ever even think about screwing with us again. I guarantee it'll be very bad for your health."

Chico needed to get the last word in. "One more thing to think about, Mr. Vargas. In a couple of days, we're gonna leave you a little calling card, kind of a reminder that you shouldn't forget about the five grand. You'll think of us when it arrives, and you'll know what we meant about persistence. We're not through with you until you're square with our friend, one way or the other."

When they left, John V. was slumped in his chair, looking at a broken and bleeding left hand resting uncomfortably on his lap.

The van was right where they agreed for it to be. They calmly got in and Blake drove off, stopping in about a mile at a previously selected spot that temporarily shielded them from anyone standing more that thirty feet away. Chico got out briefly, and when he returned, it was clear that the van was no longer the delivery vehicle for the MidTown Flower Shop.

Chapter Fifteen

The Long Ride Home

Rocky was the only one who felt like talking. This was no surprise to Wade and Chico, but they didn't realize he was going to start in as soon as the van's door closed. This time, they had decided to let him have his say, so for the next thirty minutes, Rocky talked nonstop and uninterrupted about what a great job he had done, his acting skills, his ability to think and act quickly, his improvisational skills, and whatever additional self-congratulatory remarks he could think of. He was grateful that no one was interrupting, and typical of Rocky, he took their silence as interest and approval. Fortunately, he had no clue that not only were they completely uninterested, but they were totally ignoring him.

Wade was quite experienced in tuning out what he didn't want to hear and focusing on something more important. He had used this skill countless times in endless, boring business meetings and conferences. He instinctively knew when to say, "That's right," or "Yes, good," or "I see," so that others would think he was following along. Wade had little patience with people who didn't quickly get to the point, or as a minimum, stay focused on the business at hand. But more often than not, he would eventually grow tired of those who wasted his time, and most of his business associates had often heard "Please get to the point," or "Would you please stick to the subject?"

While Rocky rambled on, Wade was actually grateful to be able to get in some serious thinking time, and promptly became absorbed in his thoughts. He made a mental note to ask Chico what he meant about sending John V. a calling card. He also spent a few minutes thinking about Stedman, and decided he would call him in a day or two to make sure he had followed through on sending the money as instructed. He decided that he also needed to see if he had gotten to a GA meeting, but felt it was best to bring this up after he got confirmation about the money, as this was the more immediate objective. Next, he made another note to ask Chico to come up with a way of determining if he had actually started with GA and whether or not he had borrowed the cash from his father. It would be easy for Stedman to tell Wade what he wanted to hear, but Wade wanted to know how he could be certain, one way or the other.

There were still more things to consider. What should be the next step after dumping FAST 1's car in the pool? How and when should they encounter John V. to collect the five grand? What should be the alternative if he doesn't come across with the money? And, always in the back of his mind, there was Guatemala. He was surprised that his team members hadn't wanted to know more details about what exactly had happened to his aunt. He had shown them the newspaper article that Paula had brought to his attention when this all started, but it occurred to him that his aunt would have a lot more to share about the situation, if he would make a point of asking.

Chico's mind was also focused on several issues that had absolutely nothing to do with what Rocky was saying. He realized that his partners were counting on him to provide plans and solutions for the challenges that they had created for themselves, and he didn't want to let them down. He had years of experience using his planning skills in his business, and that is what enabled him to achieve success and wealth. But this was different. In business, it was all about succeeding for personal reasons, but now he was part of a team. The two individuals who meant more to him than anyone, except for his family, were counting on him. He could not let them down. Every minute or two, Chico looked at Rocky and either nodded or said, "Uh huh," as Rocky continued.

But instead of listening, Chico was making a mental list of the things he had to work on. Why had he said that they would be sending a calling card to John V.? It had sounded good when he pulled it out of the air, but now he was going to have to come up with something. And he had made some progress in planning the next steps regarding Stedman and John V., but these projects needed more work. He had also come up with the next move regarding FAST 1, and he was anxious to present the plan to his team members. And he had already begun to work on a course of action for the wife beater, even though he was waiting for more information from Major Robins. He wasn't sure if he should bring this up now, or if he should wait for the additional information.

He also reviewed his comment about putting the rapist in prison and realized that he had made no progress on this project. Finally, he made a mental note to get more information about the Guatemala issue because, even though it was not a priority at this time, it wouldn't hurt to get some of the facts so that he could start working on it.

Rocky interrupted their concentration with a question, and when he got no response, he looked directly at Wade and asked it again. "So what do you think?"

Wade snapped out of his concentration and tried to respond. "Well, I…I mean…that is, I think—"

Chico came to his rescue. "Rocky, I think Spike is trying to say that we really need a little more information before we can give you a worthwhile opinion. Can you expand on this just a little?" Rocky didn't see Wade's look of relief because he was looking in Chico's direction.

"Good point," replied Rocky. "It's Angela's uncle. And I'd have to be there Saturday morning, but I don't know. What do you think?"

It looked like Chico was making some progress, but he needed to bluff Rocky into giving up a little more information in order to keep him from realizing that every word he had spoken in the last half hour had fallen on deaf ears. "Okay, we're starting to get a better idea about your dilemma. But why don't you tell us a little bit more about your wife's uncle?"

"You're right," Rocky said, still totally clueless. "I should have explained that he owns the dinner theater that is putting on the production I mentioned. The tryout for their next play is this Saturday. I just don't know if I should go for it or not. I mean it's clear to you guys that I have acting ability, but I just don't know if I should capitalize on it right now or not."

Chico had almost dug himself and Wade out of the hole, but he knew he had a little farther to go. "Why don't you tell us just a little more about the tryout, and maybe then we can come up with an intelligent opinion."

"Excellent point. I should have covered that. It's what they call a 'bit part,' and I think I would fit in perfectly. I would play a character like Don Corleone, but I would only have four lines in the whole play. But I know I'd be perfect. Do you think I should go for it or what?" Rocky asked.

Chico and Wade were careful to avoid eye contact because they knew they would ruin the point they had finally reached by breaking up completely. They discussed it later and couldn't agree which was funnier: the fact that Rocky had no idea they hadn't been listening or the fact that he was so serious about getting into acting, based on his two performances with The Payback Team.

Wade felt that he had an obligation to answer, since Chico had been handling it up to this point. "Rocky, I think it would be totally wrong for you to settle for such a small part. Why waste God-given talent on a part with only four lines?" He immediately thought that he had laid it on too thick, but when he saw Rocky give a nod of agreement, he knew he was on a roll. "Listen, this is what I think you should do. Go to Angela's uncle and tell him you want to try out for the lead, or at least supporting actor, in one of his plays. But be sure it's a part that would be right for you. You don't want to accept a role that would be out of character for you because that's the wrong way to start out."

"Yeah, I think I see your point," agreed Rocky. It was now clear to Chico and Wade that they had bailed out of a tight situation.

Since they were still making progress, Chico decided to put the matter to rest on just the right note. "Oh, Rocky, one more thing. You should put this off—at least for a while—because your value to The Payback Team is much more important right now than the dinner theater thing, don't you agree?"

When Wade saw the look on Rocky's face, indicating that he was going to yield to a higher calling, at least for now, he realized it was a good time to focus on their present situation. "Chico, how about if you clue us in on this 'calling-card' thing. What's up with that?"

"Well, I was thinking about that a little bit while Rocky was talking." His eyes met Wade's just for an instant, but they both quickly looked away, knowing that to do otherwise would result in the uncontrollable laughter they had avoided a moment ago. "Rocky, do you know anyone who can melt down a solid piece of metal?"

"Hell, yes. I know this one guy who—"

Chico wasn't interested in a long explanation. "That's okay, Rocky, you can save the story for later. You can tell it right after you remind us again about the guy with the hand grenades. And I guess I don't need to ask you if you know anyone who can make molds because I think I already know the answer. Anyway, what I was thinking is, we melt down his .357 and send it back to him in a different shape. I am convinced we need to find a way to really get his attention, short of more violence and bone breaking, to put the pressure on him to comply. I think all we accomplished today is to really make him mad. Every time he looks at the cast he will soon have on his hand, he's gonna get mad all over again. Right at this exact minute, I'm sure he's not thinking about what we want; I think he's looking at getting even. I'm thinking of something I want to say in the note that would accompany the chunk of metal, and the note will refer to something else that's gonna happen to him. Maybe the two events, together, will get him to come around to our way of thinking."

Now, Wade was more curious than ever. "Explain."

"Well, I don't want to get into it right now; it's still in the planning phase," said Chico. "But after Rocky let's us know how it went with the chopper, the Lexus, and the pool, I'll be able to give you more details. And, speaking of explaining, we really don't have a lot of details about the Guatemala deal. All we know is that some bad guys are hijacking some buses, killing and kidnapping some of the passengers, and nobody is doing anything about it. We're gonna need a lot more than this if we—"

Wade cut him off. "Yeah, I know. I already made a note to check with my Auntie Moey to get a better idea of—"

Now, it was Rocky's turn to interrupt. "Hold it a minute. You have an 'Auntie Moey'? What the hell is an 'Auntie Moey'? Is that anything like your Aunt Mary?"

"Well, we still call her Auntie Moey," replied Wade. "When we were kids, my sister and I couldn't pronounce 'Mary,' and I guess the 'Moey' thing just stuck."

85

Rocky looked at Chico and shook his head in disgust. "Jeez, Chico, do you realize our partner is a seven year old with a lisp? I'll bet—*oh, fuck!*"

Chico and Wade were startled by Rocky's abrupt change of pace. Usually, when he was pressing Wade's buttons, he didn't let up so soon. They could tell that something he had seen out of the rear windows had completely startled him. Chico was the next one to speak. "Oh, shit, we're fucked!"

It was their worst nightmare. A police car was right behind them, and Blake was pulling over and slowing down. They had no idea what the problem was, but they had rehearsed what they were going to do if things got out of hand.

They tried to remain calm while they waited to find out what was going to happen next. They lost their view of the patrolman as he walked toward the front of the van and began talking to Blake. Over the speaker, they could hear what was going on.

"I need to see your license, registration, and proof of insurance," said the cop.

"Okay, officer, no problem," responded Blake agreeably. "Was I speeding? I hope not. Mr. Wallace doesn't want any of us driving over the limit. Here's my license. Let me check in the glove compartment for the registration. If he doesn't keep it there, we can call him." Blake knew that the plates were registered to Clarence H. Wallace, and he knew it was likely that the cop had already run the plates. He also remembered that Chico had attached magnetic signs that indicated the van belonged to Austin Liquors.

The cop's tone softened a little. "All right, that checks out. Where are you heading today?"

"Well, I'm delivering twenty cases of Miller Lite to his new store up in Berwyn," said Blake. "Mr. Wallace has six stores now. The original one was on Austin Avenue in Chicago, and—"

"Okay, that's fine," interrupted the patrolman. "I just need to make sure. We're looking for a sex offender. Attacked a little girl over at Bonneville Elementary School a couple of hours ago. Reported driving a van like this one. Looks like you're okay. Got any drugs, alcohol, weapons, cannons, bazookas—"

Blake interrupted the officer with a loud laugh. The others were all glad to see that this thing was headed in the right direction. "No, don't have any cannons today. Got plenty of alcohol, though." This time, the cop laughed. It looked like this situation was going to end happily in just a few more seconds.

"Tell you what. Let me just take a quick look in back, and then you can be on your way," said the cop. So much for the happy ending.

"Hey, no problem. I'll open it up for you." The Payback Team could hear Blake's door open and footsteps heading toward the rear of the van. Just then, they heard a few words from the police radio, but it wasn't clear. It was something about an occurrence on Arrowhead Boulevard, followed by the word "urgent."

The officer's mood suddenly became serious. "We've got to wrap this up; I gotta be on the road, like right now."

Blake tried his best to stall for time. "Oh, I forgot. I've gotta press UNLOCK before we can get in. It'll just be a second." He then walked toward the front of the van, while the officer stood impatiently behind the rear doors.

Blake pressed something that made a clicking sound. "Okay, that should do it." He then walked slowly back to the rear.

The stalling efforts weren't working. "Come on, I really gotta book," the officer said.

The Payback Team had already slipped on face masks that made them look like Richard Daley, the mayor of Chicago. This time, when Blake appeared next to the cop, they could see that he had a piece of black cloth in his right hand. The cop was the only person who wasn't prepared for what was about to take place. Everyone hoped that things would go according to plan.

"Okay, you can open it now." Right after Blake spoke, several things happened in less than five seconds. As the cop opened the door, Blake slipped a hood over his head, placed his right foot on the cop's rear end, and gave a hard shove. With the cop partway in the van, Rocky grabbed his shirt at the shoulders and pulled him all the way in, quickly laying him facedown on the floor. Blake closed the door and ran to the front of the van. They were pretty sure that the cop had not had a chance to get a look at the faces of the three Mayor Daley's, but the masks were still necessary, in case the patrol car was equipped with a video camera.

As Rocky kept him pinned to the floor, Chico and Wade removed his shirt, vest, shoes, radio, and gun, and then placed his hands behind him and secured them with duct tape. There was no longer anything that could identify him as a policeman. As all this was happening, Blake had found a spot behind a warehouse that was suitable for making the switch. In just a few seconds, Chico did his thing, and the van had lost the signs and had different plates and was back on the streets.

It was time for Rocky to start his act. He placed the officer on the seat, right next to him, and spoke in a calm tone. "Okay, listen up, Officer Malone. We're not going to hurt you. You did everything right, and we respect that. We're on the same side as you, but undercover. It's a sting operation; even your chief doesn't know about it. Yeah, you guessed it, it's narcotics and organized crime. Here, take a look at this."

Rocky pulled the bottom of the hood away from the officer's face, just enough for him to look down and see that Rocky was holding some type of law enforcement badge. But he held it at an angle and then pulled it back out of the officer's limited line of sight before he could get a clear look at it. "Officer Malone, we're sorry you had to get involved with the wrong van today, but we know it wasn't your fault. You've done right by us, so we're gonna return the favor. We all need to get back to work, so we're gonna let you out up ahead, and then we're gonna drop off a package on the sidewalk a couple of hundred feet farther down. You can pick it up, it contains all your stuff, get back in uniform, and get back to your patrol car. We would appreciate it if you wouldn't disclose the details of what happened today; make something up if you can. That would help us a lot. We've put a lot of time into this, and we're real close to a big score, I mean like very big. Thanks for your cooperation, and good luck."

Since he was convinced that Malone had actually believed his story, Rocky removed the duct tape. Chico opened one of the rear doors, reached down and removed the license plate, and guided the cop out of the van. With his left hand, he pulled the hood off his head before anyone outside could notice it, and with his right hand he closed the door. As far as they could tell, Officer Malone had not seen their masked faces, and he certainly couldn't have noticed their license plate because it was no longer there.

While Chico got out a few blocks later and again changed the plates and installed new signs, Rocky made a mental note that it was time to return the set of plates they had borrowed from Mr. Clarence H. Wallace, and to ask his contact to go shopping for replacements.

When everyone finally realized that they had just dodged what was very possibly a career-ending bullet, Wade slid open the partition and started to thank and congratulate Blake for the role he had played. "Blake, we really want to thank—what the hell?"

"Name's Howie. Blake doesn't work here anymore." The driver's scruffy red beard was gone. And he was no longer bald. Instead, his short, brown hair had the marine look that they had first seen on Major Robins, and later on Art. The blue work shirt with his name on it had been replaced by a plain brown one. Finally, the birthmark had somehow disappeared.

Wade shook his head and laughed. "Well, I'll be damned," was all he could say as he closed the partition.

Chapter Sixteen

Taking a Break

As expected, the first one to speak was Rocky. "Wasn't I—"

Chico would not let him get any further. "Listen, Rocky, we're just not in the mood right now. Why don't you sit on it for a while and then e-mail it to us later?"

Now, it was Wade's turn. "Well, that's enough fun for one day. I'm not even up for a stop at our friendly neighborhood pub. Let's just be grateful we're not looking at the outside world through iron bars right now, and wrap this up for a while. Rob and Julie are coming home for the summer in a couple of days, and Paula and I plan to spend some quality time with them up at the cottage before they start their summer jobs. You know, Paula wants me to tell them about how their old man is spending his retirement. She says they should find out about it from me, and she's right. So let's plan to get together first part of next week. I hope to have some info about Guatemala by then because I will be seeing Auntie..., I mean my aunt, Sunday evening after we get back from Wisconsin. Until then, maybe we all can spend some time thinking about how to wrap up some of the loose ends."

Rocky looked disappointed that he didn't get to make another speech, but he agreed with Wade about taking time off. "That sounds good. I'm gonna check on the progress on the chopper project, and I'm also gonna ask the major to put one of those tracking devices on John V.'s car; I got a feeling we're gonna need it. And it just occurred to me that I should ask him to keep a log of where Stedman goes with his truck. That's one way we're gonna know whether he's going to meetings or casinos. Also, I'm gonna get my metal guy and my mold guy lined up. Chico, you need to let me know what kind of mold you have in mind."

Chico also liked the idea of taking a few days off. "Sounds good. Spike, I'm gonna send you an e-mail about some things you can ask Stedman, in order to see if he's doing like we told him. I'm sure he's not, but we have to know for certain. And, Rocky, I'm gonna send you an e-mail also, giving you more details about the mold. I've got a lot of things to work on, so the time off will be worthwhile, as far as I'm concerned. Getting together next Monday will be perfect."

No one spoke during the remainder of the drive, and everyone was grateful when they reached their drop-off point.

Wade decided that they would leave for their cottage as soon as his kids returned. An extra-long weekend would be just what they all needed. His family was what mattered most to him, and spending time with them was like a precious gift.

At first, his kids resisted the idea of a long weekend in Wisconsin. They had their own agenda that mostly involved hooking up with friends they hadn't seen in months, but when they understood how important it was to Wade for them to go with him to the cottage, they decided their friends could wait a few more days.

On their first night at the cottage, Wade built a bonfire down by the lake, just like he had done so many times during the twenty years they had owned the place. Julie and Rob had spent many nights with their parents around the fire, and they all realized that this night was special, as it had been a long time between bonfires.

For the first hour, Wade was silent as he listened to Julie and Rob catch them up on their recent finals, courses they planned to take in the fall, and plans for the summer. They knew that when their father was this quiet, he was waiting for everyone else to run out of conversation so that he could have their total attention. After sixty minutes of silence, they figured that it must be something extreme. They only hoped it was going to be good news.

Sensing that the time was right, he then took the next half hour to fill them in on every detail of the path that he and his team members had chosen. He finished by trying to lighten things up with a comment about how all of this was Paula's idea, so therefore, she was to blame if things didn't turn out to everyone's satisfaction. But this attempt at humor did not have the intended effect, since Rob and Julie had just heard something that was extremely difficult for them to comprehend. This was so totally unexpected that they sat in silence for almost five minutes before Julie finally decided to speak.

"Daddy, there's something I never told you. In my first year at Northwestern, we had to write an essay for English Lit about the most remarkable person we had ever known. I chose you." Then Julie paused so that everyone could let her words sink in. "You know, Dad, now more than ever, I can see that it was definitely the right choice." She stopped again before finishing. "I'm so proud of you."

During Julie's first pause, Wade had leaned forward and looked at the ground. He had a good idea of what was coming, and, as usual, didn't want his family to see the emotion that he would be unable to conceal. But just as Julie finished speaking, his plan went south, as a lone tear was illuminated by the dying fire as it made it's journey to the grass between Wade's feet. Wade waited until he thought he could get a few words out without choking up. But this plan also failed. "I...I...that is...I mean—"

Paula saw that he needed help. "I think what your father is trying to say is that he appreciates your support, and that he is grateful that you chose him as the subject of your paper. Now, what I want to say is that I was initially glad that he decided to take on this noble role of providing justice for others who have no way of getting it on their own. But now I'm not so sure. I haven't expressed, until now, how upset I was about what happened in that guy's office down in Indiana. You all could have been killed. Honey, I don't know if you saw how worried I was when I first saw you in the hospital after that guy in the Corvette shot you, but I know I don't want to go through anything like that again. I know that nothing I say can get you to forget about what you and Tommy and Michael are committed to, but please just understand that you and our family mean more to me than anything."

Wade felt there was a good chance that he could get out one or two partially coherent sentences. "Don't think we haven't thought about this. We plan to be as careful as possible."

After a few more minutes, Paula mentioned that it was past midnight and that it had been a very long day. She and Julie left and walked up to the cottage.

Until now, Rob hadn't spoken. Wade's concern about what his son was thinking was answered when Rob finally broke the silence. "Pop, I wanna be on the team." Short, simple, and totally unexpected. Rob could see that his father was working on a choice of words that would put an end to the conversation, but he decided to cut him off. "Tell you what. Instead of answering right now, how about bringing it up with Uncle Tommy and Uncle Michael?" Rob searched his father's face and realized that he was about to say "no". Before Wade could speak, Rob decided to try another tactic: change the subject. "Hey, Pop, I've been meaning to ask you something. Speaking of Uncle Tommy and Uncle Michael, I know they call you 'Spike.' You never told us why. I tried to ask Uncle Tommy one time, and all he would say was that I should call him if I ever wanted to learn how to play Texas hold 'em and not to ask you to teach me. What's that all about?"

Wade's instantaneous response was, "That little prick." Then he realized that any further comments along these lines would be inappropriate, so he stood up and took a different approach. "Okay, son, we'll go over that one day. But now I'm going to bed. You're mom was right; it's been a long day."

Realizing that his attempt to change the subject had been a success, Rob decided not to push it. Father and son got up and walked up to the cottage, side by side. As they approached the stairs leading up to the deck, Wade wrapped one arm around Rob's shoulder and gave him a brief hug. Rob knew it meant that Wade was proud to be his father.

When they walked in the door, the first thing Wade noticed was the blinking red light on the answering machine. Wade had promised Paula that he would get rid of it as soon as he retired, but now things had changed; he had chosen to be involved in a venture that needed him to be accessible just as much as ever. He pressed the PLAY button and heard a message from a very excited Rocky: *"Spike, turn on the news on channel seven. You're not gonna believe it. You're not gonna believe it!"*

It was way too late to return the call, so he would just have to wait until morning to find out what he had missed. Anyway, it was time for bed. He hoped he could get to sleep without the distraction of wondering what had caused Rocky's tone of urgency on the voice message.

When he got to bed, Paula was sleeping uneasily. Her breathing was uneven, and she was shifting her position every few seconds. Was she uneasy because of the way the conversation ended? Was she, perhaps, more concerned than she had let on?

Wade gently placed his left hand on Paula's shoulder, and within one minute she settled down, and her breathing indicated that she was now sleeping soundly. He knew, however, that it was going to be a while before he would fall asleep. There was a lot to think about.

But rather than focusing on The Payback Team's recent events, he chose something far more important. He thought about the success and wealth that he had achieved, and realized that they were nothing compared to his three priceless treasures, the ones that were, finally, sharing the cottage with him at that very moment.

Chapter Seventeen

Family Time at the Cottage

Three members of the Courtland family, along with Bosco, their six-year-old Golden Retriever, had gotten up early and taken the boat out on the lake for some quality fishing time. Wade slept in. They knew that there was no point in inviting him to join them because sitting still for three hours, other than the occasional nibble, did not suit him. His standard comment when someone asked him if he liked to fish was that he preferred to stay in the cottage and organize his slide collection of French war heroes.

At exactly 7:00 A.M., the phone woke him up. He didn't mind because he had planned to get up reasonably early in order to call Rocky to find out what he had on his mind. And that's exactly who was calling. "Spike, did you see it?" asked Rocky immediately. "This lady saw the chopper and called it in. And a guy recorded it and FAST 1 was swearing and they cut him off and—"

This was vintage Rocky, so excited that he wasn't making much sense. "Rocky, s-l-o-w d-o-w-n. Take it r-e-a-l s-l-o-w, and maybe I'll be able to figure out what you're trying to say."

"Okay, fine. Check this out..." Rocky then caught his breath and began to explain what had happened. One of FAST 1's neighbors had seen the chopper and the Lexus approaching her neighborhood. Her husband recorded the event while she phoned 911. Someone alerted the media, and the ABC crew arrived on the scene not long after the Lexus splashed into the pool. The man's video appeared on the ten o'clock news, along with an on-the-scene interview with Everett Flanagan and his wife, standing next to the pool, looking down at the Lexus. Flanagan was asked what happened, but after bleeping out most of his first sentence, the reporter cut him off and asked his wife if she could explain why a seventy-thousand-dollar luxury automobile was sitting at the bottom of their pool. It was clear to the viewers that Flanagan was so angry that he was unable to speak without the use of profanity. But she couldn't do much to help the viewers understand the "who" or the "why" of the situation.

Fortunately, Rocky had taped the news segment and promised to bring it to the Monday meeting. Before finishing this part of the phone call, Rocky said that the news segment closed with a close-up of Flanagan pacing around the pool, waving his arms and shouting something that was mostly bleeped out. Rocky then switched gears and filled Wade in on other developments. The major had called and reported that Stedman's truck had spent the previous evening at the casino. Then he explained that his contact had melted down the .357 magnum and poured it into the mold that Chico had requested. The new chunk of metal was now ready to be sent to John V. Chico had composed a note to accompany the new shape, and he wanted to share it with his team members on Monday to see if it needed any finishing touches. And at the meeting, it would be a good idea to decide on the best way to get it into John V.'s hands.

After processing all of this information, Wade's first thought was that he regretted being so far away from the action, but then he realized that he would at least be able to accomplish one or two things while he was at the cottage. And, of course, he knew that what he wanted most was to spend time with his family. Their getaway cottage was meant to be just that, a place where they could temporarily leave the rest of the world behind and sit back and unwind. The rest of the Courtlands were due back within the hour, so he decided to get a little business out of the way while he waited for their return. First, he called his aunt and arranged to get together with her on Sunday evening. Then he spent a few minutes reviewing the e-mail Chico had sent him, listing the questions he could ask Stedman to see if he had started the Gamblers Anonymous meetings. As he dialed Stedman's number, he made a mental note to begin by finding out if he had sent the money as directed.

The rest of the long weekend, including the two-and-a-half hour drive home, was relaxing and enjoyable. Paula and Wade were never sure when they would all be able to get together at the cottage again. It wasn't like when the kids were little; now, they had grown up and had their own interests and responsibilities. Although they knew that this was inevitable, it was still hard to accept.

Wade was not like a lot of successful fathers who had sacrificed time with their children in order to focus on business. He had found time to attend every school function, every birthday party, every sports event, and rarely missed a weekend with them at the cottage. As a result, this was, and always would be, a close family that cared deeply for one another.

At seven o'clock on Sunday evening, Wade was getting ready to make the short drive to his aunt's house when Rob approached him. "Pop, Mom told me why you're going over to Auntie Moey's. I'd like to come along."

"Son, I'm just not ready to involve you in this." Wade saw the look on his son's face and was surprised to see how disappointed he was. He was thinking of something more to say when Paula spoke.

"Honey, I've been thinking about this whole thing, and I've got a lot of mixed emotions. For one thing, I sometimes regret that I brought up the article in the paper about Guatemala. I don't know why it didn't occur to me how dangerous it could turn out to be. I guess I just wasn't thinking. But now that you've started, I know you're not going to turn back. But regarding Rob's request, think about it. This is exactly how you would have felt at his age. You should be proud that your son wants to be a part of what you're doing. Wade, he's twenty-one now, not eight or nine. I'm concerned about his safety, just as you are, but I'm sure you and Tommy and Michael can think of some way to involve him that would be unlikely to include violence. Why not let him go along?"

"Well, okay, I see your point, and I guess I agree," replied Wade. "But I'm not gonna make any moves like this without getting the okay from my partners. And I would expect the same from them. So, listen, Rob, here's the thing. Remember at the bonfire, when you said you'd be satisfied if I discussed this with Uncle Tommy and Uncle Michael? Well, we have a meeting tomorrow, and I promise I'll bring it up. And guess what? I'm almost positive they're gonna go along with it. That okay with you?" Wade was pleased with himself when it became obvious that he had reached a solution that everyone was comfortable with.

When he reached his aunt's home, she was not happy. "So what's so important that you're making me miss Desperate Housewives?"

"Auntie, you mean you're still not using the DVD recorder we bought you for Christmas?" asked Wade.

"Of course not, the damn instructions are in Japanese," answered his aunt.

"Listen, Auntie, the instructions aren't in Japanese. They're just a little complicated, that's all. Tell you what; before I leave, I'll go over it with you, all right?"

Aunt Mary calmed down a little, went into the kitchen, and returned with a plate of chocolate chip cookies. "Here, I made these for you, just the way you like them, baked a couple extra minutes so they're nice and crispy. Now what's on your mind?" She was more than pleased when Wade explained why he was there, but then she did something totally unexpected. "Okay, I see that you and your friends, Ricky and Chichi, want me to explain about Guat—"

"That's Rocky and Chico, Auntie," corrected Wade.

"Okay, fine, whatever. But first, I want you to do something for me. The reason I brought up those silly names you have for each other is that I've been meaning to ask you about the name they call you. That one I remember: Spike. So clue me in."

"Well, maybe some other time, but right now—"

Wade's aunt pushed her glasses down on her nose and lowered her head so that she could look over the top of the frames and give him what was known as the "Auntie Moey stare." And then she said, "Listen, Junior, if you think for one second I'm gonna give you what you want before I get what I want, then you better adjust your thinker."

Nobody ever won a standoff with Auntie Moey, so it looked like Wade was going to have to relent. But first, he decided to take one more crack at avoiding the subject. "Auntie, you probably wouldn't understand. It has to do with our annual trip to Las Vegas. Unless you understand about Texas hold 'em, there's no way it would make any sense to you."

"You mean like I see on TV, with the World Poker Tour program? What's not to understand? I watch it all the time."

Another failed attempt to outfox Auntie Moey.

"I like that Mike Sexton, and also that Daniel kid with the funny last name. And I especially like Doyle 'Texas Dolly' Brunson. Now, there's a hot number. I swear, if he wasn't married, I'd fly to Las Vegas and—"

"Auntie, please! I really don't want to hear this!"

"Hell, I'm not dead yet. Why, as a matter of fact, before he died, your Uncle Herb and I were still having sex, even up into our late sixties. And I'll tell you this—" Aunt Mary stopped mid-sentence, as she realized that Wade had put his fingers in his ears and was singing his favorite Bruce Springsteen tune. He knew that she was one of only a handful of people on the planet who could not stomach "The Boss."

"Alright, Auntie, you win. I am, like totally grossed out," Wade said. "Okay, here's what happened. We were at the Bellagio, about eight years ago, playing Texas hold 'em. Two hands in a row, I spiked a nine on the river, once to beat Tommy and once to beat Michael. The 'river' is the last card dealt, and 'spike' means to catch a miracle card to win the pot.

I should probably point out that I had been like way over-served, drinks are free in the casino you know, and I was playing like a complete idiot.

"In the first case, I had two outs, and only one out in the second hand. An 'out' is any card that can help your hand. It was later pointed out that I had zero chances of winning either hand, unless the last card was a nine. They each had a full house before the last card was dealt, so I was an extreme underdog. One of the other players at the table started calling me 'Spike', which is like a major putdown. When everyone saw that it kind of got under my skin, 'Spike' became my name for the rest of the evening.

"Then the next day, when I was trying my best to deal with like the worst hangover ever, they went at it again. The more annoyed I got, the more they kept it up. Now it's like more of a traditional, almost sentimental thing for all of us, and I'm okay with it. In fact I actually kind of like it.

"Okay, that's the story. *Now* can we get down to business?

Chapter Eighteen

The Monday Meeting

The first order of business at the Monday morning meeting was the video of the chopper dropping the Lexus in the pool. Chico and Wade had not seen it until the meeting, and they were pleased that Rocky had managed to record it. They especially enjoyed the shot of FAST 1 waving his arms and shouting obscenities, while he paced around the pool.

Now, they had to decide what to do next with FAST 1. They liked Chico's idea of using the chopper to drop the next vehicle at the front gate. If done to precision, the pilot might be able to impale the vehicle right on the gate, destroying both the car and the entrance to the estate. This would cut off access to their home, at least for awhile. FAST 1's hostile type A personality seemed to be at it's peak when he encountered any of life's many inconveniences, and this next inconvenience was apt to set him off, at least as much as the last two times. They hoped that, by now, he had received the thank you letter from the Battered Women's Shelter for the donation made with the money from selling his Corvette. It would have been nice to view a video of that event, but they would just have to use their imagination instead.

Other than his wife's Escalade, the only car left was the Mercedes Roadster. It was a vintage 560 SL in mint condition. They weren't sure if he would drive it temporarily until he could buy something else, and they discussed whether or not they should destroy such a fine automobile if he did. It was finally decided that this one was probably his favorite, so they planned to link up the major's team with the chopper pilot once again. Reluctantly, they decided that they would go ahead and drop the Escalade, if he chose to drive her SUV. They really didn't want to make life difficult for FAST 1's wife, but, on the other hand, this might upset him even more.

Then Chico came up with a twist to their plan. "You know, while you guys were debating whether or not we should eighty-six his

Mercedes, I remembered something Rocky said. He told us he found the insurance card and registration in the glove compartment of the Vette when he removed FAST 1's .38 caliber Smith and Wesson snub nose, so we know he's insured with Allstate. Let's call the claims department and inform them that the crazy guy who tried to collect on the Corvette and the Lexus is now about to demolish another of his vehicles. And we'll do this when the car is in the air, on its way to the estate. I'm sure it won't take long for him to prove that he wasn't involved, but the police and the insurance investigators will probably make his life difficult for a couple of weeks. Then, some time after that, I think it will be time to have a little meeting with him and have the discussion we talked about previously."

Everyone liked the idea, so it was approved without further discussion.

Wade then brought up the issue of his son wanting to be a part of the operation. "You'll never guess who is interested in being a part of our—"

Both Chico and Rocky provided the answer simultaneously before Wade could finish the sentence. "Rob!"

"Looks like you assholes are one step ahead of me. How did you— ah, forget it. Well, what do you think?" asked Wade.

As it turned out, they were waiting for this to come up, so they already had their answer. It was decided that Rob should be a part of the team, but would play only a minor role. Everyone agreed with Paula that he should be kept at a distance from any possible violence.

Wade thanked them for their concern and added that he thought it was the best way to proceed. Then he changed the subject. "I called Stedman a couple of nights ago, and he told me that he sent the money. And when I asked him if he borrowed it from his father, he said yes. But when I asked the first question from the list that Chico came up with, he lied. He told me he had been to his first meeting, so I asked him where it was and he told me it was in Hillside. I was pretty sure he was lying, so I checked with the report that Rocky e-mailed me. You know the one that the major provided that shows where the truck had been. Yes, it was in Hillside that same evening, but I had a hunch, so I checked with my nephew. He's familiar with the location; it's a home game. The house is owned by a guy they call Gary P., and he runs a poker game every Thursday. At this point, Stedman thinks we're through with him; I didn't let on that I felt he was lying. So now we need Chico to come up with a plan of how we can get him to do what he's supposed to do."

Chico was quick to respond. "Already got that figured out. We're gonna arrange a sit-down with us, him and his father. We're gonna hit the old man with two things. First, we're gonna catch Stedman in a lie. I'm certain that he either borrowed from someone else, or if it was from his father, he told him the money was for some other purpose. So, we will have caught him in a lie in front of his father. We're making the case that he is a sick gambler who has to lie to get money to gamble, or to pay his gambling debts, and you can bet the old man has been kept in the dark about all this. And the other thing has to do with the divorce. My instincts tell me that the gambling was an issue that came out in the divorce proceedings. My instincts also tell me that he has been careful not to let his father know about it. He probably told him it's the old 'irreconcilable differences' bullshit. Rocky, why don't you have one of your contacts look into getting a copy of the divorce records. We can drop them on the old man at the right moment to prove our point. When he sees the truth in black and white, he'll realize his son needs help, and bingo, we're there."

Rocky gave a nod of agreement, and then decided to move on to other business. He pulled out a small box and set it on the coffee table. Next, he opened it up and placed a chunk of metal in the middle of the table. The others stared at it for a few seconds.

Wade was the first to speak. "Well, I'll be damned. That's John V.'s gun, isn't it? Beautiful, absolutely beautiful. It's a donkey—no, wait, I get it! It's supposed to be a dumb ass, just like John V.! That's totally brilliant. He's gonna go ballistic when he sees this. Chico, you said you were gonna write a note to go with it. I can't wait to see it."

"I got the note right here. I wanted you both to review it to see if it's gonna get the results we want. Personally, I don't think so; all it's gonna do is piss him off more. I just don't think there's any way of getting through to this guy." Chico paused before giving them each a copy of the note. "You know what just occurred to me? We could have

Rob deliver the donkey and the note to John V. He wants to be involved, and I don't see any chance of him getting hurt, so how about it?"

After they agreed on this plan, they each were handed a copy of the note. Chico read the note out loud:

Dear Mr. Vargas,

We wanted to send you this thank you note to let you know how much we appreciated the opportunity to meet with you. We hope that you will give consideration to our proposal.

Our mutual friend, Harry, was pleased that you and Stan seemed to hit it off. He was quite surprised when we explained that Stan put both arms around you before we parted company, as he knows that Stan is usually not so emotional upon first making a new acquaintance.

However, Harry was somewhat annoyed to learn that Stan inadvertently left with one of your keepsakes, and he insisted that we return it. When we explained that the keepsake had caused you some amount of physical discomfort, he told us to make sure it wouldn't happen again. That, of course, presented a bit of a catch-22: how to return it and make sure that it wouldn't cause you any difficulty in the future.

So, our solution was to make a modification to the keepsake, as you can see. Harry liked it, and felt that, in some way, it reminded him of you. We're reserving judgment; you'll have to see for yourself. But we do hope that it will remind you of our visit, and that it will encourage you to give careful consideration to our proposal. We'll give you a courtesy call in a day or two to see if you have made a decision in our favor.

Thanks again for our visit.

Sincerely,
Allen, Mark, and Stan

P.S.

Stan wanted to offer a little business advice. He noticed the '95 Eldorado in the back of your lot and thought it should be displayed where it would attract more attention. He's working on an idea and says he'll let you know.

Chico could tell that they liked the note, although they both wanted to know what was up with the strange postscript. Chico explained that he would get to that in a minute or two. Aside from this, he was pleasantly surprised that they approved it without any changes. However, they all agreed that there was almost no chance that it was going to cause John V. to accept their "proposal." All it would accomplish, besides pissing him off, was that he would know for sure that they didn't intend to walk away from this.

Wade wanted to know what Chico thought they should do when the follow-up call proved unsuccessful. Chico said, "Well, remember when I said I had an idea how we could use the chopper, but I wanted to see how the thing with FAST 1 worked out? Well, now we know; it was clearly a success. So what we can do is this: did you notice that John V.'s building has a flat roof?" Both Wade and Rocky gave a look that said *so what?* "Okay, here's what I'm getting at. Wade, why don't you be the one to call him and ask him if he's ready to come across with the five dimes. Obviously, he's gonna tell you to go piss in your hat. Then, when we know for sure that we aren't getting anywhere, we take the next step. We get the chopper over to his place on Sunday, when they're closed. And we hook up the '95 Eldorado and we park it on the roof. That should attract the attention that was mentioned in the P.S., just not the kind of attention that John V. is going to appreciate."

Rocky expressed his approval. "That's great, but has it occurred to any of you that we're going to a lot of trouble just to get a relatively small amount of money out of some complete lowlife?"

Wade had an answer. "First, it may not be much money to us, but the original amount, fifteen hundred, is a fortune to some people, my nephew, for one. And remember, it's a little different when you're cheated out of it. You didn't just lose it, or spend it foolishly; you were robbed, plain and simple. And, more importantly, we're making progress on our first three missions, Stedman, FAST 1, and John V. You know, if we can't pull off victories on these three projects, we shouldn't even consider continuing, because the challenges are only gonna multiply. And frankly, I'm willing to admit that I'm getting a kick out of irritating the hell out of John V., and I gotta say he really has it coming."

When he saw that Rocky seemed to go along with his answer, Wade continued. "So, I guess the next order of business is to find out if Rocky got any feedback on the wife beater so that Chico can work on a plan for that project. And then there's the rapist. Any progress on figuring out how we're gonna get him in prison, where he belongs?"

After Chico shook his head, indicating that there was no progress, Rocky said that he had gotten enough information on the wife beater to determine that everything his wife had told Christine had, in fact, happened. Rocky knew a guy in law enforcement who was able to put him in direct contact with one of the policemen who had responded to a 911 call from a neighbor of the couple. Apparently, they had heard loud fighting, including what sounded like threats, along with a woman's voice pleading for someone to stop. The husband answered the door and explained that they must have had the television turned up too loud. Both officers could smell alcohol on his breath. Rocky said that the cops asked the husband what program they had been watching. Knowing that he could easily be caught in a lie, the husband became belligerent and told them that he wasn't required to waste his time answering any irrelevant questions.

At that moment, the officer could see the man's wife and young son standing in the background. She looked distraught, her hair was a mess, her right sleeve was torn, and she had a bruise below her right eye. The cop tried to ask her if anything was wrong, but the husband took control and said everything was fine, and that it was time for them to go out and catch some real criminals. The officer asked her why she appeared bruised and upset, but the husband again answered for her, saying that she had tripped and fallen down the stairs. One or two more attempts to get the wife to respond were unsuccessful, and the husband shut the door. The cop did his best to shout, through the closed door, that she could file charges if she chose to, but nothing further came of it.

After his explanation about the police incident, Rocky continued. "The major was able to obtain some information from a local hospital. She has been to the emergency room twice in the last three months with injuries consistent with bruises from a beating, but they were unable to get her to admit anything, so she was treated and released. By the way, the guy's name is Edmond Crowley, and he's got a PhD after his name. He's the principal of an elementary school, and he's on the Bloomingdale town council. He comes from money. His old man runs a big company. This was backed up by what the cop told me; the guy's neighborhood was way beyond what he could afford at his income level, and he was wearing a Rolex and a diamond pinky ring that were worth a small fortune. This is a guy who has a lot to lose; I can see the headlines now: 'Town Councilman Awaiting Trial on Charges of Beating Wife.' Beautiful. We're gonna have fun with this little weasel."

Wade was impressed. "That's what we needed to know. Chico, I guess you can start planning how to handle this guy. Now, it looks like we're gonna start getting into some really worthwhile projects. Rocky, I was thinking about what you said, you know, you were wondering if we should be spending our time on projects like Stedman and John V. I know how you feel, but I told you that it serves as preparation for what should be our real purpose. Now, we're getting ready to ramp it up a few notches. And speaking of worthwhile projects, I suppose you'd like to know what I found out about the Guatemala situation. I met with my—" Wade paused for about two seconds to make sure he didn't refer to his aunt the way he usually did, and then continued, "—aunt last night, and got the complete rundown. She was on a two-week vacation in Central America. It was a prearranged group tour, and one day, their schedule had them taking a bus on a sightseeing excursion in Guatemala. It was one of those buses like you see in the movies, held together with bailing wire and chewing gum. She was leery of the whole thing right from the start. There was a rumor that this was a dangerous area, lots of banditos who made their living by taking money and jewelry from wealthy gringos, but the driver told them that he had made the trip many times without any problems. That, by the way, is the tip-off that the driver was most likely part of the setup because she found out that that kind of thing was something of a common occurrence in that part of Guatemala.

"After the bus got to the middle of a jungle, on a road that looked like nothing more than a couple of ruts in the ground, it happened. There was a boulder that had been rolled into the middle of the so-called road, and the driver was forced to stop. Two men with guns got on the bus. One of them explained what was going to happen. His English was poor, but understandable. He explained that everyone on the bus was to lock their hands behind their heads, and anyone who didn't follow these instructions would be promptly killed. They then confiscated all the purses and anything in the overhead rack or on the floor that looked like it had any value. After that, the passengers were lead off the bus one at a time. Two more banditos with guns took each passenger down an embankment to a little clearing that could not be seen by anyone on the bus. People on the bus assumed that they were going to hear gunfire as each passenger was being executed. But, fortunately, this didn't happen.

"At the clearing, each person was told to kneel, while keeping their hands locked behind their heads. Then the last of the five banditos went through their pockets and took everything of value. He also grabbed all neck chains, bracelets, rings, and cell phones. He even had Vaseline handy to get off any tight-fitting rings. For the most part, everyone kept quiet and cooperated, with two exceptions. One elderly lady wasn't moving fast enough, so she was pulled out of line and knocked to the ground. And in one case, a man tried to resist when one of the banditos tried to reach in his pockets. He was hit over the head, and when he fell to the ground, he was kicked in the stomach. Then two of the hijackers pulled off his pants and held them up in the air and shouted something in Spanish. Most likely they were saying that this would happen to anyone else who was foolish enough not to cooperate. It was clear that they were not above harming any of the passengers, regardless of their age or sex. After they completed the robbery, each person was led back onto the bus. It was all very orderly and methodical. It was clear that they were very experienced and prepared.

"After everyone was back on the bus, the driver was told to close the door and wait five minutes. The guy then explained that they were going to leave one bandito behind and that he would shoot anyone who tried to get off the bus. They heard a vehicle start up and drive away, but they never saw where it had been parked, so there was no way to identify it."

After finishing his explanation of what happened in Guatemala, Wade decided it was probably time to bring the meeting to an end. "So now, I guess we have a lot to consider, and it looks like we're ready for the next step in a couple of these situations. Let's briefly summarize where we're at and make sure that we've got everything covered." One of Wade's strong points in business had been to get the big picture, organize and categorize what had to be done, decide who should be assigned to which task, and then develop a follow-up system to make sure that everyone's assignment was being carried out. Now, he was applying these important management skills to the challenges that faced The Payback Team.

"First, I'll take the donkey and the letter home to Rob and have him deliver them to John V.'s office. He should be able to do it tomorrow morning. He's working the P.M. shift at one of the fitness clubs, but his hours are flexible, so he can be pretty much available if and when we need him. And Rocky, it just occurred to me that he's gonna need to have one of those special wallets you got for us. We haven't needed them up to now, but I'm sure we will before long. I'll wait a couple of days after Rob makes the delivery, and then I'll make a follow up call to see if he's ready to hand over the five thousand, although we pretty much know what the answer will be. Rocky, let us know when your guys complete the Mercedes drop, or whatever vehicle he'll be driving next, and then we can plan to sit down and have a little chat with him. And be sure to bring his .38 caliber Smith and Wesson snub nose with you to the meeting. Oh, and by the way, be sure to have the major's guy call the TV station; we can't count on getting lucky again, like last time, when the neighbor called it in.

"And while we're talking about vehicle drops, go ahead and line up your guys to put the Eldorado up on John V.'s roof on Sunday, when no one's around. Then let's plan to meet with Vargas early next week to see if he's finally convinced that he should pay up. You know, I don't think it's a good idea for us to show up on his turf anymore. We need to have more control. So, Rocky, why don't you see if the major can plan on intercepting him on his way to or from work and deliver him to us? We can have him meet our van someplace, and then we can all take a little ride and have another nice chat.

"Next is Stedman. We should be able to wrap that one up as soon as we get the news from Rocky's guy in England that the money has arrived. I suggest we meet him when he leaves his apartment and drive him over to his parents' home. Oh, and I almost forgot; Rocky, we're gonna need the divorce records for the meeting, so I hope you can get your hands on them soon. My understanding was that he was living in Franklin Park at that time, so I assume that would be under Cook County jurisdiction, but I'll leave that up to your contacts to figure out.

"Now, let's talk about Edmond Crowley. Chico, if you can come up with a plan of how to handle the meeting, I'd like to pick him up this week, maybe on Wednesday, on his way home from work. We're scheduled at Indian Lakes to play eighteen holes that morning, so the timing should be perfect. We'll have plenty of time to discuss what you've come up with, while Rocky's four-putting the greens."

Rocky was not about to let that one slip by. "If I'm such a shitty golfer, then how come you dropped over five hundred bucks the last two rounds we played?"

"It's because I'm setting you guys up," replied Wade. "It's all part of my plan. Now, do you mind if we get back to business?"

Chico smiled and said, "Fine with me. In fact, I have one more thing to bring up. I thought of an idea of how we can get some money out of Vargas; although, of course, it will not be because he wants to cooperate with us. We'll need some help from Major Robins's team. I'll get his number from Rocky and set it up. I guarantee you're gonna like it. Okay, so that's about it. Are we ready to wrap it up for now?"

Rocky responded, "Well, actually, I had something to bring up. I don't know if you guys are gonna like it or not, and I don't know if this would fit in before or after the Guatemala thing, and I don't know if this is something we should pursue, or if—"

Chico was getting impatient. "Maybe if you'd come to the point, we could let you know our opinion. Get on with it."

"Okay, fine," said Rocky. "I heard about this from Angela's sister. She lives next door to an old couple who got screwed big time. It's one of those contractor scams that they like to pull on old people. They needed some roof work done on their house, and they got a referral from someone in their church. They assumed that anyone referred by someone they knew from church would have to be a person that could be trusted. So the guy came out and convinced them that they needed a new roof and had to get their chimney replaced, said it wasn't safe, played on their fear. So, he took twenty thousand up front, and then disappeared. My sister-in-law tried to help them; she contacted one of those newspaper hotlines, and also called the state's attorney's fraud division, but the guy has skipped out. Basically, they know *who* he is, but don't know *where* he is. The state's attorney's office has a couple of other active cases against him, but now they're at a dead end. Do we want to go after this one? Most likely the major could track him down. When I hear something like this, it makes me want to get in the car, go out, and find the guy and—"

Wade cut him off. "Yeah, Rocky, we all feel the same way. But let's put this one on ice for awhile. I'd like to get to it, but we've really got too much going on right now. I promise we'll look into it later, okay?"

Chapter Nineteen

Meeting with Edmond Crowley

Whack! Rocky's club made contact with the ball and sent it straight down the fairway. This was a par four hole, and yet the ball made it to within twenty yards of the green.

Wade came up with what started out as a compliment. "Rocky, that was another fantastic drive. If you had learned to putt as good as your tee shots, your career path would very likely have been much diff—"

"Put a lid on it, okay?" said Rocky. "At least part of my game doesn't suck. Now in your case, you—"

Chico decided to take control. "Okay, that's enough. We're on the fifth hole, and you two haven't stopped for a second. I feel like I'm the only grown up at a preschool playground. Now, do you mind if I bring up some business items? That's part of why we're out today, isn't it? We're supposed to meet Crowley in a few hours, and I wanted to let you know what I came up with."

Rocky needed to offer some news before Chico continued. "Let me throw in something important before you start. I've got some news I think you're both going to like. I know this one guy who owes me a big favor. He's got a manufacturing business over in the industrial park in Schaumburg. There's a garage, or maybe it's more like a warehouse, that's connected to the rear of the building. It's mostly empty, and he said we could use it any time. Think about it. It's not always a good idea to drive around in a van; look what happened when we were coming back from Indiana. So, at least for today, I am having the major's people drive him to this guy's place, and we'll meet them there. There are no windows, so he won't know where he is and won't be able to make any connection to the owner, or to us. If we like it, it's ours to use whenever we want."

Chico gave his approval. "I love it! Good job. It almost makes up for the bullshit I've had to put up with all morning. Now, let me go over how I intend to handle our encounter with Dr. Crowley. It took me awhile to come up with the right approach, but I'm satisfied with it, and I want to see if you guys agree."

Wade and Rocky stopped dissing each other's golf game long enough to listen to Chico's presentation, and then approved it without making any changes.

During the remainder of the game, several pieces of business were discussed, but for the most part, Chico had to endure the usual bickering from the other two.

Wade mentioned that Rob had dropped off the package at John V.'s business. He had told his son to park the van a couple of blocks away and to get in and out of the office as fast as he could. By no means should he wait for him to open the package or to read the note; just drop it off and go. And Wade explained that he should leave his wallet in the van, as they had not as yet secured his new identification. He was confident that Rob could get away if it came down to a chase, as his son had already become a serious runner, just like his old man. They had done a fair share of local 5k and 10k races together, both placing respectably within their age groups.

He went on to explain what happened after Rob left John V.'s office. He got to the end of the block and was about to turn down the street where the van was parked when he heard a loud "Hey!" coming from behind. He turned around and saw John V. coming after him, walking at a fast pace. "Listen, you little shit, come back here," was all he needed to hear. So he took off at near top speed, and after a couple of blocks, when he was certain that John V. had given up the chase, he slowed down to a walk. After twenty more minutes, he returned safely to the van.

When they got back to the clubhouse, Rocky gave an update on the Stedman issue, explaining that he had gotten a call from his overseas contact; the money had arrived. The Payback Team then decided that they would try to get everyone together at Stedman's parents' home on Friday.

As they were heading out to the van, Wade again had to settle up with his golf partners, handing over two hundred dollars to Rocky, and nearly as much to Chico. Rocky had his mouth open and was looking directly at Wade when Chico cut him off. "Please, enough. I can't deal with any more of this. Could we just, please, focus on our mission? It looks like we're gonna be a little early, but that's okay. I think we should be there first. And even if something happens, like Crowley stays late for a meeting or whatever, I still think it'll at least be worth seeing what this warehouse is like. It sounds like this is going to come in real handy, at least I hope so. And I almost forgot. I have to stop and pick up something at Ace Hardware on our way there." The three golfers then got into a white van that apparently belonged to Jake's Welding Service.

About an hour later, they arrived at the warehouse. They parked the van inside, removed the license plates, and took a good look at their surroundings. It didn't take long for them to agree that the place was perfect, and that they would most likely be using it frequently in the coming weeks. Someone had arranged a sitting area that consisted of four folding chairs, two comfortable, but worn overstuffed chairs, and a sofa that was big enough for three people. There was a round coffee table in the middle of the setting. Underneath everything was an old brown rug that had seen better days, but was a slight improvement over the grease-and-oil-stained concrete floor. Four orange crates, standing on end, were apparently meant to be used as end tables. For the most part, the warehouse was empty. There was an engine block in one corner and several levels of metal shelves on one wall. Except for a few paint cans and several rusty auto parts, the shelves were empty.

Rocky's cell phone rang. He picked it up, listened for less than five seconds, said "Got it," and hung up. He then called Rob and told him to make another drop-off, using the same routine as he had when he delivered the donkey. Finally, he told The Payback Team that Crowley would be arriving soon.

Within a few minutes, they heard the sound of a vehicle approaching. The door next to the large garage door opened, and three men entered. One was dressed in a three-piece business suit and was led by the other two to the sitting area. After they took off his handcuffs and went back to wait in their vehicle, Chico removed the black hood that had been placed over his head. He then motioned for the man to sit down in one of the more comfortable chairs. He made sure it was the one right next to the orange crate, where he had placed the large lopping shears that he had picked up from the hardware store. This was a heavy duty garden tool, capable of cutting through a branch two inches in diameter, or as an alternative, any one of a number of protuberances from the human anatomy.

Crowley was a scholarly looking man in his late thirties, with an average build, receding hairline, and glasses. Overall, he fit the part of a school principal or possibly a banker or even a CPA. Because of his distinguished appearance, it was hard to picture him as a wife beater. The trio, or course, realized that wife beaters can come in all sizes, shapes, and colors, and can fit anywhere along the full range of the socioeconomic spectrum.

It had been decided that Chico would take the lead this time, so after everyone was seated, he made the introductions. "Dr. Crowley, I'm Mark Miller, this is Stan Morrison, and that's Allen Harris. I'm going to get to why we're here in a minute, but first, let me put your mind at ease by explaining that it is unlikely that you are going to be physically harmed this afternoon, and if all goes well, you should be on your way back to your car and home in time for dinner. Now, I can see by the look on your face, and by the way that you keep looking at the table next to you, that you're still a little concerned. So let me start by trying to be a polite host and offer you something to drink. What would you like? We have pop, juice, and water in the cooler over there?"

"Mostly, I think I need a scotch, preferably a double, or if not, I could go for a beer," answered Crowley. "I was about to stop for a little something to take the edge off on my way home, when your two friends—"

Chico interrupted. "No, sorry. And maybe that's a good place to start, with your fondness for alcohol. That's really why we're here. Well, it's not exactly about the booze. It's what happens as a result of the booze."

Crowley only got out a few words before he was cut off. "I don't have the slightest idea what you're—"

Chico continued. "Listen, Dr. Crowley, if you're going to insist on playing dumb, two things are going to happen. First, it's going to be a long afternoon for all of us, and second, I'm going to have to rescind my earlier comment about the minimal chances of your being harmed." Chico then shifted his glance over to the lopping shears sitting on the orange crate, and paused for a few seconds to give Crowley a chance to consider what had just been said.

Now, Chico was ready to get to the point. "Everyone in this room knows that you have a drinking problem and an anger problem. And we know that you occasionally act out your frustrations, insecurities, or whatever the shrinks call it, by roughing up your wife. That's not nice. We know it, and you know it. We have 911 reports, we have police files, and we have hospital records to back up what we're saying. But we're not stupid. We realize that without your wife's testimony, they aren't enough to get a conviction. And that's why we're here: to make sure that it stops. Today, right now, we're going to help you make that decision. We're going to tell you the reasons why it's a good decision, and perhaps more importantly, we're going to explain why it would be a very, very bad idea not to make the right choice." Chico decided it was time to stop and let his words sink in. The trio looked at Crowley, trying to imagine what was going on in his head at that moment.

Finally, after almost two minutes, he began to speak very slowly. "Well...I...how did you...did my wife...?" Then he stopped and started over. Apparently, he had decided that his original approach was not going to cut it with his three adversaries. "Okay, let's say that I'm not disagreeing with you, at least not right now. Just what is it you want from me?"

Chico took his time answering, and started out by temporarily changing gears. "Listen, Dr. Crowley, the first thing for you to do is to stop thinking of us as the enemy. It doesn't have to be that way. In fact, and this is going to sound extreme, I promise you that right now, you are involved in a life-changing event. What you decide to do is going to profoundly change your existence from this moment on. Here's what I mean, and I say this because I think I know the kind of man you really are. I've been looking intently into your eyes since you sat down, and you know what I see? I see a man who doesn't really mean to hurt his wife. God knows we've dealt with plenty of sociopaths, but I don't think you fit into that category. No, my judgment of character tells me that you are a kind man, capable of loving and caring for your wife and son. But, sometimes, it just doesn't turn out that way. We know you're ashamed when it happens, but we also know that, sometimes, when you've been drinking, you're not capable of controlling the fury that is within you." Chico again paused, but this time, they were not ready for what happened during the silence.

Crowley's eyes slowly filled with tears as he stared blankly at the wall behind the sofa. He removed his glasses with one hand and wiped at his eyes with the other. Then, he lowered his head and looked at the floor for about a minute before replacing his glasses and lifting his head. Then he spoke, but it was barely audible. "What do you want me to do?"

"Well, first let's start with the positives," answered Chico. "It looks like we're all going to be on the same page here before long. Stan, why don't you put that little garden tool on one of those shelves over there, so we won't be distracted by it? And, Dr. Crowley, why don't you put your Rolex and that pinky ring on the coffee table. I'll explain more about that in a minute."

Crowley put them on the table, with only the slightest hesitation. When Rocky returned to his seat, Chico asked him what he thought they were worth. Rocky looked them over and announced that they could be pawned for around fifteen thousand dollars, since gold was nearing an all-time high. Then he put them back on the table.

All eyes were on Chico as he continued. "Okay, let's go over the list of positives. We'll assume that you want to stop hurting your wife, but we also need to assume that you're not going to be able to stop just because you want to. So, first off, you need to get into an anger management class. Next, you should join Alcoholics Anonymous, and finally, we want you to become a volunteer at the shelter for battered women. Maybe it will help if you see things from the other side, how violence affects its victims. Now, if you follow through on these requirements, you'll be halfway there. But you need to keep the consequences in the back of your mind for when you're tempted—and you will be tempted—so that you will have the motivation to keep from acting on your frustrations.

"So, here's the list of things that will happen if you ever hurt her again. And, Dr. Crowley, please note that I said 'will happen,' and not 'may happen.' First, your marriage will be over, and I'll explain how we're going to accomplish that in a moment. Second, your career is going to suffer because we're going to make sure that certain reports are sent to your school board, the parent's association, and your superintendent. And we'll make sure that all of this makes the local paper. Finally, we're going to send an associate of ours to the state's attorney's office with all of the evidence we've gathered, and he will do his best to get a case brought against you.

"Okay, so how do we go about ending your marriage? Well, I'm sure you are aware of one of the reasons why women like Mrs. Crowley don't leave their husbands. It's because of the economics involved. How would they support themselves? How would they afford an attorney? Where would they live until the divorce was settled? And since they usually feel that their controlling spouse has all the power, how could they even be sure that they would prevail in court and in the media?

"So, now, we get back to your expensive jewelry. We're going to take them to the pawnshop for you and trade them for cash. Notice, I said 'we're doing it *for* you'. This is not about us, Dr. Crowley. We want nothing out of this except justice for a woman who, I'm sure you agree, deserves it. A letter is being delivered to her right now, and the letter explains that the money from the pawnshop will be placed with an investment counselor. In one week, she is to call him and make an appointment to set up the account in her name. The money will be invested for her, and since it is her account, she can withdraw it at any time in order to take care of her needs while she is going through the divorce.

"And don't worry. I saw the expression on your face when you looked at your jewelry just now. We'll mail you the pawn ticket right away. If you're sentimentally attached, you can redeem it at any time. Now, isn't this an interesting situation? You, basically, are funding your wife's divorce proceedings! You are now the source of her empowerment! Let's hope she doesn't decide to divorce you five minutes after she gets the letter, but if she does, it will be up to you to convince her to take one more chance on you. I'm sure you've had discussions like that before, but this time will be the last.

"We know that you and your family can hire the best attorneys around, but let me assure you that we, also, can provide your wife with equally competent legal counsel. Believe me, you will be up against the best. Do not expect to win a custody battle over your son.

"Okay, you may be thinking that fifteen thousand would only last her for a couple of months, given your present lifestyle. You're right. But did you ever hear the expression 'there's plenty more where that came from'? Of course you have. Well, it's also true in this case. The letter explains that the investment counselor has access to a certain contingency fund that has been set up for her, so that she doesn't have to worry about expenses at all. She can reimburse the fund when the divorce proceedings are final.

"Dr. Crowley, we have one last thing to say before turning it over to you to find out your decision. I notice that Stan placed the garden sheers where you can still see them, and that you have glanced over there once or twice. We were going to use them to cut off your pinky ring, if it became necessary. By nature, sir, we are not violent, but if it serves the purpose of ending a much greater injustice, we are capable. But we want you to know that it is our preference that you make the right choice for the right reason."

The trio then remained silent, waiting for Crowley to speak. It only took about a minute. During that time, he again removed his glasses and wiped his eyes, but this time, he didn't lower his head. After a long sigh, he began speaking. "You're right; this is a life-changing event. You've put it in a way that really gives me no choice. I only regret that it had to be forced upon me because I should have done it on my own. I started out resenting that I was dragged here involuntarily. But, now, my only wish, besides hoping that I can become the man I want to be, is that I have the opportunity to do something like this for someone else. What a pity that I couldn't have done this on my own. I've always thought of myself as a strong, respectable…" Dr. Crowley was unable to continue. His glasses were off, his head was in his hands, and he was sobbing. When Crowley finally looked up and was able to speak, he looked at Chico and started to ask, "Why did you...?"

But Chico cut him off. "You don't need to know. Now, Stan, if you don't mind, Dr. Crowley would like to be on his way home. I think there are some things he would like to talk over with Mrs. Crowley."

Dr. Crowley realized that there was no need for any further conversation, so he simply formed the words "thank you." Then he turned toward the door as Rocky placed the hood over his head and gently started him on his journey to a new life.

Chapter Twenty

The Trip to Franklin Park

Thursday was supposed to be a day off for the members of The Payback Team. They had agreed not to get together again until the next day, when they planned to have the meeting with Stedman and his parents. There were, however, several loose ends that had to be worked on in order to keep the business of the team moving in the right direction.

Wade hadn't been on a long run in over two weeks, so he started the day with a slow and easy ten miler, during which he spent most of the time thinking about where The Payback Team was headed. He was pleased at what they had accomplished so far, but at the same time, he was concerned about the potential for violence. He was certain that they had made the right decision to involve Rob in the less dangerous assignments, even though he had recently expressed a desire to be given more responsibility. He was due to receive his new wallet within a few days, and Wade expected that would result in another request to be more involved.

In the afternoon, Wade made a call to John V., to determine if he was ready to cooperate. He listened to his ranting for a full two minutes, complete with swearing, threats, and plenty of shouting, before he very politely said, "Thank you. We'll be in touch," and hung up.

Chico went up to the Chain of Lakes, near the Wisconsin border, took his Sea Ray out of dry dock, and spent most of the day cruising at half speed, thinking about his responsibilities with The Payback Team. He never expected to be in a position where he would have to continue to use his management and planning skills, now that he had sold his business. But he didn't resent the position he found himself in, and he knew that his old friend had done something worthwhile by bringing the team together. He felt that the team was positioned to provide a very useful service to those in need, who were unable to help themselves. As he considered the power the team had to change lives for the better, or in some cases, to punish those who deserved it, he realized that they had an obligation to make certain that the team never abused that power.

He spent the remainder of his time on the water, working on plans for dealing with their current challenges, and on the way home, he gave some thought to the projects facing them later on. Before pulling into his garage, he made a mental note to recommend that the team should go after the contractor who had cheated the old couple that Rocky had mentioned earlier.

Rocky had received a call from Major Robins earlier in the week, informing him that he had gotten a copy of the file on Stedman's divorce, but that there were some items in the file that he wanted to check out before turning it over to him. He received another call from the major on Thursday afternoon, informing him that he had completed his work on the file and that Rocky should come over and pick it up.

The team was informed that the major's associate, along with the pilot from Milwaukee, had disposed of FAST 1's third vehicle. It was on the six o'clock, as well as the ten o'clock, news on all three major network stations. The same neighbor had again seen the helicopter and called 911. The major's associate had informed the TV stations that the insurance company was looking into some type of fraud on the part of the owner. This contact occurred shortly after a call was made to the insurance company. The timing of the calls was perfect, as representatives from the insurance company showed up during filming by the TV crews. In the interviews that followed, the two insurance investigators gave the usual "no comment" response, but it was clear that the owner of the demolished Mercedes was in for some serious questioning when he got home from work.

At 9:00 A.M. on Friday, the trio met at a McDonald's, not far from Stedman's parents' home. They planned to spend an hour going over several issues, the most important of which was the meeting that they hoped would take place that morning.

But it was the news report of the previous evening that initially took precedence. Although they were disappointed that FAST 1 wasn't there for the cameras, they were elated that the idea about involving the insurance company had apparently paid off. They also liked seeing that the Mercedes fell right on the middle of the gate, making it impossible to enter or exit the estate without the use of a ladder. They decided it was time to schedule an appointment to meet with him after the weekend, and it was determined that Chico should begin working out more of the details for the encounter.

Then Wade remembered his conversation with John V. "Speaking of appointments, I spoke to John V. yesterday. There's no hope of him ever cooperating voluntarily with us. He's gonna have to be 'motivated.' So let's plan on seeing him next week after we drop the Eldorado on his roof this Sunday." Wade finished by checking with Rocky to make sure that he was setting this up with his contacts.

While they waited for a call from the major's associates, they began reviewing the divorce file. The documents confirmed their assumption that Stedman's gambling problem was the underlying cause of the divorce. But, additionally, there was testimony at the hearing that, in addition to two evictions due to nonpayment of rent, he had been fired from one of his bartender jobs for stealing. Chico commented that this testimony should not have been allowed at the hearing because it was hearsay evidence, but Stedman had chosen not to be represented by counsel. He did not plan to contest the divorce, since there were no assets to be divided, so he had not hired an attorney. All he was concerned about was a chance to spend a few hours a week with his two boys, and his wife had agreed to this.

In addition to the copy of the court file, Major Robins had furnished Rocky with a report that detailed his contact with the ex-Mrs. Stedman, as well as the owner of the club where Stedman had worked when he was fired. The major wasn't able to get much out of his ex-wife, but he did find out the location of the club. The report showed that Stedman had stolen about three thousand dollars over a period of one month, and when he was confronted by the owner, he agreed to pay it back in exchange for the owner agreeing not to prosecute. During their encounter, Stedman apologized and explained that he hadn't wanted to resort to stealing, but he had received a very convincing threat. He would either have to get caught up on a gambling debt, or spend some time in intensive care.

After completing their review of the file, they agreed that they were now in possession of enough information to convince Stedman's parents that he had a serious gambling sickness. They were certain that it would come as a big surprise to them. They only hoped that they would have enough influence to get him into Gamblers Anonymous. They felt that they had been successful with their attempts to get Crowley headed in the right direction, and soon they would know if they were also going to be effective with Stedman. There was no disagreement about John V. He was probably a hopeless case.

Rocky answered his phone, talked for only a few seconds, and then informed his team members that Stedman was due at his parents' home in thirty minutes. Two of the major's associates had picked him up as he was on his way out of his apartment to head off to work. The plan was for the team to meet up with Stedman and transfer him to their van so that they would all arrive at the same time.

After a few minutes, the two vehicles pulled up next to each other, and Stedman was led into their van. According to the sign on the side, it belonged to Carson's Roofing Company.

As the van drove toward their destination, Wade attempted to start the conversation on a positive note by trying to put a friendly, upbeat tone in his voice. "Hi, Stu, remember us?"

Stedman's look made it very clear that he definitely remembered their previous meeting, but that he would have preferred never to have seen them again. Unlike their last encounter, he had no trouble getting the words out. "Why are you doing this? I sent the money like you told me to. And I started the meetings, and I borrowed the money from my dad, just like you wanted. Why don't you just leave me alone?"

Wade had an answer. "Well, Stu, I gotta say you're at least partially right, but, unfortunately, you got the part about the meetings wrong. The night you were in Hillside? Well, here's the thing, Stu, we tracked you to Gary P.'s home game. So why don't we just go inside and see how much your folks know about all this? I'm guessing there's gonna be a surprise when we compare notes on why you borrowed the two grand."

It was clear, judging by the look on Stedman's face, that he was not at all pleased with what was about to take place. Without waiting for an answer, the trio walked up to the front door of the Stedman home in the company of a very distraught young man. The lady who answered the door appeared to be in her late seventies. At first, she seemed alarmed to see three older men with Stedman, but then her look changed just enough that they knew she was happy to get a visit from him under any circumstance. She gave him a warm hug, and a brief scolding for taking too much time between visits.

She invited them in, and before anyone could speak, she turned toward the rear of the house and raised her voice. "Honey, Stuey's here with some friends. Can you finish painting later and come in the living room?" Then she turned again and said, "Would you all like some tea or some lemonade? I'd be happy to—"

Just then, Mr. Stedman, a man also in his late seventies, entered the room. It had become clear that the younger Stuart Stedman was not gong to be of any help in what was becoming an awkward situation for everyone. So Wade decided to take control and get things started in the right direction. "Mrs. Stedman, it is very kind of you to let us come into your home. And, Mr. Stedman, we appreciate that you are taking time from your project to talk with us. We've wanted to meet both of you, and we thought that this would be as good a day as any." Then he smiled and introduced himself and his friends, Mark and Stan.

After they were seated and drinks were served, the Stedmans noticed the curious looks on all but their son's faces. Mr. Stedman laughed and started to explain. "It's okay, we get that all the time, don't we, Helen? Stuey is our grandson, Stuart Martin Stedman the third. My son was killed four months before Stuey was born, and his mother didn't survive childbirth, so we have raised Stuey like our own son, right from the beginning. Are you gentlemen friends of Stuey from work?"

It had been decided that Wade would be the spokesman for the trio, since he handled most of their first encounter. "Well, actually, sir, we had hoped that Stuart might want to explain why we're here."

Stedman was no help at all. "Well, really, this is all one big misunderstanding. We shouldn't even be here. I tried to cooperate with them before, but they just won't leave me alone. And now they're here, but they have no business—"

Wade interrupted as soon as he saw that Stedman was making things worse. "Look, Stu, I think it would be much better if you explained things on your own, but I'll take over if you're going to take this conversation in the wrong direction." The elder Stedmans were becoming alarmed, and it looked like their grandson was only going to make things worse if he were allowed to continue. "Well, folks, I guess it's up to us to explain why we're here. Let me start by asking Mr. Stedman if Stu borrowed some money in the last two weeks, and if so, how much. Then maybe we can get to the point because the loan is related to our situation."

Mr. Stedman explained that he had recently loaned his grandson two thousand dollars for truck repairs. His grandson had told him that he would lose his job if he couldn't keep it running so he could get to work. "Okay, I have one more question, and then I think things are going to become real clear soon after that. Do either of you know why Stu got a divorce?"

Mrs. Stedman answered immediately. "I certainly do. It's because Stuey caught that little tramp he married fooling around with another guy. He had no choice but to divorce her. We're all glad that his attorney was able to get the child custody thing settled without any problems, Stuey can see his kids any time he wants. Why, just last week we all—"

The look on Mr. Stedman's face told the trio that he was starting to get concerned about where the conversation was headed, so he interrupted his wife. "That's enough, Helen. Just what exactly is your point, gentlemen? What's the problem here? Is Stuey in some kind of trouble?

Wade looked at Stedman and asked him one more time if he wanted to explain. Stedman simply looked at the floor. "Well, I guess it's up to me, since it looks like Stu is going to take the Fifth Amendment. Folks, we aren't friends of Stu's from work. We're actually in the collection business. That's right; we try to get people to pay up, before someone gets hurt. We often deal with people who are referred to in the novels as 'unsavory characters.' But, sometimes, we come across someone like Stu, a basically good person who made some bad decisions. If we feel we can help, we try to go a step beyond simply collecting the money and walking away. You see, Stu has a problem that you don't know about, one that will, someday, perhaps soon, hurt him real bad. You're not going to want to believe us at first, but when we prove it to you, it will be impossible to deny it."

The senior Stedmans looked at their grandson. When they saw that he couldn't look them in the eye, they began to feel that what they were about to hear was not going to make them happy. Mrs. Stedman began to cry, and Mr. Stedman walked over to her chair and held her. Even though she was clearly upset, she was nevertheless able to put together a string of relevant questions. "Is my Stuey in trouble? What happened? Please tell us? What should we—"

Mr. Stedman wanted the three visitors to get quickly to the point. "Now, Mother, be still, they're going to tell us all about it. Please continue, gentlemen. You have our attention."

Wade knew it was time to be direct. "You see, we met Stu because we had to collect a two-thousand-dollar gambling debt. When we met him, we could see right away that this was a person who needed help. You know, I think you folks have raised a fine young man here, and I am touched about how you took over when he had no one else to count on. A very sad beginning, but then you were the angels who came into his life and took over.

"So, rather than simply collecting the money for our associate, we added a little twist, one that would lead us to where we are today. You see," at this point he looked over at Chico, "one of us has had a lot of experience with addicted gamblers, just like Stu. He told us that Stu would lie to you about why he needed the money, and we knew that this lie could be the basis of your realizing that he has a problem, and of course, getting him help."

Chico felt obligated to speak. "I can tell that you're shocked and hurt that he would lie to you. But please, don't focus on the lie because that's just one of many symptoms of a serious gambling sickness, and it won't help to take it personally. Gamblers who reach the point where Stu is now will do almost anything to get money to support their addiction, just as much as other addicts need a way to continue their drug or alcohol addictions. What you need to do is to get Stu into Gamblers Anonymous. Their twelve-step program is designed to—"

Mrs. Stedman was not able to comprehend the seriousness of the situation, as proven by the nature of her interruption. "Couldn't we just talk to him and make sure he stops. I'm sure he doesn't mean to—"

Chico realized that he had to be even more direct. "Stu has made some really bad choices. You need to understand just how serious this is. Now check out what I have here." He looked at Rocky, who handed him the file. "You may look at this if you wish. It contains Stu's divorce records, and you will see that it was Jenny who filed for divorce, not Stu. There is nothing in the file about Jenny having cheated on him, despite Stu having every opportunity to tell his side of the story. And, no, he didn't have a lawyer. He and Jenny had agreed about the custody and visitation rights before the hearing.

"When Jenny had her say, she explained that they had been evicted from two apartments because Stu had gambled away the rent payments. And guess what? No objection from Stu. He also didn't disagree when she explained that gambling had cost him his last job and was the reason why he was unemployed at the time of the hearing. Finally, we suspected there was more to the story about why he lost his job. We sent one of our colleagues to talk to the guy who fired him. Folks, I'm sorry, but Stu was fired for stealing in order to pay some gambling debts. The boss gave him the choice of being prosecuted or paying back the money, and Stu chose to pay it back. The report is right here in the file." He started to hand it to Mr. Stedman, but he waved it away. Then he looked at the younger Stedman, waiting for him to look him in the eye and tell him that it was all some fantastic lie, cooked up for God knows what reason. But it never happened.

"What should we do?" Mr. Stedman made a sweeping gesture, indicating that he meant everyone in the room.

Wade jumped back in. "There is no 'we.' There's just you and Mrs. Stedman. We've done all we can, and we're about to leave. Maybe Mark can explain it better than I could, he's been through it, the Al-Anon part, I mean."

It was clear that the Stedman's didn't know anything about Al-Anon, so Chico tried to explain. "He means Gam-Anon. Al-Anon is a support group for loved ones of addicted alcoholics. The corresponding group for those connected to a gambling addict is called

Gam-Anon. You should get Stu into Gamblers Anonymous, and you need to start going to Gam-Anon meetings, so you can understand the nature of his problem. You will learn how to deal with conflicting situations. For example, how do you forgive Stu's lying without condoning his lies? How do you come to understand how gambling can turn a good person into one who lies, and how do you make sure that you are not enabling him to lie?

"Right now, you are enablers, although you don't yet realize it. If you give him money, or give him access to money, you are enabling his gambling addiction. For now, you need to understand that someone else, and that would be you, should control his resources so that he has no access to his, or anyone's, money. You need to arrange for his paychecks to come to you. You need to get him away from a job where people give him tips because, then, he has money that he can use for gambling. I know this seems extremely harsh, and maybe I've said too much, although I've lived it. Perhaps, all you should do for now is to start with Gam-Anon meetings yourself, so that you can get a clear, unbiased understanding of the reality of what I'm saying.

"There's so much you need to know, like being prepared for the inevitable relapse, even after he starts the GA meetings and appears to be getting on track." At this moment, everyone noticed Chico's eyes glistening, as he paused and tried to catch his breath. Clearly, he was reliving a nightmare from long ago.

The room was silent for a full two minutes. Mrs. Stedman was crying again, and Mr. Stedman stared at nothing in particular, slowly shaking his head, as if trying to make sense of something too extreme to comprehend.

The trio knew there was nothing more they could do. They stood up and gave one last look at Stuart Stedman, III before heading for the door. He hadn't changed position, even slightly, since he looked down at the floor more than a half hour ago.

When they got to the door, Mr. Stedman was close behind them. There was an awkward moment when no one was sure whether they should shake hands, just keep walking, or possibly offer a "Goodbye" or, perhaps, a "Good luck."

Then the unexpected happened. Mr. Stedman looked at Chico and noticed that there were still tears in his eyes. No one said a word, but the elder Stedman gave Chico a spontaneous hug—a hug that said "I share your pain." And before he ended the embrace, he said something in Chico's ear that the others were not meant to hear.

Chapter Twenty-One

Busy Days Ahead

Nothing was said for the first few minutes after returning to the van. Wade, Chico, and Rocky were each trying to process what had just occurred. Finally, after the plates and signs were changed, things began to lighten up a little. The first question, of course, related to the brief, parting episode between Chico and Mr. Stedman. Chico repeated exactly what was said: "God Bless you and your friends. We had no idea. But we'll take care of this. Our Stuey is going to be all right, thanks to you."

Another five minutes of silence followed, during which it was clear to everyone that things had gone extremely well. Chico gave a thumbs-up sign, Rocky nodded his head in agreement, and Wade just smiled.

Wade suggested that they take part of the weekend off and meet for eighteen holes on Sunday. He planned to spend part of the weekend up at the cottage. Chico mentioned that he was ready for a nice, long boat ride and Rocky had promised his daughter that he would take her and two of her friends up to Six Flags amusement park.

The last fifteen minutes of the ride were used to wrap up a few loose ends in preparation for what was going to be a very busy week. They were planning to meet with FAST 1 on Monday and with John V. on Tuesday. Rocky promised to coordinate all of the details with Major Robins so that his associates knew what to do, where to be, and exactly when to be there.

Chico had a question. "Rocky, you've got Flanagan's gun, right? And you'll be sure to bring it to our meeting? And, by the way, I think you should handle the meeting. It's about time for you to carry the ball, especially since this situation needs a little heavier-handed approach, which is right up your alley."

"Yeah, I'm planning to bring the piece. And, yes, I'll look forward to handling the meeting. I already know what I'm going to say. We already went over this, remember?"

Wade needed to explain a new development. "I've thought a lot about the approach we agreed to take with Flanagan. It's taken me a long time, but I finally reached a conclusion about what I think is the best way to handle it. He needs to spend two years in prison for what he did. Believe it or not, this is no longer about me. I'm fully recovered, and I no longer feel any trauma; in fact, I never did. My whole effort and energy were directed toward getting my health back.

"But what it's about is that someone who does something like this, forget that it happened to me, should be punished, and for two obvious reasons: first, he needs to pay for the crime, and second, the incarceration should make him see that repeating the offense, or anything like it, would be a very bad idea. So I decided I had to take a proactive approach. Our old plan was to simply motivate him to turn himself in, but this could result in an outcome beyond our control. He could simply be put on probation, or he could be given a really long sentence. It will depend entirely on how the district attorney chooses to handle it.

"Here's what I came up with. I called Sergeant Callahan and told him that I knew how to locate the perp. Naturally, he wanted to know how I suddenly came up with this info, since I had totally dummied up when he grilled me while I was in the hospital. Well, that was easy. I told him that I had been seeing a shrink, and he got me to remember the license number while I was under hypnosis. Callahan didn't go for it. In fact, he laughed so hard he started to choke. Then he said, 'I knew it, you son of a bitch. I knew you were going after him on your own. Well, okay, fine, at least you didn't get hurt in the process.' Then he gave me a long lecture about the evils of vigilante justice, but concluded by contradicting himself and saying that, sometimes, it's the only way, because the police are supposed to operate within the rules.

"You know, it's kind of funny. While he got on my nerves when I was in the hospital, I also came to respect his relentless determination and his dedication to his work. He really does want to make the world a safer place, unlike a lot of cops who are just going through the motions until they can start collecting a pension. Something tells me we're going to need him again.

"Anyway, we argued for fifteen minutes when I told him that I wanted Flanagan to get about two years in prison, providing that I could get him to admit guilt and avoid a trial. Callahan wanted at least ten years. But he finally agreed to set up a meeting with the district attorney and let me present my plan and see if he would go along with it. I saw him a couple of days ago, and everything is set, just as I asked, providing we get Flanagan to step forward and do the right thing. So, Rocky, you need to explain all of this to Flanagan when we meet with him. I really want to stay out of it. I just want to sit there and watch how you handle it, and hope that he buys into the plan. I will predict, though, that it's not going to be easy. Remember, we are dealing with a classic, hostile, type A personality."

Chico approved of what Wade had explained, and added, "That's sounds good. I like it. But, guess what? I've come up with something that is probably going to bring him around to our way of thinking. Rocky, we're going to need you to have your guy ready with one of his choppers when we meet with Flanagan. I'll fill you in on the details while we're giving Spike his usual shellacking on the links this Sunday." Wade looked like he wanted to debate the issue, but Chico waived him off with a look that said "Save it for later." Chico then turned to Rocky and asked, "Do you know anyone who owns a junk yard?"

Rocky started to reply, "Yeah, I know this one guy who—"

Chico interrupted, "Shit, why did I ask—of course, you do. Okay, fine. I need you to get in touch with him and find out if he can take a drive over to John V.'s car lot next Monday. I'll explain what I have in mind when I see you on Sunday. And we'll also need to have three or four of the major's crew on standby at the car lot while we are chatting with John V. on Tuesday, so see if you can set it up."

As they ended the drive and were about to go off in three directions, Chico concluded by mentioning that he was still working on what to do about the rapist/murderer, and that he would soon have a plan for the contractor who had cheated the elderly couple. As Rocky was getting in his car, Chico gave him his sister-in-law's number so that he could get enough information to enable the major to start tracking down the contractor.

Chapter Twenty-Two

The Payback Team Meets Everett Flanagan

Sunday was a perfect day for golf, and Wade had his best round of the season. Chico and Rocky complimented him on the noticeable improvement, as they each pocketed a crisp, one-hundred-dollar bill, their smallest score to date. Rocky complained about having to adjust his budget for the week, as he had counted on winning a lot more. Wade smiled and said something about setting them up for a crushing, costly defeat the next time out.

In addition to an enjoyable eighteen holes, they were able to wrap up several loose ends with some of their projects, and felt relaxed and ready for a productive week.

On Monday, at nine in the morning, they were waiting patiently for the arrival of Everett Flanagan, aka FAST 1. Rocky's pilot from Milwaukee was sitting in his chopper at Palwaukee airport on standby, ready for a possible quick trip to the warehouse in Schaumberg. Three of the major's associates were enlisted to intercept Flanagan on his way to the train station. Normally, it would only have required two men to accomplish the assignment, but it was assumed that FAST 1 was going to be less than cooperative.

The door to the warehouse opened, and four men entered. One of them was struggling and swearing, and judging by the appearance of his two-thousand-dollar suit and three-hundred-dollar tie, it had not been a peaceful journey. Two of the major's crew half carried and half dragged him over to the sitting area and shoved him into one of the worn, overstuffed chairs, while the third stood guard at the back door. It should have been obvious to Flanagan that resisting was a waste of energy, but it was clear that he was just too hardheaded to grasp this concept.

With the tone of voice used by someone who was accustomed to giving orders, and expecting them to be followed, Flanagan shouted, "Will someone tell me what the fuck is going on? You stupid assholes, I've got lawyers that can put your sorry asses away for a long—"

One of the men standing behind Flanagan cut him off. "This is how it's been for the last half hour. I wanted to shut his face so he couldn't talk for a month, but we did as we were told. He may look like he's been through hell, but as far as we know, nothing got broken, no thanks to him. What do you want from us, now that we've delivered the package?"

Rocky responded, "Well, you were supposed to take off, but I guess you'd both better wait with your buddy over by the back door. I'm hoping that Mr. Flanagan figures out that he has zero control and settles down."

Flanagan took the cue. "Okay, fine, I'm settled down. Now, will you please get on with it? I've got people waiting on me at the office, and I—"

Rocky interrupted. "Okay, fair enough, but you go to your office if and when we say so. Mr. Flanagan, I'll come to the point. What happens in the next few minutes is critical to your future. You need to understand that we—"

Flanagan had not figured out that submission, or at least silence, was his best option. "If you think you're scaring me, forget it. You and those simple morons over by the door are a pathetic bunch of losers. Look at this! They don't even know what to do with a pair of handcuffs! How fucking stupid is that?" The Payback Team looked down, as Flanagan pointed to a set of handcuffs that one of his abductors had attached to his right ankle.

Rocky continued. "Look, Mr. Flanagan, right now, I'm trying very hard to control my anger and impatience, and it's not going to take much more for me to put a quick, painful end to your bullshit. Now, would you like to shut the fuck up and listen, or do you want to continue on like this and wind up in the intensive care unit over at Alexian Brothers Hospital?"

Flanagan got the point. With a defiant, angry look, he gave a shrug and said, "You haven't got the balls, but I want to get out of here, so let's get on with it."

Rocky pointed to Wade and asked, "Do you know who this is?"

"I don't know, and I certainly don't give a flying fuck."

"Well, you've met before. His name is Wade Courtland, and you had an encounter with him several weeks ago. Take a good look."

It had been decided that there would be no attempt to hide anyone's identity, as was their usual approach, because Flanagan would find out soon enough when he became involved with the criminal justice system.

Flanagan gave a blank look, indicating that he didn't recognize Wade. So Rocky told Wade to roll up his sleeve and asked Flanagan if seeing the scar helped to jog his memory. After a few seconds, it was clear that Flanagan had figured out what was going on. "He's that smart-ass jogger who tried to get himself killed by running in front of my Corvette!"

Rocky continued. "Okay, now we're getting somewhere. You had a Corvette? That's nice. And can you tell us where this Corvette is right now, the one you used as a lethal weapon? Do you still have it?"

There was a long pause as Flanagan started connecting the dots. Then his eyes narrowed and filled with hatred. "You, guys—you were the ones—do you have any fucking idea what I'm going through with my insurance comp—?"

Rocky cut him off. "That's right; we've been pulling your chain for quite a while—the Corvette, then the Lexus, and then the Mercedes. But now the fun is over and it's time for you to pay your debt to society. You're going to turn yourself in, plead guilty, and serve a couple of years in prison."

Flanagan looked like he was about to laugh, but then simply shook his head in disgust. "Listen, that is definitely not going to happen. Now, I'm going to walk out of here, and if those 'wise guy wannabes' over there want to try to stop me, then bring it on. I'm finished putting up with this bullshit."

As Flanagan stood up, all three men in the rear of the warehouse began walking rapidly over to the sitting area. Rocky motioned to Chico, who pulled something out of a briefcase that was sitting on the orange crate next to him. Chico then spoke for the first time. "Mr. Flanagan, you might want to take a look at this before you lose consciousness." Then he handed him the plastic bag that contained the .38 caliber Smith and Wesson.

141

Rocky let him hold it for a few seconds, and then said, "Can you guess whose gun this is? And can you guess whose fingerprints are all over it? And would you like to know who has the slug that was pulled out of the smart-ass jogger's arm? That 'smart-ass jogger' is going to make a positive identification of you in court, and with the gun and the slug, you're going to do ten to twenty for attempted murder.

"But think about this: nobody wants to go through months, or maybe years of delays, motions, postponements, etc., before the case is finally heard. And we're not interested in sitting in court for several days while your lawyers and the district attorney do their little dance. So we've got it arranged that if you do as we suggest, you'll get two years for the lesser charge of unlawful use of a firearm, with the possibility of even less than that with time off for being a good boy. Pretty clear choice, don't you think?"

Flanagan thought about it for thirty seconds before responding. "It's pretty clear that you jerkoffs haven't thought this thing through. It seems to me that we have a classic standoff here. Maybe you can accomplish what you've said, but when I make my case about kidnapping, grand theft, malicious destruction of property, assault, and whatever else my lawyers can come up with, you guys, and your friends over there, are also going away for a long time, probably longer. So let's just say we're even and call it a day."

At this point, Rocky gave a disgusted look as he punched a couple of numbers on his cell. Then he spoke into the phone, saying, "This isn't working out. Go ahead and get that bird in the air." Rocky decided it was time to enact the plan that had been carefully arranged while they were on the golf course. "You know, Mr. Flanagan, we jerkoffs kind of thought you might come up with something like this. So here's our counteroffer. We're ready to take you to the district attorney's office where we're going to meet with him and the sergeant who is handling your case. You're going to follow the plan to the letter. Wade is going to agree not to bring charges in exchange for your guilty plea. After a couple of days to get things in order, you're going off to begin serving time. And here's the reason we're certain you're going to follow this plan: if you choose not to, we will take you for a nice helicopter ride over Lake Michigan. It will be your last mistake, and your last ride."

It looked, briefly, like Flanagan was going to go along with the plan, but then the familiar look of defiance returned as he tried to take control of the situation. "Now, that's a beautiful plan. Like I'm supposed to think that you losers have access to a chopper and that you actually have the balls to dump someone over the lake. Fuck it, I'm out of here."

Rocky nodded, and Flanagan's three abductors began leading him to the exit door. Flanagan gave a look of satisfaction and triumph and informed everyone that they were wise to see things his way. When the door opened, the roar of a descending helicopter was unmistakable. Flanagan stopped dead, and his triumphant look suddenly changed to one of horror and disbelief. His abductors once again had to use force to move him from the warehouse to the chopper. As soon as Flanagan and The Payback Team were on board, the chopper took off. Wade spoke for the first time, saying, "Don't bother with the seat belt. We'll just have to unfasten it in a few minutes when we say goodbye."

Initially, Flanagan was too horrified to speak, but after a few minutes, when they were over the lake, hovering about twenty feet above the water, he began to feel that even though they did, in fact, have access to a chopper, they were nevertheless pulling one huge bluff. So he decided to go on the offensive. "Okay, fine, dump me in the water. You know, we're only about five miles from shore. I'll be on the beach before happy hour, and then we'll see how you guys like it when the tables are turned."

Chico was the next one to speak. "You must be a good swimmer. But I doubt that it will be as easy as you think. You're going to have a little handicap." Chico then pointed to a concrete building block that was sitting on the floor. There was a wire that reached from the block to the handcuffs around Flanagan's ankle. He hadn't noticed that it had been locked onto the wire as he was being shoved onto the chopper.

While Chico was talking, Rocky opened the chopper door. Then he picked up the block and prepared to throw it into the lake. He did this slowly and deliberately, giving Flanagan just enough time to contemplate what was about to be his last moments of life. "Goodbye,

Mr. Flanagan. You've really made a bad choice. You picked the wrong 'jerkoffs' to fuck with." He then started the motion of heaving the concrete block, but was prepared to use his tremendous strength and size to grab Flanagan before the slack came out of the wire. They planned to carry through on the bluff until the last moment. It worked.

The word "Stop!" could be heard very clearly above the noise of the engine and the wind rushing past the open door.

Then, just as they had rehearsed, Chico yelled, "Fuck him! Throw it!" as Rocky once again began to discharge the block.

"No, no, please, okay, I'll do it, whatever you say. You win. Please, I'm begging you," shouted Flanagan.

Then Wade continued with their prearranged script. "All right, put it down. There's no point in dumping him just because we feel like it. He's giving us what we demanded, so let's back off. At least, I think he knows exactly what's going to happen if he changes his mind later on."

Rocky put the concrete block on the floor, closed the door, and unfastened the handcuffs. Rocky told the pilot to return to the warehouse, and then spoke to Flanagan. "You know, Mr. Flanagan, if there's a jerkoff or a moron or a loser on this helicopter, it's you. You didn't have the brains to figure out that if we could jack three of your cars—drop one of them in your pool and another one on your gate— and then grab you from the train station and transport you to the warehouse, that it was likely that we could get you up in this chopper and drop you over Lake Michigan. I have one more thing to say, and I really mean this. I sincerely hope that, at some time in the near future, you won't decide to change your mind and not go along with the plan. Because I promise you that I will personally track you down, and when I get my hands on you, Wade will not be there to stop me. I guarantee that you will wish you had spent fifty years in prison, compared to what I will do to you. You know, I was outvoted on this stupid-ass plan all along. I wanted to whack you on day one, but no, Wade got his way because he was the one who you shot. You're lucky you picked Wade instead of me, trust me on that one.

"When this chopper lands, I'm gonna walk away and I hope I never see your sorry ass again. But if I do, and for some reason you haven't served your time, I promise you will die a long, slow, painful death."

Those were the last words spoken for the rest of the ride. Flanagan was completely submissive and voluntarily entered the van for the trip to the district attorney's office.

Chapter Twenty-Three

Another Meeting with John V.

Wade, Chico, and Rocky were back at the warehouse early Tuesday morning. They were hoping that the major's crew would deliver John V., and that the encounter would be more successful than the previous meeting.

They had arrived early in order to put together a few loose ends and plan for future projects. As Chico poured everyone their first cup of coffee, Rocky began by asking what happened with Flanagan after he left the warehouse. Wade answered, "It went exactly as planned. Chico and I took him to the district attorney's office. Callahan met us there, and they verified everything I had told Flanagan yesterday morning. There was a slightly tense moment when Flanagan mentioned something about the gun, the fingerprints, and the slug, but I had clued Callahan in beforehand. I told him that I would have to twist a fact or two in order to get him to cooperate, and that he should just go along with whatever. Callahan was cool with it, but when the district attorney seemed surprised to hear about this piece of evidence, Callahan was beautiful. He said that these facts would not need to be brought up at the hearing unless, for some reason, Flanagan decided to flip. Then he promptly changed the subject. The hearing is set before Judge Amy Lockhart for the end of next week, and the DA assured Flanagan that he would end up serving only about fifteen months. He even promised to recommend a minimum security joint, so long as Flanagan continued to cooperate."

Rocky nodded his approval. "Good, that's what you wanted, so I'm glad how it worked out. Just in case you guys were wondering if I meant what I said yesterday about what I'd do to him if he didn't serve time, well, keep wondering. I'm not even sure myself. I hope we don't ever get into a situation where push comes to shove and we have to do some of those things to the bad guys like you see in the movies, but some day, we may be in that position. That's all I want to say about it for now."

Chico was the next one to speak. "Well, we're three for four. I mean we were successful with Stedman, Crowley, and now Flanagan. At least, for now, it looks like we're gonna get what we wanted from the Flanagan deal. You know, I was wondering, do you think we need to do any follow-up on some of these issues? For example, did Stedman get into GA? Is Crowley working on his anger and drinking problems?"

Wade responded, "I've also thought about this. The answer, I think is clear, and it's 'no'. I think the best we can do is try to provide justice, and hopefully, at the same time, set someone on the right course, so that doing something that hurts others comes to an end. If we try to continue babysitting for everyone we come in contact with, we'll have little or no time left for working on new cases."

Chico was satisfied. "I guess you're right. And speaking of other cases, I've come up with a plan for what to do about the rapist. It starts with finding out where he hangs out. Rocky, why don't you check with the major and have him get on this. And find out if he has anyone on his team who is Hispanic. As you may remember, this guy's name is Luis Medrano, and I want someone to start working on getting close to him, and that has to be someone he can relate to. We're going to put together a classic sting setup. When we're done with this one, Hollywood will pay a fortune for the movie rights. I'm thinking maybe this could even be the start of Rocky's professional acting career."

Rocky, at first, looked like he was about to thank Chico for the suggestion, but after a couple of seconds, he realized that they just might be pulling his chain, so he changed the subject. "How would you clowns like to spend a few days playing golf while we do a little business in Florida?"

Both Wade and Chico looked interested, so Rocky continued. "The major wasted no time locating the contractor. Funny how the government can't do it in months, but someone who really wants to find him can get it done in three days. Good example of free enterprise vs. government bureaucracy. He's in South Florida, staying at a very exclusive mobile home park. Not your typical trailer trash joint; it takes big bucks to get in. These homes are strictly high end. Not a bad setup—steal twenty or thirty grand from enough people to be able to retire early and live the good life. The major's people also checked with the state's attorney's fraud division, and they've pinned down a total of $225,000 that he has taken in deposits for work that was never done. It could be much more, but that's all they know about for sure. So, Chico, start working on a plan for how to recover it and pay these people back. Maybe we can work something out like we did with Flanagan, where he serves some time in the can, in addition to paying it back. You know what? I wouldn't mind a little R and R down in Florida. If we get in enough tee time, Spike could even cover most of our expenses."

Before Wade could get in a jab or two, Chico jumped in. "Great! I'll start working on a plan right away. And, maybe, by the time we get back, we'll be closer to pulling off the sting I have in mind for our friend, Mr. Medrano, assuming the major can find the right guy for the job."

Wade liked the idea. "Okay, Florida sounds great. But don't count on yours truly helping out with your expenses. I figured out my problem. It was the clubs. Got a new set yesterday—cost a small fortune—and things are going to be a lot different from now on. When we get down there, we can talk about making the wager, shall we say, a little more interesting. But enough of how I'm gonna get my money back, let's talk about John V. I think we've about come to the end of the line with him. After today, whether or not we make this our fourth win, I suggest we wrap it up. There's not much more we can do with him, at least not without the chance of things escalating out of control."

Rocky had something to add. "You know, I'm glad you brought the conversation back to him because I forgot to report on where we're at with respect to my junk dealer guy. He came through for us. Stopped by the car lot yesterday afternoon and gave me his report. So I've got four of the major's guys on their way over there right now, waiting for word from us. I just hope—" Right at that moment, Rocky's cell phone came to life. It was one of the major's men, announcing that they were due at the warehouse within a few minutes. And before they had time to finish their third cup of coffee, they heard a vehicle pull up to the back door. What happened next was totally unexpected.

The first person to walk in the door was Major Robins. Next came two of his associates, carrying John V. One of the men was Hispanic, so Rocky made a mental note to speak to the major later on to see if he was willing to rent him out on a long-term assignment. John V.'s hands were in handcuffs, and his ankles were shackled with a heavy chain. He was trying desperately to squirm out of the grasp of the two men who were holding him. It should have been obvious that this was useless, due to their strong grip, as well as the size of his captors. Because of the muffled noises coming from under the black hood over his head, The Payback Team assumed that Vargas had been gagged in some way.

The major was shaking his head in disgust. "Where did you find this guy? I don't know when I've seen anything like it. He doesn't seem to get it. He's not going anywhere unless we say so, but he doesn't seem to realize it. Had to stuff a rag in his mouth—wouldn't shut up about a car on a roof, among other things. Good thing you warned me, that's why I came along on this one. I think he would have gotten hurt big time if I hadn't been here, and God knows he would have deserved it. Well, here he is, in all his glory. I'll take the hood off, but I don't recommend removing the gag or the cuffs or the leg chain. Whatever you do, I think we need to hang around for awhile for your safety, as well as his, assuming you even care about his safety." Major Robins then directed his men to put him on one of the overstuffed chairs and remove the hood. As soon as he saw The Payback Team, he tried to stand up, but the major shoved him back in the chair.

As John V. continued his muffled rants, Chico announced that he got the point about why the gag should be left in place. Although he was not certain if he had Vargas's attention, he decided to try to explain the purpose of the meeting. "Well, Mr. Vargas, I guess you remember us from the last time we met. We didn't want to come to your office because there weren't enough chairs for all of us. I hope you understand.

"It seems you've noticed that we relocated the Eldorado to a more prominent place on your lot, although you don't seem pleased. Well, that's okay. But let me get to the point. There's still the matter of the five grand you owe our friend, Harry. As you know, we're in the collection business, but I don't think we're doing a very good job with this assignment, and that's particularly embarrassing, because Harry is one of our best clients, and we're letting him down. So let's try to resolve this in everyone's best interest. You know, 'win-win' as they say. We win because Harry pays us our fee, Harry wins because he gets his money, and you will be the biggest winner of all because we will go away, and you won't suffer any more unfortunate physical discomfort. So let me put it to you as clearly as I can. Can you get us the five dimes this week? And before you give us your final answer, let me point out that the consequences for a wrong answer will be severe. You can go ahead and nod your head."

Instead of the hoped-for nod, he increased the intensity of his earlier rants. The only purpose the gag was serving was that the words were indistinguishable. The volume, however, was annoying.

Chico felt he had gotten his answer. "Well, Stan, I guess you should go ahead and make the phone call. As you can see, Mr. Vargas, Stan has someone on speed dial. He's calling one of our associates. He and three others are at your place of business right now, waiting for our call. They will spend the next hour or two removing all of the tires and rims from all twenty of your vehicles, not including, of course, the Eldorado on the roof. So that makes about eighty wheels, and a junk dealer friend of ours is going to give us forty dollars each, for a total of $3200. So your debt, before adding today's expenses, will be reduced to $1800. But, because of the expenses, the new total will actually be $3,000. So, all in all, you've made another bad decision, much like the poor suckers who are in the position of having to buy one of your pieces of junk. And in case you haven't thought about it, what do you think it will cost you to replace the wheels on twenty vehicles? That's right. A whole lot more than forty bucks per. Why can't you figure out that your best plan is to do what we ask? Really, it's just simple logic."

The contorted look on John V.'s face was a blend of rage, hatred, and contempt. Submission was apparently not going to happen, not now, and probably not ever. But what occurred next—all within a span of about four seconds—was beyond anyone's wildest expectation. For some unknown reason, John V. stood up. Rocky immediately and instinctively rushed over to shove him back in his chair, and John V. wildly swung both his handcuffed arms in Rocky's direction. Normally, Rocky was exceptionally quick and agile for a very large man, but this time he was caught totally by surprise. John V.'s left hand, the one that was still wrapped in a plaster cast, caught Rocky squarely on the left temple, knocking him onto Wade's lap, collapsing the rusty metal folding chair in the process. While the major pushed John V. back into his seat, Chico pulled Rocky off the much smaller Wade, although it wasn't easy. Rocky was of no assistance whatsoever, as he was out cold.

For the first time since the three men brought their captive through the back door, the room was totally silent. Wade and Chico were kneeling on the floor, next to their fallen comrade, looking like they wanted to help, but without the slightest idea of what to do, other than to be concerned and hope for the best. Major Robins carefully studied John V.'s countenance and concluded that he was looking at a man who was enormously satisfied and proud of his violent accomplishment.

For several seconds, Wade and Chico looked at Rocky and waited. Finally, he began to open his eyes, and gradually got to his feet, with the help of his two old friends. When it looked like he was able to stand unassisted, he shook his head, as if to try to make it return completely to its former level of consciousness. Then, after another minute, he was able to speak. "Did...what I think happened...really...happen? Did he—?"

Wade answered, "Yes, it happened. Are you okay? What can we—?"

It looked like Rocky was almost back to normal. He turned to Major Robins and asked him to get his attacker out of his chair and to extend his arms out in front of him. Then, before John V.'s arms were completely perpendicular to his upright body, Rocky let go with a karate chop that snapped both bones in his left arm, a few inches above where the existing cast ended. "You are one dumb, stupid son of a bitch. Be very concerned if you ever see my face again because I guarantee it will be your last day aboveground. Now, get this worthless piece of shit the hell out of here."

Chapter Twenty-Four

A Working Vacation

At half past eight, on an early July Saturday, The Payback Team was headed to South Florida. They had decided to take the van for a couple of reasons. If all went well, they would be bringing Matthew Duncan, the swindling contractor, back from Florida, and there was a good possibility it would not be of his own freewill. Trying to get him through airport security would, at a minimum, be very complicated.

In addition, they were going to make a few stops to get in some golf, and possibly some poker at one or more of the casinos on the way. Most of the conversation was on the light side, but there were several references to business matters. Chico checked with Rocky to make sure that his contacts in Florida would be ready to assist in their encounter with Duncan at the appropriate time. Rocky assured him that everything was in place.

Then Wade asked, "You know, I was wondering, how did the major succeeded in getting the info on Duncan so quickly?"

Rocky provided the answer. "It was really pretty clever. I got Duncan's file from the fraud division because I know this one guy—"

Wade wanted him to get to the point and said, "Never mind about that. Just answer the question."

"He found the names of some of his employees, and one of them had the same last name; turned out to be a brother living in La Grange. So the major sent one of his men to his house. He waited until everyone had left for the day, and then he broke in and went straight to the computer. He scanned a few months of incoming and outgoing e-mails, going back to about the time that Duncan fell off the radar. Duncan changed his name, skipped town, and did everything he could think of to disappear forever, but he forgot about e-mail. So there it was, an e-mail, giving his brother his new name and address in Florida. And now we've got it. I can't wait to see the look on his face when we show up. I just love it when the bad guys get what's coming to—"

Chico interrupted. "Stop already. You sound like a line out of the worst B movie ever made. Anyway, I've got something to ask you. And guess what? I'm never again going to start a question by saying 'do you know anyone who…' because I already know the answer. In fact, if I ever do that again, just go ahead and slap me, okay? So here's the question. Would you look into getting a great big claw, like you see hanging from a crane in a junkyard? You know, like they use to move big piles of car parts or whatever. We're going to need this for what I'm planning down in Guatemala.

"What I want to do is suspend it from a chopper and pick up a moving vehicle. Also, we're going to need a truck, the kind you see hauling stuff to the junkyard, with sides, but with an open top. I want the chopper to put the vehicle in the truck. I don't even know if this will work the way I want it to, so I'm planning to experiment with our old friend, John V., as the guinea pig. I'm sure he won't mind. We've got to know if this will work before we try it, when the stakes are high. You can have the truck waiting at the rest stop on 294, and someone can track John V.'s trip to Indiana, and then get the truck in the right position at the right time for the drop. The chopper can pick up his car right after he gets off the interstate and gets to a less busy area. We've got to see if this will work, if not, it's back to the drawing board."

Rocky responded, "Okay, I'll get on it, but what should the truck driver do with him after he's in the truck?"

Chico had the answer and said, "It doesn't matter. He can drive him straight to hell as far as I'm concerned. But let's change the subject. I could tell by your look when you saw the Hispanic guy carrying Vargas that you were going to take this up with Major Robins. Have you done anything about it yet?"

"Yep," replied Rocky. "By the time we get back, I expect he will have a progress report for us. His name is Xavier Lorenzo, an ex-marine, naturally, and very capable of doing exactly what you asked for. The major called me back and said that Medrano hangs out at a place called Lucky Lucia's Lounge on 26th Street. Let me know what the next step is because we will be ready pretty soon."

Chico smiled. "Well, Rocky, my old friend, you're gonna love it because you're gonna be the star of our little production. I'm still working on some of the details, but I'll be ready when Lorenzo's ready. Just let me know when he has gotten close enough to him that Medrano would feel confident to take a little ride with him. It doesn't matter what he wants to come up with, just as long as he is able to get him out of the bar and into his car."

Now Wade had something to discuss. "When you brought up John V. a couple of minutes ago, I was a little surprised. I kind of assumed that we were more or less through with him. Isn't it really useless to have anything more to do with him? What's the point of any more harassment, and that's all that it would amount to because he's never going to cooperate. We should at least be grateful that we got the $3200 from Rocky's junk dealer guy. My nephew was really surprised and grateful to get his money back, first from Stedman, and now from Vargas. He never thought he had any chance of ever seeing it again. Now he looks at us as miracle workers."

Chico wasn't quite ready to give up. "Well, you're probably right, Spike, but I thought we should give it one more try. And I'm not talking about anything like the encounter we had with him on Tuesday. I was thinking we could send Rob over with a note, giving him one last chance to pay the balance. It's just possible that he's had enough and is ready to finally get rid of us. The kid could hand him the note in the poker room at Harrah's Casino, so that there would be no chance for any physical harm to anyone, especially Rob. Just hand him the note and get out of there. Period."

Wade gave a weak nod, indicating that he would go along with the idea, but that it was probably a waste of time. It was clear from Rocky's smile that he had no complaints whatsoever about anything that would further aggravate John V.

All three members of The Payback Team enjoyed the next three days of the trip. They managed to spend one afternoon at one of the poker rooms in Tunica, Mississippi and played eighteen holes just outside of Atlanta. They arrived in South Florida relaxed, enthusiastic, and ready for action.

Chapter Twenty-Five

Meeting a not so Sleazy Contractor

The mobile home park was pretty much as they had imagined it—definitely upscale, and a great last stop for old timers before heading off to some place not of their choosing. They managed to slip into the park behind a new Cadillac as it went through the security gate. Fortunately, the guard was on the phone with his back to their van, or they might have had a problem. The sign on the van indicated that it was owned by Southland Mobile Repairs, and Rocky was ready with a story to get them in; fortunately, it wasn't an issue. He was the only one in front, he was wearing a blue work shirt, and the van's Illinois plates had been replaced with Florida plates.

From what they could tell, after seeing a few senior citizens who were bold enough to venture out in the hot afternoon sun, eighty was about the average age. A few walkers and a couple of golf carts and mopeds were sitting out in front of some of the mobile homes. The trio was wondering how Duncan fit in, since he was supposed to be fifty-eight years old, according to his file.

There were four other men in the back of the van besides Chico and Wade. Rocky's contact had lined them up for the job ahead. When they got to Duncan's place, they got out and found that no one was home. One of the four recruits was skilled in the breaking-and-entering business, so getting in was no problem. The casual way in which it was conducted made it look like nothing was out of the ordinary, but as far as they could tell, no one was paying any attention.

There was nothing to do but wait. And after about two hours, Duncan walked in. Since the van parked next door was clearly a service vehicle, Duncan didn't give it any thought. But he was caught totally off guard when he walked in the door. Seeing seven strangers was not what he expected. He was temporarily speechless.

The Payback Team had seen a picture of Duncan that had been in the newspaper shortly before he disappeared, but the man standing in front on them looked nothing like what they expected. The picture in the paper was one taken by a police photographer, and as is the case with nearly all such pictures, he looked like someone who would not be welcomed in the average person's home. But this guy was different. He looked harmless. In fact, when they discussed it later that day, they agreed that he actually seemed somewhat likeable.

Wade was the first one to speak. "Sit down, Mr. Duncan, and please, let me have your cell phone. As you may have guessed, we've already disconnected your landline. You're not going to be hurt, that's not why we're here. Actually, I guess I should have said everything will be fine, as long as you cooperate. You may already, hopefully, be thinking that cooperating would be a really good idea. Anyway, the reason we're here is to get you to do what's right. Since I called you by your real name, and not the one that's on the mail box, you know that we have broken through your attempts to change your identity and remove yourself from the mess you left behind in Illinois. Now, I have lot's more to say, but you look like you want to ask a question, so we'll shift gears. Go ahead."

After a long silence, Duncan reluctantly handed over his cell phone and sat down. It looked like he was trying to figure out which of several questions to ask first. "Why does it take seven of you to accomplish whatever it is that you came here for?"

Wade continued. "Well, hopefully, most of us won't be needed at all. That's going to be up to you."

Duncan looked confused. "I don't know what you're getting at. What do you want from me?"

It's was time for Wade to come right to the point. "Mr. Duncan, first of all, I'm glad that you aren't sitting there trying to deny who you are. That would not go over well at all. These men are here to totally tear this place apart. I mean everything—the walls, the ceiling, the furniture. They're going to rip the cabinets off the walls, and tear up all of your flooring. Three hours from now, your home will just be a useless, worthless shell. The scrap value won't even cover the cost to haul it away."

The crooked contractor was horrified for a moment, and then he began to cry. As he began to speak, the words weren't distinguishable, but it was clear that he wanted to know why they would do such a thing.

Then Wade changed his tone. "Well, frankly, whether that happens is going to be by your choice. You have exactly three minutes to give us the money, in which case, we can leave your home just the way it is. I figure you can take about two minutes to think about doing the right thing, and then one more minute to get the cash from wherever you've hidden it and then hand it over to us. Or, of course, we can find it the way I mentioned a minute ago. Your choice."

Duncan kept crying, but not in the same way. A moment earlier, the tears were falling because he was thinking of how his domicile was about to be destroyed, but now he was weeping out of sorrow for the turn his life had taken, and how it had brought him to this outcome. He noticed Wade looking at his watch and decided it was time to try to pull himself together, at least, enough to get out a few coherent words. "I didn't mean for things to turn out this way. Really, I did a good job in my business. I cared about my customers and delivered value for what they paid me. I took pride in my work, and I was good to my employees.

Then two things happened that I couldn't control. My foreman quit and took most of my crew and started his own company, and my wife was diagnosed with inoperable cancer and given only about a year, at most. In just two days, my world fell apart. I had taken some upfront money for two jobs, and I had several jobs pending, and a couple of solid prospects that I had been referred to. I only cared about my wife; I no longer cared about my business. I know that's wrong, but I wasn't thinking about morality or integrity. I only knew that my wife was not going to get to retire to Florida like we had been planning. What could I do? Well, I went and bid as many jobs as I could over the next month, promising a really bargain price if they would give me half down within a week. Then I had enough money to make life as worthwhile for her as I could, until the end. We had a good life down here. She was happy. We were so close. She died peacefully two weeks ago."

What followed was a long pause, as Duncan sobbed uncontrollably. Wade had stopped looking at his watch, as the time limit had come and gone by several minutes. The men accompanying them were clearly moved, and Chico had tears in his eyes. Wade just looked at the floor, hoping that he would be able to retain his composure, and not really knowing what he was going to do next. Things had not turned out at all like he had expected.

Finally, Mr. Duncan got out a few more words. "I'm so very sorry. I didn't mean for things to be like this." Then, after another long pause, he continued. "It's just as well that you're here. I don't want to live like this. I'm so ashamed, and so tired of the charade—it's not who I am. Can you help me to do the right thing? That's what you said a few moments ago. I guess there's no point anymore. My wife's gone, I've hurt a lot of people, and I've ruined my life. At least I can try to do the best I can." After another pause, followed by a long and heavy sigh, he concluded. "There's $60,000 in a tin box under a limestone slab out in the carport. I'll get it. And there's another $140,000 in a safe deposit box in town. That's all that's left; I don't have any more. But I guess where I'm going, it won't make any difference."

Wade decided that this would be the wrong time to say anything more, although he planned to tell Duncan, at a later time, that The Payback Team would personally argue for leniency, inasmuch as he had been totally cooperative and was going to make restitution to the best of his ability. This was a good man, with a good soul, who had made some bad decisions, but what DA would not agree to a suspended sentence after hearing the whole story?

Chapter Twenty-Six

Closing Out the Duncan Project

To everyone's surprise, Matthew Duncan turned out to be a most pleasant traveling companion. They expected to drag him back to Illinois kicking and screaming, but it was quite the opposite. When they saw how completely cooperative he was when the time came to go to the bank and retrieve the $140,000, they realized that they were all going to have an enjoyable, pleasant ride home.

When they were about eighty miles from Atlanta, Rocky mentioned that it was a shame they were not going to get to play another round of golf on the course they had stopped at on their way down to Florida. There was an awkward silence, but after about a minute or two, Duncan figured out that he was the cause of their reluctance to stop. So he offered a suggestion. "Why don't we make it a foursome?"

As it turned out, the golf outing was the highlight of the return trip. The fact that Duncan beat Wade by two strokes, with rented clubs, was the main topic of discussion for the remainder of the trip. Wade tried to claim that he needed more time to "break in the new clubs," but nobody was buying it.

The next day, with only about three hours before the trip was due to end, Wade picked up his cell phone and called Callahan. He made sure that Duncan was listening, as he explained that he was bringing a fugitive back from Florida. "I would appreciate it if you could set up a meeting with the district attorney, like you did last time, so we can try to arrange for a suspended sentence. We've got almost ninety percent of the cash, along with a very cooperative, and I might add, remorseful defendant."

Wade was not surprised to hear Callahan's response. "Courtland, you are the most goddamnedest, unlikeliest vigilante I've ever known." Then he laughed his raucous laugh for a full thirty seconds before telling Wade that he would see what he could do, even though the warrant on Duncan was not within his area of responsibility.

Wade ended the call, looked at Duncan, and nodded, indicating that things were looking good. Duncan looked down at the floor. Wade could not tell if he was praying, talking to himself, or just trying to keep from crying.

Next, Rocky made a call to Major Robins. The call lasted a full fifteen minutes, and after he hung up, he filled everyone in on the details. As usual, the major was on top of things and had made progress in two areas. First, he explained about the attempt to try to pick up John V.'s car with the chopper and claw. It was impossible to do it on the interstate because there were just too many overpasses. The chopper needed more than a mile to match the speed of the car, get the claw in place, and try to drop down and grab it. Every time an overpass came up, the chopper had to climb, and then start all over. Additionally, they needed to get this operation over with quickly. The more time people had to observe this spectacle, the greater the risk. In fact, Chico realized that the whole idea was a bad one for that reason alone. Fortunately, no one had called 911; apparently, onlookers had thought it was a part of some movie project, or possibly a police exercise.

But those weren't the only problems. They tried again after John V.'s vehicle left the interstate, but because of the force of the wind on the claw that was hanging forty feet below the chopper, it was almost impossible to coordinate the movement of the chopper, the claw, and the car. There were just too many variables. And matters got a lot worse when Vargas figured out what the chopper was trying to do and began changing lanes and varying his speed. It was just not going to work. When Rocky finished explaining, Chico just shook his head and said something about getting back to the drawing board.

But Chico's attitude improved greatly when Rocky informed him that the major's Hispanic associate, Xavier Lorenzo, had made progress with the Medrano situation. They were now established drinking buddies, and Lorenzo said he was ready for whatever was expected of him. Chico then spent the next several minutes explaining the details of the plan that he had been working on. Wade and Rocky loved it and wanted to get started on it as soon as possible.

Duncan was listening to these conversations in complete amazement. "What are you guys? I mean who are you guys? I mean— actually, I don't even know how to ask. What in the hell is happening here?" Everyone just smiled and looked away, so Duncan figured that he wasn't going to get an answer. Then, after a minute or two, he simply announced, "You know, I kind of wish I had been fortunate enough to have met you guys a long time ago."

Just before the drive ended, Chico called his sister-in-law and told her that she should inform her neighbors that they would be getting most of their money back soon. Naturally, she wanted to know how Chico knew this, but he was not about to elaborate.

Over the next couple of days, Wade worked out the details of meeting with Callahan and the district attorney, turning over the money, and getting agreement not to ask for jail time. It looked like The Payback Team had scored another victory.

While Wade was finishing up the Duncan project, Chico wrote a letter that he wanted Rob to deliver to John V. in the poker room on Friday, the day he was usually there. The letter was short and straight to the point. It instructed him to call a phone number within twenty-four hours to arrange to pay the balance that he owed, and it referred to unspecified consequences if he didn't comply.

He spoke to Rocky and determined that Rob's new wallet and identity were complete, so he asked him to give the note to Rob when he dropped off his new wallet. He told Rocky to make sure that Rob knew that he was just supposed to walk up to John V.'s poker table, hand him the note, and then promptly leave. No discussion, just get out of there.

Now, it was time to turn their attention to the next major challenge: Luis Medrano, rapist and murderer.

Chapter Twenty-Seven

The Medrano Sting

There were so many people involved in pulling off the Medrano sting that even Chico, the originator of the plan, was concerned about the chances for success. Everything had to fall into place perfectly, like three acts of a play. Unfortunately, in this case, there was no opportunity for a rehearsal.

On Wednesday afternoon, everyone was ready. Xavier Lorenzo was sitting at the bar in Lucky Lucia's Lounge, talking with Luis Medrano. Two attractive Hispanic women walked in. They walked over to Xavier, and one of them kissed him and then introduced the other woman. Xavier then introduced his girlfriend and the other woman to Medrano. After several drinks, everyone was feeling pretty friendly. The second woman was starting to show an unusual amount of attention to Medrano, and he was eating it up.

Xavier was about to suggest that they go to another club where they had live entertainment, but Medrano beat him to it, suggesting that they all go out for dinner. Right on cue, Xavier's girlfriend said they would love to, but they had to take a few minutes to change and put on some makeup, so it was arranged that they would meet at a restaurant, one that Xavier was quick to recommend, in one hour.

Soon after the girls left, Xavier suggested that they leave because he had to stop somewhere to pick up some cash. Then he would have enough money to treat everyone to a night on the town, and that was just fine with Medrano. So far, everything was going according to plan, but there was still a long way to go.

When they got inside Xavier's car, he told Medrano to look in the glove compartment. He opened it up and pulled out a .40 millimeter Glock. "Holy shit! What are you doing with this?" exclaimed Medrano.

"Don't worry, it's not loaded," replied Xavier. "Go ahead, eject the magazine, you'll see." Medrano did as he was told. Now, as planned, his fingerprints were on the magazine, as well as the gun. Xavier continued. "How much do you think it's worth? Maybe around five hundred? I think I can get about two fifty for it at a pawnshop. That's why I wanted to leave right away. We can drive to the pawnshop. It's not too far from the restaurant I suggested, then we get the cash, and then we'll be on time to meet the girls for dinner. Remember, tonight, I'm paying for everything." This last comment appeared to put Medrano at ease.

When they got to the pawnshop, Xavier got out and asked Medrano to bring the gun because he didn't have a current firearm license. He told him to put it under his jacket, so that it wouldn't be seen on the street. When they got inside, the clerk in the front of the shop was occupied with some kind of chart that he was making notes on, so Rocky, who was standing in back, motioned for them to come to the rear of the shop. When they were standing across the counter from Rocky, Xavier told Medrano to take out the gun. As soon as he did, Rocky got a very concerned look on his face, as he stared intently at the gun. Then Xavier wanted to know how much he could get for it. Rocky, then, turned away from both of the cameras that had been recording everything and explained that they should go into the back room, where his partner could get a look at it.

As he led the men a few feet to the door, he raised both hands to about shoulder height. Medrano thought that this was a little strange, but for the most part, he was thinking ahead to what he hoped would be a very pleasant end to the evening.

The cameras in the pawnshop caught everything, from the moment they walked in the front door until they disappeared through the rear door. Clearly, two men had entered the shop with the intention of committing armed robbery. One of them pulled out a gun and ordered the person behind the counter to raise his hands and take them to the back room, where they apparently knew that a safe was kept. It was all very professional and well planned. The clerk in front of the shop didn't even appear to notice what was going on.

Immediately after entering the office, Rocky grabbed a heavy metal paperweight that was sitting on a desk. He waited exactly one second after Xavier closed the door and then smashed it into Medrano's forehead, knocking him to the floor. As soon as he hit the floor, Rocky put on a latex glove and grabbed the gun from Medrano. Then he ejected the magazine, pulled several bullets out of his pocket, loaded the magazine and put it back in the Glock. Next, he shouted as loud as he could, "My God, no. Please, please, don't shoot. I can't open the safe. It's on a timer." Then, as Xavier left through the back door, Rocky fired three shots: two into the wall behind the desk, and the other through the baseball cap he had been wearing. He then put the smoking gun on the floor, about two feet from Medrano's right arm, and removed the latex glove. Then he grabbed another gun from the desk and pointed it at Medrano, who was just starting to try to stand up.

The clerk in front of the store called 911 as soon as he heard Rocky yelling, and four policemen were there within three minutes. He directed them to the office, where Rocky stood, still pointing the gun at Medrano. He acted like he was frozen with fear, and one of the officers had to forcefully pry the gun out of his hand. It didn't take much explaining for the officers to find out exactly what had happened. One of them asked Rocky if he had been wearing the hat, and he answered in the affirmative, adding that he thought he had been shot. He explained that after the third shot, the gun apparently jammed, giving him time to pick up the nearest object that he could find and crash it into Medrano's forehead. That's when he grabbed the gun from his desk drawer, and he said he hadn't been able to move from that moment on.

One of the officers noticed the camera, just behind the desk, and asked for the tape, but Rocky informed them that it wasn't working. Fortunately, he explained, there were two working cameras in the front of the store that were in working order.

After one of the officers helped Medrano to his feet, he started to explain his version of events, but the cops wanted none of it. "Shut the fuck up, asshole. What makes you think we give a shit about what you have to say?" Then the same officer began to read him his rights, as he led him away in handcuffs.

As they walked Medrano toward the front of the shop, one of the officers explained that Rocky would need to come down to the station to give a statement, but he didn't have to worry because this was as close to an open-and-shut case as he had ever seen. He informed Rocky that "this is one bad ass who's going away for a very long time." Then all four officers began congratulating themselves on doing a fine job getting to the scene just in time to get another bad guy off the street. They were arguing about who was going to get the "collar" as they walked out the door.

Chapter Twenty-Eight

Meeting with Sergeant Callahan

After he returned from the police station, Rocky met Wade and
Chico at Wade's home. He had made copies of all three surveillance
videos: two from the cameras in front of the store and one from the
camera in the office that he had told the policemen was not working.
Wade and Chico were anxious to view the tapes, but they knew they
would first have to endure Rocky's soliloquy about his Oscar winning
performance. They had made a wager about how long it would take,
and set the over/under at twenty minutes, with Chico taking the over.
Twice during his retelling of the event, Rocky had to stop and ask his
two friends to stop looking at their watches and pay attention to what
he was saying. Finally, he finished, and after the second viewing of the
videos, The Payback Team congratulated themselves on the outcome.
It appeared that this had been their most important victory. All it was
going to take now would be a guilty verdict and a long sentence, and
then Medrano would be where he belonged. Rocky was curious when
he saw Wade hand a hundred-dollar bill to Chico, but he seemed
satisfied when Chico said something about finally getting paid for
Wade's loss in a gin rummy game.

Chico announced that, as far as he was concerned, they weren't
finished with Medrano just yet. He laid out the final phase of his
elaborate plan, which included a face-to-face meeting between
Medrano and the father of the girl he raped and killed. He said he
needed to give a little more thought as to how he could make this
happen. Medrano's bail had been set at $500,000, so it looked like he
would be in jail until the trial. It appeared that getting them together
was going to be almost impossible.

They spent the rest of the evening discussing Chico's plans for the
Guatemala project. This issue had been on their minds for the better
part of three months, and it looked like they were nearly ready for
action. They all agreed that they had met nearly all of their challenges
so far, and that they had gotten some valuable, relevant experience.

But they concluded that, although their projects up to this point had involved a minimal amount of danger, this was not going to be the case in Guatemala. Each of them spent a few minutes reviewing all the reasons they could think of, both for and against, to continue with the project. Their conclusion was that they were going to finish what they had started. Soon, it would be time to set a date for the trip.

The plan was for the three of them to spend a couple of weeks in Guatemala to try to get a firsthand look at what was going on. Where were the hijackings occurring? How often? Was it always the same bus driver? Was there more than one crew of banditos? Was it always the same tour bus that was getting robbed? There were a lot of questions that needed answers before they could send for Major Robins and some of his crew.

While they were getting ready for the trip, they would try to take care of unfinished business. They wanted to see if anything would come of their last effort with John V., which was planned for Friday, and they wanted to explore every possibility for arranging a meeting with Medrano and his victim's father. They each felt that if they were in his shoes, they would like to have the chance to confront their daughter's murderer face to face.

What would happen during this confrontation? They each had a somewhat different scenario in mind, assuming they were able to arrange the meeting with Medrano, and none could guess what might occur if they actually got the girl's father face to face with him.

The next day was Thursday, and at four in the afternoon, Wade got an unexpected phone call. Sergeant Callahan said he would like to talk to him. Wade said that, believe it or not, he was about to call Callahan because he had a question to ask him. Callahan explained that he would be finishing up work in about an hour, so Wade asked him if he would like to meet and grab a beer. Callahan's response was, "With a name like mine, you probably already know the answer to that one."

After they clinked pint glasses of Guinness, Callahan asked Wade what he wanted. When Wade mentioned that Medrano had somehow chosen to try to rob a friend's pawnshop and had inadvertently been apprehended in the act, Callahan paused for a few seconds, and then broke into the same raucous laugh Wade had heard when he tried to get him to fall for the hypnosis story. As before, he laughed so hard that he started to make a choking sound, and then finally, wiped his eyes and got serious again.

"Courtland, there's a lot more to you than meets the eye. But, listen, don't try to bullshit me, okay? I'm on your side. I like what you're doing. I wouldn't tell that to very many people because I'm supposed to be against John Q. Citizen trying to play judge and jury all on his own. That's what the system is there for. Only problem is, it doesn't always work the way it's meant to.

"Sure, I know who Medrano is, I know the whole story. We cops couldn't do anything about it after he got off, but apparently, you decided to step in. So cut the crap and tell me how you did it, and then maybe I will know how to answer your question."

Wade realized that, not only was Callahan on their side, but he had helped them with both Flanagan and Duncan, so if he was going to expect anymore cooperation from him on future projects, he might as well clue him in. After listening to the whole story, Callahan could only shake his head in amazement. He managed to get out just a few short words. "Well, I'll be damned." Then after a few more seconds, he added, "I guess I should be glad you're on our side. Now what did you want to ask?"

Wade got right to the point. "How do we get Medrano out of jail? We plan to let the girl's father confront him. We figure we'd want this chance if we were in his position. We haven't asked him yet. In fact, I doubt he even knows what's happened. Medrano's only been locked up for twenty-four hours."

Callahan thought about it for a minute, and then asked, "How bad do you want this meeting to happen?"

Wade didn't expect the question to be answered with another question. "What do you mean?"

"Well, if you're willing to part with fifty large, it can be arranged. Really, it's kind of simple," answered Callahan.

It wasn't simple from Wade's point of view. "Yeah, I guess we'd pay fifty grand if we had to, but how would it work?"

"Just have someone put up bail, ten percent, which is fifty grand, and get him out of the can. Make sure it's no one who can be traced back to you. And be sure to do this just a day or two before one of his scheduled court appearances, like for a motion, a continuance, or whatever. Then go ahead and have your sit down with the father. You will need to keep a tight rein on him for those couple of days because you can bet he will try to get gone for good if he has the chance. Then make sure he misses the court date, so a warrant will be issued. Then it's your choice. Assuming the girl's father doesn't rip him into little pieces, you can have a bounty hunter return him back where he came from, you can throw him under a train, you can torture him, or whatever. Like I said, it'll be your choice."

Wade was impressed. "Damn. Why didn't we think of that? That's perfect! Looks like you've come through for us. Now, how can I return the favor?"

Callahan looked pleased that he had been able to help, but then he grew serious. "Okay, here's the deal. About six months ago, a very bad man was bailed out of jail, and no one's seen him since. Bail was set at one million dollars, and the guy's mother comes down the same day and springs him. She's really the cause of the way he turned out; the kid never had to work, always got what he wanted, and never really acquired a sense of values. Every time he got in trouble—you know, drugs, statutory rape, DUI, whatever—mommy was always there. Funny thing, she thought he was just 'misunderstood.'

"Anyway, thanks to his stepfather's bankroll—he's VP of a Fortune 500 company—the kid never really saw any serious punishment from the law, and he certainly never got any at home. So things just kind of spiraled out of control, until he kidnapped a four-year-old boy who belonged to a drug buddy of his. You know the setup: worthless father, mother gets custody, father has a restraining order against him, and is not allowed to see his kid. So, Colton R. Chatsworth III, that's the perp's name, stops the kid and his mother in a Wal-Mart parking lot, punches her in the face, grabs the kid, and he and his buddy take off with the little guy for who knows where.

"But here's the thing, the kid had Type I diabetes and needed an insulin shot every day. So, after about a week, they wind up in emergency, not knowing what's wrong. Unfortunately, they can't save the little guy; he's gone within a couple of hours. The hospital staff smells a rat, the police step in, and they both get locked up, but like I said, he gets out in no time. The other guy couldn't make bail. But we can't do anything with him; he managed to whack himself in less than a week. You know, tore up a blanket in strips, made a noose, and that's the end of that. So, what we want to do is find Chatsworth and put him away where mommy can't help him. Maybe, if we're lucky, he'll learn something from his friend with the blanket, and society won't have the usual long-term expense.

"Up to this point, we have no clue where he is. No trace whatsoever. But, you know, every time I try to press the issue with the top brass, I hear about the 'budget' and 'limited resources' and 'costs,' etc. I was thinking that you and your contacts could maybe step in and find the guy. Sounds like you have less holding you back from pulling him out of his rat hole than we do. And one more thing, Courtland. This one's personal." Callahan paused and looked away for a few seconds, hoping that Wade wouldn't see the tears in his eyes, but it was too late. Wade could sense what was coming. "The kid was my grandson."

Chapter Twenty-Nine

Planning for the Guatemala Trip

During the next two weeks, The Payback Team met several times to work on plans for the Guatemala trip and to try to wrap up loose ends on their other projects. It was decided that the three of them would fly down to Guatemala and spend a couple of weeks, possibly longer, in order to check things out before calling the major. They planned to find the tour that Wade's aunt had told him about, and take several trips on the same bus, changing their appearance each time, hoping to encounter the same experience that she had. They would discuss the results of their fact-finding mission with the major in order to determine how many men he would need to send down to take care of business.

During one of their discussions, Chico and Rocky were surprised when Wade informed them what had happened at the end of his meeting with Sergeant Callahan. He had explained about their upcoming mission in Guatemala, and Callahan announced that he wanted to be included. He was close to getting in thirty years on the job and planned to retire in a couple of months. With his accumulated vacation time, he would be able to leave when the major's forces were ready to head down to Guatemala, which was estimated to be some time in mid to late August.

The Payback Team was targeting August 1st as their departure date. It was decided that they would check with the major to see if he had any objections to Callahan's inclusion on the team.

At the end of his second week in jail, the trio found out that Medrano was scheduled to appear in court the following Wednesday. His public defender had convinced him that he needed to plea bargain, due to the amount of evidence against him. Since he had a long criminal record, he was certain to get the maximum sentence, unless he pleaded guilty in exchange for a much lighter sentence, probably ten to twenty years. Plans were made to bail him out on Monday and deliver him to the warehouse where he could meet his victim's father face to face. Then they would arrange for him to miss his court date on Wednesday, so that his bail could be revoked. Then, by keeping him under watch, it would be impossible for him to vanish, which they felt would be highly likely if precautions were not taken.

Progress had also been made with Chatsworth, the guy who punched Callahan's daughter in the face and kidnapped his grandson. The major informed the trio that he was hiding out in the Wisconsin Northwoods, somewhere near the town of Land O'Lakes, and was due to be picked up in a few days. They wanted to know how this had been accomplished so quickly, but Major Robins was working on another important mission and didn't have time to go into detail. He promised to explain when he delivered Chatsworth to the warehouse, where Callahan had asked to meet with him before Chatsworth was turned over to the law.

Rob had gotten his new wallet and was ready to take a brief, final note to John V., but when he checked with the poker room, he found that he had not been there in awhile. On the second attempt, a Friday, he finally got the news he was waiting for and promptly headed down to Hammond, Indiana. Wade had given him specific instructions to hand the note to John V. and immediately leave the poker room. He was then to call Wade and let him know that all had gone according to plan, and that he was safely on his way to the parking garage.

Wade was planning to spend the weekend with Paula at the cottage, but he waited for Rob's call before leaving. Rob called at 4:00 P.M. and informed him that he had handed John V. the note as planned. He was going to stop briefly in the bathroom and then head to the garage. Wade tried to tell him to forget about the bathroom, but Rob had already hung up. When Wade attempted to call him back, Rob's cell had gone to voice mail. Wade was concerned, but Paula convinced him to stop worrying. She was anxious to leave for the cottage, as it had been awhile since they had been there.

But the weekend did not turn out to be the relaxing getaway that they had hoped for. Wade waited for what he thought was the right moment, and then updated Paula on the plans for the Guatemala mission. When she learned that it was going to take place in just a couple of weeks, reality hit her hard. She had been the one to bring up the idea months previously, but now it was no longer just an abstract concept that she had pushed to the back of her mind. Wade was going to be gone for a long time, and was going to be facing danger every day. Could she live without him? She tried to put this, along with all of her other concerns, aside, but it wasn't working.

Wade had his own set of concerns. Why hadn't Rob followed his instructions to the letter? Why couldn't he reach him on his cell when he tried to call him back? To make matters worse, he had tried calling Rob several times at home, but with no success.

Instead of staying at the cottage until Monday morning, as they often did, they were so stressed out that they headed back to Illinois on Sunday afternoon. As soon as they got home, they could see that no one had been there since they had left on Friday. Julie had gone sailing with friends on Lake Michigan, but Rob was supposed to have headed home right after his trip to Indiana. Something was seriously wrong.

Wade's first thought was to call the casino to find out if anything unusual had happened on Friday. When he was connected to the poker room, he learned that nothing out of the ordinary had occurred, other than an incident where someone had been rushed to the hospital after having passed out. When Wade asked the name and found out it was not Rob, he was relieved, but now he had no idea what to do next. His son was not the type to just disappear. Rob had always been dependable and predictable.

His next step was to talk to Chico and Rocky to see if they had any suggestions. They had known and loved Rob all of his life and were apt to be nearly as concerned as Wade was. But more importantly, they often came up with a course of action that could resolve almost any dilemma.

His first call was to Chico, who suggested that they should all get together at Wade's home and work out a plan of action. Within thirty minutes, both Chico and Rocky arrived at the Courtland residence, and Chico immediately took over. He assigned Rocky to get on the internet and look up names and phone numbers of hospitals within a thirty-mile radius of the casino. Next, he told Wade to start calling state and local law enforcement agencies in northwest Indiana. Then he said that he was going to call Harrah's Casino again to see if he could learn anything in addition to what Wade had already found out.

Even though several phone calls were placed during the next hour, no one came up with anything helpful, and everyone was becoming more tense and concerned by the minute. Paula, however, was well beyond the point of concern, as she knew, intuitively, that something was drastically wrong. She was of no help to anyone, including herself. Wade considered asking her to leave their presence, as her constant crying and pacing had become a major distraction.

When everyone was just about out of ideas, Rocky's cell phone rang. The conversation that occurred after he answered was confusing, but soon appeared to be relevant to their situation. "Hello...yes, my name is Michael...no, I don't know anyone named James Gordon." Then there was a very long pause, and everyone noticed that the look on Rocky's face had become very intense, as he was listening carefully to whatever someone was telling him.

Finally, he spoke again. "Yes, I understand. No, I don't know why that name is on the driver's license. Yes, I understand now." By the anguished look on Rocky's face, and judging by the lower, softer tone in his voice, everyone knew that Rob had been located, but where was he and what was wrong? Was he all right? Had there been an accident? Was John V. involved in some way? As they waited for their questions to be answered, they began to feel that they were not going to like the answers. Then Rocky concluded the call. "His name is Robert Courtland. I am here with his parents, and I will let them know. We will leave right away. Please do everything you possibly can."

After the call ended, it was clear that Rocky was searching for the right words, and at the same time, he was trying to get his emotions under control. Paula was about to demand answers, but Wade walked over to her and held her, preparing her for what was to come. Then they heard the words that parents only hear in their worst nightmares. "That was a nurse in intensive care at Methodist Hospital in Gary. She found my number in Rob's cell phone. He has suffered a fractured skull, and may have received a brain injury. We need to get there right away."

Chico knew that Rob's parents were in no condition to drive, so within sixty seconds, all four of them were in his car, heading to Gary Indiana. Wade and Paula were in the backseat. When Paula realized that her precious son had been in the hospital for two days, alone and critically injured, she became hysterical. Wade was of no help to anyone, including himself. Instead of trying to comfort Paula, he was rocking forward and back in his seat while pressing both hands tightly against his face. The sounds he made were muffled by his hands, but it had the anguished sound of someone who was experiencing total despair. Chico and Rocky were at a loss for what to do, especially since they, too, felt much the same way.

At the hospital, they were met by an intern who explained that they had tried to contact next of kin, but before he could ramble on any further, Rocky took control and told him to simply explain what had happened. On the way to Rob's room in intensive care, he explained that no one was certain how it had occurred, but they had assumed, due to the large lump in the middle of Rob's forehead, that he had fallen in the men's room at the casino. X-rays showed that he had fractured his skull, and there appeared to be the likelihood of brain damage. Surgery had been performed to try to relieve pressure on his brain, but it may have been too late. He had been intentionally put into a coma so that his body could rest and recover. The intern was not certain how long they intended to keep him in this condition.

As they were approaching Rob's room, the intern tried to caution them for what they were about to encounter, but this in no way prepared them for the disturbing sight that met their eyes when they finally saw Rob. In addition to the usual tubes and wires that they expected, he was hooked up to a respirator that made an annoying noise that served to remind them with every groan that this patient was very possibly experiencing his last moments of life. Rob's forehead was horribly discolored, and a white gauze bandage had been wrapped around his head, just below his hairline. He lay disturbingly still, except for the slight movement of his chest that matched the rhythm of the respirator.

Chico ran to Paula and caught her just as she was about to collapse. He put her in a chair and tried his best to comfort her. Then Wade did something totally unexpected. Rocky was the first to notice, and when he saw the distraught look on Wade's face turn to that of a wild vicious dog, ready to charge his prey, he took an immediate step toward the door. It was clear to Rocky exactly what Wade had on his mind, and he was there, blocking Wade's exit at just the right moment. Rocky lifted him off his feet and pulled him in, as if he were hugging an oversized rag doll. Wade's arms were pinned, and his feet were off the floor, so at least, for now, he wasn't going anywhere. His cries of "I'll get him! I'll kill him! Let me go!" were met with Rocky's calm, but assertive response.

"No, Wade, let us handle this. Your place is here, with your son. I promise you, we'll take care of this." Then, for the first time since they had met Rocky, Chico and Wade saw the big man cry. Finally, convinced that his efforts had dissuaded him, he put Wade down and whispered, "Remember, Rob is my godson. I'm going to finish this."

It looked like Paula was starting to settle down, so Wade helped her out of her chair, and for the next several minutes, the four of them stood by Rob's bedside, silently praying, crying, and hoping. Rob's surgeon started to walk into the room, then turned and left. He realized that this was not the right moment to discuss the details and conditions regarding taking Rob off life support.

Chapter Thirty

Forging Ahead in spite of Tragedy

After nearly a half hour of looking helplessly at Rob, it was decided that Paula would spend Sunday night in the hospital. Wade would return in the morning to spend the day with his wife and badly injured son. As the trio was leaving the ICU area, the surgeon stopped them and explained that they planned to bring Rob out of the coma on Tuesday. If he did not respond, as the surgeon hoped he would, he wanted to know who should be contacted about some difficult choices regarding Rob's future. Wade tearfully explained that he was Rob's father, and tried to get some answers from the surgeon about Rob's chances for a full recovery. In a calm and professional manner, he explained that they were doing everything they possible could, but there was no way to determine anything definite at this time. Basically, it was going to be a waiting game.

On the drive home, it was noted that the surgeon had been careful not to provide too much hope, so their mood was at a low point. Chico and Rocky decided this was not the time to discuss business, so they simply told Wade to look after his family and they would carry on the work of The Payback Team.

After they dropped Wade off, they had difficulty trying to figure out how to get through the week. They had several challenges that were coming up that wouldn't wait, but they also wanted to stay involved with the situation with Rob, including daily visits to the hospital, more than ninety minutes away in nonrush hour.

Then Chico came up with the solution: why not let Callahan temporarily fill in? They didn't know much about him, but from what Wade had said, it sounded like he could be trusted. They got his number from Wade and promptly called him.

Callahan was simultaneously elated about the opportunity to join the team, if only temporarily, and shocked to hear about Wade's son. After expressing his sympathy, he immediately offered to handle the issue of getting Medrano bailed out of jail and delivered to the warehouse. He would meet Rocky on Monday morning, pick up the $50,000 bail money, and have a third party bail him out.

It was decided that Chico would contact Ronald Gates, the father of Medrano's victim, and arrange for him to meet at the warehouse, provided he was interested in doing so. There was the chance that he wanted nothing to do with Medrano, but they felt they should offer him the opportunity.

On the next day, a beautiful, warm Monday, everything went as planned. Wade was on his way to the hospital, Chico was out shopping for some things he planned to pick up for the meeting, and Callahan was on his way to the warehouse with Medrano. Rocky and Mr. Gates were waiting at the warehouse for everyone else to arrive. Chico was the next one to enter the warehouse. He explained to Mr. Gates how he felt the meeting should be conducted, but gave him the opportunity to revise or implement anything he chose to. Then he began making a few preparations for the meeting.

Right on schedule, Callahan and another man led Medrano through the back door of the warehouse. There was a hood over his head, and his hands were handcuffed behind him. After leading him over to a chair in the center of the room, Rocky removed the hood. Medrano was bewildered and confused as he surveyed the scene before him. His chair had been placed in the middle of a ten-by-ten plastic drop cloth. There were three strangers staring at him, although one of them looked familiar. He began to think that he had seen him recently, but he couldn't put it together. Something was about to happen, but he had absolutely no idea what to expect, and he didn't have the slightest clue about where he was or why he was there. He also didn't understand how he had happened to be suddenly released from jail, and he wondered if he might have been better off if he had never left his cell. Finally, he noticed a round coffee table about three feet in front of him. When he saw a loaded .38 caliber and a straightedge razor sitting in the middle of the table, his curiosity turned to concern.

Chico broke the silence. "Mr. Medrano, I hope you appreciate that we've arranged for your release from prison. Perhaps you remember the gentleman on your right. You attempted to rob his pawnshop at gunpoint. And you don't know this gentleman in front of you, but I'll introduce him. His name is Ronald Gates. Do you recognize that name?"

When it was clear that he had no clue who Gates was, Chico tried to help him out. "Do you remember an encounter with Charlene Gates?" Once again, the name didn't register. Medrano appeared to be more concerned about Rocky's presence, as he was finally able to put the face together with the circumstances. Chico spoke again. "You know, Mr. Medrano, I must say, you truly are the classic sociopath. You raped and murdered a beautiful young girl, and it is so insignificant to you that her name doesn't even register. Apparently, after your lucky acquittal, you thought nothing more about the event. Well, fortunately, we didn't forget, and that's why we arranged for you to be in prison, awaiting trial and sentencing. And that's why we've brought you here today, facing your victim's father. Now, before I turn things over to him, there's someone I'd like you to meet, although I'm sure you'll remember him. He has a few things to explain to you."

Xavier Lorenzo had been standing quietly in a dark corner of the warehouse and hadn't been noticed by Medrano until he stood up and walked over and faced him. Xavier waited for the look of betrayal to turn to disgust and then hatred before addressing him. "I'm not going to express my contempt for you, because I know it would be wasted. But I would like to point out what the future has in store for you, thanks to these gentlemen." As he spoke, he pointed to Chico and Rocky.

Then Xavier continued. "As you can plainly see, you are finally going to get what you have deserved for a very long time. I promise you are soon going to wish that you had been found guilty the first time because you are not going to like the next twenty years. You see, this gentleman on your right has a contact in prison who is going to make every day of your life a living hell. He is going to make sure that everyone knows that you like to rape and murder young girls. My only regret is that I won't be there to witness it in person. Now, finally, I want Mr. Gates to have a chance to say whatever he would like to say to you."

A full two minutes passed as Gates looked at Medrano. He was hoping that the rapist/murderer, who was now a helpless victim, would begin to fear for his life, just as his daughter had done three years earlier. Finally, he broke the silence. "I am grateful to these men who have provided me with this moment. I don't know why they have done this, and I know it's been a lot of work, not to mention the danger and the expense. I know nothing can bring back my Charlene, but I must admit that I am enjoying this moment much more than I ever thought I could. Is that kind of how you felt when you were about to take her life? Did you find pleasure in her suffering? Is there anything you want to say before I end your life?" While he waited for Medrano to answer, he picked up the gun. At the same time, Rocky and Callahan each picked up a corner of the plastic drop cloth and lifted it up several feet in the air. Clearly, the splattering of Medrano's blood and brain fragments were going to be contained in the plastic, leaving no evidence after the fact.

Then Medrano finally spoke, but it was not what anyone expected to hear. "Okay, do it. That's better than going to prison. I could never go back there. I'm not gonna give you the chance to pull your little bullshit with your fucking contact. So fuck all of you, just get it over."

Gates pointed the gun at Medrano's head and cocked it, waiting for a look of fear that never came. Instead, it looked like Medrano was truly anxious to get it over with, just like he had said. There was no bluff involved; he saw this as a better choice than going back to prison, especially with what Rocky had planned for him.

Then another strange thing happened. Gates slowly put the gun down as it occurred to him that twenty years of unbearable suffering was clearly a more satisfying choice than instant death. He then made up a lie to suit the situation. "I just can't do it. I guess that's why they put the straightedge on the table. You'll have to do it. Here take it." He then folded the razor into the handle and started to hand it to Medrano. Rocky, following the steps of the plan that Chico had carefully laid out before Medrano arrived, unlocked the handcuffs while pinning one of Medrano's hands securely behind his back.

Medrano eagerly grabbed the razor from Gates and as he struggled to open it with his free hand, he said "Gracias, Señor. I didn't think you would be so kind. I do not ever want to go back, I can't deal with it. Muchas gracias."

Everyone watched and waited as Medrano did his best to open the razor, but Rocky was well aware that it couldn't be done with just one hand. Finally, Medrano gave up. "Por favor, can you help me? I can't get it open." Just as they had rehearsed, no one spoke, and no one moved. Medrano was now pleading for help. "Please, I can't do it. It won't open. I can't go back. Please, I'm begging you. I can't go back."

Gates was the first to speak. He was very calm, his voice just above a whisper. "Did my daughter plead with you? Did she beg for her life? Do you even remember?" Then he reached over and took the razor from Medrano's hand. "Get this piece of shit out of here."

Medrano was beyond hysterical. His screams and pleas sounded as if he were being physically tortured. As Rocky reattached the handcuffs and placed the hood over his face, the screaming got so loud that Rocky had to temporarily remove the hood and stuff a rag in Medrano's mouth.

It was clear to everyone that Callahan and his accomplice were not going to be able to get Medrano out of the building without additional help. Medrano was struggling so violently that Rocky had to step in and use his size and strength to help subdue him. All hands were busy trying to contain and control Medrano, and no one was paying any attention to Ronald Gates. He was still in his chair, holding his face in his hands, crying the tears of one who had just experienced a bittersweet revenge.

Chapter Thirty-One

Settling the Score with John V.

When they got to the door, Sergeant Callahan had a suggestion. "You know, even though you gagged him, he's still making some pretty loud noises. Let him go for a minute." After Medrano's captors released him, Callahan continued. "Listen, moron, there's no point in continuing like this. Will you please and thank you, shut the fuck up?"

This approach had no effect whatsoever, so Callahan looked carefully at Medrano's black-hooded head and guessed where his chin was. With an uppercut that came from way out in left field, he caught him at just the right point, lifting him slightly off the ground, and backward into Rocky's waiting arms. As the struggling and loud, muffled noises temporarily came to an end, they carried their prey quietly out the door and into Callahan's waiting SUV.

Before Callahan and his associate drove off, Rocky informed him that it was likely that Chatsworth would be picked up on Tuesday and delivered to the warehouse on Wednesday. Callahan thanked him and asked him to let him know the timing so that he could be there when he arrived. Then, as he prepared to pull out of the parking lot, he promised Rocky that he would keep Medrano under wraps until it was time to return him to prison. Finally, he assured Rocky that he would follow the plan for getting him back behind bars that Chico had outlined earlier that morning.

Chico and Rocky had also left the warehouse and headed straight for Indiana. During the drive, Rocky informed Chico of his plans for putting a permanent end to the John V. situation. But Chico pointed out that although he agreed with Rocky in principle, they needed to know for certain that John V. was, in fact, responsible for Rob's condition. "Listen, Rocky, I'll bet you know someone who can let us see the surveillance evidence of exactly what happened at 4:00 P.M. on Friday. I know that they no longer use videotapes and that they store surveillance information on hard drives for thirty days, so the evidence is available. All you have to do is check with one of the guys you know, and then we can find out for sure. I'll bet you can get it done in not more than four phone calls."

Rocky considered the challenge for only a minute, and then began dialing his cell phone. After just two calls, it was set. They took the Chicago Skyway to Indianapolis Boulevard and headed straight for the casino. Within twenty minutes, they were looking at the surveillance video. They saw exactly what they expected to see: Rob left the poker room, made the phone call to Wade, and then, instead of turning right to go to the parking garage, he walked straight ahead into the men's room. John V. had apparently read the note and immediately made his decision because he was only a few feet behind Rob. No one had entered the men's room for a minute or two before Rob and John V., so there were most likely no witnesses to what happened inside. Then, after about fifteen seconds, John V. left and returned to the poker room.

They continued to watch the video for another minute and saw an elderly gentleman walk slowly into the rest room, only to emerge within a few seconds, shouting and waving his cane in the air. Neither Rocky nor Chico felt like watching any further, as they would only waste time and get even more upset. They now knew for certain what they had to do.

When they got to the hospital, Wade was asleep in a chair, and Paula and Julie were standing next to his bed, talking to him as if everything was normal. After watching silently and respectfully for a few minutes, they gave their best wishes and were about to leave when Wade woke up and walked with them out into the hall. He let them know that there had been no change, but that none had been expected. The next day, Tuesday, would be a possible turning point, as the surgeon had decided to end the procedure that was keeping him in a coma. If he came out of it and responded normally, he would most likely be home within a week.

But the surgeon cautioned them not to expect this kind of miracle. More than likely, Rob would be in a kind of twilight zone for a day or two, and after that they would be able to tell if he was making the kind of progress that was hoped for. However, he put a lot of emphasis on the word "hope," as there were absolutely no guarantees; they were treading in deep, uncharted waters. Finally, Wade pointed out that, at some point, the family might have to decide whether to take off the life support from him, which meant turning off the respirator. If Rob could breathe on his own, this might mean that he could continue in a vegetative state for a long time, or it could simply bring about a peaceful end. When it looked like Wade was about to change the subject and ask about business, they decided it was time to leave. Rocky got in the final word as they walked down the corridor. "Don't think about anything except what's best for Rob and your family. We'll take care of everything else. You can expect me to keep the promise I made when we left yesterday. It's happening real soon."

As soon as they got in the car, Rocky put in a call to Major Robins and talked for several minutes. Then he called Wayne, his pilot friend in Milwaukee, and made some additional arrangements.

Chico also made a couple of calls. He checked with Sergeant Callahan to make sure that he was working on some new plans he had for Medrano, but when he placed the next call to Christine, he got some disturbing news. When Rocky was between calls, he told him what he had learned from his wife. "Well, do you remember when we talked about whether we should follow up on any of our cases? Specifically, we wondered if we should look into whether Stedman was making progress with Gamblers Anonymous and if Crowley was getting into Alcoholics Anonymous? So, guess what? Christine tells me that Crowley's wife has been beaten up pretty bad. She has had her jaw wired shut, and has a detached retina. Seems Crowley was doing okay for awhile, but then he had a relapse. She called and told everything to Christine, but, I'll be damned, she won't leave him. Can you believe it? It looks like I called this one wrong. I was sure we had turned him around. I guess we're gonna have to do a little followup work after all. I'll have to come up with a plan for how to really get this guy's attention."

During the rest of the drive back home, they agreed that the next few days were going to be tense, busy, and challenging. On Tuesday, they were going to take care of John V. Also on Tuesday, Chatsworth was going to be picked up in Land O'Lakes, Wisconsin and brought back to Illinois. On Wednesday, they were going to meet at the warehouse with Callahan and Chatsworth, and on Thursday, Chico's new plan for getting Medrano back to prison was going to be carried out. Also, somehow, they had to work in a meeting with Crowley, possibly on Friday.

They completed the afternoon by stopping for a couple of cold ones, but it was not the enjoyable event that they usually experienced. Their friend since childhood was not with them, and he was undergoing the kind of trauma that no one should have to endure. They so wished that he could happily rejoin The Payback Team and help them with their upcoming challenges. They did appreciate Sergeant Callahan's participation, but they would, of course, have preferred to have Wade back with them.

Chapter Thirty-Two

Final Meeting with John V.

On Tuesday morning at 9:00, Chico and Rocky were sitting in the warehouse, waiting for the arrival of John V. They had phoned the major the night before and made arrangements for him to be picked up on his way to his used car lot. They had also called Wayne and were expecting him to arrive at about the same time.

While they waited, they checked in with Wade. Rob was scheduled to be brought, hopefully, out of his induced coma that morning, but there was no word of any change. Wade asked to be included in some of the team's activities during the next few days because he saw no point in spending all day at the hospital. Between Wade, Paula, and their daughter, they could arrange for someone to be with Rob constantly, but it wasn't necessary for all of them to spend full time with him. So it looked like Wade was going to get back in action, at least on a part-time basis.

Before ending the conversation, Wade asked what was happening with John V. When he was informed about the video that they had viewed at the casino, Wade asked them not to do anything until he could be involved. Rocky then grabbed the phone from Chico and spoke in a very loud, insistent tone. "Listen, Spike, you should stay right where you are. You are way too emotionally involved to be able to work on this in a calm, detached manner. John V. is a dangerous man, and I don't think he is going to accept what we have planned for him without resistance. Do you remember the expression 'revenge is a dish best served cold'? Well, I think that definitely applies here. We will let you know how it turns out later today. We should be meeting up with him any minute now. You just stay with Rob, and let us know if things are looking up. Trust us—we'll take care of this."

Not long after the call ended, Major Robins and Xavier Lorenzo walked in the door with John V. Xavier's nose was bleeding profusely, and a good portion of his white tee shirt was now a bright red. Before Chico and Rocky could ask what happened, the major explained that their captive, even though his hands were tightly bound behind him, had managed to execute a perfect head butt, breaking Xavier's nose in the process. Major Robins explained, "This is one vicious, mean, ornery son of a bitch. Xavier wanted to do some major damage, but we followed your instructions about delivering him in one piece so that he would be coherent enough to understand exactly how this thing is going to play out. I'm sure that—"

He was unable to finish the sentence because John V. interrupted. "If you think that you and your stupid beaner friend here scare me, forget about it. You jerkoffs just don't understand that you shouldn't be fucking with me. By now, I'm sure you realize that I took care of your little pissant buddy who keeps dropping off your stupid fucking notes. The dumb shit never saw it coming. He was standing at the urinal with his back to me, and his head actually made a cracking sound when I pushed it into the wall." Then he grinned, as if to show everyone that he was pleased with his accomplishment. Then he continued. "Do you think you're gonna make me give you whatever fucking amount of money that you say I owe some asshole named Harry or Harvey or whatever? Not going to happen, not today, not ever. So why don't you just—"

At this point he abruptly stopped. The major had thrown him into one of the chairs facing Rocky and Chico, and as he got a good look at Rocky, it was clear that he recalled their last encounter. Rocky simply smiled at him and waited until the full impact of what was about to occur sunk in. John V. was searching for words, but could only stare back at Rocky, no doubt wondering if he really meant what he had said the last time they were face to face. It also crossed his mind that the previous time he had been brought to this place, he had been blindfolded so that, apparently, he could not retrace the drive and lead whatever authorities he chose to the same location. It disturbed him that this time, they didn't seem to care.

Chico finally broke the silence. "Well, hello, Mr. Vargas. Here we are again. I hope you appreciate that we've brought you here without any physical harm. The last two times we met, you may recall that violence occurred, but today, at least for now, we have tried to insure that you are not distracted by any pain or any more broken bones. You know, I'd like to tell you a little story. You see this man here? I had introduced him previously as Stan Morrison. His real name is Michael MacMillan. He is the godfather of the young man you put in the hospital. I've known Michael for over forty years, and I have not ever known him to say something he didn't mean. Not ever; not even once. That should concern you, Mr. Vargas, unless, of course you forgot what he told you the last time you were here. Would you like me to remind you what he said? I remember exactly, word for word and—"

John V. again interrupted. Although he was getting concerned, he tried not to let it show. "Yeah, he said the next time he saw me, it would be the last time I'd ever see a sunset, or something like that. Well, that's bullshit, and I know that none of you have the balls to follow through. Maybe you'd like to take off these handcuffs and let him try. That would be just fine with me."

Rocky was the next one to speak. "You would never guess what just popped into my head a few seconds ago. Maybe you will all find it kind of interesting. Just the other day, I read about a study that was done. Did you know that only a small minority of people would want to know when they are going to die, if they had the option of knowing? Isn't that interesting? I thought about it, and I guess I feel the same way; I don't think I'd want to know either. But, anyway, to continue, I was thinking that John, here, is one of the few people who actually, knows—well, okay, I should say he's going to figure it out real soon— exactly when his life is going to end. By the way, John, it's today; actually, this morning. Now isn't that interesting?"

John V. was starting to look uncomfortable, but decided to continue to try to seem unconcerned. "Yeah, yeah, sure. When are you guys gonna quit running your mouths off?"

The next sound that was heard was the whirring of the helicopter as it prepared to land in the parking lot nearby. Chico stood up and said, "Well, it's almost time to go. Major, would you please remove the handcuffs from Mr. Vargas's wrists and attach them to one of his ankles? He's about to take his last ride. We're going for a little cruise over Lake Michigan in just a few minutes."

Major Robins fastened the handcuffs as Chico aksed him to do, and began leading John V. to the door. John V. was a little too stunned to put up a struggle at first, but when it was time to get him into the chopper, it took all four of them to accomplish the task. As Chico, Rocky, and John V. prepared to take off, the major reminded them that he expected to deliver Chatsworth to the warehouse some time the next morning. Rocky thanked him for everything and then motioned for the pilot to get the chopper in the air. In less than twenty minutes they were out over the lake, several miles from shore.

Now, as Rocky secured the handcuffs to a rope that ran down to the floor of the chopper, to where two concrete blocks were lying, John V. was finally convinced that they were serious. In a voice that was now shaking with fear, he decided it was time to give in. "All right, listen. This is ridiculous. I'll give you the damn money. And okay, sure, I'm sorry I hurt the kid, not that he didn't have it coming. But let's just forget the whole thing like it never happened. You'll get the money; you can give it to your friend, and no hard feelings. Okay?"

Rocky looked at him and shook his head with a look that said 'no way,' and also showed how pathetic he thought John V. was right at that moment. Then he told the pilot to lower his altitude so that he was just a few feet above the water. As the pilot descended, Chico said, "No, take it up. I think we should have the fun of seeing him fall a couple of thousand feet before he hits the water."

As the pilot reversed course and began to climb, Rocky shouted, "No, damn it! This is my show, and I say we get down close to the water. If we drop him from way high up, he'll be dead the second he crashes into the water. But if we drop him close down, we get to see him struggle for a few seconds as he tries to fight the weight of the blocks. Take it back down."

John V. was unaware that this conversation had been planned by Chico the previous evening, and that the pilot was part of it. As he took the plane back down, Wayne said, "Listen, will you kindly make up your mind. Do you clowns have any idea how much fuel we're wasting?"

Chico and Rocky were looking closely at John V.'s face so that they could later describe his last moments to Wade. Fear, hysteria, horror, and disbelief were some of the words that they would later relate to their friend.

Then Chico concluded their little charade. "Hey, I have an idea. How about if we give Mr. Vargas the option? I think that's fair. I know he didn't give Rob any options when he bashed his head against the wall, but what the heck? I'm in kind of a charitable mood. How about it John? Any preference how you want it to end?"

Rocky and Chico waited a few seconds for John V. to state his choice, but John V. was strangely silent. He had been carefully trying to size up the situation to see if there was any possible way he could avoid what appeared to be inevitable. Several things registered in his mind while Chico and Rocky were having their little disagreement. He saw that the rope had been somewhat carelessly tied to just one of the blocks, and whoever set it up, forgot to include the other block in the process. That meant that the load he would be up against was only going to be half of what they had planned it to be. If he could find some way to stay afloat for just a few seconds, he felt he had a good chance of untying the knot. Then, since he felt he was a good swimmer, he might be able to make it to shore, even if it took hours, and then someday, he would even the score, and he would be rid of his adversaries for good.

He also noticed a piece of orange material under Rocky's seat, and he could plainly make out some black letters stamped on it that read U.S. COASTGUARD APPROVED. This was just what he needed, a life jacket. If he could grab it just before being thrown from the chopper, he would have a good chance of making it. The last thing he noticed was that there was a handle on either side of the exit door, about shoulder high. As soon as he was forced to a standing position, there was the chance that he could grab both of the handles and hold on tightly while he used both feet to give a powerful kick to at least one of his captors. Then, in the confusion, he could grab the preserver, jump out of the chopper, and take his chances that the rest of his plan might have a chance of being effective. John V. briefly considered the fact that none of this would be possible if he were still handcuffed. He wondered why they had been stupid enough to remove them, but then quickly refocused on his dilemma.

Then things started to move at lightning speed. Chico had grown impatient waiting for John V.'s response and told Rocky to go ahead and throw out the concrete blocks. Rocky promptly grabbed the one that the rope was tied to and heaved it out of the helicopter. John V. was jerked violently toward the door, and as he realized what was happening, made a desperate effort to grab the handles. He succeeded, but was in the wrong position to give anyone anything resembling a swift kick, as he was facing the wrong way.

Chico then ordered Rocky to end it by giving John V. a final shove out of the chopper. But John V. made one last attempt to save his life. "No, please! Wait! Don't do this! I'm begging you!"

Rocky responded, "So now you're begging us? You're fucking begging us? That's really cute. Did my godson have a chance to beg you? I don't think so. Do you know that he is in a coma, thanks to you? Do you care that the doctor doesn't know if he's going to make it? Does it matter to you that his parents were asked to sign an organ donor form? Goodbye, I'm done with you."

John V. still wasn't through bargaining for his life. "Listen, at least give me a chance. Let me have that life preserver. I probably won't make it anyway, but at least I'll have a small chance."

Chico clearly didn't want Rocky to give him even the slightest concession. "Don't pay any attention to him. Just get it over with. Do it."

Rocky wasn't convinced. "Hey, what can it hurt? That may even be better, letting him struggle above water for a few minutes before it's over. Yeah, I think I'd like to see that."

Now Chico was really getting agitated. "Don't go soft on me now, goddamn it. We didn't come out here to let him give the orders. Get it over with, *now!*"

Rocky decided to get in the last word. "Listen, jerkoff, this is my show, and I'm giving him the jacket. Just shut up, okay?" Then he pulled out the jacket and handed it to John V., who released one hand at a time from the handles and, in spite of the cast on his left arm, managed to put it on.

John V. smiled upon seeing the success of his persuasive efforts, but Chico and Rocky were unable to notice, since they were standing behind him. At this point, John V. was certain that he was about to cheat death, and he made a quick mental note to use the time it took him to get back to shore to devise a way to track down his two attempted assassins and turn the tables. "One more thing—could you drop down a little lower? If I hit the water too hard, I won't have even the slightest chance—"

Rocky cut him off as he ordered the pilot to lower his altitude. Now Chico was thoroughly enraged and shouted, "You fucking moron, why don't you just fly him home and pour him a cup of tea while you're at it?!"

John V. again smiled and said, "God bless you, sir. If by some miracle I get out of this, I'll never forget you, I promise." Then he jumped. The concrete block hit the water first, followed immediately by a still smiling John V. Chico and Rocky watched as he promptly began sinking to the bottom of the lake. The last thing they were able to see was the bright orange color of the life jacket, which disappeared from sight in just a few seconds.

Rocky looked at Chico. "Well, I guess you win. I owe you a big fat C-note. I really thought he would stay above water for at least a few seconds. I didn't think he'd drop like a fucking rock. I gotta hand it to you. That was one of your better ideas."

Chico grinned. "Thanks. But next time I come up with an idea, I'm gonna let you do all the work that comes afterward. You know, I spent over three hours last night slitting open the seams of the life jacket, tearing out all of the buoyancy material, replacing it with old rags, and then sewing the seams back up. Christine was really pissed. I was supposed to take her out to dinner."

Chapter Thirty-Three

Chatsworth Arrives

The Payback Team was together again, and ready for action. They were waiting at the warehouse with Sergeant Callahan for the arrival of Colton R. Chatsworth III, and they were all extremely anxious to find out just how Major Robins had managed to locate and apprehend him so quickly. Of the many opportunities the major had had to help the trio in some way, he had come through for them one-hundred percent of the time. But this one really surprised them.

Callahan, especially, was dumbfounded, not to mention grateful. The chance to confront the man who seriously injured his daughter and was responsible for the death of his only grandchild was about to be a reality. Now more than ever, he had come to respect what The Payback Team stood for, as well as their ability to get the job done. He was glad to be a small part of the group, and he hoped that his role would grow in the days and weeks to come. It had occurred to him that he would not ever want to be on the opposing side, as he would have no chance against the resources, determination, and dedication of these three extraordinary individuals. The idea of joining them in their attempt to solve the hijacking problem in Guatemala was very appealing, and he could think of no better way to start his retirement. He had never intended to just sit around, and now he was looking forward to a new and beneficial way to spend his time.

When Major Robins and one of his associates walked through the door with Chatsworth, they began barraging him with questions before Chatsworth was even led to his seat. The major just smiled and raised his left hand as if to say "Okay, relax, I'm going to explain everything." He removed the hood from Chatsworth, left the gag in place, and then securely tied him to a chair in front of the round coffee table directly across from Sergeant Callahan. Then he began speaking. "You know, I've spent a lot of time in the Northwoods. A lot of people don't realize that it's a great place to get lost, and it's only a five or six hour drive from Chicago. There are hundreds of square miles of forest land; both the Nicolet National Forest and the Ottawa National Forest, across the border in Michigan's Upper Peninsula, are close to Land O'Lakes. We found him there, thanks to his mommy. It's a good thing there aren't many like her, or the world would be full of fucked-up assholes like this one." Everyone, with the exception of Chatsworth, seemed amused by this last comment.

The major continued. "Mommy would send junior three grand every month and he would go to the Headwaters State Bank in Land O'Lakes, where she arranged to have it transferred. Isn't that special? Junior never has to work because mommy always took care of him.

Well, anyway, we found this out because we checked with all of the banks in Darien, where mommy lives, until we came across The West Suburban Bank of Darien, which is where she has her checking account. Then, after we juiced the right guy at the bank, we got a look at the account and found out that a wire transfer is made on the tenth of every month to the Land O'Lakes bank. The next step was finding out that he went there on the same day each month to take out the cash—that involved more juice to one of the tellers at that bank. So yesterday, we were waiting outside the bank for junior to show up and we followed him outside of town after he made the withdrawal. When he turned off the main road, we continued following him until there was no one else in sight, and then we pulled him over, and here he is. It just took a lot of creative thinking on our part, and don't forget, that's primarily what we do. We're bounty hunters. No body, no bounty.

"Well, gentlemen, I wish I could stay to see what you have in store for our little mommy's boy here, but we have to leave. I can pretty well guess what Sergeant Callahan has in that black bag next to his left foot, and I'm pretty sure Chatsworth is not going to like it. That's all for now; I know you're gonna enjoy the next couple of hours. Call me if you need me to come back and pick up the pieces or clean up the mess."

As he walked out the door, Chatsworth was looking nervously at the bag on the floor and trying to figure out what the major meant about picking up pieces. He tried to reject the first concept that entered his mind, but it kept coming back, a little uglier each time.

After the back door closed, Callahan reached into the bag and pulled out two pictures, setting one of them on the coffee table in front of his prey. Chatsworth had been following the conversation, up to this point, without uttering a sound. He was taking everything in, wondering where it was going to lead, and the more he thought about it, the less he liked it. Callahan asked him a question. "You know this gentleman on my right," he paused and made a gesture toward Chico, "made a bet with me. I said that you would recognize the lady in the picture, and he laid a hundred bucks, at two to one, against it. So, how about it? Tell us who won."

Chatsworth gave a long look and then shrugged his shoulders, expressing a disinterested look at the same time. "Well, I'll be damned. You were right. I guess you're smarter than this old cop. Okay, I owe you, but what made you so sure?"

Chico smiled and explained about sociopathic personalities. He said that they care so little about others that the harm they do is not only unimportant, but the victim is, in fact, insignificant to them. Callahan accepted this and then put the other picture on the table. "How about this one? I'll help you out a little. The first one is a 'before' picture, and this one is the 'after' picture. Now, is it clear?"

Chatsworth finally put it all together. The first picture was of an attractive woman in her late twenties, and although it was impossible to tell for certain, the logical conclusion was that the second picture was the same person after some kind of horrible accident or injury. Her left eye was swollen shut, the left side of her face was badly discolored, and it looked like the bone just below her eye had been broken, possibly even shattered. Now, he understood what this was all about. The man standing before him obviously had some kind of connection to the woman in the pictures.

Callahan continued. "Well, let me make sure you understand exactly what's going on here. The woman in the pictures is Margie Beaumont, my only child. This is what she looked like before you punched her. And this was taken the next day, before she underwent her first surgery, and before she began therapy. You know, not that it matters to you, but you didn't just shatter her face, you shattered her life. She no longer trusts anyone, can't hold a job, is addicted to pain medication, and suffers long periods of depression that can only be treated with more damn pills. She still needs more surgery, and it's all because of you.

"You know, Margie lives with me now. I'm the only one left to take care of her. My wife died three years ago. Right now, I pay a nanny to look after her when I'm working. You see, she's reverted to kind of a childlike state. But this arrangement is probably going to end soon, as she is most likely going to have to be put in a place where she can receive permanent, professional care. That will probably be better for both of us because now, every time she cries, which is often, it reminds me of Timmy, and how he must have suffered those last several days.

"It had been my goal to make you suffer for just as many days, but I'm afraid that's not going to happen. I just don't have the energy or the endurance for it anymore. So, a few hours will have to suffice.

"And this picture…" he pulled another picture out of the black bag and put it on the table. "It's a picture of a very happy little boy, about four years old." But Callahan was unable to continue for a few minutes. He turned his back to the group and walked a few steps away. He lowered his head and put his left hand to his face, apparently rubbing his eyes.

Finally, he turned around and made a little speech. "Gentlemen, I can't thank you enough. You are all starting to mean so much to me, more than I could possibly express. I only hope I can, in some way, contribute to your cause, to what you stand for." Then, after pausing for a breath, he took off his suit jacket. "If you don't mind, I'd like to spend some quality time alone with Mr. Chatsworth—a little 'one-on-one, getting-to-know-one-another-experience,' if you will." At this point, he rolled up his sleeves and loosened his tie. "Please, call Major Robins and let him know that I will need his help wrapping things up here, but not for several hours, until it's all over. I'll give him a call." As the trio prepared to make their departure, they took their last look at Chatsworth. His eyes were wide with fear, and he was struggling, uselessly, against the bindings that held him to his chair. He was trying to talk, but it was impossible to understand any of the words.

For the next couple of minutes, Callahan slowly and deliberately began emptying what was left in the black bag, item by item, making sure that Chatsworth was watching closely. He carefully lined them up in a neat, orderly row in the middle of the coffee table. As he pulled out the last item, a pair of latex gloves, and began putting them on, he noticed that the kidnaper's horrified eyes were looking intently at the former contents of the black bag: a pair of pliers, an ice pick, a hammer, and a Bic lighter. Then he spoke again as he unrolled a large, plastic drop cloth that had been sitting under Chatsworth's chair. "You know, Colton—is it okay if I call you by your first name? Maybe you'd be interested in something I just thought of as I was getting ready for our little ceremony? When I was a little kid, my mother used to take me to the dentist's office. Dr. Walker used to say 'This won't take long, and it isn't going to hurt a bit.' And then, when he started drilling, the pain was unbearable. And it seemed like it was never going to end. So he lied to me twice; it really did hurt, and it wasn't over quickly.

"Well, Colton, you probably want me to get to the point. The point is, those lies stayed with me even to this day. Why would he lie to a little kid like that? Actually, I've never figured it out; but I'm not going to lie to you, like Dr. Walker lied to me, even though you won't have nearly as much time to think about it as I have had. So, truthfully, this is going to hurt a lot. I mean a real lot, like much worse than your worst nightmare. And it's going to seem like it's lasting forever, even though it's all going to end in probably just four or five hours. He then paused to let the situation sink in. Finally, he started to reach for the hammer. "Oh, wait, Colton, I almost forgot. I've got two more things to show you. Take a look at this. That's right; it's your death certificate. Yeah, I know it's not your name, but it'll do. Those guys I'm working with are really ingenious at getting things done. Can you believe it, Colton? They've already got a signed death certificate! Isn't that amazing? Seems you were found in an alley down on skid row, all beaten up. A real pity. But you know, those things happen.

"And this is a picture of your final resting place. It's really not as nice as most cemeteries, it's where they bury the poor, the unidentified, and the forgotten. Just think about it...you'll be lying there for all eternity, but no one will know it's you! The perfect end to a totally worthless life. Very fitting.

"Now hold still for just a second, I'm going to remove the gag. You're going to want to make a lot of extremely loud noises, at least until your voice gives out, and I'm okay with that. In fact, the louder, the better.

"But okay, Colton, I know you're probably tired of hearing all of this, so I guess we can go ahead and get started. Now, where was I before I got sidetracked? Oh, yes, the hammer..."

Chapter Thirty-Four

Another Medrano Sting

Thursday was going to be another busy day for The Payback Team. Rob's family, along with their beloved friends, Chico, Christine, Rocky, and Angela, were waiting in Rob's hospital room for the surgeon to arrive. They were going to make an important decision regarding Rob's recovery, or, more to the point, his lack of any visible progress. It was hoped that he would at least have opened his eyes within a day or so after they tried to take him out of his coma, but this was not the case.

The surgeon finally showed up and spent several minutes discussing alternatives, and just as the family had assumed, it all came down to their decision as to whether or not they should disconnect Rob's respirator. Chico and Rocky and their wives made their exit shortly after the surgeon departed, as they felt that this was something the family should discuss in private.

Shortly before they left, they mentioned John V.'s name very briefly. They had wanted to give Wade a detailed account of everything that had occurred, right up until the time that the helicopter landed without him. However, they realized that the timing was wrong. As they were giving Wade a hug before leaving the room, Chico whispered a few brief words, informing him that John V. had, indeed, spent his last day aboveground.

They asked Wade to let them know of any further developments and mentioned that they had to drop the girls off and get back to meet with Sergeant Callahan and Xavier Lorenzo. Chico had decided to change course and was planning another sting that would send Medrano back to jail. Originally, it was planned to simply drop him off, but Chico had a much better idea, one that would gain Medrano many additional years of incarceration, although they doubted that he would be able to survive his first six months behind bars.

They needed to meet to go over the details of the new plan, as Callahan and Xavier were going to be handling it without them.

Callahan had been keeping Medrano under lock and key, waiting for instructions from The Payback Team. So after a half-hour meeting at a local Dunkin' Donut shop, everything was in place. As Callahan and Xavier headed out to pick up Medrano and start the sting, Rocky called one of his pawnshops to make sure that things were ready for Medrano's arrival.

About an hour later, Callahan and Xavier walked in the back door of the pawnshop. They had a tightly bound and gagged Medrano with them. They removed the bindings, put him in a chair, and then tied him loosely to the chair. If they weren't watching him closely, Medrano was pretty certain that he would be able to get out of the situation and make a run for it. But Xavier had positioned himself just in front of the rear door, and Medrano's chair had been placed up against the door to the main part of the shop. Medrano would just have to wait and see if there would be a chance to get away.

Callahan had a sadistic smile on his face, and as he removed his suit coat and hung it on a coat rack in the corner, Medrano was pretty sure what was coming next, as he had remembered the vicious uppercut Callahan had landed under his chin a few days earlier. He began speaking as he loosened his tie, rolled up his sleeves, and attached a pair of shiny brass knuckles to his right hand. "You, my friend, are about to find out how I feel about child rapists. And, oh yeah, I almost forgot. You killed her after you were finished with her. You might like to know that my grandson lost his life to another piece of shit just like you, so, in a way, I'll be getting a little extra satisfaction every time I slam this into your face." Then, for emphasis, he made a fist and smacked it into the palm of his left hand.

It looked like he was about to begin what was sure to be an extremely painful session, but then stopped for a second and removed his shoulder holster and hung it on the coat rack. Apparently, he didn't want anything restricting his ability to smash a series of well-placed blows that were likely to break most of the bones in Medrano's face.

As Callahan was about to begin the ritual, Medrano started trying to loosen the rope that had been placed around him and tied behind his back. He was going to try his best to grab the gun, kill both of them, and get out the back door. He realized that they would probably have time, between the two of them, to stop his plan from succeeding, but it looked like this was his only option.

Then something happened that Medrano could not possibly have imagined. Callahan had stopped talking and had pulled his arm back, ready for the first strike, but then he stopped, grabbed his chest with his left hand, and fell to one knee. "I...I...I can't...my pills...I left them on my desk...you've got to get me to emergency. Oh, no...not again...not now...*oh, God...oh, God.*"

Xavier looked totally alarmed and helpless. "What should I do? What about him? How can I help you? I don't know what to do!"

Callahan responded in a weak voice. "Fuck him. Leave him here and get me to the hospital. Don't stop to call 911. We gotta go...now." Xavier did as he was told and half dragged, half carried Callahan out the rear door.

Medrano could not believe his luck. He was going to get out of this. He knew just where he could go and never be found. No beatings, no trial, and most importantly, no jail time. As he got out of the chair, he smiled briefly as he thought about how Rocky's plan to have him beaten and sodomized every day, month after month, was never going to happen.

But he quickly put an end to these thoughts because he knew he had to focus on getting away. He got to the back door, but couldn't get it open. How could that be? Doors are supposed to be locked from the inside. But there was no point worrying about this; he had to consider another alternative. Then the answer came to him. He grabbed the gun from Callahan's holster and decided he would just have to confront whoever was on the other side of the door leading to the rest of the building. What chance did they have against a man pointing a gun at them? And what did they have to gain by trying to stop him? He felt that the cards were stacked in his favor.

Then he got the second surprise of the morning. As soon as he burst through the door, someone saw him and immediately yelled, "He's got a gun! Call 911!" Medrano then saw another man reaching for a telephone. He pointed the gun at him and pulled the trigger, but nothing happened. He quickly looked at the gun, a snub nose .38

caliber Smith and Wesson, and saw that it was fully loaded. So he pointed and tried again.

He was not aware that the gun was a "drop gun," a weapon that dirty cops use to plant on a suspect, and, even though it was loaded with live bullets, the firing pin had been filed down.

By this time, two men were running toward him. One of them shouted, "Get his gun!" And the other one tackled him. The man with the telephone called 911. Three policemen were there within five minutes and were promptly informed that the man pinned to the floor had broken in the back door and tried to rob the pawnshop at gunpoint. The surveillance tapes would clearly show that he had pointed the gun and attempted to fire it twice. It was only by the grace of God that it had misfired.

One of the policemen congratulated the three employees on their heroic actions and their quick thinking, and pointed out that Medrano was going away for a long time. Armed robbery and attempted murder were serious felonies, and depending on his prior record, could result in life in prison.

Within a few minutes, Medrano was being led out the front door in handcuffs, while the three cops debated which one should get the credit for his apprehension.

Chapter Thirty-Five

Preparing for the Second Meeting with Dr. Crowley

As soon as Chico and Rocky left the warehouse, they called Wade to check on Rob's situation. Wade informed them that the family had decided to remove the respirator. For the first few minutes, no one was sure what to expect, but before long, Rob began breathing on his own, and much to their relief, his breaths came normally and he appeared to be at peace; it just seemed as if he were comfortably asleep.

But, unfortunately, there was no sign of consciousness; they spoke to him, asked him questions, and Paula even gently shook him by his shoulders. There was not the slightest response. The family had been informed that this might be the case and that the next decision, in that event, would be to consider removing the intravenous drip that was providing him with sustenance. Then it would be over within days.

However, this decision could be postponed as long as they wished, even for years. The question, however, would be whether it was wise to prolong life in this manner. Wade explained that, at least for now, the family had agreed not to discuss, or even think about, this option.

Wade asked what was on The Payback Team's agenda for Friday, and when he was informed that they were going to meet with Dr. Crowley, the wife beater, he said he would like to be included, as long as they could schedule it for late afternoon. So it was agreed that they would all get together at the warehouse, along with Sergeant Callahan, at 4:00 P.M. They had heard about his proficiency with a set of brass knuckles and decided that he could be of assistance. They were all starting to appreciate him and agreed that he was becoming a valuable member of the team. The decision to meet at 4:00 P.M. would have the benefit of giving them at least an hour to discuss business prior to Crowley's expected arrival time.

When everyone was together at the warehouse, Wade brought up the topic that was on everyone's mind. "Okay, I'm sure you all are wondering what has happened to our proposed timetable for getting started in Guatemala. We are supposed to be leaving in less than two weeks. So, I guess it's clear to all of us that that's not going to happen. I'm sorry, I know it's my fault, but I have to stay here and take care of family business. Maybe you guys want to consider going ahead on your own. I know it was my project from day one. In fact, that's pretty much how The Payback Team got started in the first placed. But if you really want to know what I would like to see happen, I'll tell you. Is there another project we can work on right here, one that I can be involved in on a limited basis, until my current crisis gets settled, one way or the other? Then, hopefully, we can get back on track for Guatemala."

While Chico and Rocky were nodding in agreement, Callahan looked like he had a suggestion. But before he could begin, Chico had a question. "Okay, I can tell that you have something to say. But before you get started, do you mind telling us your first name? We've been working with you for a while now, and all we know is 'Sergeant Callahan.' Unless your first name is actually 'Sergeant,' I guess we're missing something."

Callahan laughed. "It's Sean. But that's kind of funny because no one ever calls me Sean. Would you believe that even my wife called me Callahan? I guess it just seems to fit. So, actually, Callahan will be just fine. In fact, if you ever call me Sean, I may not immediately know who you're referring to!" Callahan waited until the trio stopped laughing. "Okay, you're right, I did have a suggestion. You know, it wasn't my place to say anything about this, but I guess we all pretty much knew we were soon going to get to this discussion. So now, I think, it's a good time to bring up something that's been on my mind for quite awhile. I'll spell it out, and you can tell me if you want to pursue it. This definitely fits the criteria that Courtland just laid out."

He paused for a few seconds, and when he saw that they were all paying close attention, he continued. "You know, I was involved in a situation several months ago that I had temporarily put on the back of my mind because I was focused on the Chatsworth case. And, by the way, thanks for giving me some quality time alone with him on Wednesday. I really enjoyed the few hours we had together. The time just seemed to fly by until it abruptly ended. And your friend, Major Robins, was really effective in helping to wrap things up for us, if you know what I mean. Unfortunately, we were so absorbed in our little get together that we didn't even notice the mess we were creating. But he took care of everything. Good man.

"Oops, I got sidetracked again. Okay, here's what happened. A guy named Reed Marshall offered a ride to two teenage girls. They were both fifteen, and it was raining. They were on their way to the local Dairy Queen, just a few blocks from where they lived. They knew it was a bad idea, but it was raining, and he seemed friendly and helpful. Okay, so far, so good. But here's the thing: he takes them to his home in Orland Park and turns them over to two of the older prostitutes in his stable. That's right, he's a pimp. But not just any pimp. He's a pimp who has kidnapped four or five other girls that we know of and gotten them started in prostitution.

"You know the routine. He tells them that he knows where they live, and if they try to get away he will kill everyone in their family. There's a lot of other intimidation tactics that he uses, and of course, he keeps them under tight control, so it's nearly impossible for them to do anything but cooperate. If anyone of them does manage to get away, he simply disappears for a few days and then sets up his operation somewhere else. Fortunately, he got caught. One of the girls I mentioned a minute ago climbed out a window and got to the cops before he knew she was gone.

"Now here's where everything got fucked up. Because he takes them across state lines on occasion, the feds took over. When they found out he's connected to a larger, interstate prostitution ring, they offered him a deal if he'd give up a few names. You know, the guy was pretty well connected, had plenty of money, and got a high-priced mouthpiece to persuade everyone that he would give full cooperation in exchange for going into the witness protection program. The lawyer convinced the feds that this was necessary because his life would be worthless once he rolled over.

"Every time I think about it, I get pretty damn upset. No, that's an understatement; I want to kill him. He takes two young girls away from their families and the nice, protected life they have known forever, and changes it all in a few seconds. They are taken from a secure world and suddenly forced into pure hell, and there's nothing they can do about it. They go from, presumably, virginity to getting raped multiple times every week for over two months. And why? So the pimp can get rich off the use of their bodies. Do you think these girls, or their families, will ever get back to living normal lives? How can they possibly overcome the trauma of an experience like this?

"I'm sorry guys, but rewarding this guy with the protection of the very people who should have put him away for a really long time is a crime in itself. I only wish I could get in contact with someone who knew how to cut through this witness protection bullshit so we can get our hands on this guy. I could make him suffer like he never dreamed possible. I'd like to round up the girls and their families and get a nice audience together, and now I'm probably way off the mark. But I'm sure you get the point. For one thing—" The sergeant stopped in mid sentence. He had noticed that Wade, Chico, and Rocky had all been smiling and laughing for the last several seconds, and it looked like they were going to continue. "I'm sorry; I don't see what could possibly be funny about this. Don't you get it? What if one of your daughters—"

Chico interrupted. "Okay, okay, don't have another heart attack." Then, as he gestured toward Rocky with his right hand, he continued. "This guy, right here, can make one phone call and find out exactly what you want to know within five minutes. No problem; it will be done."

Sergeant Sean Callahan was shaking his head in disbelief. "Well, I'll be goddamned. You guys are really something. I've never known three such capable people. I'll say it again: I'm just glad we're on the same side. Anyway, that's my suggestion for the next project to work on. I've got a pretty good hunch that when we find this guy, we're gonna see that he's started the same operation all over again in his new location. I lost a bet with Chico the other day, and…oops I forgot." He stopped long enough to reach in his pocket and hand him a hundred-dollar bill. "Care to give me a chance to get my money back?"

Chico declined the offer and then asked Rocky and Wade what they thought about Callahan's idea for the next project. After a brief discussion, they enthusiastically agreed to start working on it after the weekend. The subject matter was then quickly changed because Dr.

Crowley was due to arrive soon, and they needed to spend a few minutes going over Chico's plan for how to handle the confrontation that was about to occur.

Chapter Thirty-Six

Another Meeting with Dr. Crowley

At 6:00 P.M., the backdoor opened and Major Robins and one of his team members walked in with a hooded Dr. Edmond Crowley. The major asked his associate to wait just inside the door while he walked over to the foursome, as Chico had requested of him during an earlier phone call. He handed something to Chico, and then, in a voice just above a whisper, he related the events of the last two hours.

"It was just like you guessed," said Major Robbins. "He left work at 3:00 in order to get an early start on happy hour. We followed him to a pub just a couple of miles from where he works and waited outside until he left at 5:15. We pulled up behind him when he arrived at his home and put him in our vehicle. We could clearly smell the alcohol on his breath, but you won't notice it because he pulled something out of his pocket just a few minutes ago, lifted the hood up a little bit, and then he sprayed something into his mouth several times. We didn't put the cuffs on because he was totally compliant. He even joked about knowing what was going to happen, and said he was looking forward to meeting with all of you again. He doesn't know that we saw him go in and out of the pub. So, anyway, that's the story, and here he is."

Chico then thanked him and motioned for the hood to be removed. Crowley walked over to the group sitting around the coffee table, greeted them in an unusually friendly manner and sat down. "I knew what this was all about just as soon as these two gentlemen picked me up. I guess you want to do a little checking to make sure I'm staying on the 'straight and narrow,' right?" Then he gave a little laugh, implying that they could definitely count on him to do the right thing. After he finished laughing, he looked at Sergeant Callahan and spoke again. "I see we have an addition to our little group. You probably know that I am Dr. Edmond Crowley, and you are…?"

Everyone was surprised at Crowley's familiar, friendly way of handling the situation, while being totally unaware that he was digging himself deeper with every word. Callahan responded, "You can call me Hank."

Crowley continued with his overly friendly attitude. "Okay, then, Hank it is. Nice to meet you, Hank. Well, I suppose I know the reason why we're all assembled here, but rather than being overly presumptuous, I guess I'll let you have the floor." The group continued to be amazed that Crowley was acting almost as if he were in charge, not realizing that this was far from the case.

Finally, Chico calmly took over. "Well, Dr. Crowley, if you were guessing that we just wanted to get together to make sure you were on track with the three things we asked of you last time we met, you're right. We held off from any aggressive tactics with you since you said you would comply. Why don't you give us a detailed account of how you're doing, and then we'll give you a report card." Everyone smiled at the obvious reference to the fact that he was the principal of an elementary school.

"Well, certainly, that's quite appropriate," replied Crowley. "You'll be happy to know that I've joined AA, and I've already been to two meetings. So far, I've been able to stay away from demon rum, and I plan to keep it that way. And I'm doing well with the anger management class, although I can see I need to continue with the sessions, as certain, shall we say, 'issues', have been identified that I need to work on. But so far, things are good, no, I should say better than ever with my relationship with my wife. Now, as far as your third request, helping out at an abused women's shelter, okay, I haven't started on that yet. But I'm looking into it. That's just around the corner. So, I guess I haven't earned an A+, but at least I think I'm close." His laughter quickly subsided when he realized that he was the only one laughing. Up until this moment, he had felt that he had everything under control.

As Chico had prearranged, Callahan stood up and started to reach into his left coat pocket. "Shall I do it now?" he asked.

Chico shook his head, and Callahan sat down again. Nothing was said for more than a minute. Everyone was apparently waiting for Crowley to continue speaking, but he didn't have any idea what they expected him to say, so Chico asked a question. "Before we give your grade, is there anything else you would like to add, or would you possibly want to make any changes?"

Crowley shook his head and shrugged his shoulders as if to say "that's my story, and I'm sticking to it."

Then Chico continued. "Well, okay, right now, you haven't earned an 'A,' and not even a 'B,' but let's work on it. I've got a couple of questions for you. You told us that you have been to a couple of AA meetings. Can you tell us the dates and locations? And what about the anger management class? When and where were these sessions held?"

Now it looked like Crowley's demeanor was starting to change, but he tried to recover by going on the offense. With an indignant tone, he pronounced, "Certainly, you don't expect me to remember these kinds of details? You know, I'm responsible for twenty-six teachers and almost six hundred kids in K through five. That's more responsibility than most people could handle, and you expect me to remember some inconsequential dates and addresses? I'm sure you—"

Chico interrupted. "Calm down, Dr. Crowley. There's no reason to get upset, at least not yet." He paused for a second or two and looked at Callahan, who promptly patted the bulge in his left coat pocket. Crowley's demeanor slipped another notch or two as he started to imagine where this conversation might be headed, and what might be in Callahan's pocket.

Wade was starting to look impatient, and as they had planned, he now took his turn to speak. "I see Dr. Crowley's point, I really do. But I'm sure someone of his businesslike nature would most likely have it written down somewhere. You can't expect someone of his stature to keep little things like these in his memory bank when he has so many important matters to be responsible for. I say we cut him a little slack." Crowley then gave an appreciative look, grateful that someone had come to his defense. Unfortunately, he had no clue that he was being set up. Crowley certainly had a high level of intelligence, but lacked the intuition to realize that each member of The Payback Team could not only match his high IQ point for point, but they each possessed the street smarts that he had failed to acquire.

He took the bait. "Of course, thank you for pointing that out." Then, with a smug look, as if to say "well, I guess that takes care of that," he continued, saying, "Details like that are kept in my Black—" Then he caught himself, gulped, and gave a horrified look.

Callahan again stood up and asked, "Now?" Chico motioned for him to sit back down.

"You didn't finish the sentence. It sounded like you were about to say BlackBerry." Chico reached into his pocket and pulled out the item that had been handed to him by Major Robins. "Fortunately, we have it right here. I'm sure you need to punch in your unlock code, so now, maybe you'd like me to hand it to you so you can prove what you told us earlier and earn a good grade on your report card." Crowley's failure to reach for the BlackBerry sealed his fate, and it was obvious that he was aware of that fact. It was clear that he had nothing more to say.

Chico continued. "You know, it's rare that someone fools me so completely. You put on a great show when you were here last time. I gotta say, I bought it one hundred percent. But that was then, and this is now. For the record, we know you left work early and spent over two hours in the pub. We are aware that you clobbered your wife again, and we also understand she isn't ever going to do anything about it. We tried to set up a system for her to get out on her own if you wouldn't shape up, but now we know she's not gonna change, and neither are you, at least not voluntarily. But there is just one thing I can think of that might work, and that's the approach we were originally going to take.

"You did a good job of getting us off course last time, but today is a new day. Now, we know you're a hopeless case, and no amount of being 'Mr. Nice Guy' is going to change everything. So, boys, go to work. Stan, get the tool you set on those shelves last time we were here, and Hank, you can go ahead and reach in your pocket now. You've been real anxious to get down to business, so we're gonna let you go first. Allan, kindly get Dr. Crowley out of his chair and stand him up."

When he saw Rocky place the lopping shears on the coffee table and Callahan pull a set of brass knuckles out of his pocket and start to approach him, Crowley not only began to whimper and plead, but he lost control of his bladder. Callahan momentarily paused as he looked down and saw the puddle starting to form. He said, "You know, I've seen this a lot of times. Guys who can beat up their wives and girlfriends, but when they're the ones on the receiving end, they piss and moan. I mean literally, piss and moan. Jesus, look at this pathetic little cocksucker. I'll give ten to one odds your wife doesn't act like this when you beat the crap out of her, you sick little coward.

"Now, here's what I'm gonna try to do, just so you'll know what to expect. I'm gonna try to duplicate the damage you inflicted on your wife's face." Then, before Crowley could blink, Callahan caught him right next to his left eye, and the blow came so suddenly that it knocked both Crowley and Rocky back about four feet before they both crashed to the concrete floor. Rocky got up and helped Crowley to his feet, then grabbed him from behind. Neither man was ready for what came next because they assumed that Callahan would need a second to strike again, but Crowley's jaw was broken with a punch that was as swift and vicious as any they had ever seen, or even imagined. They were again knocked off balance, but this time Rocky managed to keep from hitting the floor. Callahan spoke again. "Well, how was that? What do you guys think? Is that pretty much how you wanted his face to look? I did the best I could."

Crowley was too stunned to realize how badly he had just been pummeled. Wade grabbed a hand mirror that was sitting on the orange crate next to him, held it up to Crowley's face, and asked, "How about it, Doc? Is this pretty much how your wife's face looked?" With his only usable eye, he tried to focus, but he wasn't sure if the mirror was defective, if his eyesight had been impaired, or if the bloody, swollen, misshapen mess that looked back at him was actually his face.

Now, Rocky put him back in his chair, stepped in front of him, grabbed the shears and said, "Okay, remember this? This is where we left off before, isn't it? Listen, I want to make one thing perfectly clear. Oh, excuse me for a second. Would you guys please unroll the drop cloth? This is gonna get messy." Then he tossed the shears to Callahan. Rocky continued speaking as Wade and Chico spread out a plastic drop cloth. "You see, what we are trying to do is we are trying to send you a message. And the message, quite simply is: *Don't ever fucking do this again.*

"I hope that was clear because each time we get together, we're gonna cut off one of your fingers, until you won't have any fingers left to fold into your slimy little fist. Then, if you still don't get it, we're gonna start on the other hand. Actually, I need to correct myself, we're gonna cut off two fingers today, one for beating up your wife this time and one that you owe us from the last time you were here when you talked us into giving you a pass, remember? That's fair, don't you think?"

Rocky noticed that Crowley had placed both of his tightly clenched fists onto the arms of his chair and was clearly planning to resist Rocky's plan with all of his energy. "There you go again, thinking you're smarter than us. How pathetic is that? He thinks he has outsmarted us again. Okay, fine. Allen, would you kindly hand me that hammer?" Crowley had failed to notice that there had been a hammer sitting next to the mirror on the orange crate. As Rocky lifted the hammer about shoulder high, he said, "It's your call, Professor Genius. Do you want me to break every bone and every joint in every one of your fingers before I cut two of them off or do you want to go back to 'plan A'?" Temporarily disregarding the overwhelming pain in his smashed face, Crowley reluctantly opened his left fist. "No, sorry, Doc, you're not getting off that easy. Open the other fist—you know, your 'wife beating' fist."

Crowley did as he was told. Then he turned his head and tightly closed his eyes, as if that would somehow make what was about to happen more bearable. Then a crunching sound was heard, and Crowley's ring finger and little finger on his right hand fell to the floor. Blood poured from his hand for quite a while, but the shrieking only lasted for a minute or so. At first, it seemed that Crowley might be starting to learn to live with intense pain, but later, they concluded, that he simply had become overwhelmed and exhausted from the experience.

Chico made a call on his cell and then concluded the meeting. "Here's a towel to wrap around your hand. Your driver will be here in a minute, and I'm sure it wouldn't be polite to make a mess in his vehicle, like the one we're gonna have to clean up after you leave. Now, in case it isn't clear, we really mean it when we say that you shouldn't hurt your wife anymore. Did you ever stop to think how special she is? She will *never* leave you even though you treat her the way you do. And, yet, it doesn't occur to you to appreciate her. Let me leave you with this thought: someone who would make you cry is not worth crying over, but someone who would *never* make you cry *is* worth crying over."

Callahan couldn't resist getting in the final word as the hood was being placed over Crowley's head. "You might want to have that face checked out. It doesn't look too good."

Chapter Thirty-Seven

Rushing to the Hospital

At 7:00 A.M. on Saturday morning, Wade was walking in the door after a four-mile run. He hadn't run in eight days, so he knew that a long run was out of the question. He was glad to have gotten back on the roads because running was not only a great way to stay fit, but it gave him some "alone time," where he could work on whatever problems or challenges he was facing. He knew that the crisis his son was facing was, by far, the worst he had ever endured.

Paula greeted him with some strange news. Julie had driven her home the previous evening, after five long days and nights at Rob's side. "Bosco has been acting really weird. He's never done this before. He keeps going over to Rob's room, and he's been making kind of a howling, or maybe more like a moaning sound. He doesn't seem to be hurt because it's not really a sound like he's in pain. I can't figure it out."

Wade was about to ask a question, but the phone stopped him. Paula answered, listened for a few seconds, and said, "Yes, we're leaving right now," and then she hung up. Wade knew from the alarming tone in her voice that there was no time for a shower, and they were both pulling out of the driveway within three minutes. Paula had been informed that Rob's vital signs were slipping and there was no time to waste.

When they got to the hospital, they didn't bother to park in the lot, which was one long block from the main entrance. They pulled right up to the door, parked in a NO PARKING zone and ran straight to Rob's room. They weren't prepared for what came next.

Rob was lying face up in his bed, as usual, but a woman in a light-blue uniform was standing next to him, and it looked like she was about to disconnect Rob's monitoring devices, when she heard Paula gasp. Startled and embarrassed, the woman exclaimed, *"Madre de Dios! Lo siento, lo siento!"* Then she ran from the room, bumping into two men just outside the door who were pushing a gurney.

Before either of Rob's parents could make any sense out of what was going on, a nurse walked into the room and spoke in a low, sympathetic voice. "I'm so sorry. The patient expired just a few minutes ago. We weren't sure when you'd be here. I'll ask the men to give you a couple of minutes. They're here to take Mr. Courtland down to the organ donor lab."

Wade and Paula walked slowly to Rob's bedside. He held Paula tightly for several minutes. Both were unable to speak for awhile. Finally, Paula bent down and cupped her son's face in her hands, and in a soft voice, overcome with anguish and grief, broke the silence. "Baby, baby, Mama wanted to be here for you. I'm so sorry. I didn't want you to leave us, not like this, not alone, not now. Oh, God…please…oh, no…this can't be…"

Wade, always in charge, always in command of even the most challenging circumstances, was totally helpless. He felt he needed to do something to make things better, but on this occasion, he was beaten. Time stood still, as the senior Courtlands looked at their beloved son through falling tears, his warm personality, friendly smile, and cheerful voice forever silenced.

Chapter Thirty-Eight

A Week from Hell

The next week in the lives of the surviving Courtland family members could best be described as a living hell. It had been decided that Rob's remains, after making a brief detour to the organ donor department at the hospital, would be cremated and that a memorial service would be held on Monday morning. The traditional funeral mass had been rejected in favor of a shorter, more intimate observance.

The work of The Payback Team was placed on indefinite suspension.

Paula and Wade struggled through the weekend in a semi-delirium and were unable to function in a helpful manner, so Rocky, Chico, and Julie took over. They spent all of Saturday and Sunday at the Courtland home, taking phone calls, answering the door, assisting with airport pickups for out of town friends and relatives, and transporting dozens of floral arrangements to the church.

On Monday morning, nearly every seat in the church was filled. The front row was reserved for immediate family and just a few very close friends. The thoughts of the occupants of this pew were focused on their overwhelming loss, as Father McCarty began the eulogy.

Paula kept repeating the same words, over and over. "My baby, my baby, Mama wanted to be there for you. Mama loved you so much. My baby, my baby, why did you leave us? Mama couldn't have loved you more. My baby, my baby, Mama will always love you."

Julie reminisced through a steady stream of tears. "Hey, Bro, you were the best. We weren't like a lot of brothers and sisters, we really got along great. You know what, Bro? I just realized something: I don't think we ever had an argument! Isn't that something? But I know it's not because of me, it's because you were always patient, kind, and loving, no matter how much I tried to get on your nerves. So that's why I finally quit trying and settled in to the great relationship that we had. Robby, I want to tell you something: I tried to be there for you, but I guess I blew it. I took Mom home, and then I spent the night at Mary Lee's. But you know what? I don't feel bad because I know you'd understand. That's just how you always were and I loved you for being that way. I guess I never really told you how much I loved having you for a brother and how much I loved and appreciated you. You know, speaking of appreciation, I really am grateful for how you always stuck up for me and protected me. Remember what you did to Tommy Ross? That little fucker really got to me. How could he do that…stood me up for my Junior Prom and took Sandy Peterson instead? Did you know Mom spent over two hundred bucks for my dress? Do you remember how I cried when I finally figured out that he wasn't coming to pick me up? And do you remember what you said? I do, in fact. I'll never forget it. You said, 'No one does that to my sister. I'll make him pay.' And boy, did you ever make him pay. You asked me what was the most important thing to him in the whole world and I told you it was his stupid vintage Buick that he had restored. And when I asked you what happened to it, you just smiled, remember? I remember I kept pressuring you to tell me how you got it to just disappear—boom—just like that! Nobody ever saw it again. And you finally said, 'Okay, I promise, I'll tell you—someday.' Well, now I guess I'll never know, but thanks, Bro, that was something I'll always love you for. Man, were you right when you said you'd make him pay. I guess that car meant more to him than anyone realized. What a pity. Remember what happened after he figured out that the car was probably gone for good? He punched out his science teacher when he got under his skin about not turning in an assignment. I can't believe how angry Tommy was after his car turned up missing. Can you imagine that? Kicked out of school and sent off to a private school out of state. I heard he also got into a lot of trouble there. Well, anyway, I'll always have the memories—our memories—and I promise I'll always keep you alive in my heart. Always."

Wade wiped away a constant flow of tears, impervious to the priest's words of comfort. He tried to think about all the joy that his firstborn, his only son, had brought him, and how he was as perfect a child as any parent could ever have hoped for. Never had he and Paula experienced the kind of sorrow and heartache that many parents often face—no conferences with the principal about discipline problems, no late-night calls from the police station asking them to come down and pick up their drunk and disorderly teenager; none of these things ever happened. Rob was a leader, one whom the other kids looked up to; the one who kept others from getting into trouble, and the first one to say, "No, we're not going to do that; it's wrong." But these thoughts were overshadowed by the fact that Rob was gone and he was never coming back. And Wade couldn't stop telling himself that he was responsible for his son's demise. Why did he let Rob get involved? Why hadn't he done a better job of making sure Rob got the hell out of that casino without stopping for anything? Would he ever get over blaming himself for what happened? And how could he deal with what he was going to miss for the rest of his life: the presence of his beloved son; the many enjoyable, shared activities that were never to be; the joy of attending his wedding; the pride he would feel while holding his first grandchild; and the pleasure of having a doting son caring for his elderly father upon reaching his declining years.

Rocky was also ignoring the reverend's words. He, of course, had the expected sad thoughts about the loss of his godson, but other, darker thoughts kept coming to the front of his mind. Why didn't he have the good sense to torture John V. in the warehouse, and then throw his broken, battered, bloody, barely alive body into the helicopter? Why didn't he spend more time with John V. in the chopper, dragging out the agonizing fact that he was eventually going to end up at the bottom of Lake Michigan? Why couldn't there be some way to go back in time and finish him off the first time they had him in the warehouse? Why didn't he see what John V. was capable of and made sure that Rob would never have been hurt?

Chico, unlike the others, was actually listening to what Reverend McCarty was saying. But his reaction was not at all what the priest would likely have expected. When he said something about Rob going to a better place, Chico thought, "Yeah, fine, asshole, but did he have to leave now? What the hell are you thinking? This kid was only twenty-one years old!" Then, when he made reference to God needing Rob in heaven, Chico wanted to ask, 'What about us? Don't we count? We needed him right here, with us, where he belonged.' But when the priest pointed his finger to the ceiling and said, "You know, Rob's an angel in heaven now, and I know he's looking down at all of us, grateful that we have come here to remember him this morning," Chico rolled his eyes. Father McCarty noticed this and assumed that Chico was looking respectfully up to heaven. Pleased that at least one of the bereaved congregants was buying all of this, he paused for a second and smiled at Chico. Without missing a beat, Chico put on his most beatific look and thought, "This stupid faggot doesn't have a fucking clue." Unfortunately, these thoughts were only a temporary diversion, and he quickly came back to reality when he glanced at a picture of Rob that had been placed next to the largest cluster of flowers. Then he lowered his head and lost it. He tried to grieve quietly, but the sobs were unmistakable. Christine's hand, placed firmly and sympathetically on his shoulder, helped, but only slightly.

Wade's parents, both in their eighties, along with his sister, had made the trip from Florida, and they were helped out of the church after the service by Wade's Aunt Mary. Their health was relatively sound, but the weight of their grief had temporarily taken its toll.

Paula's father was deceased, and her mother was terminally ill and was no longer struggling against the inevitable. It had been decided to let her depart as peacefully as possible without sharing the knowledge of what they were all going through.

When the memorial service ended, twenty family members and friends drove over to a nearby animal shelter where the director had set up a catered brunch. Rob had been a volunteer there for several years and had, in fact, adopted the family's golden retriever from the shelter during his first month. Rob had become the favorite of the staff, and his parents felt that this final tribute would have pleased him greatly, so they accepted the offer.

Chico and Rocky had little to say during the meal. They were deep into the grieving process, and they felt somewhat responsible for Wade's loss. Their eyes met just once, and after this brief contact, they gave a slight nod that only two people as close as they were could understand. It was a nod that said, "We'll get through this, and we are going to help our friend get through this also. Our Team may be down for now, but we'll be back."

Chapter Thirty-Nine

The Courtland's Try to Accept and Adjust

On Tuesday, the day after Rob's memorial service, Wade got a call from Rocky. "Hey, Spike, me and Chico just wanted to let you know that we're here for you, and we'll do whatever you want us to. You wanna get together for a couple of cold ones? Fine. You want to get in eighteen holes? We'll do it. You need us to send Angela and Christine over to talk to Paula? It's done. You want us to fuck off? Well, we can do that, too. Just name it."

Wade appreciated his friends' offer. "I knew you'd call and offer something like that. Just having you guys in our lives, and knowing how much you care for us and how much you loved Rob, means a lot to us. For now, I'm gonna decline. The three of us are going up to the cottage, and we're gonna stay there and catch our breath. Could be a week, could be more. Paula and I had a talk this morning. I was afraid that she blamed me for this whole thing, and she was worried that I would think it was her fault. But, we decided that it made no sense to blame anyone. We started with the right concept—to settle the score for the little guy, the guy who got screwed, but doesn't have the means to handle it by himself. And, you know what, that's still a worthwhile goal. But now is not the time for us to even think about it. You guys go ahead and do whatever, and I'll jump back in the loop later. Not sure when, but I'll be back.

"And here's the surprising thing: Paula's all for it. You know, she wanted me to tell her what the hell happened. When I explained why Rob ended up in the hospital, I thought for sure that she would pull the plug on my involvement with The Payback Team. But all she wanted to know was whether or not we took care of John V. Can you believe it? My gentle, sweet Paula wanted to make sure he got what he had coming! So, when I told her that you guys took care of it, I thought that would be the end of it. Not by a long shot. She had to know all the details. And when I told her, she didn't say a word for a full minute. She just nodded, closed her eyes, and pressed her lips together. It's like she was saying, 'job well done, thank you.' Then she told me that Rob would want me to continue, and she said she agreed. But she asked me to hold off for awhile. That's about as reasonable a request as I could imagine. And, you know, I feel the same way, but I just need a little time to get it together. So I'll be back. And I haven't forgotten about Guatemala. Maybe by the time I get back with the team, Chico will have gotten it all figured out about how we're gonna pull it off.

"Oh, and one more thing: I know you guys are gonna link up with Callahan and Major Robins and go after the guy who kidnaps girls and gets them into prostitution. Looks like you'll be doing that one without me. But fill me in on all the details later, okay?"

Later that morning, Rocky, Chico, and Sergeant Callahan met at the golf course. Rocky related his conversation with Wade, and all agreed that they needed a plan to take care of Reed Marshall, the pimp. That's the name that Callahan had given Rocky, so Rocky checked with his source at the witness protection program and found out all of the details. Callahan was dumbfounded that Rocky could get results so quickly. They now knew his assumed name and where he was living. He had moved to Kenosha, Wisconsin, just south of Milwaukee, and his new identity was that of Milo Aranson.

Chico said he would work on a plan and that Callahan would need to fill in for Wade. Callahan said that wouldn't be a problem, as he would be available indefinitely since he was using up vacation time until he officially retired in a few weeks. He did not try to hide his enthusiasm for the opportunity to join The Payback Team and reminded them that he had asked to be a part of the Guatemala project.

After about thirteen holes, Chico announced that he probably would not be able to come up with a workable plan until he had a chance to observe Aranson's residence firsthand. This was most likely where he was keeping anyone he may have taken off the street, which had been his habit previously. They couldn't just break into the house, like the bomb and arson squad, shouting, "Get on the floor, now!" How many people are in the house? How many of them have weapons? Is there a surveillance system? How many cameras? What about motion-sensor lighting? Are there any guard dogs? All of these questions needed answers because Aranson was not going to cooperate without a struggle, knowing that, this time, he would be sent away for the rest of his life.

But there was another obstacle that they had to get around. Rocky's contact in the witness protection program had extracted a promise from him, in exchange for providing the disclosure of Aranson's name and location. There was to be no embarrassment to the agency. That meant that Aranson and his accomplices, if any, had to be eliminated, and any captor, or captors, could not provide any information that would link Aranson to the witness protection program. All of this could not be accomplished without careful planning and execution.

When the match ended, Chico and Rocky were, surprisingly, on the losing end of the betting. Callahan had taken them for over two hundred bucks apiece. As they began reaching into their pockets, there was the expected amount of complaining about being cheated, about Callahan's overstating his handicap, and most of all, about having to adjust their budget, now that Wade was temporarily out of the picture.

Before they handed him the bills, Callahan made a proposal. "Tell you what. You guys can keep the cash, in exchange for telling me about those ridiculous names you have for each other. What's with this 'Chico' and 'Rocky' shit, and what about 'Spike'—what's up with that? You know, I don't want to take part in that bullshit; I'm always gonna call you guys Tommy and Michael, and Courtland will always be Courtland. But I am curious, so what's the deal?"

Chico and Rocky just laughed as they handed over the money. Rocky finally said, "Well, Sergeant, I guess you had to be there. It probably wouldn't make any sense to you anyway, even if we did explain it. But now it's our turn. How come you always call us by our first names, but, like you said, 'Courtland will always be Courtland.' Are you ever gonna call him Wade?"

Now, it was Callahan's turn to laugh. "That's a good question. You know, when I first met him, I didn't much like him. I saw him in the hospital, right after he got shot, and he was a real smart ass. He thought I believed his bullshit about not knowing anything about what happened. So calling him 'Courtland' was, initially, a sign of disrespect. But later on, when I got to know him and found out why he clammed up in the hospital, I changed my mind. Now, referring to him as 'Courtland' is something I do because no one else does—kind of like a special, personal thing that I've created, all on my own. I guess that sounds uncharacteristic, but that's the way it is. I'll even add that I mean it with affection when I say it, but, good God, don't ever tell him I said that." Then he laughed again, even louder than before. "Well," Callahan continued, "yeah, I guess I'll call him Wade, but not until my very last breath!" Then Rocky and Chico smiled as Callahan started his raucous laugh, the one where he ends up nearly choking himself.

Chapter Forty

First Trip to Kenosha

On the second day after the golf match ended, Chico and Rocky rented a Ford in Kenosha and headed over to Aranson's home. They wanted to use a vehicle with Wisconsin plates because they intended to park on the street a couple of doors away. They realized that two men sitting in a car would attract attention after awhile, and there was certainly no point in compounding the problem by using a car with plates from another state. Rocky had used his bogus identification to rent the car because this mission had "trouble" written all over it.

When they approached Aranson's home, they got a lucky break. The home was directly across from a city park, so they could park in the lot with several other cars, and it might appear that they were just two businessmen on a long break from work. Rocky had brought a camera and binoculars from one of his pawnshops, but they planned to minimize the use of these aids as much as possible. Additionally, they had directed Rocky's pilot friend to take a couple of photos of the home from a few hundred feet up, so that they could determine the layout of the backyard, as well as the rear entrance.

Rocky handed the binoculars to Chico and grabbed the camera and took a picture of the front of the house. After looking at the home through the binoculars for less than twenty seconds, Chico shook his head. "This is a really bad setup. This guy is definitely no amateur, and he is not going down easy. I don't want to spend all morning looking through these things, but I can tell you after just a few seconds that we're not gonna get in there without a plan. There are at least three surveillance cameras, two sets of motion-sensor lights, and it would probably take a cannon to get through that front door. The storm door has steel bars—you can see that without the binoculars, and the main door is solid steel, with one small pane of glass. I'll bet there are one or two guard dogs; the helicopter might pick up some evidence of that, once we blow up the pictures, and I wouldn't be surprised if there's some heavy muscle inside, most likely armed with who knows what—

shotguns? Assault rifles? Wouldn't surprise me a bit. So, we either find a way to bullshit our way in, or we wait till he comes out. But there are two problems with waiting: first, it could take days, and we can't sit here very long before someone blows the whistle, and second, I don't think he's gonna be alone when he does come out. Right now, I just really don't have a plan."

A few minutes later, Rocky was dialing his cell phone to find out if the pilot had taken off, when Chico startled him. "Wait a minute, wait a minute, what's this?" Rocky looked up and saw that he was staring intently across the park at a black limousine that had just pulled up in front of Aranson's home. Two well-dressed men got out of the back of the limo. The driver shut off the engine and waited in the limo. As they approached the entrance, Chico spoke again. "I've got it! I've got the plan. I know exactly what we're gonna do. I know what's happening here, and I'll bet you know what I'm thinking." Chico picked up the binoculars again. "Someone's gonna look out that glass in the door, then he's gonna let 'em in, and when they come out, we're gonna find out who they are and they're gonna tell us how they got in. We need to reposition, so we can get the license number of that limo, and then we can track 'em down later and find out what we need to know. It may take a little 'persuasion,' but I'm sure...wait a minute...what's happening here?"

Rocky and Chico watched intently as the limo started up and slowly backed into the driveway and parked with the rear door adjacent to the back entrance of the home. It looked like there was a high wooden fence and a gate about three or four feet from the limo. Chico called off the limo's Illinois plate numbers to Rocky and then put down the binoculars.

Rocky promptly phoned the major and asked him to run the plates. After he ended the call, he shook his head. "This is not good. We both know what's gonna happen next—and there's just the two of us. Do we want to go for it? What do you think?"

Chico responded, "Shit, you're right, this is bad. We can't get reinforcements up here in time. But I won't be able to live with myself if we don't at least try. But we should wait until they leave, then it will be us against three of them. We don't know how many are in the house. I don't know if this Ford can keep up, but if we have to, I'll crash into them before they can get out of city traffic, and we'll take it from there. If you've got a better idea, now's the time." He paused for a few seconds and then continued. "Listen, I just thought of something. You were about to call the pilot a minute ago. Go ahead and try him again. Hopefully, he's on his way over here. Tell him what's going on and let him know that we are probably going to need him to track the limo, like real soon."

After Rocky made the call to the pilot, they sat in uneasy silence for about ten minutes. Then Rocky's cell phone finally rang, and Major Robins provided the results they had asked for. The owner's name was Garret Lawson. But the major had gone a step further and researched the name on the internet. Garret Lawson was not the garden variety pedophile; he was an Illinois state senator. He was noted as "a distinguished, fifth-term republican senator, single, respected, and well liked by both his colleagues and his constituents."

Rocky related this information to Chico, who had just one comment. "This is gonna get interesting."

Another ten minutes passed, and then the limo started up again. Within a few seconds, the gate opened up until it nearly touched the limo. Chico announced what happened next, as he surveyed the scene with the binoculars. "One of the suits is opening the door...he's getting in...I can't see very well because there's only a couple of inches between the gate and the limo, but now I can tell a smaller person, must be a kid, is being pushed into the limo...now the other suit is getting in...no, wait...he's turning back...he's reaching out his hand...I think he's shaking someone's hand...I can't tell for sure...now he's in the limo...he closed the door. Let's go!"

In less than five seconds, Rocky was backing the Ford out of its parking spot, ready to start the chase. He was planning to stay close enough so that he wouldn't lose sight of the limo, but not close enough for the driver to know that someone was coming after him. Then, before he could get onto an interstate or major highway, he would try to pull the limo over without damaging either vehicle. This entire scenario involved a lot of chance, and it only took one slight miscalculation for the plan to go horribly wrong. But they both stayed intently focused on their immediate goal: they had to rescue whoever had been forced into the limo. They knew that the consequences would be catastrophic if they failed, and that a young life would, most likely, be irreparably damaged in ways they didn't want to think about.

It didn't take long for things to start going wrong. Rocky made his first mistake by getting a little too close to the limo, and he could see that the driver gave him an extra long glance in his side rearview mirror. They couldn't see what was going on inside the limo because the rear window was heavily tinted, but they made the assumption that the driver had informed his passengers that they were being followed.

Surprisingly, the limo made no attempt to speed up, and instead of heading for I-94, which would take them back to Illinois, the driver drove just under the speed limit on local streets, intentionally staying in a residential area, making lots of turns, but never speeding and never breaking any traffic laws. There was absolutely no way to get in front of the limo, since the streets were too narrow to pull alongside and force it off the road. After about ten minutes, Chico and Rocky began to debate whether they should just ram the limo from behind and hope that they could disable it in some way. But that was not to be.

The limo came to a halt at a stop sign, and strangely, sat there without pulling forward. Rocky and Chico tried to determine the best course of action. If they got out of their vehicle, the limo would no doubt pull away, and that would be the end of the chase. Since they were stopped directly behind the limo, they could not ram it hard enough to do any serious damage, and if they tried to back up far enough to get the needed momentum, the limo would be a block away before they could start their approach.

But then the situation took a strange turn. The left rear door of the limo opened, and a large, well-dressed man got out and began walking toward the Ford. As he approached, he opened the left side of his suit jacket and revealed what was clearly a shoulder holster. Rocky opened the console in the middle of the front seat and removed a Smith and Wesson .38 caliber he had placed there earlier that morning, and Chico reached into the glove compartment and retrieved his weapon. Without a word, both men reached for their door handles, preparing to step out of the Ford and start firing. They weren't going to engage in a question-and-answer session; they were going to put down this guy, who was most likely the senator/pedophile's bodyguard, and once he was out of the way, they would have a clear shot at rescuing the kid and exposing the senator for what he was. From that point on, anyone who googled him would not see the words "distinguished" or "respected."

Their doors opened, but before their feet touched the ground, a loud, sharp voice from behind ordered, "Do not get out of the vehicle. Put down your weapons. Raise your hands and place them outside the vehicle. I repeat, do not get out of the vehicle. We will apply lethal force if you do not comply."

Rocky looked in the rearview mirror and saw two uniformed policemen, both aiming shotguns at the Ford. He looked over at Chico and started to apologize for not seeing the squad car before it pulled up right behind them, which he knew was the second huge mistake on his part. Chico read the look and said, "Listen, man, it's not your fault. This is what can happen when we have to resort to 'planning on the go.'"

After being handcuffed and placed in a paddy wagon, which arrived within a few minutes, they were taken to the police station. They assumed that they would be charged with some relatively minor traffic offense and that they would post a minimal bond and then head for home. They might have a problem with the fact that they were carrying unregistered weapons, but since their identification papers could not be linked to either of them, they weren't really too worried. This underestimation turned out to be yet another in a series of mistakes.

Chapter Forty-One

Jail Time in Kenosha

Rocky and Chico were surprised to see the limo following the patrol wagon and the squad car. They weren't sure what their point was in going to the police station, but a good guess would be that they wanted to use their clout to make sure that the maximum charges were levied against their former pursuers. If Chico and Rocky became embroiled in serious legal issues, their credibility would be diminished, and it was, therefore, less likely that the true details of the situation would come to light.

Chico had an idea. "Rocky, I'm pretty sure I can grab your cell phone if you'll turn more to your right. Then I'll hand it to you and you can try to figure out how to call the major—I hope you have him on speed dial. When it rings, set the phone down right here on the seat. Then I'm going to try to bend down to the phone and talk to him. We've got to make sure he gets that kid before it's too late."

Fortunately, they were able to complete this series of maneuvers without too much difficulty, and Major Robins picked up on the second ring. "Hello, Major, this is Tommy Martin. Michael and I are in a patrol wagon heading for the Kenosha police station. We were stopped while we were following the guy Michael called you about, you know, Senator Lawson. They've got a kid with them, and they're in a black limousine. Call the private airport where Michael's pilot friend keeps his plane and find out how to get in touch with him, and then tell him to locate the limo at the police station. He was on his way to track the limo when we lost contact with him, so he can't be too far away.

"You're gonna need about three or four of your crew to try to link up with the limo once the chopper starts tailing it. The senator has a bodyguard with him, and he's carrying. They're probably going to drive to the senator's residence; I assume you got that address when you traced the license plate, but we don't know that they will be headed there for sure. Send the girl back to her parents; actually, it could even be a boy, we weren't able to tell. Keep the other three, that's the driver, the bodyguard, and the senator on ice until we get ourselves bailed out. Could take until tomorrow, but there's no way to tell. You can call Sergeant Callahan; he'll know where to stash them until we can meet everyone at the warehouse.

"One more thing: call our attorney, Jerome Leavitt in Wheaton, and tell him to get up here ASAP. And ask him to bring as much cash as he can get together. Oh, and tell him to bring a bail bondsman with him. I've got a hunch this won't be cheap. Let him know that my name is Mark Miller, and that I am with Stanley Morrison, so that he will know who to ask for when he gets there.

"Well, that's about it. Unfortunately, you won't be able to contact us because they're gonna grab everything we own, once we get to the station. Thanks and good luck. Oh, and another thing: we appreciate everything you've done for us. I hope this one goes well. See you soon, I hope."

When they got to the police station, things went as expected. All of their belongings were put in an envelope, and they sat around for over an hour while the two policemen, their captain, and the bodyguard debated about the nature of the charges to be brought against them. While his employer, the driver, and the kid waited in the limo, the bodyguard pointed out that the senator was on official business at the time of the pursuit, and that his pursuers had intended to kill him before he could carry out some political plans that were contrary to their interests. The bodyguard's argument was that this was clearly a case of attempted assassination.

One cop seemed to go along with everything that the bodyguard brought up and he seemed impressed that he was dealing with a case that involved an Illinois state senator. He simply could not imagine the possibility that the senator could be anything but an innocent victim of some sinister political plot. The other cop appeared to have a lot more common sense and felt that the situation should be looked at more objectively, and that the stature of any of the individuals should not enter into the decision about the charges. Finally, the captain dismissed the idea about charging them with trying to assassinate the senator because there simply were not enough facts to support this argument.

The captain pointed out that the charges needed to have a reasonable chance of being believed by a jury; otherwise, the department, as well as the prosecuting attorney's department, would look foolish. The likelihood of a conviction had to be considered.

Finally, charges of aggravated assault, along with a weapons violation, were agreed upon by the captain and one policeman, Officer Monroe. The other cop pointed out that he had observed that the bodyguard had shown his weapon first. After he realized that he was fighting a losing battle, he walked away in disgust.

After the fingerprinting ritual, they were led off to the lockup. But the bodyguard wasn't finished with them yet. He asked Officer Monroe for a favor and he was only too happy to accommodate. So instead of going to the lockup, Chico and Rocky were again handcuffed and taken to an interrogation room. Once the door was closed, the officer got a worried look on his face. "Make this really quick, okay? I'm not supposed to do this, you know. If it weren't for the fact that it's a state senator, I wouldn't even—"

Before he could finish his sentence, the bodyguard grabbed Officer Monroe's night stick and jammed it into Rocky's left side, breaking a rib in the process. Next, he headed for Chico, who made his best effort to get out of the way, but there was no place to go. The blow caught him on the back of his head, knocking him to his knees. The bodyguard's face showed a contorted snarl, and his eyes were filled with hatred and contempt. "Don't you ever even think of fucking with the senator again. This is just a sample of what I'm capable of, got it?"

Officer Monroe laughed. "You know, I think he means it. Ha, ha. But listen, we gotta get outta here. Okay, you two assholes, let's go."

Rocky was able to get in a few words before they were taken to their cell. "You know, we'll meet again, sooner than you think, and I won't be wearing these handcuffs. I advise you to be very concerned. And as for you, Officer Monroe, this has been an interesting experience in how you administer justice in Kenosha. I promise you, I won't forget. The day will come when I will show you *my* kind of justice."

Both men laughed derisively, as they led Chico and Rocky to the lockup. Officer Monroe was about to place them in an empty holding pen when the bodyguard noticed that the cell directly across contained three men in their early twenties, who could only be described as typical gangbangers. The bodyguard whispered something in the cop's ear and then walked over to the gangbangers' cell. In a voice loud enough for everyone to hear, he said, "These assholes are going to keep you guys company for awhile. In case you don't know who they are, I'll explain. They're accused of raping and killing that girl from Racine who was found last week, you know, Shamiqua Rogers. But you'll only have a few hours to get acquainted because there's a bond hearing at three o'clock. Well, I guess that's it. Everyone try to get along now, okay?"

Officer Monroe gave a look of approval at the bodyguard's quick thinking as he placed his captives in the gangbangers' cell and removed their handcuffs. After he closed the door, they enjoyed a good laugh as they left the lockup area.

Rocky and Chico looked at each other and shook their heads. After forty years of close friendship, they each knew exactly what the other was thinking without having to say a word. They were both angry with themselves for committing the mistakes that had gotten them into their present situation. Also, they couldn't help but see the irony in the fact that things kept getting worse as time passed. Just when they thought that they would be able to stretch out and rest and try to start recovering from the blows they had received, this new complication was imposed upon them.

But, strangely, they weren't at all worried about their personal safety. With Rocky's size and strength, and given the fact that they were both knowledgeable and experienced in martial arts, their only concern was either seriously injuring, or possibly killing, one or more of their cellmates. If that were to happen, the chances were good that their attorney would have a difficult time getting the judge to set bail. This was going to be an interesting challenge.

They decided to take the approach of ignoring the gangbangers, so as not to provoke them. But this turned out to be another failed plan. Chico made the mistake of making eye contact with one of them, and that was exactly what he was waiting for. "What you lookin' at, white man?" Chico rolled his eyes, as if to say, "Shit, now it's starting." But he was careful not to respond since there was nothing he could say that would not further antagonize his aggressor. The gangbanger continued to escalate the situation. He stood up and walked halfway over to Chico. "I said, 'what you lookin' at, white man?'" Rocky had been pretending to ignore what was going on, at least that was the impression he was trying to give, but he remained on high alert. It looked like the big man was going to have to move into high gear with very little notice.

Chico decided that he had to say something and he hoped it would be sufficient to diffuse the situation. In the back of his mind, of course, he realized that this was probably impossible. "Well, I'll tell you what; you know, when I would get myself into an impossible situation, my mother would say, 'Junior, this time I think you've bitten off more than you can chew.' Did your mother ever tell you that?"

The gangbanger was temporarily perplexed. "What the fuck you talkin' 'bout? You fuckin' with me, ain'tcha?"

Chico was getting angry and impatient. His head hurt, he was pissed at how things had turned out, and he was very concerned about the little girl or boy whose life was possibly about to be destroyed by Senator Lawson. Sensing the inevitable, he tried one last time, although he was unable to keep the irritation out of his voice. "Well, what I'm trying to say is, you should probably go over and sit back down with your little gangster wannabe buddies and mind your own fucking business."

Immediately, a smile came over the gangbanger's face. It was a smile that said, "Okay, white man, that's all I need." He looked at his two friends and gave a nod. The nod was a signal to go into action and take out the smart ass white man. But it was not going to happen. Rocky had been intently observing, waiting to move in, if and when necessary. These three gangbangers had never seen anyone, black or white, male or female, move as fast as Rocky did. He was standing in front of the two who had been seated before they were able to stand up completely. Immediately, he put one hand on each of their necks and pushed their heads against the wall. The encounter with the wall stunned them, but they were unable to fall back into sitting position because Rocky had a strong grip on their throats and was pressing them tightly against the wall. They both clawed desperately at Rocky's huge, powerful arms, but they were no match for his size and incredible strength.

It was clear to the gangbanger standing in front of Chico that he was not about to get any help from his companions. He wasn't quite sure what he was going to do next, so Chico made his move. He grabbed his right arm, spun him around and put him in a painful hammerlock. He wrapped his left arm around the gangbanger's throat, nearly cutting off his air supply. "This is your lucky day, you little piece of shit. And would you like to know why it's your lucky day?" The gangbanger was unable to respond, prevented by pain and fear, as well as the fact that Chico had a vice-like grip on his throat. "Why don't you answer? I said, 'would you like to know why it's your lucky day'?" The gangbanger was finally able to get out something that sounded like "glmph" and Chico decided that it was meant to be "yes."

Chico continued, "It's because we're gonna be in a lot of trouble if we hurt your sorry little asses. But I'll tell you what. How would you like it if we check the court records and find out where you live and arrange for a little meeting after we all get out of here? How would you like that?" This time, the gangbanger's response sounded more like "nulck." Chico continued. "Well, I think that was a 'no.' But if you change your mind, we'll be glad to make the trip any time. Oh, and by the way, we don't know any Shamiqua Rogers. That jagoff made it up just to get you agitated, but you were too fucking stupid to realize it. So, okay then, now that that's settled, how about if we all just sit back down and try to enjoy the rest of the day?"

Chapter Forty-Two

Getting Out of Jail

The five cellmates spent the next four hours in an uncomfortable silence. Rocky and Chico, for the most part, tried to rest. They were tired and in pain. Occasionally, one of the gangbangers would make eye contact with one of them, but then they would quickly look away, not wanting to anger either of them any further.

Promptly at three o'clock, they were all called to the bond hearing. The gangbangers, predictably, were charged with selling illegal drugs and were each released on five-thousand dollar bond. The hearing took less than thirty seconds. However, in Rocky and Chico's case, it was not nearly as simple. It was immediately clear that someone had gotten through to the district attorney. He argued vigorously for a bond of one million dollars. He claimed that it was the intention of the defendants to assassinate the senator and spent several minutes talking about the potential risk that the defendants would not appear for trial.

Jerome Leavitt, their attorney, proved that he was worth the four hundred dollars per hour that he charged. His arguments were eloquent and persuasive. The judge finally agreed that there was no evidence indicating that they were planning to terminate any of the occupants of the limo, but he decided that the matter of aggravated assault, as well as the weapons violation issue, should be put before the jury. Bond was set at fifty thousand dollars for each of them. There was no need for the services of the bail bondsman as the attorney had brought ample funds to cover the ten percent cash payment that was required. The balance would, of course, be forfeited if they failed to appear at the next hearing, which was scheduled to be in three weeks. This was of no consequence to either of them, since Mark Miller and Stanley Morrison would cease to exist the moment they walked out of the building.

The attorney drove his two clients to the lot where their car had been impounded. During most of the trip, Rocky and Chico were on their cell phones, trying to find a way to turn things around in their favor. They had gone on a fact-finding mission, hoping to determine how they could wipe out a hardened criminal who was ruining the lives of numerous families, and who would continue to do so until someone could stop him. But things did not turn out well for them. Rocky probably needed to go to the hospital, and Chico wondered when the worst headache he had ever had was going to subside. Fortunately, none of their injuries was life threatening.

While speaking with the major, Rocky determined that he had learned from the pilot that the limo was headed for the senator's home in Inverness. He and three of his crew went to the senator's residence and waited for them until they arrived. They had no problem putting the driver, the senator, and the bodyguard in handcuffs and into their van. The person they had kidnapped was a boy of nine, who told them that he lived in Carol Stream. He had gone to the mall with a friend and the friend's mother and was snatched when they were briefly separated. Someone had placed a cloth over his nose and mouth that had a strange odor, and after that he didn't remember anything until he realized he had been placed in the back of a really big car that had very dark windows. One of Major Robins's men drove the young boy home and delivered him to his relieved and grateful parents.

The remaining three occupants of the limo were then blindfolded and taken to a location where Sergeant Callahan was waiting. They were in a holding pattern until they received instructions from Rocky or Chico. Rocky told them to go directly to the warehouse, and that they would meet them there shortly afterward. Before he hung up, he got the name and phone number of the boy's parents.

Chico's first call was to the pilot. He wanted to know if he had a chance to get a look at Aranson's home from the air. The pilot reported that he had flown over the house on his way back to Milwaukee after having followed the limo to Inverness. He informed Chico that there were two Dobermans in the rear yard.

Rocky placed another call to Sergeant Callahan and reminded him to bring his little black bag to the warehouse. While Rocky was talking to Callahan, Chico phoned the boy's home and talked to his father. "Hello, Mr. Parker, my name is Roland Carter. I apologize that I am unable to talk to you in person, but I am on my way to confront the man who had purchased Jimmy from the man who kidnapped him from the mall. You might be surprised to learn that he is a state senator, Senator Garrett Lawson. I know this because my colleague and I were responsible for rescuing Jimmy a few hours ago. This is why I'm calling: there is a good chance we are going to need your help in putting the senator away for a long time and I need your assurance that you and Jimmy will cooperate with us. We might get him to voluntarily plead guilty without a trial and I want to use you as leverage to accomplish this. If he knows that you will let Jimmy testify, I might be able to get him to just give it up.

"You see, we intend to go after the people who took your son from the mall, but we need a lot of information from the senator to accomplish this, and as I pointed out, we are on our way to confront him now. I hope my request is clear and I hope you will help us."

Chico was somewhat surprised when Mr. Parker not only agreed, but insisted on being allowed to attend the meeting. He had a difficult time convincing him that this would not be appropriate, but finally succeeded.

"Mr. Parker, I have one more important request. In a couple of days, maybe even tomorrow, we're going to need your permission to talk with Jimmy. We need to know details about the inside of the home where he was kept. You see, we are pretty certain that Jimmy was not the only child being kept in that home. We want to ask him how many others were with him, where in the home they are kept, and how many adults he thinks are in the home. The more information we get, the less likely it is that one of us will be killed."

Mr. Parker ended the call by saying that he and his son would do whatever it would take to put these criminals where they belonged. He made one final plea to be included in the trip to Kenosha, but again, Chico had to politely decline. Before he hung up, Chico thanked him for agreeing to cooperate and assured him that they would meet face to face within a day or two.

Chico placed his final call to Major Robins. After a quick greeting, he got right to the point. "Can you do something for me? Check on an Officer Monroe with the Kenosha police department. Find out anything you can. Where does he go to church? What kind of car does he drive? What's the license number? Where does he live? Where does he hang out? I'm gonna cook up a little surprise for him, but I'm not sure how I'm gonna go about it, so I'll need a little help. Let me know. Thanks."

Attorney Leavitt tried his best to find out why his clients were using names that he was unfamiliar with, but it was totally impossible to break through Rocky's and Chico's intense concentration on getting their mission headed in the right direction. As he dropped them off at the impound lot, they assured him that they would explain everything when they could get around to it. For now, they had much more important things on their agenda. Leavitt argued that he needed a lot more information so that he could properly prepare for future hearings, and eventually, a trial that could possibly result in jail time. He was totally unprepared for Chico's response: "Jerome, don't worry about it. The case ended when we walked out of the courthouse. It's over. Send us a bill and thanks for everything."

Chapter Forty-Three

Meeting the Senator at the Warehouse

When they walked into the warehouse, Rocky and Chico saw that all of the people they hoped would be there were seated around the large, round coffee table. The three occupants of the limo were handcuffed and seated on the sofa, and Callahan, the major, and three of his associates were also seated and waiting for the meeting to begin. Callahan's little black bag was lying on the middle of the coffee table.

It would be a gross understatement to say that the three captives were surprised to see Rocky and Chico. Rocky was the first to break the silence. "Well, Mr. Bodyguard, looks like my prediction was right on. We did wind up meeting again, and like I said, it was sooner than you expected. And guess what? Another of my predictions came true, I'm not wearing handcuffs this time. Don't you find it interesting that I'm able to make three predictions like that and they are all right on the money? Meeting again, soon, and no handcuffs—how about that? Well, I have another prediction, but I'm pretty sure you're not going to like it. My prediction? Okay, here it is: I predict that your miserable, no good, perverted life is going to end before the hour is up." Rocky looked at his watch. "Oops, looks like you've got less than twenty minutes left. Hey, I've been right with all of my predictions so far, what do you think about this one? Well, I'll tell you what, why don't you take a few minutes to think it over because I know my colleague here has something to say to the senator and Mr. Limo Driver. So, I would like to yield the floor to my distinguished associate."

"Thank you very much," said Chico graciously. "And now, if my distinguished colleague would kindly take his seat, there are a few things I've chosen for discussion at our meeting this afternoon." He motioned for Rocky to sit down and then began his soliloquy again, pausing and gesturing as if he were delivering an address on the senate floor. "Normally, I would begin by welcoming you to our assemblage, but that is no doubt inappropriate, inasmuch as you have not made your appearance voluntarily. Be that as it may, I wish to bring to your attention the fact that I have known my colleague for more than forty years, and it has been my observation that his predictions are, without exception, shall we say, right on. That being the case, Mr. Bodyguard, I urge you to heed his previous advice, that being that you should be very concerned.

"And now, I would like to address the former distinguished and respected senator from Inverness. I say 'former,' due to the fact that these attributes are no longer fitting, now that he has been exposed as a pedophile, a person engaged in human trafficking and, quite likely, a murderer. Well, we can, of course, prove the first two accusations, but it is a logical conclusion that he is also guilty of the third. I ask you, Senator Pervert, what do you do with your prey once they are no longer nubile young lads? Do you return them to their parents with a warm thank you? I think not. Do you send them off to boarding school with an admonition not to make any embarrassing disclosures? Again, I think not.

"And that, Mr. Limo Driver, is where you come in. Mr. Bodyguard will, of course, be departing very soon, so it is my considered proposal that you cooperate with the authorities and let it be known where the bodies are buried, if you'll pardon the pun. You don't have to respond just yet, but perhaps, as you observe the events that are about to unfold, you may become convinced that the suggestion is a most sound one, indeed.

"Once more, if I may, I would like to return to Senator Predator. May I be so bold as to recommend that you agree to make a full confession? What a grand idea that would be! Not only would you avoid a most protracted legal debacle, but you would, most likely, receive a somewhat less severe sentence, perhaps something like forty years with the possibility of parole, versus life with no parole. Oh, yes, Senator Pedophile, one more thing. We respectfully request that you cooperate with us fully in helping us to enter Mr. Aranson's home. We wish to have a little meeting with him also, much like the present one, you know, where one or more of the attendees are allowed just a few final, fleeting moments of existence.

"Oh, wait, there's more, I nearly overlooked something important. Two quite nasty occurrences will take place if you choose not to cooperate with these most reasonable requests.

"Uh, oh, I just looked at the time. I've let myself ramble on a little too long, perhaps not unlike some of your appearances at the podium on the senate floor. The twenty minutes referred to earlier have nearly expired. So, at this time, without further ado, I'd like to turn the floor back over to my esteemed associate."

Chico sat down and Rocky stood up and began speaking as if he were giving an important address to a large body of legislators. "Well, I do thank you for yielding the floor so graciously, and by the way, that was a most moving speech. I'm sure it could only be rivaled by some of the stirring addresses that Senator Deviant has made in the past. But now, let's get down to the business at hand, the final departure of Mr. Bodyguard."

For the first time since Chico and Rocky entered the warehouse, someone else spoke. The bodyguard stood up, shot a menacing look at Rocky, and said, "Why don't you go ahead and take these cuffs off? Let's see if you've got the balls to face me one on one."

Rocky responded, "You know, I don't remember that you took my cuffs off before you broke my rib. But you know what? I think I'd like that. Sarge, take him over there, away from the table and chairs, and remove the cuffs." All three men promptly began walking over to an open area of the warehouse about twenty feet away. But Rocky made his third error of the day when he assumed that the bodyguard would wait while Callahan removed the cuffs from both hands. As soon as one handcuff was released, he spun and landed a vicious roundhouse punch, catching Rocky square in the jaw, most likely breaking it in the process. Rocky was knocked off balance, stumbled several steps backward, and fell to the cement floor.

Callahan saw the bodyguard running toward Rocky. He drew his gun and was about to put an end to the match, but to everyone's surprise, Rocky made one of his catlike movements and jumped to his feet in no time. He stepped out of the way and grabbed his assailant as his momentum carried him right through the spot where Rocky had briefly been standing. He used the man's forward motion to work in his favor as he held him by the neck and jerked him violently to the side. A loud, snapping sound, which Chico would later describe as being similar to when his daughter cracked her gum, made it clear to all that Rocky had fulfilled his prediction.

But, unfortunately, the bodyguard's sudden demise did not occur without a price. He dropped the lifeless bodyguard, but then he doubled over on his knees on the floor next to the deceased bodyguard. Chico knew instantly that something was radically wrong. He rushed over to his fallen comrade, at first thinking he was having a heart attack. *"Michael, what's wrong? Talk to me!"*

Callahan and the major rushed over and kneeled by Rocky's side. The huge man was having trouble breathing and could not speak clearly. He had just received a damaging blow, had taken a man nearly his size, and spun him in the air. And it looked like it was too much for him. "I shouldn't have done it. I'm so sorry I did it. What the hell was I thinking?"

All three men tried to help him to his feet, but he waved them away. Callahan asked, "Is it your jaw?"

Major Robins wanted to know if he was having a heart attack. "Do you need me to do CPR?"

Finally, Rocky gave an explanation. "It's my rib. I'm pretty sure I've punctured a lung. I'm gonna need to get to a hospital. But, listen, help me get back over to a chair. Just let me sit for a minute and see if it's gonna get any better. It's hard to breathe, but I really don't want to miss anything. This is really important. But, please, go slow."

The major's very well-trained accomplices were keeping an eye on the senator and his driver, as it would have been a good time for them to try to get away. Rocky was helped back to his chair and Chico tried to pick up where he had left off. "I'm through with my speech. Hopefully, you were listening, and hopefully, you've gotten the idea that if we say something, we mean it. And, Senator Demented, just in case you missed the sarcasm, let me clearly state that we hold you in such contempt that it's really not possible to describe. Anyone who does what you do to little children is despicable. My urge is to kill you where you sit, but frankly, we need you. Remember when I said that two unpleasant events are going to occur if you don't cooperate with us? Well, now's the time for you to decide. Sergeant, if you will." Right after he finished speaking, Sergeant Callahan stood up and faced the senator. Chico spoke again. "Now, Senator, the next words out of your mouth are going to determine your immediate future. All I want to hear is that you intend to cooperate fully with us and that you plan to confess everything and ask for mercy. Anything else just won't cut it."

For the first time, Senator Lawson spoke, but unfortunately, he chose the wrong words. "I know you probably think you can intimidate me. I'm an Illinois senator, and I've got contacts who can—"

He was interrupted by an extremely loud bang that was greatly magnified as the sound reverberated off the cinderblock walls and concrete floor. Sergeant Callahan had pulled out the gun that he had taken from the bodyguard earlier in the afternoon and promptly shot the senator in the right knee. No one came to his aid as he screamed in agony. With a shattered knee cap, a hole in the back of his leg, and a pool of blood beginning to form on the plastic drop cloth that had been placed under the sofa, the senator cried out for someone to get him to a hospital.

Chico responded. "Well, that seems like a fair request, but you still haven't given us what we've asked for. You know, it seemed like such a reasonable request, your life in exchange for a guilty plea and some information. For a senator, you're really stupid. Look at the mess you've gotten yourself into, and for what purpose? There's really no way out of this except to cooperate. Listen, the little boy you bought, his name is Jimmy Parker. I've already talked to his father, and he wants the boy to testify against you. And guess what? I've got a feeling, just by looking at Mr. Limo Driver, that he will also be very cooperative in helping us put you away."

While it looked like the senator was starting to get used to living with intense pain, Rocky was not doing well at all. Chico saw him start to lean over in his chair and it looked like he was going to pass out. "Major, can you have one of your associates take my friend to the hospital? It really was a bad idea not to take him there right away. He needs medical assistance, like right now."

Without saying a word, one man got up and started helping Rocky to his feet, but this did not occur without a lot of obvious, severe pain. Chico wished that he could accompany his friend, but that was not possible at the moment.

Chico turned back to the senator and his driver. He noticed a horrified look on the driver's face, so he decided it was time to put him to the test. "How about it, pal, after all that you've seen this afternoon, do you want to help us put the senator away? As a minimum, you're guilty of being an accessory, but my guess is that there's a lot more to it than that. So it probably comes down to a long prison sentence, or maybe only five or ten years if you help us put him away. So what's it gonna be?"

Before he could answer, the senator, in spite of his pain, gave a look that said, "If you do what he's asking, you'll wish you hadn't."

Chico caught the look and decided he'd had enough. "Okay, that did it. Remember, you stupid, perverted son of a bitch, I mentioned two events that you are not gonna like. It's time for number two." Callahan promptly opened the black bag on the coffee table and let the contents fall in the middle. As everyone gazed at the contents, Callahan picked up a blindfold and placed it over the senator's head. Then he waited for a couple of minutes, hoping that the suspense of waiting and wondering what was going to happen to him might prove to be an effective form of torture in itself. Finally, he picked up the pliers and walked very quietly over to where the senator was sitting. Without a sound, he squeezed the pliers around his lower lip, and pulled it down toward his chin.

Judging by the screams, it was impossible to tell which was more extreme, the pain from the senator's lip or from his leg. While Callahan held the pliers, Chico made the senator an offer. "Tell you what: we can go on like this indefinitely. In fact, there are five of us— we can take shifts. Or would you just want to do the smart thing? If you think about it, you're going to give in eventually, why not save some time and some aggravation? If you're ready to see things our way, just nod your head, okay?" Finally, the senator nodded, more in relief than defeat. Callahan put down the pliers and removed the blindfold.

Chico looked at the driver. "Well, Mr. Limo Driver, do you want to see things our way, or do you want us to show you how some of these other little gadgets work?" The driver looked at the senator to see if he approved. It was clear that he was doing his best to remain loyal to his employer under increasingly more difficult circumstances. "Actually, there's not a lot you can do for us right now, other than fill us in on some of the details that the senator might have forgotten. Later on, your best bet will be to turn evidence against him in exchange for a reduced sentence. And here's something I want you both to know. Your lives will be dependent on our receiving correct information from you about getting into Aranson's home and rescuing whoever is in there. There are more people on our team than you have met today. If things aren't as you say they are, they will find you and you will be tortured until you die.

"One of our associates is a doctor, a specialist, if you will, and he is an expert in prolonging life beyond your wildest expectations. He will go out of his way to make sure that you don't make an early departure from the suffering we will administer. Please think about this very carefully before you start answering our questions. And don't even bother to ask to be taken to the hospital about your little knee problem. We'll take you when we're ready. Now, let's get started."

Chapter Forty-Four

Preparing for another Trip to Kenosha

Chico spent the next hour learning as much as he could about the Aranson operation. This dangerous sociopath had to be stopped and lives had to be rescued. Every day that went by was another day that some innocent child could be sold to a predator like the senator. If that happened, it was unlikely that anything could be done to prevent a life, and a family, from being ruined.

The senator and his driver were being totally cooperative because they realized that they had no choice. Lawson knew that his career was over and that his reputation was ruined. It was clear to him that he had very limited options. He could simply admit his mistakes and try to blame his actions on alcoholism. He had seen that this defense had been somewhat helpful to certain celebrities, and he hoped that this tactic might gain him some small degree of sympathy from his former constituents, and hopefully, the judge, when it came time for sentencing. The only other option that came to his mind to avoid facing the humiliation, as well as a long prison sentence, was ending his life. Although he was doing his best to cooperate, he stopped every five minutes and asked to be taken to the hospital. The bleeding had subsided, but the pain continued to be nearly unbearable.

Finally, Chico had learned just about all he needed to know and was already devising a plan for accomplishing The Payback Team's goal. When he thought about their goal, he realized that the participants would not be the ones he was originally planning on. Wade was sidelined for awhile, dealing with the emotional aftermath of the loss of his son, and it was likely that Rocky was also going to be out of commission, due to his physical injuries. Chico was not feeling totally up to par himself, but the knock on his head he had taken earlier in the day was something he felt he could deal with.

So he decided to wrap things up. "Well, okay, I guess that's about it. I certainly hope everything you told me is one hundred percent accurate. If not, what you've experienced today will be nothing in comparison to what you can expect in the future, but I think I made that clear earlier. We'll take you to the hospital shortly, but first we have to take care of a couple of details." Then he turned to the major and the two remaining members of his crew. "Guys, if you would, please use the drop cloth under the sofa to wrap up our bodyguard friend. And, Sarge, if you don't mind, find a place to stash him for a few days until I find out some information from the major about a certain policeman acquaintance of mine, named Officer Monroe. He's going to meet the bodyguard again soon, but not exactly in the way he expects.

"Okay, I guess that's about it. Senator, in a couple of days, I want you to set up a press conference. At that time, you can make your confession. I'll ask the sergeant to coordinate with you, so that he can have law enforcement present in order to take you and your driver into custody. I will also make the offer for Jimmy Parker and his parents to be present to hear what you have to say and, of course, to have the satisfaction of seeing you and your driver being led away in handcuffs.

"You know, I'd really like to set this up immediately, but there's a problem related to timing, and it's really a catch-22. As soon as your confession becomes public knowledge, there's a good chance that Aranson will put his operation on hold while he relocates to who knows where, and then our opportunity is lost for awhile. And what about the kids he has with him? No, we have to wait until after we cancel his ticket. But on the other hand, Senator, you're gonna be out of our control for a little while. I guess you could warn Aranson, but that's probably not a good idea because I don't see how that would be of much benefit to you. And, also, you know what will happen to you if you try anything like that.

"Well, anyway, I'm gonna review my notes on our little conversation, and I should be ready within a couple of days to head back up to Kenosha and finish what we started. That's it. Let's head to the hospital. I'm anxious to see what's happening with my colleague. Sarge, I don't have a car, can I ride with you? And afterward, I'd like to stop over at the Parker residence and see what information Jimmy can provide."

The ride to Holy Family Hospital took about twenty minutes. During that time, Chico outlined the plan he had come up with in order to get Sergeant Callahan's opinion. He had come to respect and trust the sergeant completely and certainly admired his effectiveness in working with The Payback Team.

Chico had learned that Aranson could only be reached, initially, by contacting his Web site. Not much could be learned from connecting to the site for the first time, but it invited the viewer to look further if he was "interested in a wild, exotic, adventure that will provide pleasure far greater than anything previously experienced." But the only way to get beyond this point was by logging in with a user name and password. It just wasn't possible for anyone to see what was really being offered without having this knowledge. Apparently, the recommendation of "satisfied, trusted customers" was the only way to find out more. And it also appeared to be a somewhat safe way for Aranson to do business. Chico couldn't wait to get on the internet and try to communicate with Aranson using the information supplied by the senator.

However, there was a complication. The senator had said that it took about a week of back and forth e-mails before he had actually been able to speak directly with him, but Chico wanted things to move along a lot faster than that. So he hoped his idea for getting it done in just a couple of days would work. He certainly had nothing to lose by trying. If it didn't work, they could always go in "cowboy style"—in other words, with guns blazing. Or they might even try the "shock-and-awe" approach, where they would drive a bulldozer into one corner of the building, and then lob in a couple of flash grenades. These techniques would probably be effective, but at what cost?

Chico decided he was going to claim that he was a wealthy businessman who would be leaving for an extended tour of Europe in three days. He had just been referred to the site that day and he wanted to have the opportunity to review the "merchandise" as soon as possible because he was in a position to make a purchase on short notice. He was going to apologize for the tight time frame and offer to postpone any purchase until he returned in three months, if that was Aranson's preference.

Naturally, he would sweeten the situation by pointing out that he could well afford the price, which in the senator's case had been sixty-thousand dollars. He hoped that greed for an immediate profit would motivate Aranson to speed up the process. If all went according to plan, he could pull up in front of Aranson's home, walk in with the major, make the deal, call Callahan, who would be driving a rental van, and have him back into the driveway just as the senator had done. But there was going to be a significant difference in Chico's approach versus the senator's experience: Callahan would not be alone in the van. After reviewing the plan with Callahan, they decided there was a good chance that it would work.

When they found Rocky at the hospital, they were not too surprised to learn that his jaw had been set and wired shut. But he was no longer in pain, thanks to the miracle of modern pharmaceuticals.

However, it was going to be a long night, because all indications prove that he had, in fact, punctured his right lung, and the doctor was about to, as he put it, "go in and have a look."

All Chico and Callahan could do was to wish him well and leave him in the care of the medical staff at Holy Family Hospital. Chico tried to make a joke about giving Rocky a big hug for moral support, but Rocky was not in the mood for humor.

The last stop before going home, after an extremely long and exasperating day, was to see the Parkers. They lived in Carol Stream, about a half-hour drive from the hospital, and they were only too happy to welcome their two unexpected visitors. Jimmy's parents talked about finding some way to express their gratitude, but Chico pointed out that the reward of seeing Jimmy safely at home with his family was more than enough. He also explained that he tried to "stay under the radar" and didn't want any special recognition, as this could quite possibly interfere with future missions.

Jimmy tried to be as helpful as he possibly could. He said that he and one other boy of ten, along with three girls in their early teens, were kept in a room in the basement. He said that the room was real long and was, in his words, "really skinny," which they assumed meant narrow. It had no windows, one toilet, no running water, and was constantly too hot. They were each given a mattress. There was no furniture, except for one small table and some metal folding chairs. The room contained one lamp that was placed on the table. He explained that one time, the lamp had gone out, and the room became totally dark. They were all very scared and screamed as loud as they could but no one came. Only when the time came to bring in food did "the nice lady" find out about it, so she sent "the mean man" down to fix it.

Chico and Callahan were perplexed when they were told that there was no door. Instead, Jimmy told them "they twisted the wall when they brought food and water." After several questions about "the wall that twisted," they gave up. A nine year old boy describes things the way he sees them, which sometimes doesn't provide an adult with a clear, logical picture.

They also tried to find out why Jimmy kept referring to the lady as "nice" and to the man as "mean." Jimmy said, "Well, the nice lady always took us out of our room after we finished lunch to give us our lessons. We went in the big room in the basement where they kept the dogs, and the mean man kept standing there, watching us the whole time. He was really scary."

This explanation, of course, raised more questions than it answered, so they probed further. They learned that the basement contained two rooms, the small, narrow room where they were kept, and the main, larger area. They surmised that the basement had originally consisted of one big area, and that, most likely, a wall had been added that created the long, narrow room where the children were imprisoned. From viewing the photos that the pilot had dropped off while they were at the warehouse, they realized that the new room was probably under the front side of the home, since there were no windows on the lower part of the street side of the house.

Then, they tried to find out what he meant by "the lessons." Jimmy explained, "Sometimes, she told us that we had to wait until a man came to take us away. There was a man who was talking to our mommy and daddy every day, and he was trying to tell them that they should take us back. They were mad at us for leaving, but then they said that we should just stay away forever. But the man was going to get them to let us go home, and we just had to wait and then it would be okay, and then he would finally take us home. But first, he would take us on a vacation for awhile to get us ready to go home. It would be really fun, and he would ask us to do some things that we had never done before. If we didn't do what he wanted, he wouldn't take us home, so we had to do what he wanted, and she said we should try to pretend like we were having fun, or he would get mad and send us back to the skinny room, and then we could never go home. And she told us that when he comes to get us, she would give us new clothes and take us upstairs and we should smile and hug him when we see him, and we should say 'it's so nice to meet you' and then we could leave.

"And then she always told us if we didn't behave while we were waiting for the man to come and get us, the mean man would take the dogs out of their cages and let them bite us. They were right there in the corner while she was giving us our lessons, and the mean man was just standing there, next to the cages, looking at us like he really wanted to make the dogs bite us.

"The girls told us that the mean man would never do that to us, but we knew he would, so we tried to behave. But one time, Josh kept crying during the lesson, and the nice lady had to stop, and the mean man picked him up and spanked him for a really long time, and really hard, too, so we knew that the girls were wrong, and that he would really make the dogs hurt us.

"The girls got different lessons. The nice lady told them that the mean man was going to hurt their family really bad if they didn't behave, and she said he would kill them if he found out that the girls didn't do what the man who was coming to take them away would want them to do." Finally, Jimmy explained that just before the senator arrived to take him away, he was taken upstairs for the first time since he had arrived. The nice lady gave him a bath, washed and dried his hair, and dressed him in new clothes. As far as he knew, the only people in the house, other than the five captives, were Aranson, the nice lady, and the very large man who looked really mean and never spoke.

After learning all they could from Jimmy, they expressed their gratitude, and as they were leaving, they asked if the Parkers would like to attend the upcoming press conference. They were not at all surprised when they simultaneously, and excitedly, answered in the affirmative.

On the drive over to Chico's home, Sergeant Callahan was naturally curious about what he was supposed to do with the body in the back of his SUV, so Chico responded by going over what had happened earlier in the day, and why it was that Rocky was in the hospital undergoing surgery. Then he said, "First, I want you to cut off his head, his hands, and his feet, and burn them until there's nothing left. Then remove his clothes, watch, neck chain, whatever, and get rid of them also. If he was any tattoos or any other identifying marks, obliterate them. I'll let you know when I get some information from the major about the cop. If he drives a car, I want you to link up with one of the major's men and find a way to put the body in the trunk—maybe while he's at church or while he's at his favorite local tavern.

"But if he's driving a van or an SUV, we'll have to think of something else. Then, after a day or so, we're gonna call the local paper in Kenosha, and the radio station, and the police chief, and there's gonna be a "leak" that the officer has temporarily stashed a corpse in his trunk, or maybe in his garage if he drives an SUV, until he can find out how to get rid of it. It will look like the guy had apparently found out something about the cop and was about to go public. And a few days later, right when he's in the middle of one huge mess, he's gonna get a call from me, asking him how he likes my brand of justice."

Callahan just shook his head. "Tell you what, Tommy. Remind me not to fuck with you—ever. Not in this life and not in the next."

When he got home, all Chico wanted was to kiss his wife and daughter and get right to bed, but there was still important business to conduct. He went on the internet and logged on to Aranson's Web site. After he punched in the password that the senator had given him, he discovered pictures of two young boys and three young girls. One of the boys was Jimmy Parker. Directly above the picture was the asking price of $60,000, and there was a caption under the photo that read: "If you want to capture lightning in a bottle, you will want to meet Billy."

There was also a notice next to the picture that informed visitors to the site that he was "No Longer Available."

Chico decided to settle on Anastasia, who, the reader was informed, "will take you beyond your wildest fantasy…look elsewhere if you have a heart condition or any other health issues." She was thirteen and "just waiting for the right person to be her master forever." Then Chico sent a response, stating that he wanted nothing more than to be Anastasia's master. After contacting a friend in California and explaining just enough to get his approval, he used his identity and invited Aranson to check him out. He knew that Aranson would do this anyway, but he wanted to show his eagerness to get things moving along since he was leaving the country very soon.

Finally, Chico's day came to an end. There was nothing to do now but hope that he would get a reply when he logged on again the next morning.

Chapter Forty-Five

Final Trip to Kenosha

When Chico logged on to check his e-mail the next morning, there was a message waiting for him. It looked like Aranson had taken the bait. He simply told Chico that he was checking him out, and that if he was interested in pursuing things any further, he would send him an e-mail. Normally, Aranson explained, he doesn't like to rush the process, and that there would be an "accommodation fee" in addition to the initial price mentioned on the Web site. He further stated that Anastasia was a "very special package" and would be well worth the extra charge.

He didn't have to wait long. Apparently, Aranson's greed had motivated him to "rush the process." He received an e-mail stating that he had been checked out and approved. The fact that he had been referred by Senator Lawson was, apparently, the key deciding factor. Aranson explained that the senator was a repeat customer and he liked to try to go out of his way to please his customers.

Aranson then engaged in a series of e-mails with Chico, discussing the details of the proposed transaction. It was agreed that Chico would arrive two days later, at ten in the morning, and would enter the house with not more than one other person. They were to have eighty-five thousand in one hundred dollar bills, they were to be unarmed, and they were to leave their cell phones in the vehicle. They would be checked thoroughly for weapons immediately upon entering the home. The driver was to wait in the vehicle until further instructions were given. It was implied that there would be consequences if these conditions were not adhered to precisely.

Chico started putting things together. He called the major and had him line up two of his men. They would need to be armed and waiting in the back of a rented Wisconsin van that Sergeant Callahan would be driving. Chico needed to get some identification documents from Rocky's contact, and he also had to get his hands on the money.

In spite of the fact that there was a lot to accomplish in a short amount of time, Chico wanted to take a few minutes to look in on Rocky at the hospital. Fortunately, the surgery had gone well, and it looked like he would be home in a day or two. In addition to wanting to see how his old friend was doing, Chico wanted Rocky's opinion about the plan that was about to unfold. Rocky said that the plan looked good and had nothing to add other than that they should get together later to review how everything went. It would be ideal if Wade could be included, but they decided they would wait until he contacted them, as they felt that it was best to give him some space for awhile.

During the drive to Kenosha, they received some very unexpected news. Rocky called Chico and told him that a news flash had just come on CNN. Senator Lawson had been found shot in the head. He was home alone, and the housekeeper discovered the body soon after she arrived. The senator's driver, who lived in a cottage behind the house, was nowhere to be found, and one of the senator's vehicles was missing from the garage. The reporter stated that the police considered the driver to be the prime suspect. Since no weapon was found at the scene, it was being looked at as a homicide.

Chico was the first to express an opinion. "Well, isn't that a kick in the ass. That slimy little weasel. Homicide—that's total bullshit. Looks like he's gonna get away with it, too. So help me God, I know he got the driver to do it. That guy adored the senator; he would never harm him unless the senator ordered him to. Remember when we had him in the warehouse? He only decided to cooperate with us because the senator finally gave him the nod. I guess this is really a case of 'suicide by limo driver'! And you know what? I can see how it's all gonna unfold. His adoring constituents are gonna think that their beloved senator was whacked by his driver. And the only way to cut through all that horseshit is if we come forward, which is not gonna happen, or if Jimmy and his folks speak up. But there's no way to prove what they would have to say, and therefore, they won't be believed, so there's absolutely no point. Talk about your conniving, slick politicians—this is one for the books. He actually pulled it off. No prison time and no public embarrassment. Son of a bitch."

After shaking his head in disgust, he continued. "Damn, I don't know how this is gonna affect our mission this morning. There's no telling how Aranson is gonna react to the news. Remember, Senator Lawson is the one who referred me to him. Let's just hope he hasn't heard about it yet. If he has, and he brings it up, we'll just have to act surprised and upset. Nothing else we can do."

Not long after receiving the news from Rocky, they pulled up at Aranson's front door, right on time. Chico and the major were dressed in business attire and, predictably, were met at the front door by a very large man, who looked like the quintessential bodyguard in an old gangster movie. Immediately after they entered through the front door, he began patting them down without saying a word. It was extremely thorough; if they had hidden a pen knife in their shorts, he would have found it. In addition, he carefully checked their identification documents. As soon as he completed the search, they were lead into the living room where they met Milo Aranson. He looked like a friendly, even likeable man. He was pleasant looking although not particularly handsome. Chico's immediate thought was that he could get right up close to a little kid at the mall without causing any alarm. He was certainly quite the opposite of someone who looked like he would want to harm anyone.

Aranson greeted them with a warm smile and a firm handshake. "I'm really sorry," he exclaimed with complete sincerity in his tone. "It's just a little ritual we have to go through. You know, we haven't had any problems yet—thanks to Leonard here—but just in case someone doesn't want to follow our instructions about not carrying a weapon or a cell phone, well, you know it's just a precaution for the benefit of everyone. Okay then, now that that's out of the way, come, sit down, tell me about your travel plans. I understand you're going out of the country for quite awhile." This guy was coming across as congenial, even charming.

Chico explained that he would be catching a cruise ship out of New York the following morning, and that six days later they would arrive in Southampton, England. Then he took a few minutes describing the rest of the proposed journey, trying to match Aranson's easy, relaxed nature. Finally, after about fifteen minutes, Aranson was satisfied that everything was as it should be and turned the conversation around to the business at hand. "Well, if you are ready to conduct a little business, I would like to show you what we have to offer, providing, of course, that you have brought something for us." When Chico pointed out that they would like to see the merchandise before presenting payment, there was a sudden break in Aranson's friendly manner. For just a second, his eyes widened, and the corners of his mouth turned into a snarl. He gripped the arms of his chair as if he was unable to contain his rage, but just as quickly regained his composure. This, clearly, was a man who had to be in control at all times, the mark of a true sociopath. He took a deep breath, and then the reassuring smile returned, although there was a slightly more authoritative tone in his voice. "Well, you see, we have procedures that must be followed. I pointed out that payment was to be brought with you and that means right here, right now. You've already seen and approved the merchandise. It was on my Web site, remember? So let's not waste any more time."

Chico smiled and apologized for his attempt to deviate from procedure. Then he nodded to the major, who promptly stood up and began walking toward the door. Leonard opened the door and waited with arms crossed over his huge barrel chest. The look on his face said, "You better not even *think* of crossing me."

Major Robins walked around to the street side of the van so that the bodyguard would not have a clear view of his transaction with the driver. He could see through the passenger's window that Callahan reached behind him and grabbed a small black bag and handed it to the major. But he was unable to observe that there were two pistols on the seat next to Callahan's left hip. While Callahan had been busy reaching for the bag, the major grabbed one gun in each hand and, shifting slightly toward the rear of the van, partially out of Leonard's line of sight, he lifted up the back of his suit jacket and placed them inside his waistband. He hoped to pass one to Chico if he got the chance. He knew that Leonard was going to promptly search the black bag, but he hoped he would not decide to perform another pat-down exercise. If he did, the only option was to waste Leonard and move to Plan B.

After returning to his seat, they all engaged in additional chatter while Leonard began counting the contents of the bag. During the conversation, Chico developed a coughing spell, and after a few seconds, the major spoke for the first time. "I think he needs a glass of water."

Continuing his role as the congenial host, Aranson smiled and said, "Oh, of course." When he was out of the room, the major checked to be sure that Leonard was sufficiently occupied with the contents of the black bag and quickly slipped one of the guns to Chico.

When Leonard finally finished counting, he looked at Aranson and nodded. Aranson then spoke to Chico. "Well, everything's in order, so I guess the big moment has arrived." Glancing over at the stairway to the second floor, he raised his voice and said, "Honey, I think we're ready for you to bring Anastasia downstairs." After a few seconds, a lady led a young girl of about thirteen into the living room. The woman looked friendly, had a warm smile, and was moderately attractive. She was stylishly dressed, wearing a cream-colored blouse, light-brown pants, and a chocolate blazer. She could have easily been mistaken for the typical "suburban soccer mom."

Aranson took the girl by the hand and introduced her to Chico. "Darling, this is Mr. Walton. He's going to let you stay with him until we are able to get you back to your parents."

Right on cue, she forced a smile, wrapped her arms around Chico and exclaimed, "It's so nice to meet you, sir."

Chico was blown away by the absurdity of the situation. Several thoughts ran through his mind while he was receiving his orchestrated hug. For one thing, he realized that something like this could have happened to his own daughter and that right at that very instant, someone, somewhere, was worried sick over the precious young creature clinging to him. And wasn't it ironic that Aranson and the other two occupants of the home were so horribly wrong to think that they were the ones in control? They had no clue that their lives were within minutes of changing drastically and irreversibly.

But these thoughts had to be put aside as Chico had to continue with his role as a wealthy pedophile on his way to Europe. His true role, both as a rescuer and punisher, could not as yet be revealed.

"Well, aren't you the pretty one!" As soon as he said it, he realized how contrived that must have sounded, but when he caught Aranson's eye, he could see that he was buying it. "Hey, tell you what, why don't you just call me Uncle Irv? And how about if I call you Princess? Because that's exactly what I thought the moment you walked into the room." Then he looked directly at Aranson and gave a satisfied, grateful look. For added emphasis, he gave a big grin and a thankful nod. It certainly looked like Aranson was convinced that he was about to send another satisfied customer out the door. He was probably already thinking that it was time to go out and find a replacement for "Anastasia," inasmuch as he could envision another referral coming his way before long.

Aranson was ready to finish the morning's business. "Well, it certainly looks like this story has a happy ending. Mr. Walton, why don't you call your driver? I know you left your cell phone in your car, like I asked you to, so go ahead and use this one. Just ask him to back into the driveway. Leonard will guide him and tell him when to stop. Then you can be on your way." As he handed Chico the phone, Leonard started to walk toward the back door.

After he made the call, Chico did his best to find out some information that pertained to the events that were about to unfold. "This is such a big home. Is it just the three of you living here?" He knew that this question could raise some suspicion, but he felt it was worth a try. But it backfired completely.

Aranson instantly showed the look that Chico had observed when he asked to see the girl before turning over the money. But, as before, Aranson was quick to recover. With a smile that was no longer warm and friendly, he responded, "Well, Mr. Walton, that's really not essential to our little transaction, now is it? Why don't we just let you go on your way? We all know that curiosity killed the cat, now don't we?" The message was pretty clear: this guy intended to stay in control, and he was capable of doing whatever it would take in order to achieve that objective.

Chico simply apologized and said that he was just trying to fill the void in the conversation while they were waiting for the van. But he could see that the suspicion was still there, and that Aranson was now watching him and the major intently. Aranson asked the "nice lady" to accompany them to the rear door as they were about to leave. Chico noticed that she reached behind her blazer and kept her hand there as soon as Aranson finished his request. Her demeanor told Chico and the major that she was on high alert.

Within a few seconds, they were all standing outside, next to the van. Callahan walked to the rear of the vehicle and opened the door. The next few seconds would determine the fate of a number of individuals, some of whom were quite likely separated from eternity by just one pull of a trigger.

Then several things happened all at once. As two of the major's accomplices, Xavier and Art, jumped out of the van, Chico, the major, and Callahan all drew their weapons and pointed them at three very surprised and stunned kidnappers. Almost in unison, Chico and Callahan shouted, "Do not fucking move!"

At the same time, Xavier grabbed "Anastasia" and immediately placed her in the vehicle, away from any weapons that had a good chance of being fired at any moment. He had been assigned to stay in the van to prevent her from trying to take off in the confusion, as she would, at this point, have no idea who meant her harm and who could be trusted. They could not allow her to get in the way of a mission that could go south at any minute.

Art began placing handcuffs on each of the three captives. The major had kept a close watch on the woman as soon as he noticed her hand reach behind her, and while he kept his gun pointed at her head, he grabbed her hand and removed a revolver. Chico then directed everyone back in the house.

"Well, since you wouldn't tell me who else lives here, I guess we'll just have to find out for ourselves," said Chico. Then he asked Art to check the entire first two floors of the house to see if anyone else was waiting to interrupt the mission, which was about to shift into high hear. He directed the three captives to sit in the living room while the search was taking place. Everyone except Leonard complied. It looked like he had a defiant streak, and Chico wondered if maybe he just didn't know how to take orders from anyone but Aranson. It wasn't a good idea, but strangely, the "mean man," in spite of being semi-immobilized by the handcuffs, gave Callahan a menacing look and took a step in his direction.

Callahan had no trouble deciding what to do next. He took two steps backward, and fired one round directly into Leonard's knee. Leonard instantly fell back into the chair that he had been directed to sit in and winced in great pain. Strangely, the loud screams that everyone expected never came, but it was clear from the contorted look on his face that he was in extreme agony. Then Callahan shouted, *"Are you fucking crazy? What the fuck is the matter with you?"*

Art reappeared and announced that no one else was on the first or second floor. Chico nodded and asked everyone to move down to the basement. But, surprisingly, the woman decided that she had a better idea. "Listen, you've got what you came for, why don't you just take back your money and get out of here? Let us proceed with our business, and we'll all just forget about what happened here today, okay?"

At this point, all four captors looked at one another with puzzled expressions, and then, one by one, they started laughing as they finally were able to put this very strange development into context. It had become clear that the kidnappers thought that this was a simple double cross: get the girl, get their money back, and get out.

Callahan waited until everyone had stopped laughing. Then, as he pointed his weapon at her knee, he said, "You stupid, fucking cunt. Don't you know what's happening here? Today is the last day of running your business. Unfortunately, it's also your last day of running anything." Then he fired.

Unlike Leonard, her vocal chords were in perfect working order. Her screams were so loud that she had to be gagged, as it was very possible that she could be heard outside, and they didn't need any unwanted interruptions from a concerned neighbor or anyone else.

Chico again directed everyone to the basement, but no one moved. Callahan then stood up and walked over to Aranson, who was apparently contemplating what to do about Callahan's comment about this being 'your last day of running anything.' The sergeant said, "Well, now I guess it's your turn. You see, there are three reasons I like knee shots. First, as you can tell, it's very painful. I mean, like it really fucking hurts. It's about the worst place, as far as pain is concerned, that you can shoot someone. Second, they're not gonna die. And that means, it's likely you're gonna have plenty of time to get what you want from them after the shot, if you know what I mean. And the last thing is that they're not gonna get up and bail. Nope. Not after being shot in the knee, that's for sure. Okay, so what's my point? Well, the point is that I've still got four knees left to blast, starting with both of yours. So let's get our asses up out of our chairs, and let's everyone help everyone else, and let's get down to the *fucking basement.*"

When everyone was finally helped to their feet, Chico sent Art out to the van to retrieve something. Then the task of moving their captives to the lower floor came. But it took a lot of time and effort to get them down the stairs since two of the kidnapers were not the least bit ambulatory. When Chico finally stepped onto the tiled floor, he saw that he was in a typical suburban recreation room. The walls were paneled in expensive, rough-sawn walnut siding, the ceiling had recessed lighting, and the furniture was comfortable and inviting. In one corner there was a well-stocked bar, along with a microwave and a refrigerator. The only things out of place were the two wire dog cages sitting next to each other by the far wall. There were two Dobermans in the cages; their incessant growling informed any visitor that he would not last long if they were let out of their enclosures.

As Chico expected, there were casement windows on three sides of the room. The remaining wall would probably not seem out of place to the casual observer. In addition to the attractive paneling, there were several paintings hanging on the wall, and two huge flags hanging perpendicularly along the middle of the wall that reached from floor to ceiling. They appeared to be from foreign countries, and they added an interesting decorative touch to a visitor's initial impression of the room.

After the captives were seated, Art returned with a sledge hammer and a pry bar. Chico looked at Aranson. "Well, are you gonna tell us how to get into that room, or do we start demolishing the wall? It's your call. One way or the other, we're going in."

The man didn't move or speak.

275

Callahan walked over to Aranson and pointed his gun at his right leg while Major Robins's colleague walked toward the wall. Callahan announced, "This won't take long. You'll have your answer in just a few seconds. If he doesn't give it up by the time I cap his knee, I'll just—"

Chico interrupted. "No, wait. Let me think for a minute." Chico had a feeling that he could figure it out. It was something about the flags. After slightly more intense scrutiny, he determined that the flags were no doubt hung at the point where the four-by-eight sections of paneling met. Thus, they were covering the points where the wall could open or "twist" in some fashion. Additionally, he noticed that the six jack posts, which had been boxed in by professionally cut pieces of the walnut paneling, were off center. They would normally be placed in the middle of the room in order to give the correct type of support to the home, but that was not the case. The wall had been added, and judging by the placement, it looked like it created a room that was only about seven feet wide. This would be the long, "skinny" area that Jimmy had referred to.

After removing the two flags, it was instantly clear how it worked. There was a space, shoulder high—about one-foot square—that had been cut out of the paneling, as well as the dry wall, behind each of the areas where the flags had been. These openings exposed a pair of two-by-four studs, and a heavy, round, metal lock bolt that had been placed through a hole in each stud, so that the middle section of wall was locked firmly in place. By simply removing these bolts, the center four-by-eight-foot section could be opened, or, more likely, could be rotated from the center, on it's axis, assuming that it had been rigged up in that fashion.

Chico smiled briefly when he thought of Jimmy's description of how the wall opened. It would be unusual for a boy of nine to have words like "rotate" or "pivot" or "swivel" in his vocabulary, so Jimmy chose the only word that made sense to him. Unfortunately, the word "twist" just didn't register in the brain of a fifty-three-year-old adult.

After he removed the lock bolts, he gave a gentle push to one side of the middle section. It pivoted from the center and revealed the hidden room. What they saw was pitiful. Three children, a boy and two girls, were sitting on metal folding chairs. They were dressed in their underwear, and it was clear that they had no idea what was going on. Instead of seeing the "nice lady," what they viewed was disturbing. She was gagged and bleeding, and it was clear that her hands had been shackled behind her. Did her captors have the same thing planned for them? Was their situation about to get even worse than what they had already endured?

Chico walked into the room, which was very warm, just like Jimmy had explained. It was also quite humid, and the air was stagnant and had a musty odor. The condition of the average prison cell was considerably better than these living accommodations. Then he addressed the frightened, disheveled children. "Please don't be afraid. Jimmy told us where you are and we've come to take you home. The girl who left here a little while ago is safe. She's outside waiting for you right now. Come on. Let's get all of you out of here." Then he motioned to Art, who promptly led them out of the room and up the stairs, to the fresh outdoors.

Chico then turned to the three adult captives. "Well, now, isn't this an interesting turn of events. Mr. Aranson, don't you find this ironic? Instead of you being in control, instead of the children being your victims, instead of your woman being free to move about and help you with your predatory little business, and instead of Leonard being able to protect you, it's all been turned around, hasn't it? I guess you could call it a reversal of fortune. Well, actually, it's worse than that. Do you remember when my associate said that this is your last day of running your business, or anything else for that matter? Now, you're going to find out that we always mean what we say. You see, you're all going in that room, and you're not coming out; at least, not for a very long time, and maybe never. It depends on whether or not the next owners find out about your little 'shop of horrors' here. But now, I guess, I'm getting a little ahead of myself.

"Major, would you mind checking in the kitchen to see if you can find some knives or scissors? We're gonna cut their clothes off and put them in that room and let them have exactly the same experience that they've provided to who knows how many little lost souls. God, you people are pathetic. I never thought, years ago, that I could do what I am about to do to all of you, but so help me, you sure as hell have it coming. When I go to sleep at night, it's gonna give me a lot of satisfaction knowing that a lot of lives will never have to experience what you have put so many helpless children through. But I digress. Let's get back to business. We've gotta get the three of you into that room, and hey, I've just come up with a good idea. Let's kill the light and see how you like sitting in the dark, like the kids had to."

After they had been stripped to their underwear and placed on folding chairs in the "skinny" room, the major's colleague removed the lamp and started to close and lock the middle section of the wall. The major stopped him. "Listen, I've got one more idea before we leave." Then he walked over to the cages and started dragging them over to the two openings in the wall. "Let's reach around and open the cage doors, and then we can push the cages into the room and close up the wall. It's really not fair to keep the dogs locked in their kennels with nothing to eat."

When the cages were in place, and the major and his helper were about to open the kennel doors, Callahan stopped them. "Wait, wait. This is not right. This is not fair. We shouldn't leave them like this. It's just not right. I'm never gonna be able to live with myself if we close and lock up this wall right now. Pull that cage out of the way, I'm going back in."

Everyone was too surprised to move, so Callahan impatiently yanked one of the cages away from the opening and promptly walked into the nearly dark room. In about five seconds, a loud gunshot sounded. Then he walked back out of the room, holding a still smoking revolver. "Okay, go ahead and finish up. It just wasn't fair that the guy who deserved it the most would get off so cheap. Besides, there's something about shooting someone in the knee that never fails to brighten up my day."

Chapter Forty-Six

Getting the Abductees Home Safely

The Payback Team, or what was left of it, was not finished with their mission. They needed to get the four frightened and confused former captives home safely. Chico's first inclination, not long after they had pulled out of the driveway, was to hand each kid a cell phone and let him or her place a call home. If nothing else, this would at least let them know that they were truly out of danger. Most, if not all, of the young passengers in the van were still not sure whom they could trust. Xavier had tried his best to explain everything to Anastasia, whose real name was Dora, but she was only half convinced.

Sergeant Callahan vetoed the idea. He pointed out that the best alternative was to simply drive them home, walk them up to their front door, make sure someone was home, and then make an immediate departure. It was possible, he explained, that by alerting the parents ahead of time, any number of things could happen. There was, for example, the chance that the media, or even the police, could be waiting for their arrival. Also, a distrustful father could, for that matter, be waiting with a loaded shotgun.

Chico knew, however, that he had to do something because Josh, the ten-year-old boy, was hysterical, and he was getting on everyone's nerves. Worse yet, it looked like one or two of the girls were about to join him. So Chico went into high-speed planning mode and quickly came up with the answer. He dialed a number on his cell phone, spoke for a minute or two, and then said, "Hey Josh, someone wants to talk to you."

The Sergeant's eyes widened. "What the hell are you doing? I thought we just agreed that—"

Before he could finish, Chico interrupted. "Don't have another heart attack, okay? That's Jimmy Parker on the phone. When he listens to what Jimmy's gonna tell him, he'll calm down right away. And let's make sure he repeats the conversation to the girls so we can get everyone settled down, and then maybe we can find out some addresses and get on with it.

Fortunately, the plan worked perfectly. They drove the van to the rental agency and exchanged it for the two vehicles they had used to get there. It was decided that the major and his associates would drop off two of the girls, Carla and Lucinda, at their homes near Milwaukee. Chico and Callahan took the other two, Josh and Dora, to their homes in Lincolnwood and Skokie, two suburbs north of Chicago.

The two Milwaukee area drop-offs occurred without incident, and four parents were, quite naturally, overwhelmed and overjoyed. They were also completely shocked when it was clear that the three men in the SUV wanted no praise, no reward, and no conversation. The parents were simply informed that the men had other business to attend to and that their daughters would explain everything. In both cases, the parents followed the major to his vehicle and were still asking questions when the SUV pulled away.

Things turned out quite differently for Chico and Callahan. When they arrived at Josh's house, a very drunken stepfather opened the door. He saw two strangers with his stepson, and he could tell that Josh had been crying. In his less than coherent state, he drew the conclusion that the two men standing at his front door were the ones who had originally abducted him and that they must have done something to make him cry. Without a word, and without any warning, he lunged at Chico, preparing to deck him with one blow. Chico simply stepped aside and watched him stumble off the front stoop and onto the sidewalk. He watched the man intently as he got back to his feet to see if he might try to reach for a weapon. The man looked harmless and appeared to be no match for either of them, especially in his inebriated condition, but it would be a different story if he was carrying. Fortunately for the stepfather, he was unarmed.

But they could tell that this "fight," if it could be called that, was far from over, at least not from the stepfather's point of view. He advanced toward Chico a second time, but this time, instead of letting him swing and fall again, he and Callahan caught him and dragged him inside. By now, Josh's mother had appeared on the scene and was holding her son, more concerned about him than the fact that her husband was fighting a battle against extremely long odds.

Once inside, they placed him on a sofa in the living room and pinned him there for a full five minutes while they explained to Josh's mother that they were his rescuers and that he was home for good. Finally, it looked like they had made their point, and they were about to ask her husband if he was ready to behave, but this would not be necessary as he was no longer awake. The alcohol had conveniently taken care of the situation for them. Callahan looked at him in disgust. "No need to see us to the door, sir, we'll let ourselves out." Then, predictably, he started one of his raucous laughs and was almost choking by the time they got to the car.

When they got to Dora's home, it was an entirely different situation, quite the opposite of what they had just encountered. Her father answered the door and was immediately overcome with emotion upon seeing his daughter. She looked healthy, happy, and relieved to finally be home. While both father and daughter were hugging and crying, it looked like the opportune moment for her rescuers to make their departure. But Dora's father wouldn't allow it. "No, no, wait, please don't go." He grabbed Chico by the hand and elbow and tried to lead him into his home. Chico considered the option of pulling away and heading to the car, but he finally decided that they would acquiesce, but only for a few minutes, given the emotional nature of the situation.

Dora's father tried everything he could to get them to open up, but all he was able to determine was that the two men standing before him were some sort of avenging angels who wanted nothing in return. He tried to offer them a reward, but Chico said, "No thank you, that won't be necessary."

He asked them to wait until he could get the media involved, but Callahan responded, "Please, that's the last thing we want." And they declined again when he asked them to at least wait until his wife returned from work.

Then, as it was clear that they wanted to be on their way, he asked the questions that they knew were coming. "What about the people who kidnapped my daughter? Are they in jail? Is there going to be a trial?"

Callahan supplied the answer that he half expected to hear. "Sir, I promise you, they will never hurt anyone again. Not ever."

As they were leaving, Dora's grateful father made one last comment. "Listen, I think I know what you guys are all about. May I just say God bless you. You know, perhaps, there is something I can do for you. I can guess that somewhere along the line, you're going to be on the losing end of one of your missions, and maybe, just maybe, I can help. Here's my card. I have a lot of contacts, both in politics and in the legal system. And, believe it or not, I know someone who would make a good addition to your cause. He's my wife's brother, and he's retiring from the marines in a couple of months. I guarantee when he finds out about this, he's going to wish he could meet you. Maybe I can repay the favor one day after all."

Chapter Forty-Seven

Planning for the Guatemala Mission

Chico and Callahan were silent for the first several minutes after they got back in the car. They were trying to come down out of orbit after an extraordinarily traumatic day. The sergeant was the first one to speak. "I don't know about you, Tommy, but this old Irishman could use like a gallon of suds right about now. Why don't we head over to the nearest gin mill and let's have at it?" He could tell by the wide grin on Chico's face that he was in complete agreement.

About the time they were starting on their second brew, Callahan asked a question. "Isn't it about time you gave Courtland a call? If I remember correctly, he said we should keep him informed about what's been going on, even though he couldn't be a part of it. And I'm wondering if maybe he's about ready to get back in the loop."

"There you go again with that 'Courtland' thing. Why don't you just call him 'Wade'?" Before Callahan could answer, Chico's cell phone rang. "Hey, Spike, we were just talking about you. We've got a lot of catching up to do. Are you ready to come out of hiding?"

Chico spoke with Wade for a couple of minutes and ended the conversation by saying, "Okay, fine, I'll try to put it together for Saturday morning, and I'll let you know." Then he explained to Callahan that Wade was returning from Wisconsin after spending several days trying to adjust to his terrible loss. He and Paula had concluded that it was best to try to get back to the process of living. They had their precious memories of their son, and that would have to sustain them; there was no other rational choice.

Wade had said that he wasn't quite ready to get back into action; that would have to wait for at least a couple of weeks. And, in addition, he had spoken to Rocky and found out that he was in no condition to consider anything but getting home from the hospital and continuing the recovery process. With a broken jaw, a broken rib, and a punctured lung, he had to focus on healing, at least for awhile. He signed off by suggesting eighteen holes on Saturday morning, and he asked Chico if he could contact Callahan and the major and see if they could make it a foursome. If he was up to it, perhaps Rocky could come along and drive one of the golf carts. Then, when everyone was together, Wade and Rocky could be brought up to date, and they could all try to decide what The Payback Team should plan for the future.

After two more rounds, they left the tavern and headed home. Callahan was all for the golf idea, so now Chico had to try to line up the other two. Rocky thought he would be able to drive the golf cart by then, but the major said he couldn't make it. He explained, "Listen, thanks for the invite, but I've got a lot to catch up on. You guys have been keeping me pretty busy. Maybe you forgot that I've got other clients, as well as you clowns. Plus, I've got to get a bill together. I haven't sent you one in over a month. But I've decided that this last little caper is on the house. I don't know when I've enjoyed anything as much as what went down with that slimy little bastard, Aranson. I wish I could be there to see how it ends. I think it's even money, whether they just waste away or if the dogs finish them off. Oh, well, either way, it's a happy ending as far as I'm concerned."

At 7:00 A.M. on Saturday, The Payback Team was ready to tee off. Rocky was glad to come along, even though it was going to be a few weeks before he could swing a club. This was going to be an enjoyable morning, although there was also important business to discuss. The four team members had been through a lot, and now, it was necessary to assess what they had accomplished—whether it was wise to continue with their mission, and if so, some sort of timetable needed to be established.

Wade was lining up for his first drive when Rocky broke his concentration. "Hold it, Spike. Aren't we going to place some kind of wager on the match? We always do. Why should today be any different?"

Wade had a perplexed look. "What? You're in no condition to even get out of the cart. And besides, you didn't even bring your clubs. How are we gonna—?"

Rocky cut him off. "No, no, Slow One. Think about it. We can still bet. Even though I can't *play* against you, I can still *bet* against you." Although still confused, Wade wanted to know what Rocky had in mind. "Tell you what, Spike, how about if I pay you twelve hundred dollars for each eagle, six hundred dollars for each birdie, and three hundred each time you par a hole? How does that sound? That's a potential win of over twenty-one large. And all you have to do is pay me a hundred bucks for any hole where you don't make par."

While Wade was apparently doing some mental calculations regarding Rocky's offer, Chico saw that Callahan was about to undertake one of his laughing episodes, so he quickly gave him a hard elbow jab in the ribs. Meanwhile, Wade finished doing the math and determined that if he had only one birdie, no eagles, and four pars, he would be ahead by five hundred bucks. Clearly, this was a chance to get back a good share of what he had lost in their last few outings. He quickly accepted the wager, teed off, nearly birdied the hole, and was on his way to some easy money. Callahan just rolled his eyes, wondering how Courtland could be so gullible. He realized that, fortunately, this weakness never came into play when The Payback Team was conducting business.

As the match proceeded, the first three holes were spent catching up Wade and Rocky on everything they had missed since they were last active on the team. The next two holes were devoted to relishing their victories regarding Aranson and the senator.

But then they addressed the topic of whether or not to continue. There had already been two major casualties, as well as a few minor ones, not to mention a couple of close calls. The issue of going to another country to solve other people's problems was also debated.

The conclusion was reached that, in reality, almost all of the projects they had worked on had initially involved "other people's problems," and that, in fact, was the whole point of The Payback Team's purpose: to help those who needed it most, but were unable to help themselves. How was Mrs. Crowley going to get her husband to shape up and stop harming her? How were Stedman's grandparents going to stop his serious gambling problem? How were the people who had been cheated by the contractor going to recover the money they had put up? How were the parents of children who had been harmed, or killed, going to achieve justice for their loss and suffering?

It was clear that they had been in the unique position to do something about all of these situations. Their mission was honorable, and they had long since ended the debate over the means that they had to use to achieve justice in many instances. The "system" was just not able to be effective on occasion, and that's where they could be of service. Hadn't the "system" failed completely in the cases of Medrano and Aranson?

After several more holes, all were in agreement that they would continue and that they would be emotionally and physically healed and ready for a trip to Guatemala in about three weeks. The Payback Team was energized and anxious to get started on what was certain to be their most challenging and dangerous mission.

As they headed back to the clubhouse, Wade reluctantly pulled out his wallet. "I can't understand it. I should've made a fortune, but I lost two hundred bucks." As Rocky pocketed the cash, Wade noticed that Chico and Callahan were laughing. "Okay, wise guys, what's the joke? Can't you see how ridiculous this is? I shot one of the best rounds I've had in two months, and I still lost. I managed to par four holes and nearly parred another four. I can't believe the bad luck."

Chico stopped laughing long enough to say, "You just don't get it. You were beat before you started."

Wade didn't get it. "Okay, genius, explain."

Happy to accommodate, Chico gave it to him straight. "Well, Shit for Brains, your first mistake was to accept a proposition bet. Generally, the person proposing the wager has an edge of some kind. In this case, Rocky's edge was that he obviously had a lot of time to think it through and come up with something he knew would probably work in his favor, and you only had about a minute. And notice how he presented it. He said you had the potential of making a huge amount of money. Spike, you were so mesmerized by this number that you failed to consider the odds. Listen, Short Bus, you've never had an eagle in your entire life, so you had no shot at winning the twelve hundred bucks. And the last time you birdied a hole, Monica and Bill were doin' their thing in the oval office. I'm amazed that you managed to par four holes today, but it just wasn't enough to overcome the steady drain of a hundred bucks on each of the remaining fourteen holes. So help me God, Spike, sometimes I have to wonder if you were around a lot of lead paint when you were little. I guess you forgot what I told you that I learned from my grandfather. He said that if a stranger with a deck of cards offers to bet twenty bucks that he can make the jack of diamonds jump out of the deck and spit carrot juice in your eye, tell him to take a hike. Otherwise, get ready to wipe your eye and pay him off."

Chapter Forty-Eight

Heading Down to Guatemala

The Payback Team spent the next three weeks getting ready for the trip to Guatemala. This journey was shaping up to be the most important, complicated, and risky venture of their brief existence. No one brought up the question of what would be next on the agenda after they returned, because they were too focused on the immediate challenge. Additionally, none of them knew for certain how many of the team would be returning.

After a few rounds of golf, as well as two or three meetings in the local pubs, Chico had finally put together a plan. He used the first couple of get-togethers to sound out everyone and get input about how they should go about it, and then tried to work it into a plan of attack. The plan had to be flexible because there were a lot of unknowns. Somehow, the team had to get to Guatemala without drawing any unusual attention. They would have nothing with them that they would need; everything, including weapons, disguises, and transportation would have to be arranged after they got there. And that's where the indispensable Rocky came in.

Chico wanted to know if he had any contacts in Guatemala, but his initial answer surprised everyone. "No, actually, I don't know anyone." He stopped talking for a minute and appeared to be mentally searching for something.

Before he could continue, Chico said, "I don't believe it. The guy who always 'knows this one guy' has hit a dead end! I knew it would finally happen and—"

Rocky shot him a disgusted look as he cut him off. "But there's this one guy I know who owes me a big favor. His wife's family is from Guatemala, and I think I can do some checking and make some connections. I should be able to get back to you within a day or two."

Right on schedule, Rocky came up with three worthwhile contacts who could handle most of their needs. Additionally, he was able to provide everyone with new IDs, including passports. He also informed them that the contacts were already working on finding a safe, out of the way place for them to stay in when they got there.

During the last meeting before their scheduled departure, Chico outlined his plan. "The only way we can find out what's going on is to catch them in the act. That means that we are going to have to take a lot of bus tours until we're on the right bus on the right day. We could get lucky right away, but it most likely will take a lot longer than that. We can't stay there forever, so I propose that we commit to three weeks, and then make a decision whether we want to continue. And we need to get our hands on some disguises because Spike's aunt said there was a rumor that at least one of the bus drivers was involved, so we have to have a different appearance every time we get on the bus.

"Now, here's the thing. I know one of you proposed just blasting away at these guys when we are finally face to face with them, but that just won't cut it. There's a good chance that one of us, or one of the passengers, is not gonna walk away if we take the cowboy approach. So what we're gonna do is, we're gonna capture one of the banditos and make him tell us about their operation—who runs it, how many banditos there are in total, where their base of operation is, what vehicles they use, and when they are planning their next holdup."

Wade couldn't control himself. "What?! What the hell are you talking about? That's the craziest idea I've ever heard. Do you really think one of the banditos is just gonna—?"

"Hey, Spike, work with me on this, will ya?" replied Chico. "Relax. I knew it would be you who would come up with that objection. Do you think I would propose something like this if I hadn't thought it through? Now, just cool your jets and listen, okay?" Chico spent the next few minutes outlining how they could accomplish this difficult objective, making sure that it was clear in everyone's mind before he moved on to what was going to happen after they got the necessary information from the bandito.

Finally, the plan was approved and everyone spent the last several days taking care of personal business and saying goodbye to their families. The time had come to head to the airport and begin their most important project, one that had started months ago as an idea, and now was about to become a reality.

After the plane had been in the air for about an hour, Rocky asked Wade what was wrong. He noticed that Wade had been extremely quiet and looked a little upset. "Hey, Spike, what's with the look? Are you worried about the mission? You know, Chico's plan has been pretty well thought out, and—"

Wade cut him off. "No, it's nothing like that. In twenty-five years of marriage, Paula and I have never had a serious fight, but things are pretty bad right now. I shouldn't have left until I found some way of resolving things, but now, if I don't come back, she'll never..." Then his voice trailed off as he sunk deeper into despair.

Rocky tried to be helpful. "Well, if you want to talk about it, I'm right here. If not, that's okay, too."

Wade was grateful. "Thanks. There's really nothing anyone can do about it. I'll just have to make sure I come home so I can straighten things out. What happened is that she got the crazy idea I was cheating on her. You've known me for forty years, and you know I'd never do anything like that. And, really, she should know it, too. But now that Rob's gone, she's just not thinking clearly."

When Rocky asked why she suspected he was having an affair, Wade explained. "It's really funny how it happened. You know, she's always been after me about two things, and I just never got around to either one. Lately, she's been on me about getting a much bigger house, something really spectacular, you know, like you and Chico did when you could afford it. I just never cared much about it. And the other thing has been going on for much longer. Believe it or not, she wants a horse. Can you imagine—a horse? She was into riding when we met, and she continued until Rob was born. So, now, she really wants to get back into it. So, I finally decided to get her a damn horse, only I wanted it to be a surprise. I've been looking into it for about a month now, and I've made a few contacts, but I didn't come up with anything until a few days ago. A mare is due to deliver any day now, and the guy said I could have it. We've traded a few calls, and a couple of times, when my cell rang, I recognized the number and I went out on the patio to take the call.

And another time, I got a call and picked it up before I realized who it was, and I promptly said, 'Sorry, I can't talk now. I'll have to call you back.' Then, when she wanted to know what was going on, I couldn't think of any good way out of it, so I just told her it was no big deal and not to worry about it. Well, the woman's intuition thing kicked in, and she thought she had it figured out that I was seeing someone. The more I try to deny it, the more she's convinced that I've gone sideways on her. But there's more. As I was leaving to go to the airport this morning, her last words were: 'I may not be here when you come home.' I know she doesn't mean it, but you can see how upset she is. Michael, I would never hurt her, I just..." His voice started to crack, so he stopped talking.

Rocky thought of several options—none of which would do any good—so he just looked at his friend with an expression that said, "I understand your pain." Then he gave a brief, sympathetic nod.

With tears in his eyes, Wade turned and stared out the window.

Chapter Forty-Nine

The Bus Rides Begin

The first two days in Guatemala were spent preparing for their mission. Rocky's contacts were extremely helpful, and the team was able to secure everything that they would need. This included a Chevy van, disguises, weapons, a place to stay, and of course, a "little black bag" for Sergeant Callahan.

It had taken a while to find just the right accommodations, but they were finally able to locate a furnished villa in a fairly secluded area several miles outside of town. It had a one-car attached garage that, with minor adjustments, would be an ideal holding pen, assuming that Chico's plan for capturing one of the banditos worked out.

The team found that, in addition to the tour company that Wade's aunt had mentioned, there was one other major competitor in Guatemala City. It was decided to alternate days with the two companies.

When they were about to take their first sightseeing tour, Chico went over some of the plans they had developed before they left. "Remember: don't take any weapons with you. We want to look like regular gringo tourists. Rocky and I will strap cameras around our necks for effect. Leave your passports in the villa, we're gonna need those to get home. And don't forget, they're gonna take everything we've got, so don't bring too much money, and be sure to use your spare set of dummy IDs. Also, put on your cheap watches and leave anything else of value behind. We have to get on the bus separately each time, and, Sarge, it's very important that you get on first so that you can sit all the way in the back. And someone else needs to make sure that he blocks the driver's view, so he can't look in the mirror and see what Callahan is setting up back there.

"Okay, then, I guess we're ready. Let's do it."

At 10:00 A.M., they left on their first trip. It was supposed to last about four hours and was going to stop at several tourist spots and end with a ride out of town to a banana plantation. Wade's aunt had explained that the holdup had occurred in the countryside on the way back from the plantation.

When Callahan got on the bus, he walked directly to the rear and gave a brief look to make sure that the driver was distracted by other passengers who were getting on. Additionally, he could see that Rocky was blocking the aisle behind him. After he sat down, he immediately pulled something out of his backpack. He had already placed a piece of Velcro on the outside of the package, and with a quick pull, he removed the peal and stick tab and slapped it on the metal underpart of the seat in front of him. Then, he sat back and looked calmly out the window.

The trip was uneventful. The bus driver did a good job of narrating the adventure, first explaining things in English, and then repeating everything in Spanish. The Payback Team was convinced that this driver could not possibly be involved; he was young, clean cut, and very articulate, certainly not like anything resembling the driver that Wade's aunt had described.

When they were leaving the bus station, it was clear that there were several ideal places for a hijacking. They were especially alert during this part of the tour, but the first day ended without incident.

At the end of the next day, Chico decided to alter their plan. The driver with the second company looked very much like what Wade's aunt had described, and he seemed to be carefully sizing up each passenger as they got on. Additionally, things looked a lot more like what they expected to see in a third-world country. The bus was tired and not well kept. It just didn't have the same professional, clean, well-run atmosphere that they had observed on the first bus. So instead of alternating days, they would be spending four hours every day on this one.

Then, on the thirteenth day, it happened. As they were leaving the bus station, the driver looked in his mirror and scanned all of the passengers behind him. It looked like he was trying to make sure that nothing was out of the ordinary, and when he appeared to be satisfied with the results, he punched in a number on his cell phone and spoke just two or three words.

With the exception of four passengers, no one on the bus had any idea of what was likely going to happen. On the way back from the banana plantation, the driver slowed down more than necessary when he approached a curve, and then came to a stop after he came out of the curve. There was an old farmer standing next to a wheelbarrow that had been full of bricks. The wheelbarrow had tipped over, and the bricks were all over the road, blocking the path of the bus. The driver opened the door and got up, apparently planning to give the old man a hand.

As soon as he got to the middle of the road, five armed men got on the bus and announced what was going to take place. Everyone was to get off the bus in an orderly, one-at-a-time fashion. They were told to keep quiet and to lock their hands behind their heads. They were to be led down an embankment where they would be robbed. They were to take everything with them, including anything they had placed on the floor or in the overhead rack. If anyone tried to hide anything, whether money, jewelry, or anything else of value, their safety would be in serious jeopardy. If everyone cooperated, they would not be harmed. Then the hijackers repeated everything in Spanish.

Although the passengers were afraid and upset, most of them did as they were told. One elderly man, however, seemed confused and was not cooperating. Apparently, they felt it necessary to make an example of him, so one of the bandito's dragged him out of his seat and forced his hands behind his head as he shouted, "*Like this, cabron.*"

The woman who had been seated next to him began to yell at the bandito, but he would have none of it. He promptly slapped her and yelled, "*Quiet means quiet, puta.*" It was becoming clear that the banditos were going to complete the heist their way, and that they had no problem taking care of anyone who got out of line.

One of the bandito's observed a young man of about twenty bend down toward the floor, contrary to their demand. The barrel of the bandito's gun came up swiftly under the man's chin, promptly straightening him up, and simultaneously knocking off his glasses.

Immediately after these cases of disobedience occurred, two shots were fired through the roof of the bus. A man holding a smoking gun shouted, "I will kill the next idiota who doesn't want to follow the rules. Now, do what you are told."

After this incident, some of the passengers were too shocked and frightened to get out of their seats and had to be prodded by some of the banditos with a shove or a slap. Although this was not turning out to be the orderly hijacking that they had hoped for, they were nevertheless able to get everyone off the bus, one at a time, with their hands clasped behind their heads as directed.

They were led off the bus, starting with the front, while three of the banditos began marching the line of passengers down the embankment. When about three-fourths of them were off the bus, one passenger at the back suffered what appeared to be a heart attack. It looked like he was trying to say something, but the words wouldn't come out. He clutched at his chest and was obviously in a great deal of pain. His level of distress was escalating rapidly, and it was clear that the two remaining hijackers had no idea what should be done. To complicate matters further, the passenger, Sergeant Callahan, had fallen on the floor and was gasping for air, and it looked like he was nearly unconscious.

The two banditos rapidly exchanged words in Spanish and finally decided that the best thing to do was to simply let him stay where he was, as he was obviously of no threat to anyone but himself. They directed the few remaining passengers to step over or around him as best they could.

When everyone except Callahan and the two men were off the bus, it was decided that one of them should stay with Callahan, just in case he was able to come to life and get off the bus and cause trouble for them in some way. Callahan waited for the right opportunity. After a few seconds, he began to groan, and then he tried to sit up. The bandito didn't realize that Callahan had been wearing a backpack, and that he had managed to twist it around in front of him when he fell. He looked up at the man and held out his hand, indicating that he wanted to try to get into one of the seats, but didn't have the strength to do it on his own. The man quickly holstered his gun, grabbed Callahan's hand, and began to pull him off the floor. It was not entirely a gesture of mercy but rather that he intended to confiscate his backpack, which became visible when Callahan started to sit up.

As the bandito got him about halfway into one of the seats, Callahan made his move. He had placed his free hand in the backpack as he was being helped up; now, he pulled the man down to the floor at the same time that his hand flew out of the backpack and pressed a chloroform-soaked rag tightly against his nose and mouth. After a brief struggle, he was out.

So far, things had gone according to plan. But now, it was time to take the next step, and it had to be done quickly. If he slipped up, it would probably cost him his life. With all of his energy, he half dragged, half carried the unconscious bandito out of the bus and then carried him over to the side of the road, away from the embankment. He dropped the bandito on the ground, in a dense patch of brush, and hurried back to the bus.

In less than a minute, one of the banditos returned and was surprised to find only one man on the bus. Callahan was now sitting up in the middle of the floor, clutching his chest, with a dazed look on his face. The man quickly summoned one of the other three banditos, and the two men exchanged several anxious words in Spanish. It was clear that they were having trouble deciding whether they should try to look for their missing colleague, or if it was best to just take off and hope that he would find his way back to their base on his own. They were obviously concerned about spending too much more time at the scene.

They decided to leave. Callahan could hear a vehicle start up and drive away. Within a few minutes, the driver and passengers began to return to the bus. They had been told to wait at the embankment until five minutes after they heard their vehicle leave.

When Rocky boarded the bus, Callahan gave him a nod and shifted his eyes over to the area where he had dumped the bandito. Then, Rocky quickly grabbed the package that Callahan had put under the seat and got off the bus. He looked back at Callahan several times when he got near the area that the sergeant had directed, and with Callahan's eye movements, he was able to zero in on the exact location. When he found the still unconscious man, he quickly took a baseball cap, a mustache, and a wig out of the package and put them on the bandito. He also slipped an army fatigue jacket over the man's shirt, and then removed his cell phone, his gun, and his holster. He gave a nod to Chico, who then distracted the driver so that Rocky could get back on the bus with the bandito. Because of his size and strength, he was able to get the man on the bus fairly quickly and pinned in the seat next to him.

Wade retrieved the chloroformed rag from Callahan, who had slipped it into a plastic bag, and passed it to Rocky, who was planning to use it if necessary because he had to keep the bandito from regaining consciousness during the return ride.

Before starting the bus, the driver spent a few minutes apologizing to the passengers and explaining that nothing like this had ever happened before. After trying his best to calm everyone down, he took his seat and began to drive.

As predicted, the driver's cell phone rang a few minutes after the bus started the return journey. Chico was closest to the driver, and he was able to hear the conversation, which lasted less than ten seconds. "No, no se. Lluego." It was clear that the driver had been asked if he knew what happened to the missing hijacker, and that he had no idea.

When the bus returned to the station, Callahan had somehow recovered completely and was able to get off the bus unassisted. He and four other passengers, including one who seemed to be having great difficulty walking, got into a tan Chevy van and drove off. The Payback Team had successfully done what everyone but Chico had initially thought could not be done: they had captured one of the banditos, and now it was time for phase two of Chico's plan to begin.

Chapter Fifty

Revising the Plan

By the time the van pulled up in front of the villa, the bandito had recovered enough to walk into his confinement unassisted. The Payback Team had rigged the garage door so that it would not open, and they had closed off the only window so that a relatively secure, makeshift jail cell awaited its first prisoner. Upon entering the garage, the bandito surveyed the sparse furnishings: several folding chairs, one table, a mattress, and a porta potty. One light hung from the ceiling.

After a minute or two, everyone except for Sergeant Callahan was seated. Callahan opened his little black bag and dumped the contents on the table. Then he spoke. "Well, isn't this a nice little get together? You're going to be our guest for awhile, so why don't we get to know each other, okay? Habla usted Ingles? Good. Now, let's get better acquainted. My name is Callahan. Como te llamas?"

The hijacker looked at everyone in the garage, and then answered the question with a defiant tone. "My name is Pepe, but listen, Gringo, you don't have to waste my time. I know what you want. And you won't need your little toys on the table over there. I'll tell you everything you want to know. But you're not going to like it. In fact, you're going to be very sorry you ever came to Guatemala. You, all of you, are the prisoners. You just don't know it. I don't think you are going to leave Guatemala alive. So ask me your questions, and do what you gotta do."

Callahan was intrigued. "Well, that was quite a speech. Why don't you tell me exactly how you expect to back up those cute little threats?"

Pepe continued. "It's simple. I'll tell you who is in charge, and I'll tell you where to find him. And then you'll go there, and then you'll die. Very simple."

Callahan spoke again. "Well, now, this is getting interesting. Why don't you tell me the whole story? It sounds like this is going to be a lot easier than I thought; although, I must say, I was looking forward to using my little gadgets over there. But go ahead, talk."

Pepe obliged. "Okay, but you're not going to like it. Maybe you should just take your gringo compadres and vamanos, comprende? The thing is: our operation is run by Tito. Tito Hernandez. He is the man in Guatemala. We work for him. You don't mess with Tito. Judges, la policia, los politicos, they all stay out of his way. Those who don't understand this...well, we take care of them, and then they are no longer a problem for Tito. Now, you see why we can do this, rob the turistas many, many times, and no one stops us, comprende? The drugs that come up from South America, they go through Guatemala, comprende? But they only get to Mexico, and then to Los Estados Unidos, if Tito says so. And Tito makes a lot of money by controlling the flow and guaranteeing delivery, comprende? This little hijacking business—that's just like a little hobby, you gringos call it 'chump change.' It's no big deal.

"Mis amigos, you don't know what you have gotten yourself into. You think you want to stop a little robbery business that is annoying to you, like a flea that is buzzing around your ear? But, no, my friends, you have stepped into a hornet's nest. There are four of you, es verdad?" He paused long enough to give a derisive laugh. "There are forty men protecting Tito. Listen, amigos, you have no chance. Go home. Hasta lluego, okay?"

Chico, realizing that his plan was now totally irrelevant, tried not to look worried. "Where is this famous Tito, just in case we don't want to take your advice?"

Pepe didn't hesitate. "He is easy to find, but you should hope he doesn't find you first. His estate is at the end of Calle Nogales. You will not like the guards, you will not like the dogs, and you will not see your families if you try to get past the gate. Buena suerte, mis amigos."

Pepe's captors tried not to show their concern as they asked several more questions. Pepe, apparently, felt there was no harm in cooperating since he knew they had no chance of getting anywhere except to their graves. The Payback Team learned that the bus driver would call one of the hijackers when the bus was pulling out of the station. He would wait for the right mix of passengers, usually consisting of a large group of Americans on a prearranged sightseeing tour. Most days, it wasn't worth the effort. Then, after receiving the go ahead, they would use a beige Humvee and head over to a three or four mile stretch of fairly desolate countryside and set up the ambush. When their work was completed, they would put their haul in a canvas bag and drop it off at the front gate of Tito's estate. Then they would return to their base, which was a hacienda, about twenty miles south of the estate. Pepe explained that when they weren't involved with Tito's hijacking business, he had other assignments for them: transporting drugs, joining Tito's contingency of bodyguards when he ventured from his estate, executing people who occasionally got in the way, and sometimes, making collections from, or payments to, some of Tito's business associates.

Chico had heard enough to know that there was no point in proceeding any further. The Payback Team left Pepe alone in his cell and adjourned to the living room of the villa. Then he asked the inevitable question. "Well, this is a whole new ball game. There's no point in taking out just the hijackers; it'll only be a matter of time before our local drug lord puts together another bunch of banditos. So, what do you want to do? Maybe we should go around the room and each one give his opinion. The obvious choice, as I see it, is either go home or take out Tito and the banditos, and maybe as many of his drug running buddies as we can."

After a few minutes of silence, Sergeant Callahan spoke. "We came here to do a job, let's do it."

Then it was Rocky's turn. "I agree, providing Chico can come up with a plan. But right now, I don't see how that's possible. Maybe this will be the one time when he strikes out. But that's okay; this is really a ball buster."

Callahan looked at Wade. "Courtland, this whole thing was your idea, initially. What do you think? Do you want to pull the plug? I will understand if you do. All of you guys have a lot more to lose than I do, so I'll go along with whatever."

Wade thought for a moment and then responded. "I might sound like I'm up on a soap box, but here's the thing. This is no longer about some people getting robbed, it's about drugs, corruption, and murder.

Will taking Tito out stop drugs from coming into the US and killing our kids? Of course not. But if we do what needs to be done here, it'll sure cut off part of the supply, at least for awhile. I don't want to spend the rest of my life remembering the time we were in a position to do something really worthwhile and just walked away. Listen, this is what we're all about. We're a team, and we're supposed to stop this from happening. Well, okay, that's my vote. If you're with me, then Chico, the master planner, needs to get to work. And my guess is that he has already started on a plan."

After another ten minutes of discussion, including what to do about Pepe, the team agreed that they wanted to go ahead. They felt that even though the stakes were much higher, and the danger factor had increased exponentially, they needed to put these guys out of business.

Chico got up and started toward the garage. "I'm gonna need some more information from our little stickup man in there. Rocky, would you come with me to help keep things under control, and would you two guys take a camera and go over to Calle Nogales and get some pictures of the estate and the surrounding area?"

When they were seated in the garage, Chico started explaining things to Pepe. "Well, amigo, this might be your lucky day. We've decided to take out your boss and all of his hired killers, hijackers, and drug runners. But as for you, if you'll—" Chico's words were drowned out by Pepe's laughter. It took him almost a minute to calm down enough for Chico to continue. "Okay, fine. I'm glad you find it amusing. But think about it. Aren't you a little surprised to be here? Is this how you were planning to end the day when you got up this morning? Maybe it should occur to you that there's more to us than you might have realized. But, anyway, here's the thing. We need some more information, and if you continue to cooperate with us, we will proceed with our initial plan for you. If not, your life will end right here in this garage before you can get out your next laugh."

Pepe had been looking at Chico while he was talking, but his head jerked when he heard Rocky cock the gun, which was less than one foot from his brain. There was no more defiant look on his face, and this time, he had no intention of laughing. It was all he could do to get the words out. "What are you talking about? What do you want from me?" Nobody answered, and nobody moved. Pepe saw the intensity in Chico's and Rocky's eyes, and it began to occur to him that there was something about his captors that he was beginning to respect. He now realized that they meant what they said, both the part about taking out Tito and the part about his chance of getting whacked on the spot. "Okay, just put down the pistola. I'll give you what you want."

Chico began his interrogation. "What I'm talking about is the fact that we were going to take the five of you, as well as the bus driver, and cut off one of your hands. You know, they do that to thieves in some Arab countries. Kind of makes it difficult to carry on with their business, if you know what I mean. So, now, provided that you cooperate with us, the worst that can happen to you is that you're going to have your hand cut off. We're gonna kill Tito and the rest of your sorry-ass friends. But I need to know a couple of things, and if you give the right answers, you will live." At this point, Rocky put down the gun, and Pepe started to loosen up.

During the next ten minutes of questioning, Chico learned enough so that he could start putting a new plan together. Pepe was not afraid to tell him everything he wanted to know because he couldn't see how they could pull it off. As far as he was concerned, his boss's fortress was impenetrable.

When they walked back into the villa, they were alone, as Wade and Callahan had left to take pictures of Tito's estate. Rocky went in the kitchen to get a beer, and Chico took out a pad and started making notes about what he had learned from Pepe. This was one of the ways that he came up with effective plans: write down all pertinent information, try to isolate the important elements, see what the pluses and minuses are for each possible solution, and then eliminate the ones with the most negatives.

He wrote that he had learned that Tito rarely left his estate, and that he had several bodyguards with him when he did. Additionally, he had at least three doubles, and sometimes, one of these look-alikes would leave with the bodyguards. A sniper would very possibly wind up taking out the wrong man. Pepe also told him that his boss never left the estate on Saturday. The last day of the week was always reserved for soccer games. Starting at one in the afternoon, five of his captains would take their places at a card table in his den, drink tequila, play poker, and watch their favorite teams on Tito's big screen plasma TV until early evening. Chico knew that this was important information, but he wasn't as yet sure how he was going to use it. He made a mental note that he would need to conduct at least one more fact-finding conversation with Pepe after he came up with a plan.

Just as he was finishing making his notes, Wade and Callahan returned with the pictures Chico had asked for. He downloaded them from the digital camera onto his laptop and enlarged each of them to full-screen size. After reviewing them in detail, he sat back, closed his eyes, and began to envision a plan.

Chapter Fifty-One

The Most Important Mission Begins

After Chico had formed the outline of a plan, he went back out to the garage and spent a few minutes grilling Pepe in order to learn more details about the mansion and its occupants. When he was satisfied with the answers, he assembled the rest of the team and began to explain how they might be able to accomplish their objective. "The only way we can get at the lion is to go into the lion's den. He's just not gonna come out when we want him to. It could take who knows how long, and even then, it could be one of his doubles.

"One thing we know for sure is that he is always in his den on Saturday afternoon. That's important information. That's the one time when we know exactly where he is. Now, we've got to get someone in there who can blow him and his captains to eternity. That's where the major comes in. We've got to get him and his whole crew down here. Obviously, the guy who's gonna go into Tito's estate will have to be Hispanic. I'm thinking of Xavier. He really did a good job for us on a couple of occasions. And we're also gonna need Rocky's pilot friend. And, somehow, he's gonna need to bring down that contraption that he used under his chopper that time he tried to pick up John V.'s car, remember? I hope he practiced the technique like we asked him to because, this time, I think we have to—"

Wade cut him off. "Hold it, amigo. Are you kidding us? Blow him up, like with a bomb? Inside Tito's estate? How in the hell—?"

Chico had anticipated doubt on everyone's part and knew that Wade would be the first to express it. He grabbed the pictures that had been taken of Tito's estate and began to explain. "Okay, I know it seems like an extreme idea, but I think I've got it figured out. Listen, just look at this picture. What do you see? I mean right here, where I'm pointing? I'll tell you what it is: it's a satellite dish. And over here is some kind of building, looks like a big garage, or maybe a storage building. It's partly torn down. My guess is that Tito has bought some of the adjoining property and intends to expand his estate. So why

305

don't we put a sniper up there and take out the transponder? You know, that's the little oblong thing right in front of the dish. Then, when they find out that their plans for watching the soccer games are in jeopardy, they're gonna call someone to come out and fix it right away. So, we wait around the corner from the approach to Calle Nogales and intercept the TV repair truck. And guess who's gonna walk in the door with the bomb at the bottom of his tool box? Xavier, of course.

"But, listen, we've got a lot of work ahead of us. What I want to do is to construct a bomb like they used on the Muir Building in Oklahoma. I remember they mixed some kind of fertilizer with some other ingredients. I'll bet the major's crew can figure it out. If we get them down here right away, they can start working on this while we're waiting for the next hijacking."

Wade had a comment. "Well, Chico, it looks like you've done it again. This could work. I should have known you'd come up with something. Let's hope the major is available."

Rocky responded. "I'm one step ahead of you. He's kind of on standby. I talked to him before we left and told him we would possibly be calling him to come down here. But I don't think I called Wayne, the pilot. He's usually pretty flexible, though. I hope he can figure out how to get that gadget down here. He calls it 'the claw.' And yes, he did work on perfecting the technique. He can pick up a car, but it has to be stopped, or at least going under about ten miles an hour."

Chico seemed pleased. "Good, that's exactly how I figured it could work. See, there's really no effective way to put them out of business other than getting all of them at once. And we can't just start blasting away because they're naturally gonna return fire. So what I want to do is to strike when they are on their way back to their base, after they drop off the loot at the estate. The timing of this is important. We want to take them out before we work on Tito because if we get Tito first, they will most likely shut down for awhile. What I want to do is to come down out of the sky, fire a couple of .50-caliber-machinegun rounds into the engine of the Humvee, and then pick them up when they slow down enough for the maneuver to work. It has to be precise, before they have a chance to get out of the Humvee and scatter or, worse yet, start shooting up at the chopper."

Now, it was Callahan's turn to ask a question. "How will we know when they are gonna do the next job?"

Chico had the answer. "That one's easy. We're gonna have one of the major's men stationed at the bus station each morning. He'll have to use a few disguises, so no one will see a pattern. It's a good bet that the driver is in the habit of making the phone call to the hijackers right after he closes the door and just before he begins his narration to the gringo turistas. We have to make certain that we get our man in just the right position to see when the driver makes that phone call, and then he can let us know that it's going down. Actually, he may know in advance when the driver is likely to make the call because we're gonna tell him what to look for regarding the makeup of the passengers who get on each day. Remember, Pepe said that most days, there just weren't enough passengers to make it worthwhile. So, I guess, that's about it. Let's get the major and the pilot lined up. Now, let's get back to the Tito issue because there are a couple more details we need to go over. I'm surprised no one asked me how we're gonna get a bomb into the estate. You can expect that no one's just gonna let Xavier walk in there without checking him out for weapons and going through his tool box. And no one thought to ask what we're gonna do about all of the guys at the estate who survive the blast. Do we just let them walk away or do we want to try to wipe out all of them?

"Okay, we'll go over all of this when I get back. Right now, I want to take a ride over to the estate to get a closer look at some of the things that caught my eye in the pictures. Rocky, I'll give you a list of things we're gonna need your contacts to pick up for us, starting with four machine guns and two really large, well stocked, tool boxes. Make sure someone keeps an eye on our little hijacker in the garage, 24/7. He can probably get out of there if he works at it. Hasta la bye-bye."

Chapter Fifty-Two

Confronting the Banditos

Both of Rocky's phone calls got results. The major and his entire crew—Art, Xavier, Howie, and Greg—would be leaving the next day to join The Payback Team. They had worked with all but Greg previously, but since Greg was an ex-marine, like the others, they knew that they would be dealing with someone who could help them get the job done.

Wayne was planning to come down a little later, as he had a lot of logistics to work on. He was planning to send the chopper and the claw down by cargo plane. The claw was rigged up via a special system that incorporated a complicated set of hydraulic controls and, therefore, could not be easily retrofitted to just any helicopter.

As soon as the major and his associates arrived, they were put to work getting a bomb together. They were handed a large, black tool box and informed that the bomb had to be designed to fit into the bottom section. The top section would consist of a removable tool tray, which would serve to conceal the bomb.

Rocky's contacts were extremely helpful, and in less than four days, they had all the ingredients. They put together an explosive device that fit perfectly into the tool box. But it was very heavy and Xavier had to practice trying to carry it in such a way that he wouldn't attract any unusual attention.

Next, it was necessary to come up with some kind of timing mechanism that could be set so that it would go off at just the right moment. This was necessary for three reasons. First, Xavier obviously had to get out of the compound before it went off. Second, it had to detonate at a time when it was most likely that the victims would all be assembled in the den. And, third, The Payback Team and their accomplices wanted to be in place at just the right time in order to finish what they had started.

When Wayne arrived, it looked like everything was in place. He unloaded everything at a private airfield that Rocky's contacts had located, but this came at a price because a large payoff had to be made. For the most part, bringing a package like this one into a foreign country could not be done without handing out with a few pieces of silver to those in charge.

All in all, this was shaping up to be a very expensive venture. When they added up all of the various expense categories, which included Major Robins's team, ingredients for the bomb, the pilot and his cargo, plus miscellaneous other items, it looked like the final bill might come close to half a million dollars. But The Payback Team had discussed this ahead of time and decided that the ultimate victory was worth many times this, in terms of the incalculable amount of suffering, as well as the loss of human lives, that would be avoided if they were successful.

After a few trials, the chopper was ready. The claw mechanism worked by attaching it to a cable that hung from the helicopter after it was a few feet off the ground. It could then be winched up under the chopper so that it could maneuver at nearly full speed to the rendezvous point. Then it could be lowered into position within just a few seconds. It resembled the large, magnetic disc at junkyards used to pick up old cars and mounds of iron, except that it had four claws that could be either extended or retracted in order to clamp on to a vehicle and pick it up off the ground.

But the tricky part was that the vehicle would ideally need to be stationary in order for the claw to do its work. This presented a catch-22, in that the thieves would therefore have the chance to exit the Humvee and become a major threat to the whole operation. Additionally, if the pilot was unsuccessful on his first attempt, while the Humvee was slowing down, there would probably not be a second chance. So, it was decided that it would be necessary to use a second chopper. This backup helicopter would be in place to start blasting away at the Humvee with two .50 caliber machine guns, if the first attempt failed. They would hope that they could take out all of the occupants before they could return fire. Major Robins had run enough missions while serving in the marines to know that this was the type of scenario that looked effective on the planning table, but usually turned into total chaos on the battlefield, with massive casualties on both sides.

While everyone was preparing for the day when they were going to take out the hijackers, Greg had been assigned to wait at the bus depot. He was able to find a bench in just the right spot where he could observe the passengers as they boarded the bus each day for the beginning of the tour. And by getting up from the bench and walking around a corner, he could also keep an eye on the driver for about thirty seconds before he was out of sight.

Finally, three days after everyone was ready, Greg, dressed up as a priest, realized that this was probably going to be the day they had all been waiting for. Judging by the number, and makeup, of passengers that boarded the bus, it looked like this would be the perfect trip for the hijackers to strike. When Greg saw the driver make a call on his cell phone as the bus pulled out of the station, he phoned the villa to let them know that everyone needed to start getting into place.

One hour before the expected arrival time of the Humvee at Tito's estate, Howie was in place on Calle Nogales, about half a mile from the estate. When he saw the vehicle approach, he notified his boss, who alerted everyone who was going to be involved.

The claw was attached to Wayne's craft, and then both choppers took off. Within five minutes after takeoff, the two helicopters were several thousand feet in the air, tracking the Humvee as it made its way back to the hijackers' base. The major was at the controls of the backup chopper, with Greg and Xavier on board, armed with .50 caliber machine guns.

Art, an experienced pilot in his own right, was flying the other chopper, while Wayne was going to work the claw's hydraulic controls. It had been determined, during practice runs back in the Milwaukee area, that it was nearly impossible for one man to work both sets of controls.

After about ten minutes, the Humvee entered the zone where the pickup was planned. Wayne and Art had made a few practice runs over the area and had figured out where the best place would be to make their approach. Both choppers had been keeping a safe distance, vertically and laterally, so they were certain that they had not been spotted.

The driver of the Humvee didn't see it coming. Major Robins brought the chopper down so fast that it was virtually on top of them when they simultaneously heard the sound of the engine and the pop, pop of the machine gun. It was not until he felt the loss of power that the driver realized that his engine block had been breached.

The hijackers were so busy looking at Major Robins's chopper, just a couple of hundred feet above and in front of them, that they failed to notice the other helicopter closing in from behind, a mere hundred feet off the ground. Two of the hijackers had their guns pointed out the windows, anticipating a frontal attack by the major's chopper, and just as the Humvee was about to come to a complete stop, they were astonished by a concurrent, violent jolt to their vehicle and a loud clunking sound on the roof. The next thing that happened startled them even more. Four large, metal hooks came in all four windows, shattering the two that had yet to be opened, and quickly turned upward, grabbing the vehicle like a shark closing its teeth around its prey. Before any of the hijackers could utter a word, they were jerked off the ground and were rapidly gaining altitude.

They reached two hundred feet before they were able to figure out the gravity of their situation. Their assumption that they were going to be turned over to the authorities vanished when an unimaginably worse scenario occurred. The jaws of whatever had crashed on top of their ride were rapidly retracting. Their trip to the ground took even less time than their ascent.

Elapsed time from contact with the Humvee until its return to earth: thirteen seconds.

Within a few seconds after the vehicle made contact with the roadway, Major Robins's helicopter was on the ground. His two armed passengers stormed the Humvee and blasted away. They had to make sure no one had survived, as an unwanted cell phone call could spoil the surprise party they were planning for Saturday.

When Greg and Xavier gave the thumbs up sign to Art's chopper, it promptly descended, picked up the lifeless Humvee a second and final time, and headed for the Pacific Ocean.

While the major and the pilot were busy terminating the hijackers, The Payback Team members were occupied with another piece of unfinished business: the bus driver. He also had to be permanently put out of business and punished for his involvement in an operation that had caused so much trauma, hardship, and even the occasional loss of life. It would be nearly impossible to calculate the immense number of individuals who had suffered over the years due to these criminals.

But it had been decided that the driver would not experience the same terminal fate as the other hijackers. Since he had played a lesser role in the operation and had not physically harmed or killed anyone, he would not pay as great a price, but one that would, nevertheless, put an end to his career in hijacking.

While Wade stayed behind to keep Pepe company, the rest of The Payback Team was in place just a mile or two from the location of the hijacking. They had rolled a large log across the road and, quite understandably, the passengers were startled to have what was supposed to be a pleasant sightseeing trip interrupted a second time.

When the driver got out to survey the situation, Rocky promptly jumped out of nowhere, moving faster than anyone could imagine, and dragged him off to the side of the road. Chico then boarded the bus and informed the stunned passengers that the bus driver had been responsible for their plight and that they were going to make sure that it never happened again. He then asked someone to repeat everything in Spanish. When the announcement was completed, Chico asked the interpreter if he could drive the bus back to the station, and he indicated that he could. After the log was removed, the bus took off.

Callahan spoke to the driver, saying, "How do you like this reversal of fortune? Let's see how you react when you're the victim. Lock your hands behind your head and start walking that way. We're gonna have a little fun."

The driver didn't move an inch. He held out both arms in a pleading motion and said, "Señor, you have made a big mistake. Those banditos...I don't know them...I promise you...I would never—"

Callahan wanted none of it. "Well, let's see who answers when I press REDIAL on your cell phone. Tell you what. Let's make a little bet. Here's how it's gonna work. I'll bet that the guy who answers is one of the hijackers. If I'm right, you lose your life. If I'm wrong, you win your freedom. How does that sound? Or, if you want, you can just stop the bullshit, admit that you are part of this whole rotten operation, and then we'll go on to the next step. What's it gonna be? Your call."

Given the alternatives, the driver changed his demeanor completely, just as Callahan was about to hit REDIAL. "Señor, I had no choice. They made me do it. I am not one of the banditos. I am only—"

He was cut off in mid-sentence, as Callahan explained what was to be his fate. "Okay, you made the right choice, although you kinda fucked it up by all the bullshit you threw in, but that's okay because the next step I referred to a minute ago is about to kick in. Now, here's what we're gonna do. First, take your cell phone back and throw it over there as far as you can. Then, lock your hands behind your head just like your passengers had to do. And then, I want you to march down that embankment." After the driver completed each of the commands, Callahan asked, "What does this feel like? Do you wonder why we're walking so far away from the road? Are you thinking that maybe you're gonna die? Did you ever consider, even for a minute, how all of your passengers felt, or were you just thinking about your share of the take?

"You want to know something? Every one of those people, they all remember what happened to them. They can't forget what you and the other banditos did to them. But, now, you will remember also. Every time you look at where your right hand used to be—that's the one I noticed you used to throw the cell phone—you're gonna remember this day. Maybe you'll also remember the harm you've caused all the people you've robbed, but I have to say I doubt it."

The driver's eyes filled with horror as he spotted the axe propped up against a nearby tree stump.

Callahan continued, saying, "So, here we are, end of the line. You're gonna be a lefty from now on. Hope you can get used to it. But, at least, I think this is gonna put an end to your bus driving and hijacking days. Hey, maybe you can get a job as a one-handed juggler!" Then Callahan started one of his raucous laughing spells as he put a piece of duct tape over the driver's mouth and a black hood over his head.

The driver's struggles and muffled protests did him no good. Within a few seconds, Rocky and Chico wrestled him over to the tree stump, and with one swing of the axe, the driver's right hand was no longer a part of him.

After everyone got into the Chevy van, the driver was dropped off at a local hospital, and then the remaining occupants returned to the villa. Not long after their arrival, Wade asked the major and Callahan if they had brought back the evidence of the results of their respective missions. When they indicated that they had, he took a few minutes to put everything together and then took his laptop into the garage. Then he addressed Pepe. "You know, amigo, you and I have been arguing for a few days now about whether or not we are capable of doing what we said we're gonna do. You also said that we don't have the cajones to remove your hand after this is all over. You know, we're only keeping you alive because that was the deal we made, and unlike criminals, such as yourself, we always keep our word. But frankly, it's becoming a nuisance to have you around. We're only doing it because you would spoil the plans we have for Tito if we let you go now."

At this point, Pepe gave a sneer and a derisive laugh. It was clear that he had no respect for his captors, or their ability to cause even the slightest harm to Tito and his band of thieves, drug runners, and assassins. Then Wade continued. "So, I've got something to show you. Tell me if you recognize anyone in these pictures. It was really a lot of time wasted on their part, but I asked two of my associates to take some shots of the jobs they just finished. Maybe now you'll shut up and start to realize that we always do what we say we're gonna do. If you're lucky, we might bring back some more pictures when we finish with Tito.

"Tell you what, I'll narrate for you. Here's a close up of the Humvee, after it was dropped out of the sky, and there's all your little criminal amigos. And look, here they go, off to the ocean to sleep with the pescados. Oh, and you might recognize this guy. But wait a minute! Where's his hand? Oh, look, there it is in this next shot, next to the tree stump. Well, okay, that concludes our little slide show for now. Hope you enjoyed it. We set it up just for you. Now, maybe the next time we tell you something, you won't act like we're full of mierda, okay?" Then he closed the laptop and waited for a response.

But Pepe was unable to speak. His face was expressionless as he stared blankly at the closed laptop. It was clear that it was going to take some time for him to process the unfathomable images that would likely torment him until his last days.

Chapter Fifty-Three

Getting Ready to Confront Tito

Saturday, the Big Day, had finally arrived. This was to be The Payback Team's denouement. Just about everything they had worked on during the previous six months was preparation for what would occur during the next several hours.

At 12:30 in the afternoon, everyone involved had gone over their assigned roles and was on their way to where they were supposed to be. The major and his four crew members, along with the pilot, were at the private airfield, getting ready to take off in the two helicopters. All four members of The Payback Team had secured a Guatemala City garbage truck with the help of one of Rocky's contacts and were on their way to the estate.

Earlier in the day, Greg, one of Major Robins's cadre had been dropped off near the estate. He then climbed to the top of the vacant building adjacent to Tito's estate and shot out the satellite dish's transponder. He then abandoned his sharpshooter's post and headed off to his next assignment. He met up with Xavier, about three blocks from Tito's estate on Calle Nogales. They only had to wait about an hour before intercepting a truck from the Gonzales Electronics Company. While Xavier continued onto the estate, Greg took the bound and hooded driver to the villa, using the Chevy van that had been parked two blocks farther up Calle Nogales.

The driver of the TV repair truck was going to be Pepe's new cellmate, at least for a few hours, until everyone, or at least the survivors, returned from their mission. One of Rocky's contacts was assigned to guard the two captives until The Payback Team, or at least those who survived, returned to the villa.

Xavier had played his role perfectly, although there had been a couple of tense moments. When he got to the estate, he was able to get inside the gate and pull up to the front entrance to the mansion without any difficulty. But as soon as he got out of the van, he was stopped by two men who had been standing by the pillars on the front porch. As he was opening the rear doors of the service van, they took a good look inside the van and then watched as he pulled out his tool box. Before he could take a step toward the residence, they asked him to put down the box and submit to a search. While one of the men patted him down. The other thoroughly ransacked the work kit. Everything was removed from top to bottom.

Xavier's body search was just as thorough. The bodyguard's hands explored every square inch of him and his clothing. At one point, Xavier was thinking that if this were a physical exam, the doctor would probably be asking him to turn his head and cough.

Now that they were intimately familiar, Xavier tried to lighten the mood by asking his frisker if he was doing anything that evening, but humor was apparently not his thing. But, at least, he had come up clean and was allowed to proceed into the building.

He was shown to the den, and he was told that there would be a large tip if he could get the TV going before the afternoon's affair was due to take place. One of the bodyguards who had accompanied him to the den explained that the soccer teams from Guatemala and Brazil were starting a big match at 3:00, and his boss and several associates were counting on seeing it in its entirety, a fact with which Xavier, the major, and The Payback Team were well aware. That was the reason why the digital timing device on the bomb had been preset to 3:20, as they knew that everyone was certain to be present in the den at that time.

One of the bodyguards left the den, and it didn't take long for Xavier to figure out that the remaining bodyguard was assigned to stay right by his side for the duration of the service call. That meant that he would have to use the diversionary tactic that they had worked out earlier, and he hoped that it would go off as planned.

Using all of the technical terms he could think of, Xavier began explaining what was wrong with the TV reception. Apparently, there had been a malfunction at the satellite dish outside, most likely caused by weather damage to the transponder, which in turn had burned out one of the lead wires in the satellite receiver inside. He made this announcement as he disconnected one of the wires inside the receiver. Then he explained that he would have to get a ladder from his truck and climb up to the satellite dish and check it out. He tried another joke by asking the man if he wanted to climb up the ladder with him, but the bodyguard just curled his lip in a snarl and shook his head—not the kind of shake that said, "no thanks," but the kind that said, "you're starting to piss me off."

He picked up his tool box and went out to the van. The back door was still open, so he climbed in and started rummaging around, looking in bins and opening drawers, apparently trying to find just the right component for the next part of the job. As he expected, the bodyguard grew restless after a minute or two and backed away a few steps to light a cigarette. During this brief few seconds of inattention, Xavier pulled out a bin on the floor, under one of the shelves on the left side of the vehicle, and deftly switched tool boxes. After another few seconds, he found the transponder he had been looking for and grabbed the ladder and headed for the post next to the mansion where the satellite dish was located. Knowing that it was likely that the transponder that was needed for replacement might not be in the repair truck, The Payback Team had done the necessary research, located the right part, and made sure it was placed in the tool box. Additionally, Xavier had practiced removing and replacing the transponder so that there would be no slip ups when the time came to make the switch. Within a few minutes, he was able to install the new transponder, and as far as the bodyguard could tell, this was the work of an experienced technician.

When he got down from the ladder, Xavier explained to the bodyguard, who had become his virtual shadow, that he had, indeed, found the problem. Next, they needed to go inside and see if the TV was working, or if there was also a problem with the receiver, as he had previously mentioned might be the case.

Once inside, they determined that the receiver would need to be serviced, as the TV was still not working. So Xavier headed back out to the van to get his tool box, with the bodyguard not far behind. When he stepped out of the van, tool box in hand, he decided to take the initiative, in hopes that he could avoid another search. Placing the box on the ground, he said, "Okay, I guess you want to check it out again. Here you go, take a look." Then he opened the top of the box and stepped back. The bodyguard could tell that the contents looked exactly the same as when he had left the mansion previously. Apparently, he was satisfied, as he gave a motion with his arm that indicated he should get on with his work. Fortunately, the bluff worked as planned. Xavier picked up the box and proceeded to do everything he could to make it look like he was carrying the box just as before in spite of the fact that it was more than thirty pounds heavier. His luck continued, as the bodyguard was paying more attention to his second cigarette and didn't notice any difference in Xavier's stride.

Xavier opened the tool box, took out a screwdriver and a pair of pliers, and started working on the receiver. He had reached the moment when he had hoped to be alone in the den, but that was not to be, so it was time for the preplanned diversion. He took out his cell phone and appeared to be calling his shop to ask for a little advice. While the bodyguard heard nothing but technical jargon, Greg, on the other end of the phone, knew that it was time to get to work, as Xavier obviously needed a distraction as soon as possible.

Within a minute, an extremely loud explosion occurred on the front grounds of the estate, just inside the entrance gate. Greg had been waiting in the Chevy van, not far from the compound, and promptly drove up and lobbed a flash grenade over the wall of the compound.

As expected, the bodyguard hurriedly left the den to see what had happened, and to see if any of his colleagues needed assistance. He returned in less than a minute, after determining that everything outside was under control. During the short time Xavier was alone in the den, he removed the bomb from the bottom of the tool box and placed it where it was least likely to be discovered. He had carefully surveyed the den and determined that it should be put on the bottom of the polished mahogany cabinet under the bar. He moved several boxes of supplies out of the way, put the bomb in the rear of the cabinet, and then put everything back in place.

When the bodyguard returned, Xavier asked, "*Que paso?*" But the bodyguard, who was clearly a man of few words, gave a wave that clearly said, "This is nothing for you to worry about, just keep working."

As planned, Xavier reconnected the wire in the receiver and the TV promptly came to life. If he had expected any kind of appreciation from the bodyguard, he was disappointed. The man simply led him to the front door of the mansion. When he got outside and started heading to the repair truck, the bodyguard gave a nod to another man, who thanked Xavier and handed him a tip of two hundred pesos.

With his work completed, Xavier slowly drove away from Tito's compound. If the bomb stayed in place until 3:20, and if Tito and his captains were where they were supposed to be, they would be denied the pleasure of seeing the conclusion of the soccer game.

Chapter Fifty-Four

The Culmination of the Guatemala Mission

At about the time that the major and his troops were taking off from the airfield, The Payback Team was approaching Tito's estate in the garbage truck. They parked a couple of blocks away and waited in silence.

Each member of the team was focused on fulfilling his part in the extraordinary scenario that would be unfolding within the hour, but they also couldn't help thinking that they were glad that it would soon be over. Chico was looking forward to getting home to his family, and for just a moment, he also thought about the absurdity of the situation they were in. Instead of spending the fortune he had earned from his consulting business in the style of the typical retiree, he was living like an undercover CIA operative in a third-world country. The question of whether or not it was worth it could only be answered after the outcome of the mission was evaluated; provided, of course, that he survived.

Rocky also thought about his family and planned to call them as soon as he got back to the villa to let them know that he would soon be on his way home. He briefly looked at the other members of his team and hoped that every one of them would be with him on the flight back to Chicago the next morning. The entire experience with The Payback Team, from the very start, had been one exhilarating day after another, right up to the present moment. He hoped that nothing would stop them from continuing their quest after they got home. Certainly, the others would want to take a little time off, but he planned to be ready for action almost immediately.

The most important thing in the world to Sean Callahan was his daughter. He figured that after his wife died, she was the only thing keeping him from becoming a raging alcoholic, who would one day drink himself into oblivion. He was thinking how much he was going to enjoy getting back home and heading over to the nursing home that was now caring for her. He only wished that she was of sound enough mind to look forward to the visits as much as he did. Briefly, his thoughts drifted to the new dimension that had found its way into his existence, and that was his recent inclusion on The Payback Team. He felt that their purpose was extremely worthwhile, and he was thoroughly enjoying the camaraderie with his new teammates, as well as the action. The next day, on the plane ride home, he was planning to present them with a list of future projects that he had prepared. He hoped that they would want to continue and that they would decide to take on some of his suggestions.

Wade was very concerned about the possibility of not making it back home. Although Paula had calmed down somewhat, and had apologized for the thoughtless remark she had made when he was leaving for the airport, he could tell that she still harbored concerns about the infidelity issue. He knew that the problem would be solved the minute he presented her with the surprise he had been working on, but that, of course, was dependent upon his safe return. Additionally, he thought about Rob, and along with his deep sense of loss, he tried to relish the love they had shared for twenty-one years. He vowed that he would spend some time, every single day, remembering how much he loves and misses his beloved son, right up until he finishes taking his final breath. Just before they turned on to Calle Nogales, Wade decided that he would arrange a meeting of The Payback Team members within a day or two after getting back home to decide if they wanted to continue with their mission. He had absolutely no idea how they would vote, and for that matter, he wasn't even sure if he wanted to continue.

At 3:10, on a hot and humid Saturday afternoon, everyone was again focused on the mission. The garbage truck was parked two blocks from the estate, and the two choppers were high in the air, making wide circles in preparation for just the right moment.

At 3:19, Tito and his five captains were doing exactly what they do every Saturday, but they were enjoying this particular Saturday more than usual because their team was leading the Brazilian team by one goal. At precisely 3:20, one of the Brazilian players made a well-placed kick that was heading straight for the opposing goal, and an uproar promptly broke out as the six men in the den simultaneously jumped up from their poker game yelling, "No, No!" They would never learn the outcome of the goal attempt.

A tremendously violent blast not only destroyed a large part of the mansion, but rocked the ground within a quarter-mile radius of the estate. In addition to hearing the blast, it was so powerful that The Payback Team felt the garbage truck quiver slightly. Upon hearing the explosion, they promptly took off and headed for what was left of Tito's compound. At the same time that the truck crashed through the entrance gate, the two choppers descended upon the compound. Greg and Howie, in one helicopter, and Xavier and Art, in the other, began firing their machine guns at anything that even remotely resembled a human being—starting with the two men at the guardhouse, and then turning to three others who were running from the front porch.

Then, one of the choppers went around to the rear of the mansion, and more machine gunfire could be heard. After one minute, it looked like everyone outside had been taken out. After another minute, it looked like the cloud of dust that had been stirred up by the blast had settled down enough for the garbage truck passengers to begin their part of the mission. Wearing bright emerald-green shirts and orange baseball caps, they all began running up the steps to the mansion, nine millimeter Glocks in hand, along with two additional, fully loaded clips. They planned to enter the building and put two bullets into every occupant, whether they were alive, dead, or dying. There were to be no survivors.

The two choppers continued to hover just outside both the front and rear entrance, and the four machine guns were ready to take out anything that exited either door that wasn't wearing a green shirt and orange cap.

A major concern of Chico's was the issue of collateral damage, but during his most recent session with Pepe, he had learned that there were never any children in the mansion, and that individuals such as the chef, housekeeper, gardener, and others did not work on weekends. The only individuals who would be present at the estate were those directly involved in Tito's crime cartel.

When they got inside, they split up and tried to check every room on both floors as quickly as possible. At first, it looked like nearly everyone inside the building had not survived the blast, but two shots were fired into each brain, just to make sure. When Sergeant Callahan reached what had been the den, he did not find it necessary to fire a single round, as most of the body fragments were not much bigger than one of the bullets in his Glock.

There were seven or eight men alive and dazed in some of the outlying rooms and, in each case, their existence was summarily terminated. In total, it was likely that about eighteen men inside and nine men outside had been eliminated. When taking into account the deaths of the hijackers, it appeared that Tito and about three-fourths of his band of criminals had been eliminated, assuming that Pepe's earlier comment that the gang consisted of forty men was accurate.

When they were certain that their work was complete, The Payback Team boarded the helicopters and promptly vanished. They had timed their exit perfectly, as several police cars were just starting to arrive. The policeman were going to have great difficulty getting into the compound, however, since Rocky, who had been driving, had backed up the garbage truck and blocked the entrance immediately after he crashed the gate. This had been planned in order to give The Payback Team a little extra time to get away in the choppers in the event that the law arrived sooner than expected.

An hour later, when the band of vigilantes returned to the villa, the major declared that it was "Miller Time." Everyone went for the idea, with the exception, surprisingly, of Sergeant Callahan. "Listen, you guys go ahead. There's a little unfinished business regarding our little amigo in the garage, something about ending his thieving days for good, remember? I'm gonna take care of it, then I'll drop him off at the hospital, and when I get back, I propose we have us a little chugalug contest. And don't forget, someone's gotta put the hood back on our favorite TV repairman and get him back to his truck." Then he slapped his hands and rapidly rubbed them together gleefully. "Well, okay, then, I'm off to the garage. Now, let me see. Where did I put that axe?"

Chapter Fifty-Five

A very Uncooperative Hijacker

Callahan found the axe and proceeded toward the garage. He looked over his shoulder and made a request. "Rocky, if you don't mind, follow me into the garage and hold this little fucker still while I perform a little surgery on his right arm. And, Courtland, why don't you take our little TV compadre back to his truck." Both men nodded, put down their half-finished bottles of Dos Equis and got up from their chairs.

A minute or two later, Wade was on his way toward the front door with a hooded and handcuffed repairman, along with the man who had been assigned to guard the two abductees. At the same time, Sergeant Callahan approached Pepe, holding a laptop in one hand and the axe in the other. "Well, Pepe, while you're still able to use both hands, take a look at this. We've got some interesting pictures to show you. As you will see, you are one of the few remaining survivors of—"

Before he could finish his sentence, Pepe shouted, "Take a look at this, *cabron!*" He lunged at the sergeant and buried a five-inch hunting knife deep into his gut. Callahan's countenance reflected horror, shock, and pain, simultaneously. Within just a second or two, Rocky pulled Pepe away and threw him violently against the garage wall, temporarily knocking him senseless.

At about the same time that Pepe hit the ground, Sergeant Callahan sank to his knees and then fell in a heap on the garage floor. Rocky shouted into the villa, "Spike, stop. Bring that son of a bitch back here." He knew that the only way Pepe could have gotten a knife was if the repairman had given it to him. Apparently, no one considered it necessary to frisk him, other than to grab his cell phone. Rocky could see that this had been a horrible, costly mistake.

The major promptly yelled at Wade to bring back the repairman.

When Wade returned to the garage with the repairman, he saw Callahan lying face up on the floor with the knife still protruding from his midsection. Blood was already oozing down to the garage floor beneath him. As Rocky grabbed the repairman, he shouted, "Xavier, get an ambulance over here! Callahan's down!" Then, he took the repairman back into the villa, leaving Wade temporarily alone with Sergeant Callahan and Pepe, who was lying motionless, next to the wall.

Wade bent down and spoke to him. "Listen, it's gonna be all right. We've sent for an ambulance, and you're—"

Callahan cut him off. "Listen, Courtland, don't bullshit an old bullshitter, okay? When he stuck me, he twisted the blade and I know he cut the artery. I won't be around for long, and I've gotta tell you something. Call Hiram Morton at Harris Bank in Roselle—let him know what happened. I've got a fund set up to take care of my daughter...he'll know what to do. My daughter...she's at the Pine View Care Center in St. Charles...go and tell her that Daddy took care of the bad man who hurt little Timmy...and tell her that Daddy's gone to see Timmy and Mommy, and we'll be waiting for her...then we can all be together again." At this point, he was having trouble getting the words out, and his voice was fading. He motioned for Wade to bend down closer. "And listen...look in my little black bag...there's a list I put there...I wrote down some projects I wanted us to tackle when we get back in operation again...but now I won't..."

By this time, some of the occupants of the villa had entered the garage. They could sense that Callahan was nearing the end, so they simply maintained a respectful silence so that he could conclude what he was trying to tell Wade.

Sean Callahan was having great difficulty speaking and it was clear that he was in a lot of pain. In nearly a whisper, he said, "One more thing...don't feel bad about this...you guys gave me the best ride I've had in a long time..." He was slipping away rapidly. With one final effort, he looked up at Wade and, nearly inaudibly, whispered, "Thank you...Wade..." Although his eyes were still open, Wade knew that he was gone.

Chapter Fifty-Six

The Guatemala Mission Comes to an End

Wade stood up from the garage floor with tears in his eyes. The others instantly knew what that meant, and what followed was a moment or two when no words were spoken and no looks were exchanged. Xavier picked up the phone and quietly told the ambulance service that it had been a false alarm.

Finally, with a heavy sigh, Chico broke the silence. "Well, we knew something like this could happen. I was just hoping..." his voice trailed off as he walked back into the villa. Then he began again. "Okay, now, we have to think this thing through. This situation is definitely not covered in 'Planning 101.' Rocky, first off, bring Pepe in here. I don't care if he is unconscious, drag him in here or chop him up and bring in the pieces. I don't care one way or the other. I just want him where we can see him." After taking a deep breath and slowly shaking his head in disbelief, he continued. "There's a lot to think about here. For one, what do we do with this little bastard who slipped Pepe the blade and is responsible for our loss? And what are we going to do with that piece of shit that Rocky just dumped in the middle of the floor? And then there's the issue of how do we get our fallen teammate back to the US? You know, when we stopped at a bar in Lincolnwood a few weeks ago, he opened up a little. He told me that when his time comes, he wants to go out in his policeman's uniform. And he told me he has a brother in Michigan City who will make all the arrangements. We need to honor these requests, no matter what it takes. He was a stand up guy, we all can agree on that.

"But right now, I'm gonna have another Dos Equis in his honor, and I'm gonna sit here in silence while I figure this out. We've got a lot to resolve before we can get out of here. I doubt if it will be tomorrow morning as planned." After he opened the bottle, he put his fingers to both temples and began rubbing as he closed his eyes and lowered his head.

Within a minute or two, Pepe began to come to life. Rocky grabbed his gun and promptly pointed it at Callahan's assassin. It was obvious to all that Pepe's brain was about to be disassembled, but Wade abruptly stopped him. "No, Rocky, we need to see what Chico comes up with. Let it wait."

This commotion seemed to bring Chico out of his meditative trance. He began with a question. "Did anyone touch the knife?" After everyone responded in the negative, he continued. "Good. Then I think I know what we're gonna do, and I think it's our best option. First, Rocky, you need to check with your contacts and find out how many people we have to pay off to get Sean on the cargo plane, along with the chopper and the claw. I'm sure there's all kinds of red tape to cut through." Then, he turned to the major. "Would you bring the knife in here, and put on a pair of latex gloves first? The only sets of prints I want on that weapon are what's on there now, Pepe's and the guy it belongs to. And, Greg, would you find out where the repair guy kept the knife? My guess is he's got a sheath strapped to one of his legs, just below the knee. And be sure to use a latex glove. "See, here's what we're gonna do."

He stopped and looked at Pepe, who by now was fully conscious and sitting upright on the floor, listening intently. "Now listen up, Pepe, because this next part concerns you. You are going to play an important role in all of this. You get to play the dead guy. That's right, you're gonna get to lie down in the rear of the repair van with a knife in your gut. Fortunately, we have one handy, you were using it just a little while ago, remember?"

At this point, Pepe stood up and was about to protest. Rocky promptly wrapped both of his huge hands around Pepe's throat, lifted him off the floor, and began shaking him violently. Before he put him down, he shouted, "You're being very impolite. My friend's trying to explain something to you. How will you know what you are supposed to do if you're not listening?" Then he dropped him back on the floor and gagged him.

Chico smiled at Rocky. "Thank you, my friend, that was very helpful. Now, if I may continue. There's going to be a lot of blood on the floor of the repair van, just like in the garage, thanks to you. But since we don't have anything that we can use that would look like blood, we're going to ask for your help. I hope it won't be too much trouble. Anyway, here comes the really neat part. Our helpful repair guy here, you know, the one who helped you out in the garage, is gonna insert the knife. Isn't that fascinating? Well, okay, he won't, actually, physically do that part, but what the heck? With his prints all over it, who's to know the difference after the fact, if you know what I mean? So that's how it's gonna work. Put the hood over the repair guy, drop him off a few miles from here, take off the hood and the cuffs, and turn him loose. Then we leave Pepe in the van with the knife in his gut and the sheath on the floor next to him." Pausing for a breath, he looked at Pepe and said, "Now, Pepe, I know this got a little complicated. Do you think you can convincingly play your part, or do you want me to go over it again?"

Pepe gave a muffled sound that Chico interpreted as a "yes."

"Okay, good," replied Chico. "I guess we only have one thing left to settle. Now, who wants to be the one to carefully insert the knife in Pepe's belly?" Everyone in the room, other than the two whose hands were shackled, promptly raised a hand. "Well, okay, I guess I'll have to decide. Spike, you get the job. You were the first one to meet him, and you brought him onto the team, so you get the honors. I know you'd probably like to practice a little, but we're gonna do this in one take. Okay, does everyone know how this is going down?" Then he looked at Pepe and the repairman. "Are you guys clear on this?"

Before they could respond, Rocky pointed to the repairman and asked a question. "Why does this guy get a pass? Why don't we whack him, too? As a matter of fact, I'd kinda like to grab that little black bag over there and let both of them find out about Sean's type of justice, firsthand."

Chico was ready with an answer. "Yeah, I thought about that one. You know, think about it. We would have probably done the same if we were in his shoes. I mean, someone snatches us out of our van, locks us in a garage with a guy who says he's gonna be killed if we don't help him, what are we gonna do? But, I know, that doesn't change the fact that our comrade is dead because of it. So, I say we set it up the way I outlined and let fate take over. If he finds a way out of it, you know, a dead guy in his van with his knife in his gut and his prints all over it, what's gonna happen next? Jail time? Can he find some way out of it? Let's allow him take his chances. I just know he doesn't deserve to get whacked, because he had no way of knowing the whole crazy story about what went down before we grabbed him. So, at least he gets a pass as far as his life is concerned, but my guess is he's gonna be in one hell of a lot of hot water before long. I just wish I could see the look on the faces of la policia when he tries to tell his side of the story. Seems like it's gonna be pretty hard to prove— think about it.

"One last thing: we need to draw straws to see who is gonna clean up the mess in the garage. We want to leave this place as we found it, you know, make it look like we were never here."

As everyone began to get started on their individual assignments, Rocky retrieved Sean Callahan's lifeless body and carried it into the villa. Wade looked directly at his face, which was now at peace, and declared, "Well, Sean, you did your part, and I promise you, old friend, I will take care of everything, just as you asked. But first, I am going to make sure that Pepe meets up with you again, *muy pronto.*"

Chapter Fifty-Seven

Going Home

Although it didn't seem possible, Wade, Chico, and Rocky were able to get to their plane on time as originally planned. For a while, it had looked like they would have to delay their return by at least a day or two, due to the horrible complications that had occurred on their last full day in Guatemala.

Major Robins and his crew, along with Wayne, were also at the airport, making arrangements to load the chopper and its accessory onto a cargo plane, prior to boarding the Continental Airlines flight back to Chicago.

Thanks to Rocky's contacts in Guatemala City, the remains of Sergeant Sean Callahan were due to be flown to Philadelphia the next day. The surviving members of The Payback Team were impressed with how the arrangements were handled. One of Rocky's contacts had pointed out the obvious fact that it would be nearly impossible to get a dead body, one that had been brutally murdered, prepared for burial and flown out of the country. The issues of legal procedures, customs, and documentation would somehow have to be addressed, and that could take an indeterminable amount of time.

As expected, Chico went into his thinking-and-planning mode and came up with the solution in less than ten minutes. After he explained his plan, the contact immediately began calling mortuaries within the greater Guatemala City confines. On the tenth attempt, he located the owner of the Morales Funeral Home, who said that he had been commissioned to prepare a deceased gentleman for transportation to Philadelphia. After the completion of the call, the contact announced that it was time to load Sergeant Callahan's remains into the van and head over to the funeral home.

The sergeant's blood-soaked shirt had already been removed, burned, and replaced with a fresh one, so within thirty minutes, the van, along with Xavier, who was to act as interpreter, pulled up in front of the funeral home. It was not difficult to get Mr. Morales to go along with the exchange of the two caskets, especially since he was rewarded with twenty thousand pesos for his effort and cooperation. This compensation also covered the next step, which was for Mr. Morales to contact the mortuary in Philadelphia and let them know that an error had occurred and to inform them of the location where the casket should be sent. Then, of course, he would promptly forward the correct casket and its contents to Philadelphia. Problem solved.

While waiting for their flight, Xavier bought a few copies of the morning paper and distributed them to his fellow travelers. While they looked at the pictures on the front page, he interpreted the headlines and accompanying text. The paper reported that the largest drug cartel south of Mexico City had been dismantled by way of a violent drug war. It was estimated that there were more than fifteen deaths, but the number could not be determined for certain due to the extensive amount of widely scattered body fragments that were present at the scene.

A few minutes before boarding their flight, a video clip came on the news, and once again, Xavier explained what the narrator was saying. It was speculated that a rival drug cartel from Mexico City had dropped a bomb on the compound, and then their forces had entered the estate and executed the survivors. It was announced that Tito Hernandez had most likely not been at the residence at the time of the incident, and that he would probably seek retribution for the attack. Since Tito had previously escaped numerous attempts on his life, it had been assumed that he had probably avoided death on this occasion as well. It was estimated that more than one-half of all drug shipments from south of Guatemala were, at least temporarily, halted from flowing north. Finally, the announcer informed the viewers that it was probably only a matter of time before Tito could reassemble his organization and get back in business.

Not long after the flight took off and everyone was finally heading home, Wade showed Chico and Rocky the list of potential future projects he had taken from the sergeant's little black bag. He asked them to simply look it over without forming any conclusions because this was not the time to try to make any decisions about The Payback Team's future. But as they reviewed the list, he said, "Listen, let's get together a couple of days after we get back and discuss where we want to go with this. I, for one, am not ready to make any commitments or decisions, one way or another."

Both of his comrades nodded in agreement and then continued to look over the list.

Wade settled back in his seat and closed his eyes. He was planning to get a couple of hours of sleep, but that probably was not going to happen due to the jumble of thoughts that were spinning around in his head. He had gone from what looked like the start of a quiet life of early retirement to a man possessing forged identification papers and driving vehicles with stolen license plates. He had also become a kidnaper and a killer. And, finally, he had lost a son along the way. For most of the rest of the flight, he tried to make sense of it and was doing his best to conclude that the results were what counted. But was this a case of using the ends to try to justify the means? He knew that Rocky had no reservations about their mission and that Chico probably felt the same way, but he knew he was in for a lot of soul searching before he could say for sure if he wanted to continue.

He also knew that it was going to be impossible, as long as he drew breath, to forget about the carnage inside Tito's estate. As he closed his eyes, he could vividly picture each shot he had fired into the skulls of other human beings. But, most of all, he could envision Pepe's terrified eyes looking up at him as he plunged the knife into his belly. He could still remember the warm sensation as Pepe's life fluid made contact with the latex glove covering his right hand. Did Pepe deserve to die? Should he have been the one to bring about his demise? Wade's last thought before finally drifting into a fitful sleep was that he wished, just for a moment, he had the sociopathic ability not to worry about matters of conscience.

Chapter Fifty-Eight

Wade's Infidelity Issue is Resolved

After they cleared customs at O'Hare Airport, the original Payback Team members were greeted by their wives. It had been a long, dangerous, challenging, and costly trip. But it was over, and it felt really good to be back.

Wade refused to talk about the trip during the car ride to their home, but he promised he would open up at a later time. He was more interested in catching up on what Paula had been up to while he was away, in addition to hearing about how Julie was doing in her last year at Northwestern University.

Finally, when they walked in the door, Paula begged him to at least share a few details of his trip. Wade dropped his travel bag and looked at her. In his most dramatic tone, he replied. "Honey, I'm sorry, I just…I mean…I didn't want to…oh, well, I guess, I better just come out with it." Then he paused, while a very concerned look came across Paula's face. "Listen, I guess you need to know. I picked up a case of SDD while I was away. It looks like Chico, I mean Tommy, and Michael have it also. Apparently, we spent too much time in Guatemala. I'm sorry. I was going to tell you sooner or later."

Paula's voice was trembling as she asked, "What is it honey? What's SDD? Please tell me…I've got to know."

Wade replied, "SDD stands for 'sexual deprivation disorder.' I've got a really bad case. It's not fatal, but they say in some cases it never goes away and that the symptoms can sometimes pop up almost without warning."

Paula was not only relieved but offered help. "Listen, Big Boy, I think I can provide some therapy for your 'condition.' Come with me, right now." Then, she promptly took his hand and led him to her private therapeutic parlor.

Early the next morning, Wade and Paula were seated at the breakfast table. Wade knew what was coming, so he took control. "Listen, Paula, I know you're about to ask me for the details of our trip, but here's how it's gonna work. First, let me have my coffee and read the paper. I've been looking forward to sitting here with my coffee and newspaper almost as much as I was looking forward to the really effective therapy session you provided last night. Nice moves, girl, I'm feeling much better. But don't forget, my condition may last for quite awhile. Then, after breakfast, I want to take you for a nice, long ride in the country. I've got something cooked up that I think you're gonna like. And while we're driving, I'll tell you all about our little vacation in Guatemala. How does that sound?"

Paula liked the idea and went off to get ready for the drive.

During most of the forty-minute ride, Wade kept his word and explained in detail what took place in Guatemala. Then, when they were about five minutes from Wade's destination, he asked Paula to put on a blindfold. "Trust me, you'll thank me later."

Wade pulled up to a ten-acre estate in Barrington Hills. There was a white, wooden fence surrounding a large, brick, country estate home, complete with white pillars and an expanse of beautifully manicured lawn. Off to the side was a pasture containing two horses, a mare and her young foal.

After he opened the door for Paula, he led her over to the fence and asked her to place her arms over the top rail. Then, he told her to open her hands. "No, not like that. Turn them so that your palms are facing up." Then he placed a sugar cube in each of her outstretched hands, as he began to whistle loudly.

"Wade, what in the world—?"

Wade cut her off. "Just wait a minute. Okay, here they come." Then, when both animals were just a few feet away, he removed Paula's blindfold.

She gasped as her eyes took in the complete picture. With the green lawn, the horses, and the estate all in front of her, she knew it was a picture she would never forget. As the mother and her offspring munched on the sugar cubes, she spoke without diverting her gaze from the magnificent scene in front of her. "Oh, Wade, it's so beautiful. Thanks for bringing me here, I just love it. I'll never forget this moment."

"Honey, I guess you just don't get it," said her husband. "The horses are yours. I got them for you. It's what you wanted. That's what I was doing on the phone, when you thought I was up to no good. I wanted it to be a surprise."

Now, Paula finally looked at her soul mate of more than twenty-five years, her tears flowing uncontrollably. "Oh, Wade, I…they're so beautiful…I'm so sorry I—"

Wade cut her off. "You don't have to say it. I know. I just want you to be happy. I love you so much."

"Oh, my God, Wade, this is too much. I didn't expect anything like this. I didn't even think you were listening all those times I talked about getting a horse. And just look at this place. This is exactly the kind of place I had hoped we could have some day. But the horses will do just fine. I'm so happy. Honey, you're the greatest."

"Well, I'm really glad you like the place because I bought that, too," Wade said, smiling. Paula's eyes widened; she was making an effort to say something. Wade wasn't certain if she was unable to speak or if she just couldn't find the right words, but he decided not to wait. "Listen, you don't need to say anything. We've got to get going. We're closing in two weeks, and we've got a lot of packing to do. And, besides, I think I'm getting another SDD attack."

Paula smiled.

About The Author

W. Ward Neuman lives with his wife, Pam, in Illinois and Arizona. His background is in real estate investing and he has published three books about managing income property. He has also written numerous articles that have appeared in running, finance, and poker magazines.

After a lifetime of concern about injustice, he decided to write his first novel and has put to life on these pages some of his fantasies about how the bad guys should be made to pay for harming the good guys, especially when "the system" has failed.

He can be reached at his e-mail address, willster@amerilink.net.